WINTER'S DAUGHTER

www.penguin.co.uk

WINTER'S
DAUGHTER

Val Wood

bantam

TRANSWORLD PUBLISHERS
Penguin Random House, One Embassy Gardens,
8 Viaduct Gardens, London SW11 7BW
www.penguin.co.uk

Transworld is part of the Penguin Random House group of companies
whose addresses can be found at global.penguinrandomhouse.com

Penguin
Random House
UK

First published in Great Britain in 2022 by Bantam
an imprint of Transworld Publishers

A CIP catalogue record for this book
is available from the British Library.

ISBN 9781787635616

Typeset in 11.75/14.38pt New Baskerville ITC Pro by Jouve (UK), Milton Keynes
Printed and bound in Great Britain by Clays Ltd, Elcograf S.p.A.

The authorized representative in the EEA is Penguin Random House Ireland,
Morrison Chambers, 32 Nassau Street, Dublin D02 YH68.

Penguin Random House is committed to a sustainable
future for our business, our readers and our planet. This book
is made from Forest Stewardship Council® certified paper.

To my family with love,
and for Peter as always.

There is wealth in this ancient town. There is poverty, too, where people without any means or hope of survival take refuge in doorways until the break of day.

There is also a cellar, known as a safe haven for those who have nothing. Safe, until the rains come. And it is here that a child is found.

She speaks little, and when she does it is in a foreign tongue. Her mother, reputedly, wore exotic silks, was beautiful with fair skin and hair, and took great care of her daughter; so where is she, and why would she leave the little girl in this soulless place?

CHAPTER ONE

November 1856

'Come on! Come on! Get these children inside. Quickly!'

James Ripley, fair-haired, stockily built and above average height, carried one child in his arms and another on his back as he urged on the other men who were steering the children and old women towards Hull's ancient Holy Trinity church. More women followed, their arms piled high with thin blankets, old cushions and baskets of belongings, all wading through the rush of water that was overflowing from the drains and had poured down the cellar steps threatening to drown them, and trying to avoid the large pools that had gathered in the dips and troughs and potholes in the street, while screaming and crying to others in the bedraggled crowd to hurry or die.

Above them a storm raged. Lightning fissured, lighting up the sky, the street, the pinnacles and towers of the old church; thunder cracked and pounded and women shrieked at each reverberation, crash and thud as the sleety, spiky rain fell in torrents, drenching them when they thought they couldn't get any wetter.

James had been woken early by someone tapping on his bedroom door, the sound becoming increasingly louder as he was slow to respond. He slipped into his dressing gown and went barefoot to open the door, mumbling huskily, 'I'm coming, I'm coming!'

Mrs Evans, their housekeeper, in her dressing robe and nightcap, held up a smoking candle stub on the dim landing and croaked, 'Sorry, sir. Mr Howard, I think it was, sent a lad to say can you go fast as you can as 'cellar is flooding. He didn't say which cellar.'

'Oh, dear Lord!' he'd muttered. 'It's all right.' He'd cleared his throat. 'I know which one.'

'Will you have a pot o' tea first?'

He'd shaken his head. He wasn't at his best in a morning. 'No. A cup of tea if the kettle is boiling, but not if I have to wait. No!' he'd added decisively. 'Go back to bed, Mrs Evans. It must be urgent for someone to come so early.' The clock on his bedside table showed five o'clock exactly.

Hurriedly he'd thrown on warm clothes and left by the kitchen door, wishing he had picked up his hat, and turned up his coat collar to stop the rain trickling down his neck as he ran across the High Street, through narrow Church Lane and crossed the normally busy road of Market Place, now empty save for a single wagon trundling from Lowgate. He turned in to North Church Side and came to the infamous cellar where already there were men helping women and children up the stone steps through the murky water pouring in from the flooded street. These were men with no place to live but the one they had just vacated, and no hope of work; many were vagrants with no hope at all in their lives.

Holy Trinity church had been a place of sanctuary since its beginnings, over six hundred years before, but these people were in need of food and warmth as well as prayers, and were urged on towards the open door.

'Has anyone tried the almshouses?' James called out to no one in particular. 'Watson's or Greggs'?'

4

'They're full up,' a familiar voice called back. It was Nicholas Howard, with his arm in a sling. 'Sorry to drag you out,' he said, stepping inside the church door. 'I'm a bit hampered; I've broken my arm.'

James wished that Charity Hall had still been open; in the centre of Hull it had been easier for those town dwellers at rock bottom in their lives to turn up at the great wooden gate to ask for succour and shelter and keep on knocking until someone answered. They didn't always get in – there were rules to follow before they were admitted – but many were.

The inhabitants of the workhouse had been moved out of town two years before, into a modern building on the long road to Anlaby which was much admired by those who had contributed to it, including James himself. The accommodation was better, the food more nourishing and the children's uniforms more suitable, but nevertheless it was a long walk from town when footwear was non-existent and hunger slowed the steps.

One of the young boys shook off the hand urging him on and shouted out, 'I'm not going to Charity Hall. You can't make me!'

'It's gone,' James called back. 'It's empty. The workhouse has been moved to a new building, much better than the old one,' he said encouragingly. 'We're going into the church for now; it's only temporary, just for tonight or until the storm blows over.'

'Will there be soup?' the boy persisted.

'I hope so,' James answered, muttering under his breath, 'Please God.'

He did hope so; there were always some women who were prepared to deal with any emergency and be ready with pans of hot soup and hunks of bread for those in need. This was a fishing and shipping town where the residents were used to tragedies and calamities, mostly in the fishing industry when ships already battered by severe seas could sink negotiating the turbulent waters of the northern ocean as they tried to enter the Humber Estuary.

'I can't go in.' Still the boy held back. 'I'm Catholic.'

'It won't matter. Come along,' James urged him, trudging up the path and through the open door. 'The soup will taste just as good, no matter the belief.'

James approached the women who had brought in bread and ready cooked sausages, and was told that the verger had refused to allow a brazier inside the church. One was being set up outside the door to heat the soup and boil a pan of water for hot drinks, but some people were complaining that it wasn't healthy, being too near the graves which held the town's many cholera victims, including recent ones, and what was more the rain was so heavy it was putting the fire out.

James slid the child on his back to the floor, but the other was still clinging like a limpet to his coat collar when he went to find the verger and discovered him drinking coffee in a tucked-away corner.

'Sir.' James caught him in mid-slurp. 'We must bring the brazier inside the door. I'll set a man on especially to watch it doesn't fire any of the church property, but these people, these children, are in great need of Christian salvation. For God's sake, they need food and hot drinks.'

The man swallowed and mumbled, 'I don't have 'authority to allow it.'

'Then tell me where I can find the vicar and I'll ask him myself, or else turn your back so you don't get the blame if God or those who represent Him choose to say you've committed a mortal sin by helping these children.'

Whether the verger caught the bitter sarcasm in his voice or his own conscience got the better of him, James couldn't tell, but there was no answer and he took it as a silent agreement.

The child patted his cheek and he wondered where her mother was; at least, he thought it was a girl but he wasn't totally sure. The long dark hair gave no clue, for who would have cut it down in the hellhole from which these children had been rescued?

The deep brick cellar had been used as a shelter for decades; James recalled his father talking of it, telling him that it had once been a warehouse before it had burned down when he was only a youngster himself. He had gone to see the burnt-out embers: there was little left of the original building. The roof and top storey had almost gone, and some of the floor above the cellar, but part of that lower floor and the chimney stack had survived, ensuring that at least some of the cellar could be kept dry, even though there was always the danger of the rest of it collapsing on top of those beneath it.

Once, those who were at the rock bottom of their lives had been forcibly turned out of this fine accommodation, as it was regarded as being unsafe. The low entrance was boarded up with stout planks, for the original wooden door had long gone as firewood, and lodgings were offered in various workhouses and almshouses depending upon where those seeking help came from and if they qualified for support. As many did not, within a few weeks the planks were down and those not used for fuel made into another door, packed with damp straw to keep out the whistle and draught of the wind, and they were home again.

Their system remained the same. The women and young people, with or without parents, settled at the back where there were some low brick walls, effectively creating several small 'rooms' where privacy could be assured. They could bring their bedding, such as it was, and, most vital, could feel safe. The men were at the front, where they kept out drunks and prostitutes, for although some of the women living here plied that particular profession it was an unwritten rule that

7

they didn't bring their customers back. Any man who took too much drink whenever he could beg or steal coins to buy it was not allowed in until he was sober. Consequently, there was a good community spirit, and they watched over each other as best as they could, tolerated one another's faults and short-comings and turned out those who didn't follow the rules.

When James had picked up this child where he or she sat on a very wet blanket, he'd asked, 'Whose child is this?' but no one had answered, such was the hurry to get out to some other shelter before the rain pouring down the steps filled the cellar and drowned them all.

He asked the boy he had spoken to outside, who was wait-ing for the soup to heat.

'She's a girl. The women call her Lay-lah. It would be an odd name for a boy, wouldn't it?' He dug his fingers into his pockets and rubbed them to clean them. 'I don't think she has a mother; at least I've never seen her with one. She hasn't been there long, and a few of the women have fed her, don't know whether from their dugs or with pobs.'

James heaved a breath; here was life in the raw. 'Does she never go out? Does she stay in the cellar?' Surely, he thought, she can't have spent much time underground without fresh air or seeing daylight?

The boy shrugged. 'Dunno. I think she was taken out on dry days, but not if it was raining or if it was very cold; they asked the parson if she could sleep in the church one night, but he only let one woman in with her, and none of the men.'

'What's your name?' James asked this fount of knowledge. He didn't think the boy was local: he had a different accent from Bob, the odd-job boy who worked for him.

'Tom, sir. I don't know my second name,' he added hastily. 'I think the soup's ready.' Abruptly, he rushed off to be first in the queue.

James looked about him. The women who had come in

8

with them were busy housekeeping: they'd found their own places on the pews away from any draughts and put down damp blankets to keep their space; some had sacking pillows, probably filled with straw, where their children immediately curled up with their cold hands beneath their cheeks and closed their eyes.

James went up to one of the women. 'Can you tell me who is the mother of this child? Leila, I believe she's called.'

She shook her head. 'I've nivver seen her wi' anybody. She's not been here long.'

'Does no one know how she came to be here? She must have come in with somebody.'

'There was Peggy. She'd been here for a long time an' she looked after her – she'd look after anybody's bairns, would Peggy, but she wasn't her ma; then Peggy was took bad onny a few days ago and died afore 'morning. She wasn't a relation; look,' the woman went on, pointing at the little girl in his arms, 'she mebbe isn't English. Look at them dark eyes. I've got brown eyes, but not like that bairn's eyes. What I think, mister, is that she should go to 'orphanage or 'workhouse. She'll get food and a cot and warm clothes. There's nowt for her in yon cellar; onny dreams of hunger and a ride wi' ferryman.'

She lifted her head and called in a muted voice, aware of being in a church, 'Lizzie! Come 'ere a minute, will you?'

An older woman came over; or at least James thought she was older. It was difficult to know, as most of the women had lined faces, scrawny necks and bedraggled hair and some lacked any teeth; they could be twenty or fifty. 'What d'you want, Dot?'

'This gennleman is asking about Lay-lah. Can you remember when she came to 'shelter? Was she wi' her ma?'

'Aye, she was. I saw her. Peggy brought her in.' The woman sat down on the pew next to James and heaved a weary sigh.

'She were lovely; blonde-haired, dressed like a foreigner – you know, wi' a long silk frock and a scarf over her head. Don't know what they're called. It's onny mebbe three, four days back, a week mebbe, I'd say. Time rushes by when you're having such a nice time livin' in 'cellar. She didn't talk much, mebbe shocked to come so low, cos she seemed like class, you know?'

'So where is she now?' James asked. 'She can't have abandoned such a young child. Not in conditions such as those . . .' He shook his head, feeling sick at the thought of it.

'Who knows?' Lizzie said. 'Folks come and go, but I think she left 'bairn wi' Peggy; she'd been lookin' after her own young grandbairn, had Peggy, but he died, and so she fed Lay-lah wi' whatever crust she had. I think 'bairn's ma might have given Peggy money for food. We thought she was mebbe going to look for work; she won't have found any and I can't think what a woman like her would be able to do, except – you know, but then . . .' She paused as if not wanting to state the obvious.

'Anyway, she told us she was lookin' for her husband and asked Peggy to mind 'bairn,' she went on. 'She went out, but she didn't come back, and Peggy died just after and we didn't know what to do about 'bairn, but we took it in turns to give her a crust.'

She shook her head and looked up at James. 'There's got to be summat better than this, hasn't there? We're like rats in a box, ants under a stone. We're worth more than this, surely to God?'

She looked about her, at the weeping marble angels, the fine arched windows, the beautiful stained glass. 'Such splendour,' she muttered. 'All for 'glory of God while His people suffer. Well, I've had enough. If it's stopped raining by tomorrow, I'm off to 'workhouse. Me, Lizzie Chambers! I vowed I'd nivver end up in there, but my old bones ache, I'm hungry

10

and I'm tired. I'm fifty-two years old and I'm going to say I'm older cos I expect I look it and I hope that they'll tek me in.'

She glanced again at James. 'I'll tek 'bairn wi' me, unless you've any plans for her, sir. I'll tell authorities that she's my granddaughter. Nobody'll dispute it. Why would they?'

CHAPTER TWO

James brought soup for the child and for the two women. Lizzie took the little girl on to her knee, spooned some of the hot liquid into her own mouth and then, taking another spoonful, gently blew on it and put it to the child's lips.

'How do you think she will be treated at the workhouse?' he asked Lizzie. 'Will she be accepted?'

Lizzie gave a nonchalant shrug. 'I'm prepared to lie,' she said. 'I'll say my daughter was married to a . . .' again a casual shrug, 'I dunno, a Turk, whatever, cos if you look at 'bairn's eyes you can see summat foreign in her; I'll tell 'em that he left and my daughter died of – I dunno,' she said again. 'Not cholera cos they might not let us in; mebbe starvation, cos that would be possible.'

'Do you have a daughter?'

'Nah! Four lads.' She sniffed. 'You'd think I'd be in a better place, being mother to four grown men, wouldn't you? Two of 'em lost at sea alongside their da. One killed in a brawl and 'youngest went off to find his fortune. He's either found it and spent it on a good life or lost it gambling, cos I've never seen sight of it or him either and he's been gone five years or more.'

She shook her head and sighed. 'I'm still living and breathing,' she said, 'and never thought of ending it, though I've come near a time or two.' She gave him an almost toothless grin. 'Neither have I done owt to be ashamed of, so I'm still pure!'

He laughed. 'You were never tempted?'

'Not since my old man. Best feller I could have wished for. We'd have been all right, him and me, till 'end of our days, but it wasn't meant to be.'

'Do you – do you not receive any kind of pension?'

'Seamen's Sixpence. Aye, my old man paid into it since he were a lad and there was enough to pay 'rent or eat, but not both, so I decided that I'd collect 'money and eat and come to live in 'palace we've just been washed out of: wi' a bit of imagination I could be anywhere in 'world. But now? Nah.'

A faint shadow of unease swept across her face, and he thought that he could see the woman she once might have been, strong and determined but now battling with something else that perhaps she was unable to deal with.

'Look,' he said quietly. 'If you agree, after I've made some enquiries and talked to people who might be able to help, I'll take her home with me. You need not fear for her safety with a stranger; I have a wife and a son, and I'll tell you where I live, which is in High Street, and tomorrow I'll come back and let you know what I decide to do about her. She can't go back to that cellar; she should be with her mother, but how to find her? I'll discuss the situation with my wife.'

'You're giving me references?' she mocked, and looked at Dot in astonishment, as if she'd never known such a thing.

'Well, you don't know me,' he said in mitigation. 'I could be anybody – someone who intended her harm.'

She looked at him and bent towards him. 'I'd know,' she said softly. 'I know men and their ways and whether or not they're lying or if they've got evil on their minds, even if they're well dressed and well shod, like you are, sir; believe me or not, every one of them folk in 'cellar would seek you out if

13

you harmed any child known to us – or not – and you'd finish up injured but alive in 'estuary wi' a brick tied to each foot and another round your neck.'

She nodded and gave a small smile. 'Tek her,' she said softly, 'and if your wife don't want her, cos some ladies might not want another woman's child, especially from such a place as she's been living in, then bring her back and I'll tek her wi' me to 'workhouse. She might be sent to 'orphanage, seeing as she's so little, but she'll be clothed and fed and mebbe her ma will come back to look for her one day.'

He nodded and stood. He unbuttoned his coat, picked up the little girl and wrapped her inside it, then fastened it up again whilst she looked curiously at him from her large dark eyes.

'James Edmund Ripley,' he said to Lizzie. 'My home is in High Street, as I said.'

She gazed up at him. 'I reckon I know you, sir. Or at least your name. Shipping, I think?'

He nodded. 'I'll come back tomorrow and let you know the outcome.'

His stomach rumbled with hunger as he left the church. He'd been out most of the morning, and he'd missed breakfast, but he'd done what he could to help matters by persuading the vicar to agree that the homeless could stay in the church for the time being.

The child peered around his neck as they left, as if looking for the two women, but she didn't cry or wave or shout, and he thought he had never seen such a child, who seemed so accepting of what life was offering, though he admitted to himself that he didn't know many children. Certainly, going off with a stranger wasn't something his own son, eleven-year-old Matthew, would have done; the boy was wary of unfamiliar people, even of those invited to their home until they had been introduced.

That's because his mother is cautious of strangers, James considered, as he walked away from the church and passed the cellar, which had already been boarded up. He shuddered, hoping it had been thoroughly checked to be sure there was no one left inside.

Matthew was at school in York. Moira's father had been a pupil there and was very keen that his grandson should attend, as was Moira's mother, whose brothers had been there. He'd offered to pay the school fees and Moira had agreed before discussing it with James, who would rather have had Matthew at the old-established Hull Grammar School, situated in Market Place only yards away from Holy Trinity. He considered that the boy was too young to be away from his family, and had agreed with his father-in-law's proposal only on the proviso that Matthew could transfer if he didn't want to stay.

James had muttered under his breath that the Grammar School had been good enough for Wilberforce and Andrew Marvell, as it had been for him. Privately, he was determined to have his only son back here and close to home as soon as the time was right.

The rain was still torrential and he kept his head down and his collar turned up, trying to shield the child. He crossed Market Place to cut down Church Lane and turned into the ancient High Street. After just a few minutes of hurried walking, dodging the deep puddles and the avalanches that poured down from leaking gutters, he approached his house. He didn't reach for his key or ring the front doorbell, but turned down a narrow lane known as a staith, of which there were many in High Street which led to the rear of the houses, the warehouses, the yard gates and eventually to what the locals still called the Old Harbour: the original narrow dock that now carried shipping in from the estuary towards the newly named Queen's Dock, in honour of the Queen's visit two years before.

The door wasn't locked and he frowned as he stepped inside to the small boot room where rubber boots and shoes were neatly stacked and outdoor coats and black gamps were kept for him and the servants to use in bad weather, but not for his wife. If Moira had an appointment on a day that was wet or stormy or even just cold, then a message would be sent and the appointment cancelled. Besides, to his knowledge she never used the back door, and neither did Matthew, who rarely went anywhere without his mother.

'Mrs Evans!' he called.

The housekeeper was sitting at a clean, scrubbed table in the kitchen drinking tea, and she jumped and stood up. 'I didn't hear you come in, sir,' she apologized.

'Sit down and finish your tea,' he said. 'The door was unlocked; why was that?'

'Onny cos I'm here, sir. I'm waiting for Bob to come back from an errand and then I'll lock it again.'

She was halfway to sitting down and then rose up again as she saw the dark head of the child inside his coat. 'Well I never! What – who have you got there, sir?'

He unbuttoned his coat and the little girl looked about her with interest. She saw the teapot and a plate of biscuits and stretched a hand out towards them.

Mrs Evans reached for the biscuits. 'Can she have one, sir?'

He nodded. 'Yes. I would guess that she's hungry.'

'Whose child is she? Is she lost?' The housekeeper picked up a biscuit and offered it to the little girl, who took it and pushed most of it into her mouth. 'My word, you are hungry.'

To their astonishment, the child leaned towards her and stretched out her arms. Mrs Evans took her. 'Ah, cupboard love, is it? You're a bonny little thing.' She put her nose to the back of the child's neck and sniffed. 'She doesn't smell too savoury, sir. Where's she been?'

James pulled out a kitchen chair and sat down. 'I came in

by the back door purposely,' he began, not at first answering her question. 'She needs a warm bath and her hair washing; I don't want Mrs Ripley seeing her for the first time like this. Do you have anything she can wear? The clothes she has on are only fit for burning.'

'Not in my kitchen range sir,' Mrs Evans said firmly. 'They need to be burned outside in a dustbin or suchlike, but they might wash. Are you, erm, what are your intentions, Mr Ripley? Is she a waif and stray? Is she stopping?'

He leaned his elbow on the table and looked at them both. The little girl was obviously used to being handled by women and sat quite comfortably on Mrs Evans's lap eating another biscuit that the housekeeper had given her.

'I understand that she has, or had, a mother. She was rescued from that cellar on North Church Side. It's been flooded and the occupants have had to flee to the church. There are women there handing out bowls of soup.'

Mrs Evans looked across at him. 'You're not telling me it's 'same cellar from all them years back? The one that they said was full o' folk wi' nowhere to go and where some bairns were born and some died?'

'So they say. My father used to talk about it. He remembered it from his boyhood.'

She nodded and replied, 'I recall my ma telling me and my brothers about it. She used to warn 'lads that's where they'd end up if they didn't behave.'

They were easy with one another. Mrs Evans had begun work here as a kitchen maid for his mother's cook when she was fourteen. Young Josephine Evans was quick and efficient and soon made her way up the servants' ladder; she could also, if it were required of her, help out with the cooking, and one day James's mother came down to the kitchen to speak to her and offered her the position of either cook or housekeeper, as the present ones were about to retire. Josephine had said she would be both if she could have a housemaid or a kitchen maid and a lad to chop wood and bring the coal in, and she'd teach them her immaculate standards. Those who couldn't reach them were replaced immediately, without any sentiment, and although she had never married she was always given the respectful title of Mrs Evans.

The household had then consisted of young James, his older brother Daniel, who married when he was twenty-one and left to set up his own home, and their undemanding, easy-going parents. Over the years, housemaids and kitchen maids came and went but Mrs Evans stayed and didn't ever consider leaving, for she had never met anyone she considered worthy enough to be swapped for her comfortable employment. She had her own room, good food, weekends off if she wanted them, which wasn't often, and a week's holiday every year when she visited her sister who lived in Goole.

The new Mrs James Ripley couldn't find any fault with her, even though she sometimes tried, but Mrs Evans missed the elder Ripleys, who on Mr Ripley's retirement bought a small house in Scarborough and went to spend the rest of their days by the sea, whilst Daniel took control of their small but efficient shipbuilding empire to do with as he wished as long as he didn't bankrupt it.

James, after intense study, became second in command; besides being a first-rate draughtsman he was efficient in finance and soon became financial director of the company, which suited him perfectly. He had never enjoyed having to take occasional test voyages on their newly built smacks and barges, for he was not over-fond of turbulent waters.

They employed a marine surveyor, who checked out everything that a former Navy man who had re-invented himself as a ship's designer could, and they couldn't fault him. He and James worked well together and, with a foreman, a ship's carpenter and an apprentice, made up the company's workforce.

18

Daniel himself had learned his trade with a fishing fleet, catching sole in the Silver Pits, but he moved from the deep waters to dry land when he realized that their father would eventually need a successor to run the company. It was clear that the business of building smacks to trawl from the teeming water-pantry of Dogger Bank was bound to succeed.

'So after her bath and finding suitable clothes, and mebbe feeding her, for she looks half-starved to me,' Mrs Evans continued, 'what next? Are you expecting Mrs Ripley to look after her until her ma appears? If you'll beg my pardon for enquiring, sir.'

James swallowed. 'To be honest, I'm not sure, but I couldn't leave her. At present the people from the cellar are sheltering in Holy Trinity. I saw two women who had been looking after her; they have no food, no dry blankets . . . nothing, that's what one of them said. The other, who was older and alone, is going to try for a place at the workhouse—'

'Well good luck to her,' Mrs Evans murmured.

'And told me,' he went on, 'she was willing to take the child with her and pass her off as her granddaughter.'

Mrs Evans let out a breath and seemed to rouse herself, but with that the outer back door opened and they heard a clattering of buckets and the sound of boots being hurled to the floor before a drenched boy came into the kitchen in his bare feet.

'Get changed into some dry clouts afore you catch your death,' Mrs Evans told him. 'There's some in 'bottom cupboard next to 'range; and hang your wet stuff up to dry.'

The boy touched his forehead at James and did as he was told, taking out dry breeches and a jumper from the cupboard, and grabbing a towel from the range rail to dry his hair before going back out to the boot room. He emerged a few minutes later fully dressed and hauled down the wooden dryer hanging from the ceiling, draped his wet clothes over the rails and hauled it back up again.

The door leading upstairs to the main house opened and a young girl came in. She dipped her knee to James and then stared incredulously at the little girl sitting comfortably on Mrs Evans's knee.

'Rosie! Just 'person we want,' Mrs Evans said. 'Go and fetch 'small tin bath hanging outside 'door and bring it in.'

'It's chucking it down, Mrs Evans!' Rosie said, aghast.

'Yes, and? It won't drown you. Everybody's wet. Master here is wet, Bob's wet, this bairn is wet; do you want me to fetch it?'

'No, mum,' she mumbled. 'I'll get it.'

James hid a smile. Mrs Evans was definitely in charge, and the girl, Rosie, was back in no time at all.

'Now listen to me, Rosie.' Mrs Evans got up from the chair and handed the child back to James. 'I want you to tek 'bath upstairs and then come back down for a jug of hot water that I'll give you and you'll tek it up again and fill 'bath up. It'll tek half a dozen jugs at least, I'd think, and then between us we're going to bath this bairn and get her into some clean clothes; is that understood?'

'Yes, mum,' she said.

'And for 'last time, I'm telling you not to call me *mum*. I'm Mrs Evans and that's what you'll call me. Is that clear?'

'Yes, mu— Mrs Evans,' the girl said, and the housekeeper raised her eyebrows and sighed in James's direction as if to say *This is what I have to contend with!*

CHAPTER THREE

With Mrs Evans carrying the little girl, and Rosie carrying the final jug of steaming hot water for the bath tub upstairs, James drew the kettle on to the hob to boil again and found cups and a tin of tea leaves in the cupboard.

He looked at the boy, who was sitting silently at the table. 'Would you like a cup of tea?' he asked, and Bob jumped up immediately.

'Yes please, sir.'

'Sit down,' James said quietly. 'I know how to make tea. I've known since I was your age.'

'I've never learned,' the boy answered. 'Never had tea afore I came here.'

'Never?' James asked, and it occurred to him that not everyone could afford tea. 'Do you live at home?'

'I live with my auntie Lil; my ma's dead and I don't know where my da is. Sometimes he comes to see my auntie, but not often; she's his sister. Last time he came he said I should find a job o' work cos he has to pay my auntie for my board and lodgings. That's when I came here.'

'And when was that?'

The boy gazed into the distance. 'Erm, I can't remember,

sir. About a week, or mebbe two, mebbe it was three. I think it might have been three.'

James asked him how old he was, but he said he didn't know that either. 'Mrs Evans said we'd settle on eleven, sir.'

'Do you know a boy called Tom? He lived in the cellar on North Church Side.'

The boy's face lit up. 'Aye, I do. We're best mates. He's older than me, I think.'

'Did you know everyone's been washed out of the cellar? It's flooded. That's why the little girl is here.'

'No!' Bob was aghast. 'Where've all 'folks gone? Little bairn's called Lay-lah; funny name, in't it? She was allus shouting it out. They don't know where her ma is, nor her da. What they all gonna do?' He seemed appalled. 'I nearly went to live there, cos I know me auntie dun't really want me. She says she's enough to do wi'out me being there, but now I've come to work here and give her me wages, she feeds me a bit better.'

'So it was Mrs Evans who took you on, was it?'

A wary look came into the boy's eyes. 'Er – yeh, and she pays me wages.'

'Ah, good,' James said, 'that's all right then,' and saw the relief in in the boy's face. 'Do you know who I am?'

'Erm, yes, sir. You'll be 'gaffer, I expect. Mrs Evans said I hadn't to go upstairs except to carry hods o' coal first thing in 'morning, cos Rosie can't lift 'em, and she's useless.'

James didn't answer. He was deep in thought, assessing Mrs Evans's power in this household, and he believed she was using it kindly.

'What do you do for spare clothes? Those you're wearing are very large on you.'

'Don't know who these belong to. Those are mine up on 'dryer.' He pointed up to the ceiling, where his ragged trousers and a thin jacket were steaming and James thought of his own son's wardrobe, filled with a week's daily change of clothing, but too small, he thought, to fit this boy, who was taller, although much leaner.

'Mm,' he murmured. 'I'll have a word with Mrs Evans. You could do with something warmer. Where do you sleep?' he asked abruptly. 'Here?'

Bob shook his head. 'No, I have to go back to my auntie's house; she says she needs to keep an eye on me so's I don't get into mischief.'

'And do you?' James probed. 'Do you get into mischief?'

The boy drained his cup and stood up. 'Never have done, sir. It's just that she's seen gangs of lads about when she goes shopping and thinks I'll join 'em. I won't,' he said adamantly. 'But they're all right. They're just beggin' cos they've no money. Some of 'lads have lived in 'cellar; 'older men don't want 'em there, but there's nowhere else they can go.

'It's best in winter when 'food stalls get set up,' he went on, 'and they can have soup or sausages, but then all 'doorways get filled up wi' down an' outs an' beggars an' that . . .'

He seemed to run out of steam with what he had to say, but then the inner door opened and Mrs Evans came in with a pink-faced, damp-haired child who was wrapped in a large soft towel and peeked out from the safety of her arms.

'Is it all right if I go now, Mrs Evans?' Bob asked.

'Don't you want to stop for some stew? It's simmering in 'oven.'

James felt hungry; lunch upstairs would have been and gone. 'Why don't you stay and have something to eat here?' he asked the boy. 'You could tell your aunt that you were waiting for your clothes to dry, which would be perfectly true,' he added persuasively, lifting a finger up to the ceiling rack.

'Will that be all right, Mrs Evans?' Bob asked. He obviously took his instructions from the housekeeper.

'Are you thinking you might get into trouble with your aunt?' she asked, and he nodded and pressed his lips together.

'Sometimes I have to run a few errands for her when I get back,' he admitted, 'especially if it's raining, cos she dun't like getting wet.'

James was beginning to dislike this boy's aunt, even though he had never met her. 'I'll write her a note,' he said, 'telling her I had an important errand for you; how would that be?'

'Oh, thank you, sir. What is it?'

'What is what?'

'The errand, sir.'

'Ah!' James was caught out. The boy was obviously not used to subterfuge. He was honest. 'Mm, I'll think of something,' he said, and a grin escaped his lips but Bob didn't notice.

James held the little girl again whilst Mrs Evans took the hotpot out of the oven, a tantalizing aroma of beef and onions rising from it. 'We could do with a small chair for her,' he murmured, and Mrs Evans cast her eyes swiftly towards him.

'Rosie's upstairs looking for something for her to wear, sir. We've got a cupboard up in 'ironing room where Master Matthew's clothes are kept from when he was little.'

'Boy's clothes?'

'They're all 'same when they're little bairns. Lads don't get breeched until they're four or five; we've plenty of nightgowns and little smocks that'll fit her. It's just a matter of finding 'em.'

'Is there anything up there that would fit this young fellow?' He indicated Bob. 'His are drenched. He can't possibly wear them before they're dry.'

'He can go home in what he's wearing; nobody else will want 'em and I don't know where they've come from. But first he can have something to eat; I dare say his aunt will have cleared 'table by now and there'll be nowt left but bread and cheese. Am I right?' She looked at Bob, who nodded.

'Bread an' drippin'. She hasn't allus got cheese. Mr Ripley, sir, could I work for you? On your ships, I mean?'

'You know we're shipbuilders, don't you? We're not shipping merchants or trawler owners.'

'I know that, sir. But I like mekkin' stuff out of wood. I'd like to be a carpenter but my aunt said she wasn't going to be paying out for an apprenticeship cos my da would never give her 'money back.'

'But wooden ships are being phased out. We do still build from wood but also out of iron, and some shipbuilders are using steel.'

The boy seemed disappointed and bit on his lip. James asked him what else he liked doing.

'Dunno. It's just that I like 'feel of wood. I know how to whittle and carve and I think I'd be good at it.'

'I know someone who has a joinery business, but you do realise you're too young to become an apprentice? We have one, but he's older than you. Maybe in a few years? Can you measure accurately? Read instructions?'

Bob shook his head. 'No, sir,' he answered in a low, disappointed voice. 'I haven't had no schooling.'

'You haven't had *any* schooling,' James corrected without thinking.

'No, sir, I haven't,' he agreed, and James let slip a little sigh.

'I have a son about your age, did you know?'

'Aye, I think somebody said. How old is he, sir?'

'Maybe a little younger than you. He's almost eleven. He's at school in York.'

'Does he have to sleep there?'

'He does, because it's too far for him to come home every night. He'll be coming home next weekend. It's one of the oldest schools in the world.'

'It'll be a bit of a wreck, then, if it's that old. Couldn't he have gone to 'Grammar School? That's onny across 'road in Market Place. Though that's old as well.'

James hid a smile but didn't reply as Mrs Evans placed the

hotpot on a mat on the table and Rosie came through the door, triumphant that she had found a pile of clothes suitable for the little girl to wear. She pulled out a flannelette nightgown, popped it over Leila's head and buttoned it up.

'Mr Ripley.' Mrs Evans had the ladle in her hand, ready to serve the hotpot into four bowls. 'Were you thinking of going upstairs to tell Mrs Ripley that you are home, or shall I dish up?'

James cleared his throat. 'Erm, I think I'll have something to eat first. Rosie, will you run up and tell Mrs Ripley that I'm home and I'll be with her shortly, just as soon as I have changed out of my wet clothes, and . . . erm, yes, that will do, I think.'

If I told her that I had forgotten, he mused, because my thoughts were on other matters, my dearest wife would not fully comprehend their seriousness. Yet I know those matters are not my concern alone but that of society in general.

And with that resolution made, he looked into the sharp eyes of Mrs Evans, who gave a quick nod and murmured to him and Bob, who was also waiting, 'Eat!'

CHAPTER FOUR

'I'm sorry to be so long, dearest.' James bent and kissed the cheek his wife had proffered.

He'd eaten well and had smiled when he saw young Bob tucking in eagerly though not greedily.

'You're a good cook, Mrs Evans,' James had told her. She was sitting on a bench opposite him with the little girl beside her and spooning small helpings of broth into her open mouth. 'I'm pleased you've stayed with us all these years and not thought of moving on.'

She'd acknowledged his remark with a nod, answering, 'I'm a plain cook, sir, but a good one. I knew if I could please your mother, which I did, I could think of this place as my home. I've everything I need here.'

He'd taken another bread roll, and with an eye on his young companion broke off a piece and dipped it into the delicious savoury gravy, saw the boy's eyes open and heard the soft intake of breath. He leaned towards him and whispered, 'We're allowed to dip our bread when we're at home, but we don't do it if we're dining out, or have company.'

Bob had flushed and whispered back, 'Aunt Lily dun't allow it, Mr Ripley; she says it's not polite.'

'Well, she has a point,' James agreed. 'We do need good

manners at the table, but as long as we know when and where we can let them slip a little, I believe it's all right.' He'd glanced at Mrs Evans. 'Would that be right, Mrs Evans?'

She raised her eyebrows. 'If you say so, Mr Ripley. But best to learn manners first, in my opinion.'

'So where have you been all morning, James?' Moira asked him. 'You were up very early. I heard you leave. Could you not have cancelled your meeting?'

'It was cancelled.' He sat back on the sofa, stretching out his legs as Moira poured the coffee that Rosie had brought up. 'We cancelled as soon as we realized there was an emergency. The Humber bank broke through; the town is flooded. The drains couldn't contain the water. We're very lucky to live upstairs and have a sound basement, unlike those poor folk who don't have a roof, let alone a home.'

Moira blinked. 'What?'

'The people I've seen today don't have work so they haven't money for food, let alone for rent or any place to shelter. They've been living in a cellar for weeks and now it's flooded.'

'In a cellar! No! So where are they now?'

'Sheltering in the church. The women of the town have answered the call to arms as usual and set up a brazier to heat soup, and they've brought bread and other foodstuffs as well as blankets and towels so that the poor folk can get dry.'

'They are eating in church?'

He felt the heat of annoyance; did she really not understand, or was she choosing not to? He realized he was taking out the frustration and helplessness that he felt so strongly on her innocent remark, yet continued in the same vein.

'Where do you think they should eat or rest?' he asked testily. 'Isn't shelter in a holy place the best place to be? Or I could have brought some of them home, I suppose. Why didn't I think of that?'

It was not his wife's fault that she was an innocent; he knew that very well. She was not a woman of the world, as he had discovered on their wedding day; she had been carefully brought up by her parents, her mother essentially, and given no tutoring in real life. He shouldn't speak so; she was gentle and caring and he was just looking for someone to blame.

She too sighed. 'I don't think we have sufficient room, James.'

'Well, the child that I've brought home, Leila I think is her name, won't take up a lot of space. She's still an infant,' he muttered. 'About four years of age, although no one seems to know for sure. Mrs Evans said she can sleep at the bottom of her bed.'

'What! Are you teasing? You are, aren't you?'

He put his hand to his chin and scratched his short curly beard. 'Actually, Moira, no I'm not. It's a very serious situation and it bothers me no end to think of people without food or shelter and we're not yet into midwinter. We have snow and ice yet to come.'

Her face saddened. She was not an unfeeling woman, that he knew, but as her next words showed, she didn't comprehend how others lived, being only aware of their own family situation.

'We can't help them all, James,' she said softly. 'If some people are unable to manage their lives successfully, what can we do to help?' Then she added, sadly, 'A child, of course, can't help itself and certainly not at so young an age. Have you really brought her home? Where are her parents? They should be looking after her.'

He sighed. He could almost hear her mother's voice. Moira had a wet nurse ready and waiting when Matthew was born; her mother had advised her that that was what she should do and arranged one for her, engaging a nursery maid too, and as he knew nothing of babies he hadn't objected.

The result was that Moira had had very little to do with the baby except to coo over his cot every morning and evening, though she was anxious over every little sneeze, always fearful that James would drop him while lifting him from his cot, and never ever sat him on her knee without first placing a freshly washed cot sheet over her spotless gown in case some germ that might be lingering there would be passed on to him.

'What about sleeping clothes? Is she dry? We don't have anything suitable for her to wear in case of little accidents.'

'Mrs Evans and Rosie have found things for her to wear,' he assured her.

'A rubber sheet,' she pronounced. 'That's what she should have for the bed; Mrs Evans won't want it to be – to be—'

'I know,' he said wearily. 'It's all in hand, Moira. They'll know what to do.' He was secretly pleased that she had not objected to the child's being here but was only concerned about the inconvenience to Mrs Evans, which was a benevolent gesture at least.

'What did you say her name is? Leah?'

'No one knows for sure, but the women call her Lay-lah. She keeps shouting it out. It's probably Leila.'

'Why would she call out her own name?' Moira gave a puzzled frown. 'Has anyone asked her what it is? If she's four, she'll know it. She would surely call out her mother's name, not her own?'

He pondered. He was so tired. Before coming into the sitting room he'd washed and changed into dry underwear and put his dressing gown over the top of his cord trousers and shirt, but he still felt cold and shivery in spite of the large helping of warming hotpot that Mrs Evans had put in front of him. He would dearly like to go to bed and catch up with some sleep, but it was only mid-afternoon, in spite of being so dark outside.

'You could be right,' he agreed. 'But she doesn't speak.'

Lizzie and Dot hadn't mentioned the name of the child's mother, he recalled. Maybe they hadn't heard it, or perhaps she hadn't offered it. It was very strange that a woman would leave her child behind. Perhaps she had gone to look for work, as one of them had suggested; but why hadn't she come back, even if only to pick up her daughter and take her somewhere safe? Even the workhouse would be better than the cellar. Or maybe she had trusted the woman – Peggy, was it? – to take care of her?

'James.' Moira's voice came as if from afar. 'You should go to bed for a rest. We'll talk later, or tomorrow. It's Saturday; you can take time off. We'll discuss the child's situation then. Shall I ring for Rosie to put a hot brick in your bed?'

He mumbled yes please, and vaguely thought that it would be nicer to have a warm body next to him rather than a solid brick, but that wasn't on offer. In an afternoon! How decadent. But beggars can't be choosers, he considered, trying to work out how long it had been since he'd shared Moira's bed. A week? Two? Neither had she come to share his.

Moira caught Rosie on her way down to the kitchen after having put hot bricks in Mr Ripley's bed. 'Fire is burning nicely and 'room is nice and warm,' the maid told her.

'Thank you,' Moira said. 'Erm, what about the little girl? Is she asleep? Mr Ripley said she was going to sleep in Mrs Evans's bed.'

'Yes, ma'am, that's where she is now. She's fast asleep already. Would you like to tek a look at her?'

'Oh! Would Mrs Evans mind? I don't . . . erm, I – would she?'

Moira never entered the servants' rooms and certainly not the housekeeper's. Mrs Evans had lived in the house longer than she had, and after Moira's marriage to James and the senior Ripleys' departure to their new abode, Mrs Evans had shown her all of the house from top to bottom: the attics, the servants' quarters and the kitchen, bathroom and laundry room as well as the formal rooms where the family lived and slept.

The housekeeper, in the opinion of her young mistress,

had rather a proprietary manner and had murmured to her, 'So there you are, ma'am. You don't have to bother your head about anything now that you've seen it all, apart from your own private rooms of course, and you can be certain that we'll make sure that they are all exactly as you'd like them to be.'

So now Moira gazed keenly at Rosie to see if the offer was appropriate, but happily was saved by Mrs Evans's coming upstairs.

'Is something amiss, ma'am?' the housekeeper asked.

'No, not at all, but I was enquiring about the child that Mr Ripley brought home. Mr Ripley implied that she was sleeping in – in your room?'

'She is. Would you like to tek a look at her, ma'am?' Mrs Evans asked. 'She's a right bonny bairn. You can come up and look and welcome. I don't think she'll waken. Poor bairn, she was exhausted, and hungry too.'

She turned to climb the next flight of stairs and Moira followed her, whilst Rosie went on her way down.

Mrs Evans quietly turned the doorknob. A lamp was burning low on the top of a chest of drawers and a small fire glowed in the grate; next to it was an easy chair with a soft cushion. A single bed was placed alongside the inner wall and thick curtains were closed against the window with a chest of drawers beneath.

'This is very cosy, Mrs Evans,' Moira whispered. 'Very nice. Is there anything else you require? Pictures for the wall perhaps?'

Mrs Evans shook her head. 'No, thank you, ma'am. Pictures gather dust, nice as they can be. I'm quite happy with what I have.'

Moira nodded. 'Well, do ask if you think of anything.' She tiptoed to the end of the bed, where the top of a small dark head showed above the sheets.

To Mrs Evans's surprise, her mistress knelt beside the bed to gaze at the little girl before looking up and murmuring,

'She's beautiful, isn't she, Mrs Evans? I don't think I have ever seen a more beautiful child.'

'She is,' Mrs Evans agreed. 'She's a right bonny bairn. Anybody who could leave her in that awful place must be either uncaring or in a desperate situation herself.'

Moira nodded. 'I quite agree,' she said softly. 'I can't believe that she has been abandoned. Something has happened to her mother, and what about her father – where is he?'

Mrs Evans had no answer to the question.

CHAPTER FIVE

When Mrs Evans woke the next morning, she opened her eyes to see the little girl sitting up and gazing at her from the deepest brown eyes fringed with long dark lashes.

'Hello,' the housekeeper said croakily. 'You've had a nice long sleep.' She stretched out an arm and put her hand under the bed to pull out a chamber pot. 'Do you need the potty?'

The little girl looked at it and then at her, and pulling back the blanket, put her feet to the floor, pulled up her nightgown and sat down on the pot.

'Good girl,' Mrs Evans murmured, and was surprised when the child got back into bed again next to her and slid down the sheets. 'Oh, we're having a sleep in, are we? I should think so too, considering where you've come from.'

She had slept all night long, and the housekeeper considered that the warm bath and the supper she had eaten had comforted and relaxed her enough to send her off into a deep, much-needed oblivion.

She tucked the child beneath her arm. 'What's your name?' she asked quietly. Patting her own chest, she said, 'Evans,' and then patted the child's, but the little girl pressed her lips together and pointed to the door. 'Lay-lah!' she said.

The housekeeper patted her own chest again and said, 'Evans,' and then tapped the child's. 'Leila?'

But the little girl shook her head. Her eyes welled up with tears and her lips trembled, and pointing towards the door she called softly, '*Lay-lah!*'

Josephine Evans knew nothing about children. Her two older sisters had already left home and her two brothers were no longer children when she was born; she was the last child in the family and her mother had died when she was five.

Her life would then have been mapped out for her had she toed the line and submitted to being maid of all work for her father and brothers as she grew older; at eleven she took stock of her role and at twelve on finishing school she took matters into her own hands and applied to be a scullery maid in one of Hull's big houses, having decided that if cleaning, scrubbing, washing and some cooking was to be her role, then she might as well do it for some other family and be paid for it and get free food and lodging and possibly even occasional time off.

She would forgo marriage, she'd thought as she climbed the ladder of success from scullery to kitchen to housemaid, moving to different employers when they offered better terms, for wouldn't it be exactly the same thing, looking after a husband rather than the father and brothers she had left behind? It wasn't that her family had been unkind, just careless of her feelings and never, ever asking her what she might like to do.

But children, no. She didn't know any, except for those who had been at school with her, a few girls and noisy lads that she avoided: not until she met James Ripley, who was about her age when she came to work for his mother, did she realize that some were kind and considerate, and as he was mostly at school, their paths rarely crossed.

But this child, with her dark appealing eyes and sweet mouth, she could have loved; she would have liked to sit her on her lap and put her face against her cheek to comfort her, for the little girl was missing someone and it could only be her mother.

It was six o'clock. She rose from the bed, washed and dressed and put on a freshly ironed apron, and pulled a chair up to her wash stand. She emptied the bowl of water she had used into a bucket and refilled it with fresh, then picked up the child and sat her on her knee whilst she wet a clean flannel and washed her hands and face, letting her splash her hands in the water.

Then she took her own hairbrush, which was always clean, and attempted to brush out the knots in the long curly hair.

'My word,' she murmured. 'I think you're going to need a little trim to get rid of these. We don't want to pull, do we?'

The little girl shook her head as if answering, and sat perfectly still whilst Mrs Evans dressed her from the selection of clothes that Rosie had found.

'The only thing we haven't got is shoes and stockings. I think Mrs Ripley will have to go shopping.' She paused. 'Unless, of course,' she said softly, 'you're being taken elsewhere to live.'

She felt saddened, but thought practically that there was every likelihood the child would be taken to an orphanage if her mother couldn't be found.

An hour later, after she had fed the little girl with porridge, poached egg and soft toast, James Ripley came down to the kitchen.

'Good morning, Mrs Evans, and good morning to you,' he added, bending to speak to the child, who was drinking a cup of milk. 'How are you this morning?'

She looked up at him and licked her lips.

'We'll have to give you a name.' He smiled down at her and turned to the housekeeper. 'I can see a change in her already,' he murmured. 'Good food and a warm bath has made such a difference. Did she sleep? And did you?'

'Yes,' Mrs Evans told him. 'We both slept all night, but I confess I tossed about quite a lot, worrying about what was in front of her. She's a dear little thing, but she needs some – some . . .'

'Constancy? Stability?' he offered.

'Aye, stability I suppose I was meaning, sir. What's going to happen to her?'

The little girl was watching with interest, first one and then the other, and then she pointed to the door. 'Lay-lah!' she said in a determined voice. 'Lay-lah!'

James bent towards her. 'Where is Leila?' he asked gently. 'Where is she?'

She looked up at him and then clasped her hands together. 'Gone!' she whispered.

'Oh!' the housekeeper gasped, and murmured. 'So she can speak!'

'The women didn't say that she couldn't,' James said softly. 'They just said that she didn't.'

He sat down on a kitchen stool and pulled a clean white handkerchief from his pocket, and as the little girl watched he swiftly rolled and knotted and turned it into a rabbit with floppy ears and handed it to her. It was something he used to do for Matthew when he was that age.

Her face lit up into a big smile as she took it. 'Mine,' she said. 'For Floris.'

'Ah,' he breathed. 'So is that your name?'

The door leading to upstairs opened and Rosie came in carrying an armful of sheets. She dipped her knee on seeing James. 'Sorry, sir,' she mumbled.

James put a finger to his lips. 'Come here,' he murmured. 'Stand by me.'

'Floris,' he said in a louder voice. The child, enraptured by the rabbit, looked up.

James pointed to the maid. 'Rosie,' he said, then turned to

the housekeeper and pointed again. 'Evans,' and the house-keeper patted her chest.

Then he patted his own chest and said, 'James.'

The little girl looked down at the handkerchief and then showed it to James, holding it up for him to see. 'Rabbit,' she said gleefully.

He could barely contain himself, but held out his hand to her. 'Floris?' he asked.

She opened her mouth, and placing her small white teeth on her bottom lip blew gently. 'Ff-loris', she giggled, and they all clapped their hands.

'Oh, my goodness,' James breathed. 'A step forward. I must tell my wife.'

'Indeed, sir.' Mrs Evans looked hugely thankful. 'It doesn't help in finding her mother, but knowing 'little bairn's name is such a relief. What will happen next, sir? I could grow to be very concerned for her.'

'I know.' He nodded and stood up. 'So could I.' He pondered for a moment. 'I'll chat to Mrs Ripley, Josephine,' he said, without thinking, and added quickly, 'Sorry – Mrs Evans.'

'That's all right, sir, I don't mind, but I was wondering, didn't you say there was a woman willing to tek her to 'work-house and pass her off as her granddaughter?'

'Yes, I did; she did.' He ran his hand across his face. 'What sort of time do you think she might set off? Any idea? It's still relatively early, isn't it?'

'Well, she might have gone already if she was hoping for a cooked breakfast,' she said practically. 'But on the other hand, she might be waiting for you to go back.'

He gave a deep sigh. 'I think – I think I'll speak to my wife before I go to the church.'

She nodded. 'Why don't you have your breakfast first, Mr Ripley? I'll cook it now. You'll think better on a full stomach.

And how would it be if I make a bacon sandwich for this poor woman who is willing to tek somebody else's bairn to 'work-house with her?'

He smiled. 'You're a marvel,' he said. 'Don't ever leave us, will you?'

'No, sir.' She raised her eyebrows. 'I won't.'

He ran upstairs. It was still early, but, unusually, Moira was already coming down.

'Is it too early for breakfast?' she asked. 'I rang the bell, but no one answered.'

'Rosie's seeing to the laundry and Mrs Evans is cooking breakfast now. Someone will be up with it shortly.' He opened the dining room door. 'Let's sit down until it comes. We must talk; there have been developments.'

'Oh,' she said quietly. 'We're talking work, are we? I've hardly slept all night. I'm so concerned about the little girl.'

'I meant the little girl. Her name is Floris,' he told her.

'Floris? How pretty. How do you know?'

'She told me,' he said gleefully. 'I told her who we all were down in the kitchen: Rosie, Evans and then James. I made her a handkerchief rabbit, do you remember, like the ones I used to make for Matthew? And she held it up and said "Rabbit".'

'And her name?'

'I asked her and she said it and we all clapped.'

She looked slightly crestfallen, and it came to him that she might be thinking she'd missed out on a treat.

'I want to talk about the options for her, which are few. I'll ask Mrs Evans to bring her up; she seems like a different child from the one we rescued from the cellar.'

Moira shuddered. 'I can't bear to think about it,' she said in a low voice. 'It's so horrid. The children could have drowned. How or where do they eat?'

'Well, mostly they don't,' he said grimly. 'I think they go into King Street and the market area when the shops are on the point of closing and ask for stale bread, or hope to find an apple or a fallen carrot that they can chew on.'

She gazed at him. 'I hope you are exaggerating, James,' she said with an edge to her voice. 'People can't survive on what you're suggesting.'

'That's right, they can't,' he agreed, and got up to open the door for Rosie, who was on the other side struggling with the breakfast tray. James took it from her.

'I'll fetch 'coffee and tea up, sir,' Rosie said. 'Shan't be a minute.'

'No rush, Rosie,' James said. 'Will you ask Mrs Evans to bring Floris up in about ten minutes – after we've eaten breakfast?'

She dipped her knee. 'Yes, sir,' she said, and left, closing the door behind her.

'What options are there for Floris?' Moira asked as she served him with eggs and bacon from the side dresser; he shook his head at the offer of sausages.

'Only one, if her mother doesn't turn up: one of the women – an older woman, Lizzie Chambers – has offered to take her to the workhouse. She's going this morning, hoping to be admitted herself, and she says she'll take Floris with her, pass her off as her granddaughter.'

He paused, thoughtfully. 'Perhaps we should give her another name. Floris is quite an exotic name, don't you think? It doesn't go with Lizzie. Maybe Mary or Hannah might be more suitable,' he mused.

'Let me see her first,' Moira interrupted him. 'I only saw her asleep. Perhaps . . .' She paused, and took a sip of coffee. 'Perhaps her mother might show up. Perhaps she's been sheltering from the storm.'

James shook his head. 'She hadn't been seen for a few days. She had left Floris with another woman, who unfortunately died. The other women have been feeding her with whatever they had, but they know nothing about her mother. Lizzie thought that the father might be foreign, because of her dark eyes. Not that it makes any difference,' he added with a shrug.

'Oh.' Moira pressed her lips together. 'I've only seen her when she was asleep.'

'She does have dark eyes, so her father could be any nationality, as could Floris, depending on where she was born,' he said, adding, 'Would it be a problem for you, if she stayed with us for a short time?'

CHAPTER SIX

Moira hesitated, and James glanced at her; what kind of response would she give? After over a decade of marriage he didn't feel that he really knew his wife; she was almost as much of a mystery to him now as she was when he had asked her to marry him.

He had been introduced to her at a friend's social gathering and had thought how sweet and shy and unassuming she seemed. She was with her parents, and as he knew her father, Bertram Denham, he was introduced to both his wife and his daughter, a daughter who proved to be as different from her mother as anyone could be.

Mrs Denham had looked him up and down as if he were a fish on a slab, deliberating on whether it were fresh or not; he immediately disliked her and, oddly, felt protective towards her lovely daughter for being saddled with such an arrogant parent.

Bertram Denham, however, had sought him out on another occasion and questioned him on his ambitions and on his personal life, asking if he intended marrying, to which he had responded that yes, he did, when he had reached his majority and was earning enough to support a wife and family, if he had found someone to love and be loved by in return. The last condition wasn't at all what Denham had expected from the young man, not knowing that James's parents had had loving relationships not only with each other but with their sons too, and that such a family was normal in James's eyes.

'Your father hasn't retired yet?' Denham had asked. 'I suppose you and your brother will be taking over the business when he does?'

'Not yet, he hasn't,' James responded, and wondered about Denham's interest. 'My brother will run the general side of shipbuilding eventually; I will probably look after the financial aspect, as that is what I'm studying. But Pa isn't ready to give up on business yet, and neither are we ready to begin. Maybe when Daniel gives up seagoing, but he's only twenty-two and I'm nineteen and still at university.'

He saw curiosity in Denham's eyes and knew he was sizing up his prospects, and thought that the marriage stakes could be the only reason. He wasn't ready for that, even though he was attracted to Denham's seventeen-year-old daughter, as he was to any other young and pretty female.

He was surprised, though, when Denham began to question him about Daniel. Was he anxious to marry off his daughter, he'd wondered, and had he been put up to it by his odious wife?

'Daniel is about to be engaged to be married.' He'd told the white lie knowing that Miss Denham would be unsuitable for his ambitious brother. Daniel *had* been giving a particular young woman some attention, but there were others too, for he was looking for an aspiring wife to match him in temperament.

But that was then, and subsequently James had met Miss Denham on other occasions, and continued to think of her as shy and pretty, and began to have tender feelings towards her as he discovered her likes and dislikes, her love of music and dancing and hatred of noisy parties and brash people; and he learned that she was not at all like her mother with her arrogant manner, and more like her father, who it turned out was quite a mild-mannered man under the thumb of his haughty wife.

'And so,' he began again now, 'would you object if she came to live with us for a time? Until we find out who she is and where her parents are?'

Moira moistened her lips. She shook her head and his spirits sank, but then she murmured, 'No, I wouldn't object at all, if you thought it would be the right thing to do.'

He breathed out. 'I will be in my office, you realize? She would be with you most of the time.'

'Yes,' she said. 'I realize that.'

Someone knocked on the door and he called out for them to come in. It was Mrs Evans and she held Floris by the hand. In the child's other hand was the white hanky rabbit.

When the little girl saw James, she held up the rabbit for him to see, and then turned it to show Moira. To James's relief, Moira smiled and put out her hand; Floris waved the rabbit in front of her and said, 'For Floris. Mine,' she added gleefully.

'I think she's known love, James,' Moira said softly. 'She isn't afraid of people, even those she doesn't know.'

'I think you're right, ma'am,' Mrs Evans broke in. 'She's been brought up to trust people.'

'Yes, I agree.' James got to his feet. 'We'll keep her with us then, shall we?' he said decisively. 'At least until her parents show up?'

He saw the relief on Josephine Evans's face, and Moira smiled and nodded, her eyes on the child.

'Right,' he said briskly. 'I'll nip round to the church and catch Lizzie now,' and he followed Mrs Evans towards the door.

'James!' Moira called. 'Do you think we should give this woman some money? She seems like a good person, and – and

44

she might like to buy something warm to wear, or a blanket, for who knows what sort of place she might be going to.'

He nodded. 'It was my intention.'

'And I've packed up a parcel of food, ma'am,' Mrs Evans said, her hand on the doorknob. 'I hope I did right? She might not get anything to eat till dinner time.'

'Of course,' Moira said. 'That was very thoughtful of you.'

James slipped out, glancing back to see Floris sitting on the rug by the fire chatting to the rabbit, and Moira looking down at her and smiling.

'Will you come through 'kitchen, sir,' Mrs Evans said, 'and pick up 'parcel of food? I've put 'leftower sausages in too; I thought 'others there might like to share them.'

He grabbed his mackintosh from the hall stand and cut down the kitchen stairs. 'I'll give the sausages to the young lads or the children,' he said.

'Aye, good idea. Just in case 'women haven't come wi' soup.' She sighed. 'It's still bucketing down wi' rain. What'll they do tomorrow, or 'rest of 'week? Do you think they'll be allowed to stop in 'church?'

He shook his head. 'I've no idea, but I'll ask.'

Bob came into the lobby just as James was reaching for the doorknob. 'Phew!' he said. 'It's teemin' down.'

'So I see.' James looked at the boy as he shook himself like a young pup. 'Seeing as you're already wet, do you want to come with me to see what's happening at the church?'

'I'd best ask Mrs Evans first, sir,' Bob said. 'Just in case she's got a job waiting on me.'

James hid a wry grin. Never mind that I pay Mrs Evans's wages, he thought, she seems to have more authority than I do.

As he opened the back door he heard the housekeeper chastising the boy and telling him to 'go wi' maister if he needs you', and when Bob joined him outside he urged, 'Come on. I want you to look out for your best mate Tom and find out where he spent the night.'

'A shop doorway, I reckon,' Bob said. 'He didn't want to sleep in 'church.'

'Would he go to St Charles, the Catholic church?' James asked. 'He told me he was a Catholic.'

'Did he? I didn't know that.' Bob frowned. 'Mebbe he was just saying it in case he had to go to a church service.'

'Would he do that?'

'Yeh!' Bob said in a matter-of-fact manner. 'He would. He don't like being tied down to anyfing.'

James sighed. Anyone trying to teach Bob the rudiments of the English language would have their patience well tested.

'Look at that.' Bob pointed down one of the narrow lanes that they were about to cut through. 'It's like a river, all sparkly.'

'So it is.' James smiled, but his smile soon faded, for it was no laughing matter. There were no drains in this particular street to take away the rush of water and it was fortunate that there were no houses down here either, just the backs of office buildings, otherwise the occupants would be severely flooded.

'Let's go down the next one,' he said, and was pleased that he had put on his rubber boots. He noticed that Bob was wearing a pair of old and shabby boots that didn't look fit for use even in dry weather.

'Who buys your clothes?' he asked him. 'Your auntie?'

'I dunno,' he mumbled. 'These boots aren't mine; they belong to one of me cousins and he grew out of 'em, so when he got a new pair – not new,' he added, 'second-hand new – my auntie said I could have these cos they didn't fit our Simon. He's 'next one down of my cousins,' he explained. 'They're too big for me and too small for him, cos he's fourteen, so I've packed 'em wi brown paper.' He grimaced. 'They give me blisters, though, cos 'insides are all torn.'

James mentally made a note of a pair of waterproof boots and a mackintosh; if Bob was going to work for them the least they could do was provide adequate clothing. Mrs Evans and Rosie had clothing supplied for them, therefore so should he.

The Hull women had turned up with baskets of food for the people bedded down in the church. Some had made bacon sandwiches and there had been a rush for those; others had brought fresh bread with potted meat or cheese, and some had brought cake. Within minutes it was all consumed.

James looked round for Lizzie and Dot and eventually found them bedded down on one of the pews at the back of the church. They hadn't had any of the food, Lizzie said, as she was so stiff she couldn't drag herself to the door.

'Just as well that I brought breakfast,' James murmured. 'This should keep you going until you get to Anlaby Road.' He somehow couldn't bring himself to utter the words 'the workhouse'. He glanced at Bob and saw him lick his lips at the sight of the sausages which had been intended for Tom or any other children.

'Have you seen the boy Tom?' James asked Lizzie. 'Did he come inside the church last night?'

Both women shook their heads. No, they hadn't seen him, but they confessed they'd dropped off to sleep quite quickly.

'Do you want to look outside to see if he's there?' he said to Bob. 'He'll mebbe come in if you're here.'

'Aye, all right,' the boy muttered, still eyeing the sausages.

'Have you had your breakfast?'

'Just a bit o' bread,' Bob mumbled. 'Me cousins are both working so they have to have breakfast afore they go. I told me auntie I might get lucky and get dinner at your house, sir.'

James nodded. 'I'm sure you will, but you're hungry now?'

'Starvin', sir.'

Lizzie had been listening as she tore into the bread and sausages. 'Nay, you're not starvin', lad. Starvin' is when you've

47

had nowt to eat for days and no possibility of any food coming. If you've got a chance of some dinner today, then count yourself very lucky.'

She took another bite of sausage, and then offered him the remainder. He shook his head. 'No, you're all right,' he mumbled. 'I've had a bit o' bread. I can manage.'

'I'll have it.'

They all looked up. Tom had appeared seemingly out of nowhere. 'I rushed up to 'door when I saw 'women with their baskets,' he said breathlessly, 'but I was too late.'

He had a feverish look in his eyes as he gazed at the remaining food.

'Here you are, lad.' Lizzie leaned towards him with the half sausage in her hand, and he took it eagerly. 'Eat it slowly,' she told him. 'Mek it last. You'll throw up if you eat too fast.'

Dot was delving into the now flattened paper parcel. She brought out a slice of bread and handed it to him. 'Here you are, ducks. Riches!'

Dear God in heaven, James thought. This won't do. This really won't do at all.

CHAPTER SEVEN

Moira sat in an easy chair and watched Floris playing on the floor surrounded by soft toys that had been Matthew's; she delighted in watching the little girl quietly chatting to them. She had asked Rosie to go upstairs and bring down a toy box that was stored in what had been the nursery and was turned into a schoolroom when Matthew had had a tutor; it was now a depository for toys and games for which he had no further use, but he refused to give any of them away.

She is such a pretty child, Moira thought, studying Floris unobserved. Quite beautiful, with her dark eyes and olive skin, which had lost some of its pallor after a good night of sleeping and eating well since James had brought her home. Mrs Evans had washed her hair after bathing her, and now it was shiny and turning up at the ends in soft waves since Moira had trimmed out the tangles.

She wanted to ask Floris where her mama was, but dared not. Suppose she began to cry for her; whatever would Moira do to pacify her when she didn't have an answer? Who is she, she thought, and who are her parents, and where are they now? The little girl hadn't been abandoned or ill-treated, you could tell by her demeanour. She wasn't frightened of anyone; it was obvious she was used to people from her willingness to go with Rosie or Mrs Evans and James in particular; she would put her arms up to him when he came into the room.

Perhaps because he brought her out of that dreadful place? How on earth had she come to be there?

I wasn't able to completely relax with Matthew, she recalled. When he was an infant I was afraid of letting him fall. I wasn't used to children, and when he cried I didn't know what to do to pacify him. He was only wanting food, she remembered, or changing, and she used to ring for the nurse to take him, the woman who picked him up so easily and whisked him away, and she felt now that the nurse had pitied her.

'Well, that's over and done with,' her mother had sniffed when she first looked into the crib at her grandson. 'You've done your duty. A son, that's what a man always wants. James won't be bothered about a daughter so you can relax now and won't have to worry about the wretched business of begetting them.'

Moira had cringed. But James wants more children, she'd thought. What about his feelings? He was thrilled with Matthew and lifted him out of his crib on the day he was born so that he could look at him more closely. He must have thought that we would never have a child, she pondered, as I was always so frigid, and yet he was so patient with me. I had always thought that I'd like to have a daughter, a little girl to play with and take out shopping with me, but it was so— She brushed away the notion of conception. Her mother had pooh-poohed the idea of having another child.

'Your father wanted a son, of course,' she had said. 'As I say, every man wants to turn a son into his own image. He was very disappointed that you were a girl.'

Moira had felt shocked and belittled. It wasn't her fault; there was no power on earth to decree whether a child would be a girl or boy.

She had wanted to retaliate that James didn't want a child to form into his image, but dared not. Her mother always had the last word; otherwise she went into a sulky, impatient mood. James had said he wanted to bring Matthew up to be a good human being, and had also said that his son could follow whatever path he wanted as long as it was honest and honourable.

She knew too that when it had come to the time of choosing a school for him, James had only given in to her father after learning that Mrs Denham's brothers had gone to the same school; it had had nothing to do with her parents paying the school fees, but was because Moira would never hear the end of it from her mother if he didn't agree.

James had told her what her father had said – that it was a good school and he had enjoyed his time there. 'But he's your son and you must decide,' her father had added, 'even though my wife is set on it. That's why she suggested that we offer to pay the school fees.'

At this point in her thoughts, Rosie brought in a pot of coffee on a tray, a glass of milk for Floris and a plate of biscuits, and placed them on a low table by Moira's chair. Floris immediately jumped to her feet when she saw the milk; she held a rag puppet by one leg and stood waiting, her eyes on the biscuits. Suddenly, she spoke to Rosie in a language that neither the maid nor Moira could understand, although both knew it to be a question, as Floris put her head on one side in an enquiring manner.

'What did she say, ma'am?'

'I have absolutely no idea!' Moira answered. 'It sounded like – well, nothing I have ever heard before.' She leaned towards the child. 'Floris?' She smiled. 'In English, please!'

Floris looked at her and then at Rosie, and then at the milk and biscuits, and jumped up and down. She dropped the toy and clapped her hands together. 'Biscuit for Floris, please!'

Moira put her own hands together and clapped. 'Good girl,' she said, and nodded to Rosie. 'Put a biscuit on a plate, please, Rosie,' she said, and smiled at Floris. 'Sit down, Floris.'

The child immediately did so, and Rosie draped a napkin over her knees and gave her the biscuit on a plate.

'Would you like milk?' Moira asked, and Floris glanced at the glass and nodded, putting the biscuit to her mouth.

'All right,' Moira murmured. 'We won't bother about the please this time. Thank you, Rosie.'

'Isn't she lovely, ma'am? And speaks two languages! Isn't that just so clever.'

'Yes, indeed. It's not French, and neither do I think it's Italian.'

'We get Dutch and German sailors coming into 'Hull ports, ma'am, but it don't sound like either of them.'

'No, it isn't. At least we now know that she has mixed parentage, but that doesn't help us one jot in knowing where they are!'

She asked James when he came in later. He had come home to ask Mrs Evans for more food, but he couldn't help as Floris didn't use the strange words again.

'It was a rolling kind of language,' she said. 'Not guttural. It wasn't anything I had heard before, not that that is surprising as I haven't travelled further than France.'

'I'll get a map,' he said. 'That might help us.' He stopped as he reached the bookshelves and turned towards her. 'Could it have been Greek? That's unintelligible to most English speakers.'

She shook her head and laughed. 'As if an unschooled young woman like me would learn such a language!'

'True,' he admitted. 'Unless you were a scholar, but at school we learned Greek and I managed to grasp an understanding of some of it.'

He took an atlas from a shelf, one he had had as a schoolboy, and sat down with it on his knees. Floris put down her toy and came to stand next to him. 'Story,' she said. 'Please.'

James looked at her and smiled, and then, moving the atlas, picked her up and sat her on his knee.

'Pictures,' he said. 'Not a story book.'

'Story, please, Baba,' she said, settling herself comfortably against him, and Moira gazed at them, emotion flooding through her. Not only because the little girl sat so at ease on James's knee, but that someone, her father, perhaps, had told her stories. So where was he, and why was Floris alone in Hull?

Moira's mother was coming for luncheon, so they had only a brief discussion about the possibilities of Floris's homeland and parentage before the dining room table was set at midday. Mrs Denham didn't yet know about Floris, and wouldn't have heard anything about the flood, or the rescued people in the church.

Mrs Evans had put a bowl, a spoon and a fork on the table and a cushion on a chair so that Floris might sit with them; they had done the same for Matthew once he was old enough to leave his high chair, and after that he always ate with them, much to the surprise of his grandmother.

'You'll rue the day,' she had said to Moira when she had been invited to lunch when Matthew was only a toddler, and been startled to find that a place setting had been made for him. 'Surely he should eat in the nursery? You always did when you were his age.'

'But that would mean that James wouldn't see him,' Moira had explained patiently. 'He's generally at home for luncheon, and at the end of the day Matthew is ready for bed when James comes in, so he doesn't see him for more than a few minutes. Just as it always was for me,' she added bravely. 'I hardly ever saw my father except at weekends.'

Her mother had stared at her in astonishment. 'But that is the way things are done,' she'd said sharply.

And for the first time in her life, Moira had answered back. 'Not in this household, Mama,' she had said, and had felt the thrill of victory. 'We eat together as a family.' She had seen the look of approval on James's face as he'd poured her and her mother a glass of wine and a tumbler of apple juice for Matthew, freshly pressed by Mr Evans.

But today, James, on hearing that his mother-in-law was coming for luncheon, remembered that he had much to do and would not be able to eat with them.

'Do give your mother my sincerest apologies' – he bent to kiss Moira's cheek – 'but I'm sure she'll understand. I'm going back to the church to deliver the food and see Lizzie, and then I have a meeting with Daniel until well into the afternoon,' he said, which was only partly true, and grinned, pretending he hadn't heard her hiss of 'Traitor' in his ear.

'But what will I tell my mother about Floris?' She saw a cabriolet pull up outside the front door. 'Oh, she's here! Quickly, off you go!' She gave him a push and he fled down the kitchen stairs before anyone answered the doorbell.

Mrs Denham brushed herself down as Rosie opened the door, and Moira came into the hall to greet her. 'Mama,' she said nervously, giving her a peck on the cheek. 'How are you today?'

Her mother sighed, and Moira knew she would hear a dreary litany of the morning's events.

Her parents lived in Hessle, a small village by the estuary on the outskirts of Hull, and came into town once a week to amble along the fashionable shopping streets of Whitefriargate and Silver Street, where, however, she rarely bought anything, preferring to tell her husband what she had seen and would like to be given. Unfortunately, he often didn't listen and seldom bought what she had wanted, which necessitated her returning to the shop to exchange the gift for the one she really desired.

'You pander to her, Papa,' Moira had told him. 'Why don't you go with her and let her choose what she wants?'

He shook his head. 'That would spoil it for her.' He smiled. 'She enjoys telling me that I have no idea what her preferences are, even after so many years; and by doing it my way I get an afternoon all to myself without any interruption.'

Is that how marriage works? she had asked herself in the early days. It wouldn't work for me.

'Please come through, Mama,' she said now, when Rosie had helped Mrs Denham off with her coat, though she kept on her hat, a dark red felt with rather bedraggled feathers. 'There's someone here that I'd like you to meet.'

'Oh! You have company?' Mrs Denham's eyebrows shot up and her mouth turned down.

'Not exactly, but someone I'd like you to meet.'

She led her mother into the sitting room, where Floris was lying on her stomach on the floor looking at the upside-down atlas. She looked up as Moira came back into the room, followed closely by Mrs Denham, and sat up.

'Mama, I'd like you to meet Floris; she's staying with us for a time. Floris,' she coaxed, 'come and say hello to my mama.'

Floris obediently got up from the floor and then hid behind Moira's skirts. Moira put her hand out to her. 'Can you say how do you do?'

Floris peeped out, took hold of Moira's hand, and then shook her head.

'No? You're not shy, Floris,' Moira persisted. 'Won't you say hello?'

The child put her fingers to her mouth and shook her head again. 'Want Baba,' she said plaintively.

'Whose child is it?' Mrs Denham said grimly. 'Not well brought up. That's what happens when a child is allowed to mix with adults. They don't know how to behave. They have to be taught.'

'Mama, she's still an infant,' Moira protested. 'Probably only three or four years old.'

Mrs Denham drew herself up. 'Then she should be in the nursery, not sitting with adults. Whose child is she, anyway? A waif and stray? Some orphan that James has found wandering the streets and brought home, I'll be bound. In fact I'd put money on it!'

CHAPTER EIGHT

James waited at the end of the staith until the cabriolet that had brought Mrs Denham to the front door had set off on its return journey before briskly walking away. He avoided Church Lane, where the excess water was still standing, and crossed the busy Market Place, which was humming with pedestrians, hand carts and loaded rullies despite the heavy drizzle. Hunching into his mackintosh, he hurried down North Church Side, avoiding glancing at the boarded-up doorway, and turned towards Trinity Church. He was keen to see Lizzie before she set off to the workhouse.

Inside the church there were several men from various committees he attended, some of them talking to the vicar; most of them were retired from their business lives, hence arriving earlier than James.

'Ripley, there you are.' Harold Bell greeted him at the entrance as he stepped inside. He was one of the most successful men in town, though you'd never realize it by his casual mode of dress. 'We were hoping you'd come. What are we to do with these people? They can't live on the streets. It isn't fair that they should have to, yet they don't want to go to the workhouse. I've told them that the new place is a big improvement on Charity Hall, but they're not convinced . . . and we do know, of course,' he added as an aside, 'that they won't all get in. They're not all from his area, you know. There are at least two from Lincolnshire! There's just one woman who has agreed to go, but she said she's waiting for you.'

'Yes.' James had spotted Lizzie amongst some of the other women who were sitting in the pews, quietly talking. 'She is. That's Lizzie – Mrs Chambers.'

Lizzie was nodding at him and gave him a brief gummy smile.

'Why her in particular?' Bell asked curiously. 'Is she a special case?'

'I think she probably is; she's a Hull woman so she will be allowed in. I also think that she's had enough of the life she's been living and her only needs are food and a bed to sleep in, where she can probably end her days; she's too old to work and not fit enough in any case.'

Bell's face creased. 'There are a few like that, so why . . .'

'She's been looking after a little girl,' James told him. 'She doesn't think she's been abandoned, but no one knows where the mother is. The child was left with another woman in the cellar whilst she looked for work, or so the story goes, but then she didn't come back; the other woman was suddenly taken ill and died. Lizzie took over and has offered to take the child to the workhouse with her and pass her off as her granddaughter.'

'Dear God,' Bell exclaimed. 'So the little girl was left alone? Where is she?'

'She's staying with me and my wife for the moment.'

'How come?' Bell asked curiously. 'Temporarily?'

James sighed and nodded. 'I'm going to try and find her parents. She's not the usual ragamuffin you might find on the streets scratching about in the gutter. She's maybe three or four, or perhaps more, but anyway too young to be left alone. But at the moment I don't know where to start. I was hoping that Howard might be here, but I expect he's hampered by his broken arm.'

He glanced up at Lizzie, who was getting to her feet as if she might be leaving. 'I'd better go and tell her,' he muttered. 'It's not right, Bell. I'm particularly worried about the children – there's a boy, twelve, thirteen maybe . . . we have to do something, find a place where they can shelter, have decent food—' He broke off. 'I won't be long. We must talk.'

'Well, Mr Ripley,' Lizzie croaked as he approached her. 'You haven't brought 'bairn wi' you. Your wife was happy to have her stay, was she?'

'Indeed she was. Her name is Floris,' he said.

'Florence?' she said. 'Your wife?'

'No, the child is called Floris. She told us.'

'Floris?' she repeated. 'Never heard of such a name. Pretty though, en't it?'

'Yes. It's Latin. It's from the word for flower.'

'Ah,' she said meaningfully. 'I knew she was a wanted child. You don't give a bairn such a name as that without having love in your heart.' She put her head to one side and gazed at him. 'Have you got bairns of your own, Mr Ripley?'

'I have a son. He's away at school just now.'

'Ah,' she said again. 'Bit of a handful, is he? What will he think of a little lass tekkin' his place?'

'She isn't taking his place,' he said abruptly. 'School isn't a punishment for him. And – and it's only temporary.' He didn't know where that statement or the next came from. 'He'll soon be going to the Grammar School.' He pointed across the square. 'That's where he'll be going, just as I did.'

She nodded. 'Aye. If you're going to have bairns, you need 'em near you. No use letting other folk bring 'em up.'

'I quite agree,' he murmured. 'So, are you still of the same mind? You're still going to ask for a place at the – the workhouse?'

'Aye,' she said. 'I'd rather end my days under a roof than on 'street, especially as winter's on its way, and there's no other option.' She gazed at him. 'Thank you for your concern, Mr Ripley. I'll not be there long, so you needn't worry about me.'

He handed her the parcel that Mrs Evans had given him. 'I've brought you some more food.' His voice had suddenly become hoarse. 'And my wife said would I give you money to buy a warm blanket, in case you were cold.'

'That's right kind of you, sir, and your lady wife. But if I have a nice new blanket wi' me – well, I reckon I wouldn't have it long afore somebody else took a shine to it. No,' she said firmly. 'I'll go in as destitute and then they'll not deny me.'

He nodded. 'Well, let me at least save you a long walk and get you a cab. You can get out of it anywhere you like if you don't want anyone to see you arrive in style.'

He whistled to a driver standing by his vehicle and the man climbed on to his seat, shook the reins and drove towards them.

'Take this passenger to wherever she wants to be, please.' He pressed coins into his hands and then handed Lizzie into the cab.

'Is it all right if I tek a little drive to 'pier first?' she asked. 'I haven't been there in years. Too far for me to walk any more. I miss seeing 'estuary and 'waves coming over 'top of 'pier.'

She handed the parcel of food back to him. 'Give that to Dot, will you? Her need is greater than mine. I expect I'll have supper or a cup o' cocoa tonight.' She sat back against the seat, making herself comfortable. 'God bless you, sir, and your lady wife, and may good fortune always attend you.'

He watched her being driven away in the direction of the pier but didn't hear the conversation as the driver called down, 'Now then, you old hag, not going to throw yoursen in 'river, are you? It wouldn't be good for my reputation.'

'Don't you give me any lip,' she called back. 'That gent is a friend o' mine. He'll check up in 'morning to find out if I arrived up 'road in one piece. So 'pier first so I can see 'estuary for 'last time, a little tour round 'town, and then – and then halfway up Anlaby Road, somewhere near to Argyle Street, and I'll walk 'rest of 'way and present myself at 'palace. They'll have 'welcome committee waiting for me, I don't doubt.'

'Right you are, Ma,' he laughed. 'Would you like me to pop into 'Vittoria while we're at 'pier? I can fetch you a pint of ale or a glass o' gin?'

'Ooh!' She breathed out noisily. 'Wouldn't that be a treat? But no, ta, buy yourself one out of 'change. It wouldn't do to turn up pleading poverty wi' drink on my breath, would it?'

He drove her to the pier and waited whilst she got out to look over the horse-wash and gaze down at the estuary; when she came back to the carriage, he saw tears glistening on her cheek.

'You all right, Ma?'

'Aye, I reckon I am.' She stood staring out at the turbulent estuary. 'Just reminiscing, you know. Me and my old man used to walk down here of a Sunday when he was home from 'sea. We'd pop into 'Vittoria, he for a pint of stout and he'd buy me a gin. That was afore we had our bairns.'

'Where are they all now?' he asked.

'One died in a brawl, others tekken by 'ocean, 'cept for 'youngest, and I don't know what happened to him.'

'What was his name?' the driver asked. 'If ever I should come across him, I'll tell him where you are.'

'Highly unlikely,' she said. 'But Jack Chambers is his name. I reckon he went to sea like his da and his brothers and has gone to join 'em.'

The man nodded. 'Sorry to hear that,' he said. 'But I'll keep my eyes and ears open, just in case.'

She sighed. 'Aye, do, and if you ever come across a young woman, a lady no less, who's hit hard times and is looking for her young daughter, direct her to James Ripley, that gennle-man who paid my fare to ride in this fine carriage.'

'Ripley of 'shipbuilding fame?'

'Summat like that, I reckon,' she said wearily, and climbed back into the vehicle. 'I'm ready to go now, young man, and thank thee kindly for tha patience.'

He closed the door for her and touched his hat. She looked done in, he thought as he climbed aboard and picked up the reins. I must call in on my ma, he mused. Not seen her lately.

CHAPTER NINE

Moira's mother expressed her opinion of Floris quite forcibly. The child, she said, was quite obviously an incomer, a foreigner or even a refugee.

'And?' Moira said. 'What about it? She's a child, Mama!' Moira was visibly upset and her mother raised her eyebrows. 'Her mother is missing. She's far too young to be out alone.'

'Have you enquired at the police station? Or you could take her to the workhouse to be looked after. She's not your responsibility, Moira. She could be diseased or – or full of fleas!' She looked towards the little girl, narrowing her eyes. 'Although she's wearing reasonable indoor clothing.'

Moira shook her head, not bothering to explain that the clothing that Floris was wearing had once belonged to Matthew. She reached out to the bell on the wall and pressed it. 'Come and sit down, Mama. Lunch will be up in a moment. We're having pea and ham soup and cold chicken and salad. How is Papa?' she asked, wanting to take the conversation elsewhere. 'Is he well?'

Floris came to her knee and clasped her little hands together. 'Papa?' she said eagerly.

Moira picked her up and placed her upon her knee, and

shook her head. 'My papa,' she said softly, tapping her chest, and Floris lowered her head and looked sad.

'What does she mean?' her mother said abruptly. 'She's got a father, then? At least that's a relief to know; that she's not a – not—' She cleared her throat.

'You mean born out of wedlock? Illegitimate?' Moira asked bravely, using language that her mother never would. 'It wouldn't matter anyway, not to us. It wouldn't be the child's fault.'

Moira was saved from her mother's tight-lipped answer by Mrs Evans and Rosie's coming in with the luncheon trays. Rosie carried the cold food and set it out at the end of the table, whilst Mrs Evans placed the soup in front of Mrs Denham and Moira, then tucked a white napkin beneath Floris's chin. Smiling at the little girl, the housekeeper placed a deep bowl on the table in front of her whilst Moira lowered her into her chair.

'Evans,' the little girl cried gleefully. 'Soup!'

Mrs Evans patted the top of her head. 'Clever girl,' she whispered, and Moira put her hand to her mouth to hide the smile that had erupted when she saw her mother's expression of derision.

'It wasn't a very happy occasion,' she told James later, as she ate a light supper and James a heartier one. 'Mother left early, making out that she had lots of shopping to do, which was plainly untrue as she would have brought someone with her to carry her parcels. She doesn't like to be seen carrying her own.'

She paused a moment, and then said softly, 'I think she realized that she had said the wrong thing. Floris behaved so beautifully at the table, didn't spill a drop of soup, and after I cut up her chicken for her she ate all that was on her plate, except for the salad, and said please and thank you in such a quaint way.'

James listened quietly. He would have liked to have made a cynical comment on his mother in-law's remarks, but didn't. He wondered how such an obnoxious woman could ever have given life to such a gentle, mild-mannered daughter as Moira. Had Moira been downtrodden as a girl, not allowed an opinion of her own, and was she only now finding her voice and her feelings?

'Where is Floris now?' he asked. 'Not bedtime already?'

'Not quite,' Moira answered, 'but Rosie has taken her upstairs for her bath. She seemed quite sleepy. I suppose she is still recovering from her ordeal in the cellar. Rosie will bring her down before bedtime. How were they at the church? Did you find Lizzie?'

James nodded. 'I was going to tell you. Lizzie has gone to Anlaby Road, but the people who are still there are reluctant to leave. It's still raining; who would want to go outside in this weather?'

'Can they stay for much longer?'

He sighed. 'They were moved out whilst a funeral service was held, but went back in again when it was finished. The verger stayed with them. I think he was bothered about the silver candlesticks disappearing.'

'Then he should remove them,' Moira said firmly. 'Shelter for homeless people should be the priority, not silverware!'

He smiled; she did have a mind of her own after all, in spite of her mother.

'I wanted to discuss Matthew and his schooling with you,' he said, changing the subject. 'I'll bring him home next weekend. If he likes the idea, I'd like him to leave the York school and start at Hull Grammar next term.'

'Oh!' Her face lit up. 'Will there be a place? I'd love him to be at home.'

'Would you?' He felt enormous relief. He'd been reluctant to insist, but it was what he wanted above all else. 'I met one of the masters recently and asked him what would be the chances. He said that as I was a former pupil the response would be favourable. They like the continuity of the generations. Of course, Matthew might want to stay on at York. He might have made friends there.'

Moira shook her head. 'I don't think so, not special friends. Last time he was home I asked him if he was enjoying school and he said it was all right. I think he missed the boys he knew from the private school in Hull; they had all gone on to the Grammar School.'

'Do you think you can stand up to your mother?' he asked guardedly. 'She was the one who wanted him to go to York, because her brothers had been there.'

'I know,' she said, breathing hard and deciding to speak her mind. 'But my uncles wouldn't care one way or another how we educate Matthew; they would think it our concern and nothing at all to do with them. Which it isn't.'

James was astonished. 'So we'll discuss it with Matthew when he comes home?'

She gazed at him. How was it that they had drifted so far apart since their marriage that they were being so formal? This wasn't what she had wanted for their life together. Had she been so much under her mother's thumb, and her father so acquiescent that he hadn't noticed? And yet James had seen the effect of it: she had copied her mother's views on marriage and how a child should behave, instead of following her own instincts. What was it that had made her more positive now?

It came to her instantly: it was Floris. The vulnerable child living in such dire and distressing circumstances had appealed to her protective, caring instincts, perhaps particularly because her own son was living away from home, when really she wanted him here with her and James.

'Yes, please,' she whispered, and her throat thickened.

'I don't want him to think that we don't want him when we do. I don't know how we came to this, James. He's our son and we love him and he should be with us at home.'

He rose from his chair and strode across to her, taking her hands and drawing her up to stand close to him, then tenderly touching her face.

'Of course he should,' he said quietly. 'The time will come when he will make up his own mind about future education and we can help him decide.'

He kissed her lips, and then moved back as they both heard the knock at the door and Rosie came in carrying a rosy-cheeked and sleepy Floris in her arms.

'She's almost ready for bed, ma'am,' Rosie said. 'Shall I just heat up some milk for her?'

Moira sat down and held up her arms to take Floris on her lap. She nodded, and kissed Floris on the cheek. 'Please,' she said softly. 'Then I'll put her to bed.' She turned to James when Rosie had gone. 'I was thinking, perhaps we could redecorate the nursery and bring down Matthew's little bed for her? Rather than having her sleep at the bottom of Mrs Evans's bed?'

'Be careful, Moira,' he said quietly. 'She's not our child. If we find her mother, she'll be leaving us; don't break your heart over her, even though she's an absolute treasure. She came to us because I couldn't think of anywhere else to take her, and . . .'

She nodded. 'I know . . . and has stayed,' she whispered, her voice full of tears. 'I keep telling myself that, but she is a darling, and what if we don't find her mother, or her father either?' She looked down at the sleepy little girl whose dark eyes were flickering into sleep. 'We would have to keep her then. She would have nowhere else to go.'

Rosie brought the cup of warm milk and James looked on as Moira held the cup steady so that Floris could drink from it.

We have set ourselves a problem, he pondered. He couldn't

trust himself to speak. Whether Floris stays a short or a long time with us, sooner or later we'll have to give her up; she is not ours. It is our duty in honour to find her parents, no matter who they are, and return her to them, for they must most sorely be missing her.

CHAPTER TEN

The following day James met his father from the Scarborough train at Paragon railway station. He'd hired a hansom cab in which they continued their journey, driving towards Hessle, where they would view the ongoing work at the shipyard that James's grandfather, a former ship's carpenter, had built up and his father had continued. They would then follow on with a business meeting and lunch at his brother's Hessle residence.

On the journey James, from the driving seat high above the cab, spoke to his father through the gap in the canopy made especially for the purpose, and told him about Floris and the people they had rescued from the cellar. 'It's disgraceful, Pa, that people should have to live like that. Nowhere to rest their heads but on a pile of old sacks, no means of earning money to buy food, and therefore reduced to begging; and as for the children . . .' His words dried up in his powerless anger.

'The workhouse?' his father suggested, lifting his head and turning his body to speak to him. 'Is that the only option?'

James raised his voice as they rumbled through traffic. 'Yes. One of the older women has gone there; she offered to take Floris with her, but I took her home. I'm going to try to find her parents, or her mother at least.'

'You took the child home? What did Moira make of that?'

'She agreed with me that the workhouse is no place for a child. Floris is only, I don't know, perhaps four, maybe less. So sweet; Moira has become attached to her.'

'Hmm,' his father grunted, and then raised his voice. 'Don't get too involved. If her mother turns up you'll have to give her up.'

'I know, I know,' James said testily. 'We're aware of that.'

The roof of the hansom was lowered. The day was dry, but grey. His father glanced up at him. 'You're in the wrong business, James, my boy. There's no sentiment in shipbuilding or accountancy. You have to deal only in facts.' He sighed. 'There should be an organization to deal with people in poverty; for people who have no means to shift for themselves even if they want to.'

He was silent for a while, and then went on, 'You must have some time on your hands; you're very efficient in looking after the company's assets. You can surely find some like-minded people who would join you in forming a group or an association to help these people. Set up a charity, why don't you?'

James had been listening. The traffic had lessened as they moved to the Hull outskirts and turned on to the Hessle Road, an area that housed fishing families. His father had always been an ideas man, able to look at different options; he had been influential in enabling Ripley and Sons to become even more successful than his own father had made it.

James raised his voice. 'PIP.'

'What?'

'People in poverty, you said.' James laughed. 'Would you mind if I did? I would still do the same as I do now for Ripley's.'

'Tell you what,' his father called up, 'although we'd need to gain Daniel's approval too, as a company we could put our name to it. Sponsor it. Not immediately; first we'd have to see

69

that the charity worked legitimately and wouldn't fall at the first hurdle. It would be to the company's credit if we were seen to be helping the have-nots.'

'Maybe set up an apprenticeship scheme?' James said. 'I know a young lad who wants to be a carpenter, but can't read or write.'

His father began to shake his head, but James interrupted. 'I know there are schools who can teach them, but not everyone knows how to access them, and without a stable home life it must be extremely difficult.'

After driving for a few more miles in silence, he saw the shipyard ahead. 'We're here,' he called, and drove into the yard. 'We'd better put our shipbuilding hats on now. Next time I'll hire a trap so we don't have to shout.'

'You should buy one, or a governess cart or some such. Then your wife could get out and about too.'

I'm not sure about that, James thought. Not sure if Moira would be brave enough.

Moira had asked Mrs Evans to come upstairs, as she wanted to discuss arrangements for Floris. Rosie had taken the little girl up to the former nursery where she could play with Matthew's old toys.

She had decided to ask the housekeeper for her opinion; she had realized that although Mrs Evans was a single woman without children, she had grown up with brothers and knew more of the world around them than she did.

'Please take a seat, Mrs Evans,' she said. 'I would like your opinion on our plans for Floris. James and I have decided that we will keep her here for the present, rather than sending her to a children's home or the workhouse. Although we are sure . . .' she hesitated, '*almost* sure that she would be well looked after in either, it will be no hardship for us to keep her safe here until we have news of her parents.'

70

Mrs Evans gave a rare smile, and sat down opposite Mrs Ripley. 'I was hoping that you would, ma'am. She's a dear little thing. You'll have to be careful, though, that you don't become too attached to her, or you won't want to let her go.'

'I know.' Moira looked down at her tightly clasped hands and eased them slightly. 'It will be difficult, but our ultimate aim is to restore her to her parents.' She paused. 'But in the meantime I was going to ask if you would supervise Rosie in cleaning the old nursery. Then we'll bring Matthew's bed in there for her and buy him a new one before he comes home. He's growing so fast.

'I'm also going to buy her some warm clothes. Matthew's old ones are rather small for her – they're baby things, really – and then she'll at least look presentable when her parents are eventually found.'

Mrs Evans nodded. 'Those that she was wearing, I'd guess she had had them for a long time,' she said thoughtfully. 'I wondered if her parents had been travelling. Her underslip and pantaloons were very worn and dirty, but they were silk. I washed them,' she explained. 'They were, or had been, very good quality.'

'Travelling? You mean – as a gypsy?' Moira asked.

'Oh, no, ma'am! I doubt that a gypsy or a Romany would be able to afford such fine silk. I meant travelling abroad. Maybe there was a mishap on their way back from a foreign country. You just don't know wi' foreigners; there are a lot of wars going on, so mebbe they were escaping from somewhere.'

'You could be right, Mrs Evans.' Moira pondered. 'Did Rosie tell you that Floris spoke another language to us? I have no idea what it was. Not French or Italian – something I hadn't ever heard before.'

'No, she didn't say, ma'am, but 'little girl has such dark eyes, hasn't she? And if you're going to buy her some new clothes,

71

just to tide her over, there's a children's clothes shop in White-friargate and they're not that expensive.'

'Yes, I'm going today. I'll get her some wool dresses and some underclothing, too; flannel, perhaps, as the weather is getting very cold. And a coat and bonnet!'

Moira realized that she was getting carried away in her eagerness to clothe Floris, but Mrs Evans was nodding away in agreement and making suggestions such as a pair of indoor slippers, and some stout shoes for when Floris went outside.

'I don't know her size, of course,' Moira murmured. 'I'll have to measure her feet.'

'Maybe a pair of rubber boots, too. Mr Ripley said he was going to buy a pair for Bob, and some decent working clothes.'

'Bob?' Moira said vaguely.

'The odd job lad, ma'am. His clothes are in rags.'

'Oh, dear!' Moira said distantly. 'Sorry. It's not right, is it?' She looked pensive for a second. 'Send him up when he comes in, Mrs Evans, will you? I hardly ever see him.'

She had her coat and hat on, ready to go shopping, when a tentative knock came on the sitting-room door. It wasn't Rosie's sharp tap, nor Mrs Evans's bold one.

'Come in,' she called, and the door slowly opened to reveal a boy in a misfitting jacket and trousers with a too-large shirt hanging out of them. On his feet he wore boots without laces.

He pressed his lips together and then mumbled, 'Mrs Evans said as I had to come up cos you wanted to see me. Am I in bother, miss? I try to come in quietly when I bring 'coal hod up of a morning.'

'You're Bob, aren't you?'

'Yes, miss – ma'am – Mrs Ripley.'

Moira gazed at him. But for the grace of God, this could be my son wearing someone else's old clothes, she thought.

'No,' she said, 'you're not in trouble. But I like to see who's working for us. You're very useful, do you know that? Bringing the coal hod and the logs up every day is most helpful and very much appreciated.'

She saw the boy visibly relax. 'I'm very strong,' he said. 'Rosie can't lift 'hod when it's full o' coal and I can and don't ever drop it.'

'I wanted to see you because I'm going out shopping, and although Mr Ripley will take you for some new boots, I thought I'd buy you some shirts and trousers and maybe a jacket to wear, so I wanted to see your size.'

The boy's mouth dropped open. 'My auntie won't have to pay, will she, miss? She dun't have any money.'

'No,' she said, 'she won't. But if you're working for us, you'll need to be more presentable than you are now.'

Bob hung his head. 'Yeh, I know miss – ma'am,' he said. 'It dun't look good, does it?'

'No, Bob, it doesn't, but now that I've seen you I think I know what to get.' She reached to her sewing table for her tape measure. 'Can I just measure you round your chest? Lift up your arms. That will be all, thank you.'

What on earth is James thinking of, she wondered as Bob went out of the door, touching his forehead with his finger. How could he have a boy working here dressed in rags? And Mrs Evans – what was *she* thinking of employing a boy like that, however worthy? She really should have asked me first, or at least asked if she could have money to buy him new clothes.

CHAPTER ELEVEN

Moira often walked into town alone. Before her marriage, her mother insisted on accompanying her; she told her that young women should never walk alone but always have an escort, either a maid or a mother. Although many women, young and older, observed this rule, Moira discovered that the truth in her case was that her mother didn't care to be out alone and so tagged herself on to Moira.

As a young woman Moira had had friends who would have liked to join her for afternoon tea or shopping, but on discovering that her mother would be coming too they soon made excuses not to accept her invitations: a headache, perhaps, or some such malady. Eventually, neither did they ask her to join them. As a married woman she had decided that now she was free of her mother's influence she would shop without a companion; Hull after all was a small though influential town, and she would keep to safe areas and always arrive home before nightfall, especially in winter. The High Street was a dark and narrow street with only a few gas lamps to light the way, and many alleyways and gloomy courts which had the potential to harbour villains within them.

She had discussed the matter with James, who had said that his own mother was a free spirit and went wherever she wanted, but shied away from narrow cut-through passages and walkways, of which there were many in Hull. Now that she was living in Scarborough she did the same; she did not cut through the Bolts, the narrow steps that ran down from the town to Sandside where the fisherfolk lived and worked, but in that case not because she was afraid, but only because they were very steep and made her catch her breath. She was a Hull woman used to the flatlands of her birthplace who was now walking up and down the steep hills of a seaside town.

'Aye,' her husband would say when she asked him to slow down if they were out walking together. 'You need a good deal of breath for Scarborough.'

Moira walked briskly into Whitefriargate, the ancient main shopping street of Hull. She knew where she needed to be, a small shop not far from Parliament Street and opposite where the Charity Hall workhouse used to be until recently. She had looked into the shop window often, drawn to gaze at so many pretty clothes for babies and small children, velvet dresses for little girls and sweet white, blue or pink clothing for baby boys or girls in the historical French fashion.

I must be practical, she told herself as she entered the establishment. She is not my child; she is only staying for a little while.

Nevertheless, an hour later, she turned for the shop door clutching many parcels containing three little dresses – two in fine wool, one in crisp cotton because she couldn't resist the embroidered smocking across the bodice – three pairs of white cotton pantaloons with frills round the ankles, three white flannelette nightgowns, one wool dressing gown and a pair of little fur-lined slippers. A red winter coat and matching bonnet, two pairs of lace-up bootees (for which she had the promise that she could bring them back if they didn't fit), and three pairs of warm wool buttoned leggings that came from the foot to the knee.

She turned back to the assistant. 'I've just remembered that I have other parcels to collect, so would you kindly deliver these?'

She had almost forgotten that she was to buy boys' clothing too, and gaily waving goodbye to the assistant, who she was sure would be delighted with the sale, headed off further down the busy street to a different kind of shop to buy trousers, shirts and a jacket for Bob.

I won't be as enamoured with workaday clothes as I have been buying for Floris, she thought, and she knew that in her heart she had loved buying clothes for a little girl, even though she had kept reminding herself that Floris wasn't her daughter. She caught her breath. I'm missing Matthew, she thought. I really do want him back at home.

She passed a shop selling men's and boys' clothes but resisted going in, reflecting that that would be a treat for James. She marked a tweed jacket that she thought Matthew might like, but then reconsidered, thinking he would like to choose for himself, and walked on towards a shop promising clothes for the working man on a sign above the window.

These she did carry home, for she felt that the boy's need was urgent, and as the weather was becoming much colder she had bought him wool jumpers and flannel shirts, a pair of cord trousers, a jacket, and several pairs of socks. She had left the purchase of boots and a waterproof coat for James.

She arrived home at the back door, something she rarely did, and Mrs Evans was astonished to open the door to her.

'Ma'am!' she said. 'Is everything all right? Can I take your parcels?'

'Perfectly all right, Mrs Evans,' she said, stepping inside. 'But yes, you can take the parcels; that's why I came to the kitchen door. These are for the boy.'

'The boy?'

'Erm, Bob? Or is he Robert?'

'No, ma'am, he's Bob.' Mrs Evans looked at all the parcels. 'Are they all for him?'

'Yes. The only things I didn't buy,' she lowered her voice, 'were undergarments. I know what to buy for Matthew, but I wasn't sure if boys such as Bob would wear the same.'

Mrs Evans's mouth twitched. 'I – I could get those for him,' she said. 'There's no need for you to bother yourself, ma'am. I understood Mr Ripley to say he would get him a waterproof coat and boots.'

'He did,' Moira affirmed, at which Mrs Evans cleared her throat and said, 'He'll think all of his Christmases have come at once.'

Moira sat down on a kitchen chair. 'He will, won't he, poor boy. He's such a ragamuffin, and really, Mrs Evans, we can't have him looking as he does when he's working for us, it doesn't befit our circumstances. Besides,' she said sorrowfully, 'he's still only a child. I'd hate to think of Matthew being cold and wet and wearing someone else's boots.'

Mrs Evans nodded. Perhaps she'd had the mistress wrong after all. She'd thought it was Mr Ripley who had the heart and understanding, and yet his wife was the one who had gone straight out after meeting the boy and bought him warm clothing. It must be nice to be rich, she thought, and then mentally chastised herself for such negative thoughts.

'Mrs Ripley,' she said, 'seeing as you're here in 'kitchen, would you like a pot of tea?'

Moira gave her a wide smile. 'Mrs Evans, I really would.'

Mrs Evans ran a hot iron over the new flannel shirts and pressed the trousers to take out the creases. Bob came in whilst she was doing so.

'Just 'lad I was looking for,' she said, not looking up at him.

'I did your errands, Mrs Evans. 'Butcher said he'd send his lad over in 'morning wi' your order.'

'Did you tell him I wanted it early?'

'Yeh. He said it'd be here by eight o'clock or mebbe sooner.'

'Good lad.' She put the iron to cool at the back of the range where it was out of reach. 'Now then, when Mr Ripley gets home he's going to tek you out to buy you a new waterproof coat and boots.'

She saw the boy's mouth drop. 'D'ya mean brand new or nearly new?'

'He said new so I'd suppose that's what he meant,' she said dismissively. 'Some lads are very fortunate.' She gazed at him keenly. 'Not only that, Mrs Ripley has also been out and bought you some new clobber. So whose birthday is it today?'

'Must be mine,' he said in a strangled voice. 'Is that what those are?' He nodded to the shirts on the wooden clothes-horse in front of the range.

'Well, they're not mine and they're not Rosie's.'

'And – and they're not for Mr Ripley's son, I suppose?'

'You'd suppose right. Nor are these fine breeches.' She picked up the trousers hanging over a chair. 'So what I want you to do now, whilst everybody's out or upstairs, is to fill that bowl wi' hot water out of 'kettle and have a good all-over wash. I'll lock 'back door so nobody barges in. Rosie's upstairs look-ing after Floris so she won't be down, so there's onny me, and you needn't be bothered that I'll see owt that I haven't seen afore. Do you understand?'

Dumbly he nodded. 'You mean under me arms an' that?'

'Yes,' she said. 'Under your arms and *especially* an' that.'

'And then – then can I wear 'em?'

'You can. You can wear 'trousers, a flannel shirt and a wool jumper over 'top, or 'jacket, whichever you want. Then I'll ask Mr Ripley if we can get you some vests and long underpants for winter, and then he's going wi' you to see your aunt.'

'Oh!' He huffed. 'What for?'

'Don't know,' she said, although she did. 'So come on, get a move on. I'll see to 'kettle. Don't want you to scald yourself.'

She ran cold water into the metal bowl and topped it up with hot and then turned her back, just as she used to do when she lived with her father and brothers, and busied herself with preparing the family's supper.

When James came home after dropping his father off to catch the Scarborough train, he whistled when he saw the boy standing in the kitchen in his socks but no shoes, with his hair brushed, his face scrubbed clean, and wearing his new clothes.

'Who is this, Mrs Evans? What happened to the other boy who used to be here? He hasn't left us, has he? He was a very useful boy.'

'No, it's me, sir. Bob. Mrs Ripley got me these new clothes.' He stroked the wool jumper that he'd put on over the shirt while Mrs Evans had pulled the collar up over the neck and folded it down. 'I'm ever so warm, even me feet, but I don't want to get me new socks dirty wi' me old boots.'

'We'd better get you some more boots then, hadn't we? You can come upstairs with me to show Mrs Ripley and then we'll decide what to do next. Just a light supper for me tonight, Mrs Evans,' he added as an aside. 'I've eaten a hearty lunch at my brother's house.'

After Moira had duly admired his new clothes and marvelled that everything fitted, James sat down and addressed the boy.

'What we've been thinking, Bob, now that you're on the staff here and kitted out in appropriate clothes for what you do in your work . . .' Both James and Moira observed how the boy stood up straighter and lifted his chin as he listened. 'We wondered if you'd prefer to live in, so that you're on call, as Rosie and Mrs Evans are?'

'I'd have to ask me auntie,' he muttered. 'And where would I sleep, sir?'

'There's a room on the top floor that you can have,' Moira answered for James, 'and we wouldn't expect you to agree without asking your aunt's permission first. She is your guardian, I suppose?'

'Does that mean being in charge o' me? Cos if it does, then yeh, she is. I think so, anyway, but she might be glad to be shut o' me.'

Moira flinched, but James interceded. 'Well,' he said, getting to his feet, 'shall we go and ask her?'

CHAPTER TWELVE

Bob's Aunt Lily opened the door and was about to give Bob a sharp rebuke for being late, but she held her breath when she saw James Ripley standing behind him.

'This is Mr Ripley, Aunt Lily,' Bob told her. 'He wants to talk to you.'

The woman groaned. 'Oh! Have you been in bother?' she began, but James interrupted.

'May we come in?' He stepped over the doorstep straight into the parlour; at least he thought it was the parlour, but he guessed that it was the only room in the house, except perhaps for a scullery behind the half-open door at the opposite side, where he glimpsed a stone sink and a back door.

'He hasn't been a bother at all,' he said quickly. 'He's a very willing and agreeable boy. You are the aunt who's been looking after him whilst his father is away, so he tells me?'

She nodded, and James saw how weary she looked. Her hair was thin and lanky, her face flabby and grey, and her neck and hands were wrinkled; and though he suspected that she wasn't so very old, her features told of a hard life.

'Won't you tek a seat, sir, and tell me why you're here, if Robert isn't in trouble?'

'So, Robert is it, and not Bob after all?' James looked down at the boy, who hung his head.

'I like Bob best,' he mumbled.

'Sir,' his aunt said sharply. 'Don't forget your manners.'

Bob's head sank lower and James sat down on the only vacant chair, the other being piled high with clean washing. He went on swiftly, 'The lad is worried about how you'll manage if, as I propose, he comes to live in alongside our other staff. We keep a maid and a housekeeper,' he explained. 'Bob is very helpful with keeping the coal hods full and the wood store filled with chopped wood ready for the fires. But there are other jobs he could assist with if he lived in: running errands, or cleaning boots and shoes, for instance.'

'Well, I've no objection, sir,' the aunt muttered, 'and I dare say he'd work a lot better if he had a full belly, cos I find it difficult to feed three growing lads; I've two of my own, sir. Both working now but onny bringing in a pittance.'

'Bob will still receive the same wages,' James told her, 'but with the addition of bed and board, so you won't need to feed him.'

'You could have me wages, Aunt Lil,' the boy said eagerly. 'I shan't need any spending money.'

'And he could come and see you, say once a fortnight,' James added. 'I'll ask the housekeeper about that; she rules the kitchen and the staff.'

'Aye, I gathered so.' The woman permitted herself a thin smile. 'Strict, is she?'

'Shall we say she runs a tight ship,' James agreed. 'She's been with our family for many years and we have never had cause to complain.' He stood up. 'So, if you agree, Mrs Walters, Robert can start immediately. We'll provide suitable clothing; as you see, underneath the coat he's wearing he has a new warm jumper and trousers. Next, we'll get him fitted with a waterproof coat and boots.'

The woman's eyes filled. 'I'm sorry I couldn't do better for him, sir. When he told me he was applying for work, there was nowt else but hand-me-downs to dress him in.'

James assured her that it didn't matter and that his house-keeper had seen his potential. 'Where is his father?' he asked. 'Can he not help you out?'

She shook her head. 'He could be at 'bottom of 'sea for all I know.'

'Then write down his name, age and which company he's working for and give it to your nephew next time you see him, and I'll try to find out for you.'

'Casual labour,' she said, and he could hear the emotion in her voice.

'Nevertheless, we can try.' He put his top hat back on, tapped his finger on the brim and turned to the boy. 'Have you something to say to your aunt?'

Bob reached up and kissed his aunt's cheek and she bent towards him and gave him a hug. 'Be a good lad, won't you?' she said huskily. 'And don't forget me.'

'I won't do that, Aunt Lily, an' I'll come an' see you like Mr Ripley said,' he said bravely, and then thrust his hand into the pocket of his new trousers. 'Mrs Evans give me this,' he said, producing a sixpence. 'I want you to have it.'

'Quite touching, really,' James told Moira later when they arrived back home; he had taken the boy to the shop in White-friargate where he bought him a waterproof coat – one that he could grow into – a pair of strong boots and a peaked woollen cap.

Rosie brought in a tray with a plate of chicken and pickle, slices of bread, a pot of coffee and a slice of fruit cake for James's supper.

'Perfect,' he said to the maid. 'Thank Mrs Evans for me, Rosie. This is just right.'

Moira continued with some mending until James had

finished eating, when he gave a deep sigh. 'It's been a strange day,' he murmured. 'A mixed range of events. Meeting Pa, viewing the ongoing work at the shipyard, discussing finances; we have the possibility of two new ships for a client, and I must spend the next few days working out the costings and expenditure. We might have to take on additional men to complete them.'

'What sort of ships?' Moira asked.

'Two smacks,' he said briefly. 'One for next year, the other for the year after and the possibility of more. And then there was the meeting with Bob's aunt. I had formed the totally wrong impression of her from the boy's description. I had her down as a harridan from how he had described her, but what I found was a woman worn out by drudgery who was trying to bring up a family of three boys with no husband and very little money.'

'She'd be pleased that Bob now has live-in work and she has a mouth less to feed?' Moira offered.

'I'm not sure.' James teased through his beard. 'I think she might have felt guilty that she couldn't have done more for him than she had.' He heaved a breath. 'They're living in a one-up one-down house in a court off High Street, not five minutes from here, yet it's a different world. From what I could make out, I think there might have been a yard at the back, maybe somewhere to throw out slops. I know that area; I remember first going down there with my mother when I was a child. She always carried a basket. I didn't realize then that she was taking food for the poor. I think the yard abuts another yard in a court at the back of it,' he went on, 'so there's no—'

'No way out?' Moira interrupted softly, and he shook his head. 'So, erm . . .' She hesitated. 'What about the' – she dropped her voice to a whisper – 'the night soil men?'

He leaned forward towards the fire and cupped his chin in his hands. 'Through the house,' he muttered, barely opening his mouth. 'There's no other way.' It wasn't a matter he would normally discuss with his wife, but he wanted to make her aware of where the boy had come from.

'It's wrong that people should live under those conditions!' She put down her sewing. 'No matter who they are, it's not decent or fair. And how would they escape if there was a fire?'

'That might be a rare occurrence,' he answered bitterly. 'In that house at least, they had such a low fire that they'd have to burn one of the old worm-eaten chairs to have the chance of a blaze, for there was no coal in the hod nor kindling in the hearth.'

'It's upset you, hasn't it?' she asked. 'James, you have rescued two children in this last week and perhaps saved some lives from disaster . . .'

He looked up at her questioningly and she went on more calmly.

'Floris you rescued from the flooded cellar, and other people and children too, whom you took into the church where they would be safe and dry, and you've improved Bob's life enormously.'

'But it's not enough,' he murmured. 'We know that it isn't.'

Moira reached for his hand, a gesture unusual for her; she was often shy of showing emotion. 'It's a start,' she said softly. 'We must find others; other people with a conscience who can together make a difference to these people who have nothing.'

He gazed at her and wondered. Had this concern for others been there all the time and he hadn't seen it? Moira had led a sheltered life, and although her father seemed to be benevolent her mother certainly wasn't; a more self-centred woman would be difficult to find.

His dearest wife, shy and unassuming, without any prompting from him had finally found her own voice.

CHAPTER THIRTEEN

'Shall I explain to Matthew about Floris?' James asked Moira before he set off for York, early on the Saturday morning.

Moira considered. 'I think so. So that he's prepared for a little girl in the house. Will you . . .' She hesitated. 'Will you also discuss with him the possibility of starting at the Grammar School?'

James nodded as he shrugged into his winter coat and then picked up his driving gloves. 'Yes; he should be asked which he'd prefer. Daniel and I were both asked inclinations, and for university the choice was ours entirely.'

'I hadn't realized that Daniel ever went to university.'

'He didn't. He dithered over it, and then said he'd prefer to go to sea, not in the Navy but on trawlers. When Pa agreed that he could, I believe he thought that one voyage would put Dan off the sea for life, but it didn't. He loved it. He was told that he'd make a great skipper if he stayed in trawling, but by then he had ideas on how to improve some of the ships he'd sailed in and discussed them with Pa, who found them innovative and suggested he joined the company.' He picked up his top hat and bent to kiss her.

'Take care on the road, won't you?' she said anxiously. 'Whose carriage are you hiring?'

'The usual fellow; he's very reliable. Don't worry, we'll be home before dark.' He blew her a kiss as he left the room and was gone.

He'd often thought of buying a carriage, but living in town, working from his home office, he didn't need a vehicle every day, so he was satisfied to hire one when needed from reputable livery stables where the carriages were well sprung and comfortable and the horses were in tip-top condition.

For today's journey to York he'd hired a two-wheeled trap in which he and his son could sit comfortably next to each other and chat as they drove home, with room for Matthew's wooden box behind them.

'Pa, can I drive?' Matthew asked as they set off back on the Hull road.

Pa is it now, James wondered? Too old for Papa? Our boy is growing up without us; we can't have that. I want to influence him, not leave it to schoolmasters, no matter how clever they are.

'On a straight run of road you can,' he told him, 'when we've gone through the villages, and when there are no other vehicles.'

'It's fairly quiet now,' Matthew pointed out, adding, 'Some of the other boys drive home.'

'Older than you? Or about the same age?'

'Mm, well, most are older, but they're farmers' sons so they'll be used to driving, I suppose. Are traps expensive?'

'Not too much,' James said. 'It's the upkeep of the horses that costs the most, feeding, stabling, shoeing and veterinary bills and so on, so if you're not driving every day it's more economical to hire.'

'Oh, I see! And I suppose just coming up and down to York now and again, it wouldn't be worth it?'

'Not really. And doing it this way we have a choice of hire carriages, don't we, for whatever the weather? However, whilst we're on the subject . . .' How opportune, James was thinking; I was wondering how to bring up this matter. 'Your mama and

I – although it would be your decision, of course – well, as we rather miss you at home, miss you a lot as a matter of fact, we were wondering if you'd prefer to be at Hull Grammar School and come home every day?'

Matthew turned to look at his father and seemed completely stunned. 'Do you mean it?'

James laughed. 'Of course I mean it! Your mama and I have discussed it often since you started at the York school.'

'So why did you send me there?'

'The school was highly recommended by your grandfather – Grandfather Denham, that is, not Grandpa Ripley. My father was educated at Hull Grammar School, as your Uncle Daniel and I were; but when we agreed that you should go to York, your mama and I hadn't reckoned on the fact that the house would feel so empty without you.' James glanced down at his son, just as Matthew let out a great gush of breath, and saw that his lips were trembling. 'Are you all right?' he murmured.

Matthew nodded, but his voice faltered. 'I thought that you didn't want me at home all the time; that's what some of the other boarders say about their parents.'

'Well, it absolutely isn't true about us!' James put his hand round Matthew's shoulder and squeezed it. 'We thought that you might like to try out being independent, but then we wondered whether we had made a *big* mistake, that perhaps you weren't quite ready.'

'I'm not! I'd rather be at home,' Matthew said in a small voice, 'and some of my Hull friends are at Hull Grammar School so I miss seeing them.'

'Oh, well, that's splendid!' James felt hugely relieved. 'Shall we arrange that? Your mama will be delighted, and so am I!'

'So, need I go back? I'll have to write to Jonathan and Cyril to tell them. They're my best friends there; they're a bit older than me, so I don't suppose they'll mind too much.'

I will never again in my life allow anyone to influence me

about my family, James resolved, angry with himself for having been led into a situation where he had never been totally at ease. He glanced down again at Matthew, saw the big smile on his face, and drew in at the side of the road.

'Come on then.' He stood up, moved over, and handed the reins to Matthew. 'Easy does it; just up to the crossroads should be enough to give you a feeling for the pull. Trot on,' he called to the horses, and murmured to his son, 'Shake the reins, that's it, and off we go.'

Matthew was ecstatic. After a mile, he slowed the team and handed the reins back to his father. 'Mama won't believe it, will she? She'll be so surprised when I tell her!'

'Indeed she will. And I'd almost forgotten,' James fibbed, 'I haven't told you what's been happening at home.' He went on to tell Matthew about the great storm and the people in the cellar who had to be rescued from the flood, and Matthew drew in his breath.

'And so what happened to the boy Tom, and the old lady? Where did they go? They wouldn't be able to live in the church.'

'No, they couldn't.' James's voice dropped. He was particularly worried about Tom, who seemed to have disappeared; Lizzie, he knew, could live by her wits, having had a lifetime of training, and should by now be settled into the workhouse. But Tom could be desperate enough to steal or take any kind of risk in order to eat, or find shelter, or even just to stay alive.

'But we were able to rescue a little girl,' he added in a brighter voice, after telling Matthew about Lizzie going to the workhouse, 'and brought her home. We don't know where her parents are, so there was nowhere else for her to go, and at present she's sleeping in Mrs Evans's bed—'

'She could have mine, Pa!' Matthew broke in. 'Mama said last time I was home that mine was getting too small for me; if I have a bigger one we could put my old one in the schoolroom and make it into a nursery again!'

James felt choked. Matthew was the same boy he'd always been, but no longer too shy to speak up with his own opinion – the school in York had taught him that, at least – and he was coming home.

Floris gazed curiously at Matthew when they arrived, and Matthew crouched down next to her and said, 'Hello, Floris. I'm Matthew!'

She looked at him, and then at Moira. She pointed at Matthew and said, 'Boy!'

'Yes.' Moira laughed. 'My boy! Matthew. He's been away at school.'

Floris turned round and picked up a book that had once been Matthew's and handed it to him, then took his hand and said, 'Story please, Maff.'

To Moira's astonished delight, both children sat in one chair and Matthew began to read to Floris. Moira thought that he might have been embarrassed to read to such a little girl, but he wasn't at all, and each time he paused Floris gave him a little nudge to keep going. As Moira also listened to the story, she realized why he kept on reading. It was *Robinson Crusoe*, a book that had been written over a hundred years before, and one of Matthew's favourite adventure stories. It was far too advanced for such a little girl, but she seemed entranced, glancing up constantly into Matthew's face.

Rosie knocked and came in. 'Shall I bath Floris, ma'am?' she asked, and then noticed Matthew. 'Hello, Master Matthew. It's nice to see you home again.'

'Thank you, Rosie; it's nice to be home. Shall I read some more, Mama, or is it bedtime for Floris?'

'Five minutes more,' she said. 'We can skip bath time tonight, Rosie, and Floris can have some warm milk before she goes to bed, and maybe tomorrow, Matthew, you could help to move your bed into what will be Floris's nursery and you can sleep on a palliasse until we get you another bed. Will that be all right? Do you mind?'

He got up from the chair, squeezing out from Floris, and put his arms round his mother's waist. 'No, I don't mind at all. I'm so pleased to be home, Mama, and part of everything again. Pa told me that I can attend the Grammar School and I'm so excited.'

Floris climbed down from the chair and put her arms round Matthew as far as they would stretch, and that was how James found them, with a smiling Rosie looking on.

Later, after they had eaten supper and Floris was fast asleep at the bottom of Mrs Evans's bed, James glanced at the mahogany bracket clock that was ticking on the mantelpiece; it was just after seven o'clock. He got up from his chair and went to the window. It had stopped raining, but the night sky was heavy with low dark cloud.

'You're restless, James. What is it?' Moira was concerned. It seemed as if he couldn't settle.

'I think we'll have more rain and I'm bothered about the boy.' He sat down again, but gave a sigh.

'Which boy? Not Bob? Surely he isn't out! We shouldn't allow him out in the dark.'

'No, no, not Bob. The boy from the cellar. Tom. Bob knows him, says he's a mate. He has nowhere to live, now that the cellar is boarded up.'

Matthew looked up; he was still reading *Robinson Crusoe*. 'The boy who came to the church? What did he sleep on? Did he have a bed?'

'No, I shouldn't think so; a sack of straw maybe if he was lucky, but it would have been soaked through when the cellar was flooded.'

Matthew didn't speak, but neither did he go back to his book.

'You want to look for him, don't you?' Moira stared at James.

James got to his feet and went to the window again. 'Yes, I do. I think I'll ask Bob if he'd like to come with me; he's more likely to know where to find him than I am.'

'Will there be any policemen about, do you think?' she asked.

'Bound to be,' he said, turning round. 'I can ask if they'll keep their eyes open for him, but I'll tell them he's not in trouble. I don't want them thinking he's a troublemaker just because he's out on the streets.'

'Can I come, Pa?' Matthew put down his book. 'Would he be more likely to show up if there are boys with you? I don't know Bob, do I?'

'No, you don't. Mrs Evans took him on when he came to the door looking for work.'

James glanced at the clock again, and then at his wife, who was looking very anxious. 'Yes.' He made a decision. 'You can come,' he said to Matthew. 'You needn't worry,' he told Moira. 'There won't be any ruffians about. It's far too early. They wait until people start turning out of the hostelries. We'll only be an hour or so.'

CHAPTER FOURTEEN

They were wrapped up warmly, but even so, the chill bit into them as soon as they stepped outside. A shrieking, whistling wind coming off the German Sea, streaked through the Humber mouth, straight down the lashing waters of the estuary and into the River Hull, where it tossed every boat and tug, straining every mooring, then slid round corners of the old town, tunnelling through alleyways, scattering rubbish, lifting broken tiles and rattling loose window frames and door latches.

Bob was snug in his new coat and woollen cap, and Mrs Evans had found him a thick scarf in a drawer. Matthew too had on his warmest coat and a similar cap to the one that Bob was wearing.

'Stay by 'master,' Mrs Evans had said, wrapping the scarf round Bob's neck and pulling up his coat collar. 'No going off on your own unless he tells you to.'

Bob had nodded; his eyes were bright with excitement. He hadn't seen Tom since meeting him in the church after the flood, and wondered if he had found somewhere else to shelter; and, he worried, what was he doing for food? It seemed now that Mr Ripley thought Tom might have gone missing, and – Bob lifted his chin purposefully – was giving him the very important job of helping to find him.

He'd glanced at Matthew but didn't speak until Matthew asked him, 'Are you Bob?'

'Yeh. Are you Matthew?'

'Yes. I've never been out in the dark like this before. Have you?'

'Yeh, but onny to my auntie's. She dun't allow me out when it's as dark as this.'

'Don't think of wandering off, either of you; stay by me,' James said, treating them equally, as they crossed Market Place, holding on to their caps as they headed for the church but this time passing across it and turning into South Church Side, where there were several narrow streets that a child could shelter in and not be seen.

'Do you know this side of the church?' he asked Bob.

'No, not really. There's an owd folk's hospital and some houses down Vicar Lane, but it's a bit dark so I daren't ever risk it. I think 'Three Crowns is down here, and Tiger Lane, but I an't seen any tigers!'

'Tigers!' Matthew exclaimed. 'I didn't think there were any tigers in England!'

'There aren't,' his father said, 'except maybe in a circus or a travelling zoo.'

'I've seen wild animals when Hull Fair comes to town,' Bob told them, his voice carried away by the squall. 'Lions and elephants and a man wi' a monkey on his shoulder, but I an't nivver seen a tiger! My, wouldn't that be summat?'

'You talk very strangely,' Matthew told him. 'Are you from a foreign place?'

'Me? No!' Bob gazed at Matthew in astonishment. 'I thought that you was!'

James gave a sigh. 'Quiet now, both of you. I want to listen for Tom. I'm going to call out his name, and then I want you to do the same, Bob, and tell him who you are and that he's not in trouble.'

Bob put his shoulders back and straightened his spine. 'Right you are, sir.'

James cupped his hands to his mouth and shouted out towards the narrow entries. 'Tom! Tom, are you there? It's James Ripley here. Are you all right?'

He nodded to Bob, who then cupped his hands to his mouth in the same manner. 'Tom! It's me, Bob! Are you all right? You're not in trouble. Can you give us a shout? Have you got somewhere to stop?'

'Now then, now then! What's afoot here?'

A single lamp was swinging wildly and in its glow they could see a truncheon held by a gloved hand and an arm clad in dark serge.

'We're looking for a young lad' – James peered forward – 'erm, constable? I wonder if you've seen him about? He was rescued from the flooded cellar on North Church Side the other morning – were you there?'

'No, sir, I wasn't. I wasn't on duty on that filthy night, I'm happy to say, but my fellow officers told me about it, that 'folk who were rescued went into 'church.'

'Most of them did and some stayed the next night, but the boy, Tom, didn't. I have reason to feel uneasy about him. He has no parents, no means of sustenance and no shelter.'

'Has he been in any trouble?' the officer asked. 'That's 'onny reason we'd know of him.'

'No,' Bob broke in. 'He hasn't. He's got nowhere to go, 'cept 'workhouse, and he won't go there.'

'Will you watch out for him?' James asked. 'And bring him to me if you find him? James Ripley, High Street; my name is on a brass plaque outside my door. We'll give him shelter.'

'Ah! You'd be as well to be careful, sir,' the constable said bluntly. 'You never know what these down and outs might get up to. You'll probably lose your fine silver or your lady wife her jewels.'

James heard Bob's drawn-in exasperated breath and quickly stepped in, saying, 'We know all the risks, officer, and the boy isn't one. I'll bid you goodnight and we'll continue our own search.' He turned away, drawing Matthew and Bob with him and muttering something that he wouldn't have liked them to hear or repeat.

They continued their search and James, under his breath, called himself an idiot for not bringing a lamp, for the narrow streets alongside the church were pitch black.

He knocked on the door of Lister's Hospital to enquire if a boy had been seen asking for food; someone peered from inside a thin gap as the door was opened as far as the heavy chain across it would allow, and said they didn't admit anyone during the night hours except in an emergency. 'We have elderly residents who cannot be disturbed,' a croaky voice said, and James couldn't be sure if it were a man or a woman who was speaking, but he apologized profusely for troubling them.

After searching down Vicar Lane and enquiring at the Three Crowns public house and then the Fleece Inn, they turned round, as to go on would have led them to the wider thoroughfare of Mytongate and James didn't think that Tom would be there. They paused outside the Grammar School to check the shallow doorway and then crossed the church concourse towards an inn with lights ablaze, and a row of shops with their windows shuttered against the night. It had started to rain again, and James was wondering whether to head back home with the two boys and come out later on his own, or to gather some men he knew who might continue the search with him.

It was still early, and although usually there would be many people about, now because of the cold, wet, miserable conditions there were but a few huddled into their coat collars, scurrying towards Whitefriargate.

'Come on,' he resolved finally as they walked past the dark shop doorways, empty but for a stray cat curled into one corner that didn't even look up as they passed. 'We'll go as far as Parliament Street and take a look up there, and then head back home.'

'Yeh!' Bob said eagerly. 'He might have gone down Winter's Alley, or even down Land o' Green Ginger. He'll know it; all of 'Hull lads know those entries.'

Letting Bob lead the way, as he claimed to know all these narrow cut-throughs, and after turning back occasionally when they came across a brick wall bordering someone's back yard, they finally came to a pile of old clothing heaped in a corner with the boy, Tom, huddled inside it.

James scooped him up into his arms, and put Bob in charge of finding their way out on to Lowgate, where they crossed over and hurried towards High Street and home.

He was worried. He couldn't hear or feel a breath of movement from the boy, and when they emerged on to Lowgate he was horrified to see, under the gaslight, the pallor on his face.

He stopped. 'Bob, I have one more task for you.'

'Yes, sir?'

'I want you to turn round and go as fast as you can to the doctor's house at the top of Albion Street.' He gave him the number. 'Will you tell him that Mr Ripley says it's very urgent and can he come at once?'

Bob looked at him and pressed his lips together. 'Tom's not going to die, is he, sir?'

'I don't know.' James thought there was no use pretending. 'I hope not, but that's why we need the doctor, so run as fast as you can and then come straight back home, and don't stop to talk to anyone.'

Bob nodded and set off. He'd know the quickest way, James was sure, but he'd have to retrace some of their steps and go round the Town Dock to get to the elegant street of fine houses where many of the town's doctors and surgeons made their homes in close proximity to the General Infirmary.

'Wish I could have gone too,' Matthew said in a low voice.

'Oh, I need you for something else,' his father said. 'Just as soon as we get to High Street.'

'All right,' Matthew said, gathering himself together in preparation.

They hurried on and turned down a narrow lane to reach the top of High Street, where James said, 'Now I want you to run like the wind to our kitchen door and ask Mrs Evans to get out the warmest blankets and put the kettle on to boil. Can you do that?'

'Yes, Pa,' he said, and James watched him running off at great speed until he turned the corner of their staith and disappeared.

He hugged Tom closer to him as he followed his son, speaking to him in soft whispers, reassuring him that he'd be fine when he'd had a bowl of soup and was sitting by a grand fire, but the boy didn't answer and James felt his anxiety increasing until at last he reached the kitchen door, where Mrs Evans was waiting for him.

'Don't lock it,' he said breathlessly. 'I've sent Bob to fetch the doctor, but he'll probably go to the front door. Matthew, will you run upstairs and tell your mama that we're back and will she listen out for the doctor?'

Matthew turned for the stairs as Rosie came down with an armful of blankets. 'I'll wait with her, Pa,' he said. 'Shall we come down again?'

'Bring the doctor down when he comes,' he told him, and went to help Mrs Evans take off Tom's wet clothes and then wrapped him in several warm blankets whilst she poured warm water into a cup and put a spoonful of honey into it.

He looked across at Mrs Evans as he took the boy and sat with him on his knee near the fire while the housekeeper knelt and put a spoonful of the honeyed water to his lips, but Tom didn't sip or swallow. She rubbed his fingers and toes to bring back the circulation but still he didn't stir.

'Here's 'mistress, sir,' Rosie whispered as the staircase door opened and Moira came in, dressed in her night clothes.

'Let me take him, James,' Moira said. 'I'm warm; I've been sitting by the fire.'

James nodded and stood up so that she could take the chair. He was beginning to shake with cold and distress, but he wrapped Tom and his wife in blankets and Mrs Evans filled the stone hot water bottle and placed it beside them.

'How long is it since we came in?' he asked no one in particular. 'I hope Bob found the doctor. I should have taken him straight there.'

'No, you did right to bring him here, sir. Listen,' Mrs Evans answered. 'That's a horse and trap. It'll be 'doctor.'

CHAPTER FIFTEEN

'How long has he been like this?' The doctor held his stethoscope to the fire to warm it before slipping it between the blankets to listen to Tom's chest and then his back. The boy was like a rag doll, unable to move of his own accord.

'I don't know,' James murmured. 'We found him in an alleyway and brought him straight home; we wrapped him in blankets immediately and tried to give him water, but he's – he's not responding.'

Matthew was standing by the staircase door and Bob close to the back lobby, as if ready to make his escape.

'Matthew,' James said, 'take Bob upstairs, will you, and both of you wait in the sitting room until we come up.' It was a command rather than a request and the boys did as he said without a word. Rosie followed them.

The physician straightened up and sighed. 'I'm afraid it doesn't look too hopeful. His pulse is weak, and he seems to be on the point of starvation.' He rubbed his chin. 'By rights he should be in hospital, but I daren't risk moving him.'

'We'll take care of him,' Moira said softly, holding him closer to her.

The doctor nodded. 'Just keep him warm, as you are doing, and give him sips of warm water if he'll take it, but I can't give you much hope. I would say he's been without food or shelter for some time.'

'How can this happen?' James asked in an angry whisper. 'This is supposed to be a civilized country and yet there is no provision for children like him.'

'He could have applied at the workhouse,' the doctor murmured. 'Unfortunately it has a reputation for being harsh, yet children do survive there and grow up into decent adults, although . . .' His voice wavered. 'I agree some fall by the wayside.'

He emitted another deep sigh. 'Just do what you are doing; if you can get him into a bed or on to a mattress he might rest easier, but . . .' He paused again. 'I'll call again tomorrow.'

When the doctor had gone, Mrs Evans put the kettle on the hob. 'Tea, ma'am, sir?' she asked in a low voice. 'Kettle's on 'boil.'

'Not for me,' James said. 'I'll pop up to see the boys.' He smiled at Mrs Evans. 'Do you need Bob for anything else?' he asked.

'No, sir, he can go to his room.'

'I'll bring a mattress down,' he murmured to Moira. 'It can go by the range. Will it be in your way?' he asked the house-keeper, who shook her head.

'Yes, please, Mrs Evans,' Moira said as James quietly closed the door behind him. 'I'll join you in a pot of tea. Don't set a tray,' she added, 'straight from the pot will be fine, thank you.'

She settled back in the chair and adjusted her seating position to accommodate Tom and ease the cramp in her arm where he was resting.

How can this be? she wondered. We have two lost children here – Floris of an unknown nationality asleep upstairs, separated from her parents: how did she come to be here? Is it fate that brought them here, to be cared for by us?

'I'll stay with him, Mrs Evans,' she murmured. 'I don't want to leave him alone. If he wakens he'll wonder where he is and might try to get up.'

Both women knew that the probability of that happening was low.

'Somebody must know him.' Mrs Evans poured the tea. 'How can a bairn like that have nobody in 'world who cares for him? It's not right. Not right at all.'

Moira sighed. 'It certainly isn't right. No grandparents, no uncles, aunts, cousins? A whole family wiped out? How?'

'I can't imagine.' Mrs Evans shook her head. 'Some tragedy; an accident? How old can he be?' She pondered. 'Perhaps he's older than we think. Mebbe he's been in 'workhouse and got to 'age when he had to leave and find work; or,' she paused to consider, 'he could even be a runaway, left home as some young lads do—' She stopped speaking when they heard James's footsteps on the stairs and he came in, hauling a palliasse alongside him and more blankets in his arms.

'It was in the laundry room,' he said quietly. 'Rosie found it. She was sitting in there, not knowing where to go; I told her she could go to her room but she said the laundry room was warmer.'

'So it is. We always keep a low fire in there to keep 'laundry aired.'

'Is there not a fire in her room?' Moira asked.

'Onny in winter, ma'am,' Mrs Evans answered. 'Generally in December.'

'But it's winter now! She must have a fire, and so must you, and Bob too.'

'Very good, ma'am. I'll get Bob to chop more wood in 'morning.'

James placed the palliasse in front of the range and covered it with a blanket, and then he lifted Tom from Moira's arms and laid him on it, covering him with more blankets. 'He's lost that chill he had on him,' he murmured, crouching down beside him. 'He was icy when I picked him up from that alley.

What a good thing we found him when we did. He wouldn't have lasted the night.'

'I'll stay with him, James,' Moira told him. 'I can sleep in this chair, and if he needs a drink—'

'No, I won't hear of it,' James said. 'I'll—'

'No! I insist.' Moira spoke over him. 'You've been out searching the streets. You'll be worn out – you *are* worn out; you've had a harrowing time lately and need some rest. Who knows what tomorrow might bring.'

Mrs Evans nodded, agreeing with the mistress; and James admitted to himself as he climbed the stairs to check on Matthew and Bob, and tell Bob that he could go to bed whenever he was ready, that not only was he tired, he was also worn down with concern and fury. How could it be that a boy like Tom, not so much older than his own son, could be alone and friendless with nowhere to rest his head, no food or drink, and could so easily have lost his life in a flooded cellar, only to be saved to sleep or die in a cold wet alley?

To his astonishment the two boys were playing chess. Matthew often played when he was at home, but Bob?

'He's very good, Pa,' Matthew said. 'He hasn't played before but he got a grip of it straight away, didn't you?' Bob grinned with pleasure as he nodded.

'Well, I'm off to bed,' James told them. 'You're finished for the night, Bob,' he added. 'Mrs Evans doesn't need you for anything more, but don't be late to bed. When you go down in the morning you'll find Tom asleep in the kitchen. Mrs Ripley will be with him, so knock before going in.'

Bob had stood up when James had come in and Matthew did too. 'It hasn't been a pleasant homecoming for you, Matthew,' he said wearily. 'I'm sorry about that. Let's hope that tomorrow will be better.'

'I hope so too, Father,' Matthew said solemnly, 'and that Tom recovers well.'

James nodded and left them, too tired to say more, but guessing that Bob had told Matthew more about Tom than perhaps he would tell him, and thinking that both boys, but his son in particular, were learning about real life right here in front of them.

He fell into his bed, warmed by the hot water bottle that Rosie or Mrs Evans had filled for his comfort, and was grieved that such a crime – for Tom's condition, he considered, was exactly that – could happen here under the very noses of people who with their comfortable homes and full bellies wouldn't even notice.

A house, he thought as he tossed about, unable to sleep while his mind was so active. A house, a place of safety where children or young people without anyone to care for them could find food and shelter and somewhere to lay their heads other than a dark alley.

But who would pay for it? Not the town corporation, for they would impose too many rules and stipulations; and besides, they would say there was already the workhouse or children's homes for young abandoned children such as Floris.

A community house then, reliant on donations from those able to give, and run by others who did not have money to spare but were willing to give their time instead. He closed his eyes and saw the women who turned up with soup and bread whenever there was a tragedy or snow on the ground. Some were rich, but not all, not by any means; they were just aware that some folk needed a helping hand when they couldn't help themselves.

He felt himself drifting into sleep. But we'd need money to rent a house ... maybe a sponsor, a company maybe, like ... like Father ... what was it he'd said?

Moira woke, or at least something awakened her. The kitchen was dimly lit; Mrs Evans had left a lamp burning low enough for her to see that Tom was sitting up and gazing at her, and she felt joy easing into her wits.

'Tom!' she whispered.

'Yes.' His voice was croaky and low.

'Would you like some water?' She reached for the covered jug on the small table next to her and the cup beside it. She poured just enough to half fill it. The doctor had said a little sip at a time.

She was wearing a dressing gown and threw off the blanket that covered her and knelt beside him on the floor. 'Just a little sip,' she said quietly. 'You've been unwell.'

'Who are you? Are you an angel?'

She smiled and offered him the cup but he didn't reach out for it. 'No,' she murmured. 'I'm Mrs Ripley. You know my husband, James Ripley.'

There was no recognition in his expression. 'Are you my mother? I don't remember you. Mother might be dead and it would be my fault.'

She held the cup to his dry lips and tipped it slightly so that he had to open his mouth to take a drink, which he did, and then another.

He looked around the kitchen. 'Where am I? I'm not in the workhouse, am I? Is this your house?' His words came out fast and low, hoarse and dry. 'I think you are an angel. You look like an angel. Am I in heaven?'

'No, Tom. I'm not an angel and you're not in heaven. My husband and Bob – you know Bob, don't you? He's your friend, I think – they found you outside. You were very cold and they brought you inside to get warm.'

He looked around him. 'It's cold outside. Am I dead? I should be dead.'

'You're not!' Moira said, and wished that James would come down, or Mrs Evans; something wasn't right. Tom had a remote look on his face, his limbs were shaking and his eyes were roving around the room as if looking for somebody or something.

'Would you like something to eat?' she asked. 'Hot milk or cocoa?'

He narrowed his eyes and lowered his voice and stared at her. 'Have you got any poppy?'

'What? What do you mean? Will you have a biscuit, or bread? Bread and warm milk? That would be nice, wouldn't it? Or would you like to sleep again?'

He threw off the blankets. 'I have to go.'

'Oh, but where? Please don't go out! It's so cold. You'll make yourself ill again. It's dark.'

But he was on his feet, unsteady, holding on to the chairs and the table and making his way towards the clothes horse where his clothes had been drying. 'Have to go. Have to go,' he repeated, and she too stood up.

'Please don't go,' she implored him. 'I'll fetch James. He can take you.'

He turned to her. 'Where? Where will he take me?'

'Anywhere! Wherever you want to go!' She was edging towards the staircase door. 'Please wait, and I'll fetch him. He won't be a minute. He'll be pleased to see you looking so much better.'

She ran up the two flights of stairs, lifting her nightgown and dressing robe so she didn't trip, and quietly opened the bedroom door. 'James! James!'

Her whispers instantly woke him. 'What is it? Is he worse?'

'No!' Moira's heart was hammering. 'He's awake. He says he's leaving. He's not listening, James. He's – he's – I don't know, acting strangely. He won't have food or milk and I – I think he's going to get dressed.'

James was already out of bed and putting on his nightrobe, leaving behind his slippers and heading for the stairs and then down to the kitchen.

106

The flame of the lamp was quivering and a draught of cold air was blasting through the kitchen from the door of the boot room, which was swinging on its hinges; the outer door was wide open.

They both looked round and then at the empty clothes horse where Tom's ragged old clothes had been; missing were the blankets that had covered both him and Moira.

The kitchen was empty. Tom had gone.

CHAPTER SIXTEEN

James closed the outer door and bolted it; he picked up the fire tongs and took a large lump of coal from the hod. Opening the fire door of the range, he placed it inside on the banked-up coals.

Moira watched him. 'You're not going to look for him?' she asked.

He shook his head. 'By the time I'd dressed and put on my galoshes he'd be gone somewhere I'd never find him.' He took a deep exhausted breath and, sitting down in Moira's vacated chair, he stared into space. 'No,' he muttered. 'If he wanted warmth and food and safety he would have stayed. There was something else that he needed more than what we had to offer.

'He seems like a street urchin,' he went on, 'and yet I don't know; it's as if he knows nothing else besides life out there, but he speaks well, and . . .' He sighed. 'There's something about him . . .'

Moira picked up a cloth and lifted the lid of the range to place the half-full kettle on the hot plate. 'When I offered him warm milk or cocoa he asked if I had any poppy. I didn't know what he meant.'

James groaned and put his head in his hands. Of course she wouldn't know. How could she?

'It's laudanum,' he murmured. 'People often take it when they're at a low ebb. Some give it to their infants to help them sleep; sometimes they give them too much and they don't ever wake up. Adults who take it or chew it mixed with tobacco to help them through their dreary lives eventually can't do without it.'

'Oh!' Moira put her hands to her mouth. 'My mother has taken laudanum when she's been unwell. When I've asked her what it was she said it's just something to help her sleep!'

James nodded. 'She'll be all right. Physicians recommend small doses sometimes.'

She made tea and poured them a cup each. James drank his and then stood up. 'Come on.' He held out his hand. 'We can do nothing more. Let's go to bed. Tomorrow is another day.'

Moira lit a candle and followed James upstairs. He turned the doorknob and went to his room and sat on the side of the bed, his hands clasped, his head lowered.

She hesitated outside the door. He looked so sad, so dejected. He lifted his head and turned to gaze at her; he held out his hand and without hesitation she took a step inside, closed the door behind her and went towards him.

CHAPTER SEVENTEEN

Leila's Story

Leila Mackenzie was born in Hull's Albion Street, the only child of Henry and Dorothy Mackenzie. Her birth had temporarily halted her parents' journeying across Europe and beyond; their joint attraction had been their mutual love of travelling the world.

Before meeting Henry, Dorothy, as a lone woman, had been forced by convention to be accompanied on her travels by some other female as adventurous as herself. These, sadly, were few in number, and at the age of twenty-five she was as delighted to meet Henry as he was to meet her, and they decided to marry.

Their love of travel far exceeded any physical passion, but they were fond of one another, and for two or three years they were the perfect companions, until after imbibing too much red wine under a star-filled Egyptian sky they discovered that Dorothy was with child.

'Such a to-do, dearest,' Dorothy exclaimed to her husband as she straightened up from heaving into a sick bucket outside their tent in the land of the Pharaohs. 'And I must say that I'd far rather give birth on a comfortable bed in England than in a canvas tent in a desert; all this sand between one's toes and in other tender places, or a mountain of scratchy bracken and chirping crickets, is simply not conducive to comfort!'

'Of course you would, my darling,' Henry agreed. He was a very amenable man and was quite happy to return to England and stay at home for a year or so; they could plan their next trip and put their affairs in order, for their lives would inevitably change once they became parents.

Leila was born in December, when the sky was filled with flurries of snowflakes that landed gently on the steps leading up to a Doric porch in a row of the finest three-storey houses in what was known as Hull's Georgian area; houses built around the end of the eighteenth century that were intended for the wealthy.

They had called the child Leila in honour of her beginnings, as the Arabic word meant dark night or red wine, even though she was born with hair the colour of honey. She had the fairest of English skin, and her parents worried that she might burn when they eventually returned to the eternal sun-filled skies once they began their travels again, which they had planned for when Leila turned three. In the event, her skin became golden and her hair bleached almost white in the sun, despite the *hijab*, or *shayla*, she always wore in hot climates.

Over the years she was educated by her parents; her mother taught her to read, write and spell, and gave her lessons in history and geography as well as English, whilst her father taught her mathematics, statistics and languages, which she picked up very easily, having met many people of different cultures and nations.

Until Leila was twelve there were only rare short visits back to England; her father needed to ensure that his assets, including the house, which was occasionally rented out, were still in order. And then, whilst they were travelling in India, Dorothy caught an unidentifiable malady, and despite a hurried journey to the city of Calcutta, where she was given excellent treatment, she weakened rapidly and died within a month.

Knowing she was dying, she had begged her husband not to give up on his travels, and urged him to ensure that their daughter continued to receive an education. Clinging to Leila's hand, she told her that she could do whatever her heart decided, that she must not be held back simply because she was a woman, and in due course she should defy convention and plan her own life and future.

Too shocked by Dorothy's sudden death to consider travelling far, Henry and Leila remained in Calcutta for several months. The city was the major trading post of the East India Trading Company and was growing fast.

Henry Mackenzie, however, was a man of scruples, and had watched with alarm as the company expanded, abolishing local rule and assuming full sovereignty, which he considered might someday trigger a rebellion of which he wanted no part. He conferred with his daughter and decided that they would journey back to Europe and live quietly for a while, giving Leila time to further her education before embarking on their next expedition.

They packed their bags and hired a driver and a bullock cart. Having taken note of Leila's fair hair and complexion beneath her flowing shayla, the driver rigged up a canvas top and fastened it carefully over the cart before they set off.

At dusk, they came across a group of other travellers who had stopped for the night and were cooking over a fire, and the driver drew up.

'We stop to rest,' he told Henry. 'And better to keep with others. Bandits at night!'

He had brought a small canvas tent for his passengers and positioned himself outside it. Henry walked Leila to a clump of trees where she could be private, and then he too relieved himself before they joined the group and were invited to eat with them.

The next morning they were on their way again as dawn broke. Late in the afternoon they came to a village where they were offered food and accommodation for the night, and their driver exchanged places with another man who would drive them for the next two days.

'How far is it to Mumbai, Papa?' Leila asked him one day. 'I can't recall how long the journey was when we first came to India. It's a pity there are no trains for us to travel on.'

'Mumbai?' Her father smiled. 'That city has been called several things over the centuries, you know. Bombay is its official name at the moment, and Hindi speakers call it Bambai, but no doubt it will change again one day. As for transport, there is talk of passenger trains in the future, but as yet there are only goods trains carrying building materials. I understand that the East India Company is considering commissioning a passenger service and building special trains for it, but it won't be in time for us.'

'You didn't say how far it is,' she reminded him.

He pursed his lips. 'It will take us months, my dear, but we will break our journey regularly on the way.'

'How far?' she persisted.

'I believe close on two thousand miles,' he admitted. 'India is a very large country. But remember, for most of our married life your mother and I undertook journeys of hundreds of miles at a time, and every country we went to became our home. When we finally arrive in Bombay, we will rest in a hotel for a week or two before boarding a ship for Oman.'

She nodded. It was the only life she had known. She was a nomad, a rover like her father, and as her mother had been, constantly travelling from one place to another, one country to the next. She could never think of herself as being from any fixed abode.

'I was born in England, wasn't I?' she asked, covering herself more closely with the long veil that draped over her head and shoulders. It was almost midday and the sun was beating down; soon they would be stopping for shelter.

'You were. In our house in Hull, which you have seen when we have been home. We were in Egypt when your mother discovered she was pregnant, and she decided she would rather travel to England and give birth in a comfortable bed than take her chances in a foreign land! Besides, better by far for a child to have a British birth registration than none.'

They travelled onwards by bullock cart, canal boat, dhow and steamer, over numerous waterways and through landlocked mountainous country, Henry marvelling at Leila's resilience and endurance, until at last they reached their destination. There they rested for almost two weeks before boarding a dhow to take them across the deep shining water to the Musandam coast of Oman, where the sun created deep shadows in the rocky mountainside and snow-white clouds floated in the brightest of blue skies.

'This is beautiful, Papa,' Leila murmured, so low that he barely heard her, but he could see she was entranced from the joy on her face.

Disembarking, they travelled on to Riyadh, a walled city of palaces, mosques and fine places to stay, as Henry had remembered from a previous visit with Dorothy, and took the opportunity of pausing awhile. Leila brushed up on her language skills and read English novels. Her father set her maths tests, and geography too, and tried to explain the intricacies of the English language. In this she did not do well. 'Such a difficult language to learn,' she said crossly.

They stayed for a month and then moved on towards Europe. Henry was becoming jittery over the changing political situation; alliances were shifting and different states forming as various factions vied for power.

Leila had decided she would like to finish her education in France before leaving full-time schooling; she was by now sixteen, having spent four years without her mother's hand to guide her, but with her father always discreetly by her side to advise and keep her safe.

Whilst she was at school in France, Henry travelled alone to England, to check once more that all was as it should be with his house and assets, and his young daughter grew in independence without him.

'Two years, Papa,' she'd said. 'That should be enough time to complete my schooling, and then – and then, do you think that we might visit the Ottoman Empire? I've been reading about Turkey and it sounds fascinating.'

Henry did not agree. 'We have already touched upon the empire, and indeed it has much to offer,' he said. 'It might sound exotic with the beautiful mosques, and the mysterious women behind their veils, but it is a volatile region and I think we should stay away.'

She listened, but she didn't learn, although she smiled and nodded at her father in agreement. One day, she thought, that is where I will go. I have already fallen in love with the sound of it.

CHAPTER EIGHTEEN

James was lost in thought. Moira sat in the opposite chair with Floris on her knee, reading from a book of fairy tales. They had had supper and Floris was in her nightgown and warm dressing gown; this was her quiet time before bed. She pointed from time to time at images in the story book, her dark eyes wide open and her lips parted.

Matthew was sitting at a small table by the window where the heavy winter curtains were drawn to keep out any cold draughts. He was working on a puzzle; he had brought the book downstairs from his bedroom shelf for his mother to read to Floris.

'It has lovely pictures in it, Mama, and it's in colour, and Floris might like the story of Aladdin.'

Floris clapped her hands together in delight. In the short time she had been with them, she had lost the pallor she'd had when they first took her in. Though she would sometimes look towards the door and ask for Leila, she was also learning to trust them, and since Matthew had come home she had taken to greeting him by rushing towards him when he came into a room and wrapping her arms around his legs.

He didn't mind. In fact, he was very good with her and had searched in the nursery cupboard and his old toy box to find things she might like to play with, like rubber balls and hoops, though she was as yet too small to manoeuvre a hoop. Toy soldiers and horses she liked, but best of all she loved books and having a story told to her.

James and Moira had gone together to the police station to alert them to the fact that Floris was staying with them, and asked that if they should hear from anyone who had lost a child they should immediately apply to them. So far, there had been no one.

James looked up as he heard the front doorbell chime, wondering who it might be, and saw Floris point at a page of the book. She gave a huff of breath. 'Baba,' she said huskily. 'Baba!' Moira had heard the doorbell too, and looked across at James, who gave a little shrug.

Floris shook Moira's arm and pointed again. The page showed a man with a short dark beard and a pleated turban on his head; he wore a loose blouson and wide silk trousers that were tight around his ankles, with a pleated sash wound round his waist.

'It's Aladdin!' Moira smiled at her. 'Do you know the story of Aladdin?'

'Baba!' she repeated.

'I thought Aladdin was a Chinese story.' Matthew looked up. 'Is Floris's father Chinese?'

His mother gave a little shrug. 'We don't know anything about him,' she said, 'but looking at Floris – I don't think so.'

'I thought the story came from the Arabian Nights,' James interrupted. 'It's a made-up story, in any case, isn't it?' he added, and grinned at Moira's sham look of horror.

'Of course not!' she exclaimed. 'Of course it's true!'

'Baba!' Floris said again, and Moira saw that her eyes had filled. 'Baba!'

Moira turned the page that had reminded Floris of her father just as a quiet knock came on the door, and it opened to reveal Rosie standing half inside and half out. 'Sorry, sir, ma'am. There's a constable at 'door. He said as could you come down, please.'

James stood up immediately. 'I'll go. No need for you to come,' he said to Moira when he saw her beginning to stand. 'Whatever it is, I'll deal with it.' He followed Rosie out on to the landing where she waited for him to go in front, and didn't ask her what the constable had said or wanted, but ran quickly down to where the man was waiting in the hall. 'How can I help you?' he asked.

'You might remember that we met one night, sir, and you asked if I'd seen anything of a boy.' The constable looked at Rosie, who was hovering on the bottom step of the staircase.

'Thank you, Rosie,' James said, without turning round. 'That will be all for the present,' and the maid scurried down the kitchen stairs. 'I do remember,' James told the constable, not adding that he had found Tom, or that he had disappeared again.

'We've found a body, sir – a lad, close by 'River Hull. He'd not been injured, not in a fight or anything. He's been tekken to 'mortuary. We wondered if it might be 'lad you've been lookin' for and if you'd be willing to come and identify him.'

James shuddered. Would it be Tom? And would he recognize him, skinny and wasted as he would be, probably not only for lack of food but also by the effects of laudanum or any other unknown drug that he might have taken to ease his misery.

'We'll put 'details in tomorrow's paper if it isn't 'lad you know,' the constable added, 'and try to find out who he is.'

James nodded. 'I'll come, but I must explain that I don't know the boy well; he was one of the young people rescued from the flooded cellar.'

'Ah, I see! Were there many of 'em?'

James shook his head. 'Not boys of his age. Some older,

some young men, but mainly women and little children. Just give me a minute.'

He ran upstairs again and put his head round the door to speak to Moira. 'Just have to slip out; won't be long.'

Moira looked up enquiringly and so did Matthew. James shook his head. He didn't want to explain anything in front of Matthew. Then he suddenly thought of Bob. Where was he? Was he in the kitchen with Mrs Evans and Rosie?

He ran downstairs again and saw that the constable had seated himself in a hall chair. 'Won't be a moment,' he muttered as the man stood, and ran down the kitchen stairs and opened the door.

'I need my galoshes, Mrs Evans,' he said. 'Did I leave them down here?'

He glanced around the kitchen as Rosie dashed to get his galoshes from the boot room. 'Where's Bob?'

'He's gone to see his auntie,' Mrs Evans said. 'I've told him not to be long.'

James nodded. 'Ask him to come up and see me when I get back, please,' and seeing Mrs Evans's frown he added, 'He's not in trouble. I just want a word.'

'Very good, sir.' She continued with her task at the sink, and James took his galoshes from Rosie with a word of thanks and ran upstairs again to join the policeman.

'This is a bad business, isn't it?' he muttered as they went out.

'It is,' the constable agreed, 'but summat we get used to. Some of these lads with nowt else to do wi' their time get mixed up with other gangs of lads and start drinking spirits or taking poppy and then start fighting.'

'Where do they get the money for such indulgences?'

'Gin is cheap. They pinch stuff from shops, for instance, where you'd need eyes in 'back o' your head to catch 'em, or push into folk and snatch a wallet. They ain't particular where 'money comes from cos they're hooked on 'poppy and don't know 'time o' day, most of 'em. Want locking up in my opinion, and that's what happens if we catch 'em.'

But it's not a solution, James thought as he followed the man towards the police station and the adjacent mortuary.

He was led into a small cold room where a body was laid out, covered by a sheet. The attendant lifted the sheet and James drew in a huff of breath as he gazed down at the thin, bruised face.

It wasn't Tom. It was a boy of about the same age, maybe a year or two older, but definitely not the boy he knew as Tom.

He shook his head; he felt sickened. Such a waste of a life. This lad was someone's son, someone's child. Had he been loved, or had he been so bad that he had been turned out of his home? Surely not the latter; he was too young to be considered worthless. Was someone searching for him? He didn't know the answer to any of these questions, but knew that someone somewhere must know him. A boy of his age must be known by his name, whatever it was.

'No.' His voice cracked as he spoke. 'Not the boy I was looking for. I would like to report him missing. His name is Tom.'

Back at the front desk the duty sergeant licked his pencil. 'Surname?'

'I don't know.'

'Address?'

'I don't know.'

The sergeant looked up. 'Of no fixed abode?'

'I imagine so.'

'A relation o' yourn?'

'No.'

'Why you botherin' then, sir, if you don't mind me askin'.'

'Someone has to, don't you think, sergeant?'

The sergeant gave a lift of his shoulders but his lips turned down. 'We get these young fellers, ne'er-do-wells, regularly. Creep out of their holes as soon as 'weather turns.'

James wanted to turn his bitterness on the sergeant, but knew it would be useless. The man must have seen so many desperate, out of work, jobless, homeless people that he had become hardened; not because he didn't care, but because he had no solution to the problem, so the best thing to do was ignore it; otherwise he wouldn't be able to do his job.

James bade him good evening and left, turning up his coat collar and pulling up his scarf. It was becoming much colder, though not yet cold enough for snow; just damp, with a biting wind which cut through to old and young bones alike, and how much worse if you were not wearing a wool coat. He recalled then that when Tom had left their house he had taken with him the blankets they'd put over him to thaw him out.

He gave a muffled snort. So that's how they survive, these boys and men, and probably women too, who live on the streets: they use every opportunity to steal in order to keep warm, to eat and to save themselves from starvation.

Suppose there was a place, a house, a room, a shed even where they could go to eat and rest, where no one would ask questions; a refuge to accommodate those who had nowhere, no shelter to keep them from the worst of the weather.

If only we could speak to some of them, ask what they want from life, and whether there was someone who would pay for the provision? His father's conversation came back to him. He must speak to him again. But his own views were decided: food would be needed, someone to make soup and bread; they'd need blankets and mattresses. He thought of the women of the town who were always ready and willing when there was a tragedy: a ship going down, a house fire, or even a flood like the one in the cellar.

But would they be willing to help on a regular basis? Winter was coming and more people would need food and shelter; would they themselves be willing to help others if facilities were provided?

There was the rub: would they, or would they simply take what they needed and disappear into the night again, just as Tom had done?

CHAPTER NINETEEN

James walked home briskly, head down, but aware of shadows shifting in doorways. Although he wanted to ask the occupiers of these shelters why they were out in the night, why they did not have a home to go to, he was also mindful that he should keep a clear head, alert to any danger, because he was alone.

He headed into High Street and towards the lamp outside his own front door, and in front of him saw someone scurrying down the staith towards his yard gate.

'Who's there?' he called out and the figure stopped and turned. 'Bob? Is that you?'

'Yes, sir.' The voice quaked. 'Is it you, Mr Ripley, sir?'

'Yes, I'm sorry if I startled you.' He turned his steps towards him. 'Come inside. I don't like you being out when it's so dark.'

'It's not late, sir. It just gets dark in 'winter.'

'It does indeed.' James reached over for the top inside bolt of the gate; it wasn't bolted. Bob, shorter than him by several inches, must have left it undone when he went out. 'I want to have a word with you, so off you go inside.'

He followed the lad through the gate and shot the bolt, hooking a chain across further down so that no one could reach it from the outside, although the back wall would be easy enough to scale.

Mrs Evans looked surprised to see him coming through the lobby door and looked at him with raised eyebrows, but without explaining where he had been he simply said, 'Mrs Evans, I'm not happy about Bob visiting his aunt after dark. I know' – he raised his hands as she opened her mouth to speak – 'it isn't late, but nevertheless, I'd like him to be able to go out at a different time of day. What about a Saturday afternoon? How often do you visit your aunt, Bob? Once a fortnight?'

'Bob fills all the coal buckets and chops wood on a Friday and Saturday, ready for the weekend, sir,' the housekeeper answered for the boy.

'And my auntie finishes her ironing on a Saturday,' Bob added. 'She wouldn't want me to be there then.'

James sighed. 'Well, choose another day, but I don't want you wandering about after dark, is that clear?'

Both Bob and Mrs Evans nodded and said, 'Yes, sir,' and James shrugged off his damp coat and ran upstairs to hang it on the hall stand to dry out.

Moira was alone in the sitting room. Floris was in bed, and Matthew elsewhere. 'I quite agree,' she said, when James had finished telling her about the boy in the mortuary and his worry over Bob visiting his aunt in the dark. 'That poor boy,' she went on, 'the one who died. Maybe his parents are waiting for him to come home. Do you think someone attacked him, if his face was bruised? Or perhaps he suffered a fall? I wouldn't like young Bob to do the same.'

'Both of those things.' James poured himself a small glass of brandy from the decanter. 'Or neither.'

He sat in a chair by the fire and stretched out his legs and feet to the heat. 'It is both *nothing* to do with us and *everything* to do with us. Practically outside our own door, there are people in distress.' He remained quiet for a while, and then looked around him. 'Has Matthew gone to bed?'

'No, not yet, but he's gone to his room,' Moira told him. 'I think he's enjoying having his own place, and not having to share with school friends.'

James nodded. 'We have an appointment at the Grammar School next week. He's maybe preparing himself for questions; they're sure to ask him some, or even give him a test.'

'He'll be all right, won't he?' Moira seemed anxious.

'I would say so; he's bright, and the fact that Daniel and I were pupils there must go in his favour.'

Rosie brought up a jug of hot chocolate and a plate of buttered scones. 'Shall I ask Master Matthew if he'd like anything, ma'am?'

'Please do, Rosie, and tell him he can join us if he wishes to.'

Rosie dipped her knee and left the room as Moira poured the frothy chocolate for both of them.

'I've made a decision.' James took a drink, leaving a thin moustache of foamy chocolate on his top lip. 'I'm going to write to my father tomorrow and call on Daniel to ask him the same question.'

'What question?'

'My father came up with the idea that a company such as ours could sponsor a place of safety for young men and boys who are roaming the streets of Hull; a danger to themselves and potentially other vulnerable youngsters.'

'Only young men and boys?' Mora questioned. 'What about girls and young women? They are even more defenceless than males.'

'That's true, but we can't mix them; we'd soon be accused of setting up a house of ill repute!'

Moira blushed and muttered something.

'There are more young men roaming the streets than there are girls and young women,' James went on. 'I've seen young girls selling flowers in Whitefriargate, so they are at least trying to make a living, though I admit it's probably only a pittance; but perhaps there are more opportunities for girls, such as in the flour or cotton mills.'

Clearly, Moira wasn't convinced, adding that young girls were given difficult and dangerous jobs cleaning beneath moving cotton frames for very little money, but although James agreed it was wrong, he was also confident that if they were able to put young men and boys on the right path, the young women would probably follow.

Moira submitted. 'So you'll need a house.'

'A building of some kind, with cooking facilities, and large enough to put in beds.' Distractedly he ran his fingers through his hair, making it stand on end.

'A house then,' she said again. 'With a fireplace or a cooking range. Maybe a rented property in the town centre that's easily accessible.'

'You're right,' he said. 'No one would want to walk out of town. I'm going to call on Nicholas Howard. He's the one who alerted me to the people in the cellar. He has quite a lot of influence in the town, and I'm fairly sure he would also be a sponsor. He's a committee man and we'll need to form a committee.'

Someone knocked on the door. James called 'Come in' and Bob appeared. 'Mrs Evans said you wanted to see me when I came back, sir.'

James frowned. 'Did she? Ah, yes, I did say so. I just wanted to be sure you were back, that's all, but of course we met downstairs, didn't we? But whilst you're here, does your aunt go to church? No? So would it be convenient for you to visit her on a Sunday morning? If you went once a fortnight, say, at about ten o'clock, you could stay until twelve noon. How would that suit you, m'dear?' he added, turning to Moira. 'Would you need Bob during those hours?'

Moira covered her mouth to hide her amusement. Here was her husband taking on the role of housekeeper and mistress of the house. 'I will discuss it with Mrs Evans,' she said, her smile breaking forth. 'I'm sure she'll have an opinion on the matter.'

James cleared his throat. 'Of course, of course. But, erm, Bob?'

'Yes, sir?'

'You get round the town on your errands, don't you? Have you seen any buildings – shops, houses and such – with *To Let* signs outside?'

Bob pondered. 'Are those 'ones that have big letters at 'beginning o' words, sir?'

Oh, heavens, James thought. I'd forgotten that he can't read.

'Those are the ones, yes. Perhaps I might have a little job for you in the morning. I'll ask Matthew to go with you.'

Bob looked confused, but only said, 'Right you are, sir. Will that be all?'

James swallowed. 'Yes, thank you. I'll see you in the morning.'

When Bob had gone, he turned to his wife. 'I'd completely forgotten that he couldn't read. That's no good. We'll have to find someone to teach him.'

Moira raised her eyebrows. 'One thing at a time, James! You can't solve every crisis. And what's this about Matthew going somewhere with him?'

'Bob knows all the ins and outs of the streets of Hull and we agreed that we would need a place in town, so I thought that if we explored suitable places before forming a committee, we'd be a step ahead.'

Moira stared at him. 'And you're thinking of sending Bob and Matthew on this search? On their own?'

'They'll be all right,' he said, wrong-footed. 'It will be day-light!' He stared back at her and began to laugh. 'Do you know, you sounded just like your mother.'

'Oh, no!' she said, and started to laugh with him. 'That's too unkind.'

CHAPTER TWENTY

James wrote to his father, asking him when he might be coming to Hull as he had a project in mind that he'd like to discuss. Not a shipping venture, he'd added, but a social one, concerning the homeless of the town.

A reply came in which his father said that he and James's mother would be in Hull the following weekend, as they had received an invitation to a celebratory party on Saturday. James grinned on reading it.

'My parents are becoming partygoers,' he told Moira. 'They can fit us in on Sunday morning before they return home.'

'I'll write and invite them for luncheon,' Moira said. 'I haven't seen your mother for some time, and she hasn't yet met Floris, or seen Matthew since the summer.'

'That would be nice,' he said. 'I want to talk to Pa about setting up this scheme for the people from the cellar; he's always able to give sound guidance.'

'Without being overbearing,' she agreed. 'You're very lucky to have such agreeable parents.'

He nodded. He knew that he was; they had always been amenable, never pushy or arrogant, and never gave advice unless it was asked for.

They arrived on the Sunday in time to chat before sitting

down to eat. The senior Ripleys greeted Matthew effusively –
because of his York schooling they had missed seeing him for
nearly twelve months – and were introduced to Floris, who
gave them a little wobbly curtsey. She wore a white dress which
came to mid-calf, and white stockings and red shoes which it
gave her much pleasure to show off.

Caroline Ripley lifted her on to her knee and wound a curl
from the little head around her finger. 'Well, sweetheart,' she
murmured. 'Where have you come from, I wonder?'

Floris gazed at her with parted lips, then leaned towards
her. Touching her mouth to Mrs Ripley's cheek, she breathed,
'Lay-lah!'

Mrs Ripley nodded and whispered back, 'Oh, and where is
Lay-lah?'

Floris pressed her lips together and solemnly shook her
head. 'Gone!' she whispered. 'To find Baba.'

After luncheon and before the Ripleys went off to catch their
train back to Scarborough, James took his father into his study
to discuss the possibility of setting up a charity to help people
who were living on the streets whilst Moira and Caroline settled
down for a chat. Matthew, having given his paternal grandparents chapter and verse on his schooling in York and telling
them of his hopes of attending the Grammar School, asked to
be excused as he was going on an errand for his father.

'Just as a start, Pa,' James was saying, 'I've asked Matthew
and Bob – the house lad who does odd jobs for us – if they'll
walk round the town to look for vacant properties.'

He saw the frown on his father's forehead and explained,
'Bob can't read; he's never been taught. He missed out on any
kind of schooling, from what I gather, but he knows all the
streets in the districts I'm thinking of.'

'Streetwise, is he?' Elliot Ripley commented.

'I suppose you could say that,' James concurred. 'I've asked

129

Matthew to go with him and take a notebook and pencil so that he can write down the names of suitable streets and alleyways – as a kind of project,' he added.

'Is it safe?'

'Yes.' James nodded. 'There are always people out walking during the day, especially around Whitefriargate or Parliament Street, or even here in High Street, but it won't be too busy as it's Sunday and the shops are closed. I've suggested they come back home in an hour.'

'Well, it's good that they can see what life is like for folk on the bottom rung,' his father commented. 'They should be taught to be aware.'

'Bob is already aware; he lived with his aunt and her sons before coming to work for us, because his father is a seaman and hardly ever at home. He had barely any clothes to his back when he came, although I think his aunt did the best she could.'

'How did you find such a lad?'

James laughed. 'I didn't. Guess who?'

His father leaned back in his chair. 'Not our Josephine?'

'Exactly so!'

'Well, I'd say that when you set up this charity you should ask Mrs Evans to be on the board. She'd soon sort everybody out and wouldn't stand any nonsense.'

'I agree. Strong women, that's who we need!' He paused. 'But can I rely on your approval, Pa? If we can offer the backing of our company as sponsors, we might pick up others, such as Nicholas Howard.'

'Good idea,' his father declared. 'Spread the cost of starting up the project; get members of the corporation involved so it looks as if they are giving their approval. Be careful about suggesting the money is coming out of the pockets of corporation ratepayers, though; appeal to the fulsome liberality of the Hull public, who are well known to be the most generous in the country.'

'Exactly!' James replied. 'I couldn't have put it better myself.'

'And the little girl? Floris, is it? What are you going to do about her?'

James shook his head. 'I don't honestly know. Her mother seems to have disappeared completely, although she had been sheltering in the cellar with Floris for a day or two. It's difficult to get a full picture or even a time scale, but she apparently asked a woman in there if she would take care of Floris whilst she went . . . well,' – he shrugged – 'who knows where? No one is sure what Leila said to the woman because she was taken ill and died shortly after, leaving Floris alone.'

He gave a deep sigh. 'I can't sleep for thinking of the conditions in that cellar, Pa. Diabolical; a death trap. I think the building might have been a wine merchants at one time and that's where the barrels were kept; there was a musty smell when I went in, but it might have been the smell of damp. There are probably drains running beneath, I don't know,' he finished hopelessly.

He put his elbows on his knees and rested his chin in his hands, and his father was silent for a few minutes before saying, 'It was a wine merchants. I remember the fire from when I was young. Completely gutted. I also remember the building being cleared out once before; there were people with cholera in there, children begging for food who had no other place to shelter and refused the workhouse.

'You won't remember the Masterson and Rayner shipping merchants, who once had a property further down High Street,' he went on without waiting for an answer. 'One of their sons, or grandsons more likely, set up something such as you're thinking of to help the poor. There has been no shortage of altruistic people willing to help others in this fine town.'

James nodded, but didn't raise his head. 'I know,' he mumbled. 'But it's never enough.'

'No,' his father said quietly. 'It isn't. "The poor are always with us." I remember my father saying that, and his father before him.'

He paused, mulling things over and patiently waiting for James to recover himself, then said, 'The woman who died, the one who was looking after Floris, did you say her name was Leila, or have I got that wrong?'

James sat up. He had been thinking not only of the distress of the people in the cellar but also of the boy Tom who had refused help and disappeared, as well as the unknown boy he had seen in the mortuary. Everything seemed to have come to a head, and his grand scheme of saving them all was just a ridiculous pipe dream.

'No,' he said, clearing his throat, and feeling embarrassed at his own stupidity in imagining he could solve anything. 'The woman who died was called Peggy, I believe. I know nothing about her.'

'So who was Leila?' his father persisted.

'Leila? Did I say that?'

His father nodded.

'She – erm . . .' James frowned. He couldn't recall mentioning her name. 'She's Floris's mother. The child was crying for her and the women in the cellar thought it was her own name, but of course it wasn't. She was calling for her mother.'

'Ah,' his father murmured. 'Mm. Well, I wonder . . .'

James sighed and stood up. 'Shall we go and enjoy a pot of tea with our ladies?'

His father remained sitting. 'Yes, good idea,' he said vaguely. 'I must ask your mother, she might remember. Years ago,' he went on, 'a *lot* of years ago, a rather odd couple had a house in Albion Street. They used to travel extensively and sometimes rented out the house. I've not seen or heard of them in, oh, I don't know, twenty years or more. They used to come home now and again, stay a short time, and then go off on their travels again.'

He put his head back as he reminisced. 'Yes, I've got it. They came back one time and she – Dorothy, that was her name – gave birth to a child and called her Leila.' He pursed his mouth. 'Never heard of such a name before; perhaps that's why I remember it. '

He nodded and rose up from his chair. 'Your mother will recall; they do, don't they? Leila. Pretty name.'

CHAPTER TWENTY-ONE

'Yes, I do remember them,' Caroline Ripley said. She and Moira were relaxing in the sitting room with Elliot and James. 'At least, I remember Henry Mackenzie; he was quite a catch at the time, but was hardly ever at home after his father died. The old man left him a fortune, and then after he married Dorothy they just travelled abroad. Not that she was a fortune-hunter; she most certainly wasn't. Her father had an estate out on the west side of Hull. A former banker, I believe; bankers generally went west and the farming people went east. So what about them? They haven't been seen for a number of years, or at least I haven't heard mention of them,' she mused. 'They had a daughter; she must have travelled with them, unless they put her into school.'

'It's just that I recall the Mackenzies giving their child the name of' – Elliot Ripley lowered his voice and spelled it out – 'L.E.I.L.A. I remembered it as it's rather unusual.'

'Really?' Moira exclaimed. 'And would she now be old enough to have a child of her own?'

'Oh, yes!' the elder Ripleys said in unison. 'Indeed she would be,' Elliot added. 'The house has been rented out from time to time; don't know if it still is, as of course we haven't seen it since we moved to Scarborough. Henry Mackenzie would be about my age, I suppose, or maybe a few years older, so who knows, he might not be in the land of the living. We're at a dangerous age, aren't we, old gel?' He raised his eyebrows at his wife.

'*You* might well be,' she answered briskly, 'but don't count me in on your reckoning. Come summer you'll find me in a bathing machine on Scarborough sands.'

'Their daughter would be about your age, Moira,' her husband went on, not listening to his wife, 'or maybe a bit younger; I forget. Time moves so swiftly. So it could be that she has returned, or perhaps just a strange coincidence. Unusual name, though.'

'It begs the question, if she was born into riches,' Moira said sadly, 'what was she doing in a flooded cellar?'

Floris looked up and gazed from one to another; they all looked at her. She couldn't have understood what they were saying, Moira thought, as they had avoided using names, except for Henry and Dorothy Mackenzie, and surely she wouldn't haven't known those.

James's mother smiled. She leaned towards Floris and gently stroked her cheek, then patted her own knee. 'Would you like to come up on Grandmama's knee?'

Floris gazed up at her from her dark-lashed eyes and then shook her head and turned to look at Elliot Ripley. She pointed to him and giggled. 'Maff's grandbaba.'

They laughed. 'We must say goodbye to Maff!' his grandfather said. 'Where is he? In fact we'd better get a move on, old girl, or we'll miss our train. We'll come through again before Christmas, won't we?'

He looked at his wife, who replied that they would, and said, without thinking, 'You must come over to us too, Moira. Bring the children and we can have a stroll on the sands.' Then she glanced up at the window, where the rain dashed against the glass, and added ruefully, 'That is, if it ever stops raining!'

James got to his feet to ring the bell. 'I'll ask Bob to fetch you a cab; there are generally some waiting by St Mary's. People shelter under the archway to wait for them.'

'Thank you, m'dear,' his mother said. 'I hate sitting in wet clothes, and if we walked we'd be soaked by the time we reached the railway station. But isn't it just *wonderful* that we can now travel right into Scarborough rather than catching a cab home from Bridlington? The new line will do wonders for the local trade in summer.'

James nodded and agreed. His mother was always so enthusiastic, so eager to hear the latest news and always read the newspapers when her husband had finished with them so that she might keep up to date; she was naturally curious about how people managed their lives, and if they were not coping very well she would be the first to give a helping hand, without ever prying or snooping into anything that didn't concern her.

Matthew came downstairs to shake hands with his grandfather, and kissed his grandmother as he said goodbye. Floris watched him and she too put out her hand to shake Elliot Ripley's. He smiled and bent low to take hers, and said, 'Goodbye, Floris. I hope we'll see you again soon.'

To everyone's delight, she gave an unsteady but graceful curtsey and bowed her head to him. Moira watched fondly as Caroline kissed her cheek tenderly and again Floris dipped her knee and head.

That isn't anything I've taught her, Moira thought. She has been shown by someone else to do that, and not recently. The people she met in the cellar would not have had such social graces.

After the senior Ripleys had gone, Matthew asked his father if he'd like to hear about the places he'd seen whilst out with Bob.

'I would,' James said. 'Where did you get to?'

'To places I didn't know existed,' Matthew said. 'We went down some alleyways like the one where we found Tom, but came back as they were too narrow and creepy and there weren't any buildings for let or sale in any case. But then we found somewhere in' – he took a notebook from his jacket pocket and looked at it – 'Winter's Alley. At least, we didn't find it, but Bob knew it was there. He said the sign had been up for a long time. I suppose it was too dark an area and the building in too bad a condition for anyone to want it.

'We crossed over to Junction Dock and looked at some of the buildings down there, but they're all occupied,' he went on, 'and then we cut across Market Place to Blackfriargate and looked round there, but didn't find anything. Next we went down Rotten Herring staith to come home because it was getting really cold, and did you know that there's a fishing smack tied up on the opposite bank of the Old Harbour? It looks deserted, and I wondered why it was there. It must belong to someone!'

'It surely will,' his father agreed. 'I know the one you mean. It's been there for a while. Someone must own it.' He gazed at Matthew. 'Why, what had you in mind?'

'No, not me,' his son said. 'It was Bob. He said it would make a good shelter if no one was using it, and if anyone did, it would be better on this side of the water, so it would be easier to get on to. I think he meant more accessible,' he added, 'but he might not have known the word for it.'

James nodded. He liked the way Matthew accepted Bob as he was, not judging him at all for his lack of vocabulary. Everybody had to learn.

'Many of the buildings down by Junction Dock are owned by Trinity House,' he said, 'as are many in Whitefriargate. Did you know that?'

'No, I didn't, though I knew the Trinity House school was

there. Once when I was home from York I followed some of the students in their uniform just to see where they were going, and saw some of them doing their drill. They looked very smart.'

'What kind of shelter was Bob thinking of?' His mother had been listening in to their conversation.

'Not really a shelter, more like a soup kitchen. He was sure there'd be somewhere to cook – a galley, he called it; would that be right?'

'It would,' his father answered. 'You might like to come with me to Hessle sometime and see how the ships we build are kitted out.'

'Me too come?' a small voice intruded. 'Floris can come?'

'Of course you can come,' Matthew said, and put his arm round the little girl as she came up close to where he was sitting. She held the by now rather grubby rabbit hanky clasped in her hand. 'Perhaps we'll wait for a nice day, shall we?' He looked across to his parents for an answer, and they both smiled and nodded.

'It's of no use saying *Yes, if all goes well,* or *Unless someone claims you,*' Moira said later, when Floris had gone with Rosie to be made ready for bed and Matthew had gone down to the kitchen to have a word with Bob, mumbling that he wanted to ask him something. 'She won't understand what we mean. Whatever are we going to do about her, James?' She had a catch in her voice, and she put her hands to her face. 'I can't bear to think of her going to live in the workhouse.'

'Nor can I,' he said in a low voice, 'but neither can we expect to give her anything but a temporary home until someone, her mother or another relative, comes to find her. Perhaps we should keep mentioning her mother's name so she doesn't forget her.'

He remained silent for a while, and Moira knew he was mulling over past events. Then he cleared his throat. 'Maybe

I'll take a walk down Albion Street and try to find a clue there about the family my father mentioned. And whilst I'm about it, I feel we should set out a plan for forming a committee of people who feel the same as we do about housing.'

'People in poverty,' she murmured. 'That's what your father called them, didn't you tell me?'

He nodded. 'People in poverty. House the homeless. Homeless in Hull. Whatever we call it, the name doesn't matter; what matters is that we must get them off the streets before winter strikes even harder and more young people succumb to starvation.' He felt overwhelmed with good intentions, but did not know where to start. They needed money, for one thing, and that would probably be the most difficult hurdle to cross.

He'd just finished speaking when Matthew rushed in. 'I've been talking to Bob and Mrs Evans.' His face was flushed with excitement. 'We thought if we could find out who the old ship belongs to and if they'd let us borrow it or rent it for the winter, we could set up a soup kitchen, and Mrs Evans said she would make the soup and that other women would too, if you were willing to set it up. I mean, organize it.'

James and Moira both raised their eyebrows. 'Ask Bob to come in,' James said. 'I know he's there.' He'd caught sight of a figure outside the door when Matthew had burst in, and rather sheepishly, when Matthew opened it again, Bob stepped inside.

James felt incredibly proud and somehow uplifted that these young boys were willing to do this. It was a start, he thought.

'A brilliant idea,' he said. 'I'm sure there'll be plenty of goodhearted men and women to support you.' He stood up and gazed at them. 'We could call the venture Bob and Matt's Soup Kitchen.'

CHAPTER TWENTY-TWO

Leila

At seventeen, almost eighteen, Leila decided that her education was complete, and wrote to her father to say so. Whilst Leila was safely in a French school, Henry had returned to Hull and given his solicitors instructions that if he should die they should put the Albion Street house in Leila's name and she could claim it once she reached twenty-one, when she would become the only beneficiary of his Will.

Mindful of the fact that if she took a husband he could legally inherit everything she owned, at least in English law, he put in a proviso that if she married the terms would be rescinded and any property pass to her children if she had any, or to certain named charities if not, although she was to be allowed to live in the house in Albion Street for her remaining days.

He received Leila's letter on his return to Nice, where he had rented a villa in this popular old town and was becoming used to his new lifestyle: he slept late, rising to enjoy long days of lounging in the sun on his balcony, which naturally overlooked the sea, reading books and newspapers; imbibed good wine and champagne, ate delicious food which his cook prepared for him, and occasionally took a restorative swim in the sea. In the evenings he might visit a local club in the old town, where he played bridge or chess, drank coffee and brandy with men, and sometimes women, from all orders of life, and enjoyed debating political matters.

There were hangers-on, of course, who had sniffed out the scent of money, and he was generous to a fault, but he was oblivious to the charms of women and men who made a bee-line for him for this reason, and their flattery and blandishments slid off him like soft soap in a warm bath.

He had had a good marriage with Dorothy. They had understood one another, and he didn't want anyone else in his life apart from his daughter. Neither, he mused as he poured himself another glass of wine whilst he lounged on his balcony, did he want to travel any more. The thought bothered him, as Leila had repeatedly written telling him how much she was looking forward to travelling in the Ottoman Empire with him when she had finished her education.

Perhaps she doesn't realize how big an empire it was and still is, he considered, nor how many countries and nationalities have been involved, and how many have broken away and become independent of the sultan. There could be trouble; there had already been discord and conflict, and I don't want to be caught up in any of that.

But, inevitably, Leila had made up her own mind about her future, and after saying *au revoir* to the friends she had made at school, though without any intention of meeting them again, she set out from Paris immediately after breakfast one morning, travelling by local train and various coaches, and arriving at his door five days later. He came out of the villa to greet her in time to see her luggage being unloaded from a hired trap by an obviously besotted young man, who turned out to be the brother of one of her school friends and had accompanied her all the way.

'Papa!' She smiled sweetly, giving him a hug. 'Can Pierre

stay the night? There's no transport back to Paris until tomorrow, and would you be a darling and give him his fare? And maybe some money for bringing me all this way?' She spoke in English, knowing that Pierre didn't speak or understand it.

Her father hummed and hawed and said, 'There are only two bedrooms, Leila, you know that, and he's not sharing with me! I'll take him to *la pension* and he can catch a coach in the morning; perhaps the proprietor will know from where. This is not England, you know, where you can just hop on to a train. France's transport system is lagging way behind every other country in Europe in spite of the third Napoleon's efficiency.'

'I know!' she said fervently. 'It took us *ages* to get here, but Pierre won't mind, he's an absolute darling and has been very cooperative and extremely useful.'

Her father was taken aback by her description of Pierre, especially when tears came into the boy's eyes when Leila briefly kissed him goodbye, murmuring that they would keep in touch. Henry thought that extremely unlikely, as he had no intention of allowing any young man to trail after them wherever they went, or even if they stayed in Nice, which was what he really wanted to do.

He returned an hour later, having paid for Pierre's supper, a room, and a wagon or coach ride the next day, and given him enough money to pay for a train journey back to Paris if he could get one. Dorothy and I would have walked, he thought, or gone by mule or canal boat. Youngsters are made differently these days; they expect transport all the way to their destination.

Leila had unpacked her valise and bags, and put her school clothes into a cotton pillow slip ready for washing. She had decided that she would not wear them again, but give them away to a family who perhaps couldn't afford to buy such good material. And I shall *not* wear a corset as my friends will when

142

they finish school, she mused; they will follow their mothers' style, whereas I will wear cotton slips and cover them with silks, georgette and floaty cotton after the style of Arabian or Indian women in saris. They cover themselves from the heat of the day and prying eyes, and yet look attractive and desirable. But I will be careful not to imitate women from a high caste, if that's the word, but create my own comfortable style for travelling, and always, *always* cover my hair with a hijab. Otherwise I will be known immediately as an English or Scandinavian woman.

'Your mother always wore a large straw hat,' her father said, when she told him that they should go shopping. 'Best thing for keeping the sun out of your eyes and off your face.'

She considered this, for it was true: she would burn. 'It's not as if we're going to India!' she said.

'Ah, well, are you sure of where you want to travel? The Ottoman Empire once covered a huge area, but now much of it is dissolved and countries have become independent. The Greeks broke away a long time ago and are now free; Egypt, Syria – there's hardly anyone left. Serbia has gone, as has Moldavia, and everyone is keeping an eye on Russia's advance. As for the Turks, they're scattered throughout what was the empire, but have little influence nowadays. Many of them are still nomadic.' He pressed his lips together. 'So where do you actually want to go?'

'I have been thinking about it, Papa,' she murmured in a little girl's voice. 'I think we should begin in Turkey.' She lowered her eyes. 'I will be guided by you, of course, but I believe that Turkey is safe?'

Hm, he considered. From what I hear from the fellows at the club, the Turks have completely lost their power, though the sultan once ruled practically all of Europe; now there is conflict everywhere. Paris has street fighting in spite of Napoleon; and in these strange days, conflict is not only about possession of land, as it has always been, but also about commodities and trade routes, and military power, and the control of the Danubian countries.

Hm, he thought once more. Maybe it's time to go home. Is England home? It is for me, or it was once. We felt safe there. But for my daughter? For Leila? She doesn't know it at all.

'Oh, and Papa . . .' Leila clasped her hands together and brought them up to her face. 'I would have said this to Mama, had she been here.' She lowered her eyes, her lashes touching her clear fair skin. 'I really want to fall in love one day.'

He gazed at her, his beautiful young daughter. In love? What does that mean? With a foreigner? But no! We're the foreigners. We're travellers in foreign lands. Nomads, like the Mongols, and the Turkish tribes who were scattered throughout the empire along with the Serbs, and the Albanians who were considered to be the brigands of the mountains.

But now the whole world is on the move and it's difficult to know for sure which land is ruled by whom. For six hundred years most of southern Europe was under the rule of the Byzantines until it became the Ottoman Empire, and after that the sultans probably let the different tribes get on with their own religion and customs and so on, but now?

He gave a deep sigh. Who knows what will happen next? The Russian border creeps ever closer, and countries are falling out with each other when once they were friendly neighbours. The more I think about it, the more I think my travelling days are over. I'm too old for possible conflict.

'Leila,' he said, 'I will take you to Turkey and the city of Constantinople. You can see the mosques, the obelisks, the minarets, the spires and the steeples, and the bazaars, and then, whether or not you fall in love, dearest girl, we will return home to England.'

Though she smiled sweetly as she thanked her father, she did not agree. She had only vague memories of England, for they hadn't stayed long on any visit. She recalled drenching rain and dark gloomy nights, and neither she nor her mother had suitable clothing because her mother had forgotten too. Leila cried when she got a soaking, and her father had to carry her.

I will find a rich and handsome husband, Turkish or Greek or Italian, and live with him in sunshine regardless of my fair skin.

'Papa,' she said aloud. 'Why do you not buy this villa, or have it on permanent rental? You would be near enough to take occasional trips to England, stay for the spring or summer, and come back to Nice for the winter.'

He shook his head. 'The house in Hull needs to be lived in; apart from tenants who have stayed from time to time, it's lain empty for close on ten years. It needs updating, and I'll either make it my home or sell it and buy another.'

He seemed a trifle melancholy, she thought, especially when he added, 'I need a settled existence now, Leila, and after this trip to Turkey I will go home. To Hull.'

CHAPTER TWENTY-THREE

Moira stood by the front window looking out over High Street. The rain was relentless; gutters on the buildings on the opposite side of the street were overflowing, and volleys of gritty rain cascaded down the walls so that pedestrians had to step into the centre of the narrow road, which mercifully was empty of wheeled traffic.

She gazed up beyond the rooftops: was that a bright spot amongst the grey? She hadn't been out for several days, and neither had Floris, but the little girl seemed happy enough, lying on the carpet and drawing with crayons on a plain sheet of paper that Moira had found for her, along with a flat piece of board to rest it on.

It had been Matthew's idea to give Floris a box of crayons to keep her occupied rather than constantly begging for someone to read her a story. He didn't mind reading to her, but she had a tendency to always want the same stories, and he was bored with them. Also, he was busy. The Grammar School had sent him a paper of set questions on several subjects to complete before he sat the obligatory entrance examination the following day.

James had left early for a meeting with his brother to discuss monetary matters and crucial work in hand. He was still waiting for an answer following his enquiries about ownership of the old ship; he had his hopes pinned on being able to rent it and use it, as the boys had suggested, as a soup kitchen.

He had discussed the idea with Moira of finding a building to house those who had no other place to go and suggested that it would have to wait until he made further enquiries. 'One thing at a time,' he'd murmured.

'But winter is almost on us!' she'd exclaimed. 'It's raining now, but it's getting colder, and soon we'll have sleet and then snow and what will happen to people who have nowhere to shelter? The thought of the cellar is abominable, but it was a roof over their heads!'

'I'm doing my best,' he said irritably. 'I can't do more. I have a job to do and that won't wait either.'

I've never known him so worked up about anything, she reflected, her gaze wandering up and down the street below. I feel so useless, but what can I do? I don't know anyone I could ask. I don't know any owners of property, at least no one who would want to let it to someone who would allow those who have no money or possessions to live in it.

Who would own such a property? There must be someone. She looked down into the street again, but without seeing, until two women walked by, hunched up together, their shawls pulled over their heads in a useless endeavour to escape being drenched. One of the women was thin but walked rapidly and Moira's attention was caught as she was reminded of Mrs Evans, who was always brisk even when in the kitchen, as if she had to get on with whatever she was doing before starting immediately on the next.

Has James discussed this matter with her? He does talk to her. He's known her for so long; longer than he's known me, she mused. Would she know anyone? Or would Bob's aunt? *She* might. Yes, of course! She would know landlords, the good ones and the bad. Should I call and ask? Would she mind? Would James mind?

She turned to look at Floris and said impulsively, 'I'm going down to see Mrs Evans. Want to come?'

Floris scrambled to her feet. 'Yes please.' She looked down at her drawing and then picked it up. 'For Mrs Evans. For biscuits.'

Moira wanted to laugh. Was she bargaining? A picture for a biscuit?

'Matthew come too?' Floris said.

'Matthew is busy,' she told her. 'You'll see him later.'

Floris tucked the picture under her arm as if she was going on an outing, and followed Moira out of the door and towards the back stairs. She knew her way around the house now. She seemed to be settled in, no longer crying out for Lay-lah, as she had done when she had first arrived. This concerned Moira: if the name was her mother's, Moira thought that perhaps, as James had suggested, they should mention it from time to time so that Floris didn't forget her.

'Will you knock on the door, please, Floris?' she said, a subtle way, she hoped, of teaching her manners. Floris tapped with her knuckles. 'A little louder,' Moira said, and this time the child banged harder.

Rosie opened the door. 'Who's knocking at our door?' She pretended to look about her before looking down. 'Oh!' she said, as if startled. 'If it isn't Miss Floris come to call.'

'And Matthew's mama,' Floris piped up. 'Matthew is busy, but we've come for a biscuit.'

Rosie opened the door wider to let them in, dipping her knee to Moira, who smiled. How everyone loves this adorable child, she thought; and how we'd miss her if – if ... She decided not to think about losing her. Difficult enough to cope with if or when it happened.

Mrs Evans had her hands in a bowl of flour and was rubbing a knob of shortening through it. 'Sorry if I don't stop, ma'am,' she said. 'I want 'pastry to rest afore I make 'pie.'

'I don't want to disturb you, Mrs Evans. I just wanted to ask you a question, and Floris has something for you too.' Floris was hopping from one foot to another as she waited for Moira and Mrs Evans to stop talking.

'A picture,' Floris said, surveying the table, which held a bag of flour, a slab of butter in a dish and another plate bearing a lump of lard. She pressed her lips together and held up the picture, which was now becoming creased around the edges. 'Cake!'

'My word,' Mrs Evans exclaimed. 'That looks just like the ones that I make. Rosie,' she said, 'bring out 'cake tin and we'll compare them; and mebbe Mrs Ripley'd like a cup of coffee and a slice of cake to go with it?'

'Coffee, yes please,' Moira said, 'but no cake for me.' She briefly wondered what her mother would think if she chanced to call and found her daughter in the kitchen having coffee with Cook. She had the rare and happy sensation that she didn't really care.

'May I sit down, Mrs Evans?' she said. 'I came with a purpose.'

'Course, ma'am, and there's a little stool for Miss Floris.'

Floris placed the picture on the table and sat down, her eyes following Rosie as she went to the larder to bring out the cake tin and then made coffee and heated milk on the range.

'I wanted to ask you about the fishing smack on the other side of the Old Harbour,' Moira went on. 'Do you know the one I mean? It seems to be abandoned.'

'I do know 'one you mean, ma'am,' Mrs Evans said. 'But I don't think it's abandoned, although it's been there a month or two. It set out to go to 'fishing grounds, so I heard, but 'owner was took ill and crew brought her back into 'Old Harbour so he could be tekken off to see a doctor, and nobody else has 'authority to do owt— erm, anything about it. Though I suppose 'port authority could do summat if they had a mind to.'

'I see.' Moira pondered. 'We wanted to rent it,' she said, and Mrs Evans looked up. 'Is it an old vessel?'

Mrs Evans shrugged. 'Mr Ripley would know better than anybody.'

Moira nodded. 'He would, it's just that he's too busy right now for me to bother him.' She felt useless as she sat sipping coffee, whilst Floris tucked into a small slice of cake. 'I'll have to wait until he comes home; we really must try to find out if we can use it.'

'I could find out for you, ma'am,' Rosie piped up. 'I could ask my da. He works on trawlers, and goes out on fishing smacks. He might know 'name of owner and if he's recovered.'

Mrs Evans raised her eyebrows. 'If young Bob and Master Matthew are still keen to turn it into a soup kitchen, ma'am, wouldn't it be as well to find out who's going to supply and make 'soup and owt else the poor folk would like to eat, sausages an' bread an' that sort o' thing? That needs to be organized so that they've got all 'ingredients to hand as soon as they're ready to start.'

'Hm,' Moira murmured. 'Actually, I rather think the boys want to sort out the food themselves.'

Mrs Evans harrumphed. 'Beggin' your pardon, ma'am, but has Master Matthew ever cooked anything afore? Cos I'm certain sure that Bob never has; who could trust 'em to cook precious food without wasting any?' She looked at the mistress's pink face, and went on, 'I dare say that Bob's auntie might lend a hand, and then 'lads could hand it out to those who need it.'

Moira could tell by Mrs Evans's manner that she thought the whole project a complete waste of time. I have to do something, she thought. Here I am with time on my hands when people are starving and desperate for somewhere to live. All right, I'll ask Bob's aunt and risk her thinking I'm a fool, and if she gives me the names of landlords I'll try to find a philanthropic one who is willing and able to help.

CHAPTER TWENTY-FOUR

Moira debated whether or not to tell James about her plan to visit Bob's aunt, but she was heartened when he came home in a much better mood than when he had left that morning, and with news for her too.

He put his arms round her waist and swung her round. 'Guess what?' he said gleefully. 'Pa and Daniel have agreed that the company can sponsor the opening of a house of charity, or whatever we decide to call our refuge for the homeless.'

'Oh, that's wonderful!' she said. 'What a great start. But not that name, please. Let's call it something more optimistic, so that those who don't believe in what we're doing won't look down their noses.'

'We don't care what people like that think!' he objected.

'Perhaps not,' she said quietly. 'But the people who will come to live there perhaps would prefer something more liberal-sounding.' She considered for a moment. 'What do you think about the Happy House? If we can find something appropriate and at a reasonable rent, we could maybe make a dormitory for the men, and— oh, you said not women and girls! So what about women like the elderly woman you met – Lizzie, was it? We wouldn't be able to accommodate someone like her, and that seems unfair; they were all living together in the cellar, weren't they?'

James nodded. 'I understand they had rules, and those breaking them were turned out.'

'So they supported each other and friendships were made?' They looked at each other and the name of the proposed refuge came immediately to them both.

'Friendship House,' they said in unison, and smiled and nodded. 'Perfect!' James said.

'Wonderful,' Moira agreed, and then told him her plan of enquiring about landlords and property owners in the town. 'I'm going to ask Bob's aunt if she knows which landlords we should approach.'

James opened his mouth to speak, but she went on, 'I realize that you might know of several from your business contacts and colleagues, but they might not know how they treat their tenants or maintain their properties.'

'Just what I was going to say,' James murmured. 'I've heard of some dreadful property owners; men who hold respectable positions in other companies or industry, and I have never discussed with you, for the subject is nauseating, the way some people have to live only yards from our very own house.'

'Here? On High Street?'

'Not actually on High Street, for many of the houses here, as you know, are now used for offices or warehousing, but the courts adjoining Whitefriargate and Silver Street are quite simply not fit for human habitation.'

'But I shop regularly in Whitefriargate,' she said. 'And you sent our son and Bob to look at those places for a suitable property!'

'Yes, I did, but during the day. I would never suggest they go down there after dark. I am not saying that people of ill repute gather there, but those without any means of making a living or even a bed for the night might, and we shouldn't put temptation in their way.'

As he spoke, a vision of Tom huddled beneath a pile of old clothing came to mind and he felt ashamed that they hadn't tried harder to find him since he ran away.

Moira's forehead creased. 'But why would we look for property in those areas if they're not fit to live in? I don't understand your reasoning.'

'Because we'll repair any dwelling that we rent, and make it comfortable, and word will spread that it is a safe place to live, and those who come will maybe have a chance of a better life.'

'Oh, I see,' she murmured. 'Because in more salubrious areas, those at rock bottom wouldn't come at all.'

'Exactly,' he beamed. 'Those are my thoughts, but we can't do it alone; we must find workmen to repair and decorate it, and we must have a committee to help us run it. But first of all we must find somewhere suitable.'

Moira gave a sigh of satisfaction. 'Good. I was thinking I might visit Bob's aunt tomorrow and sound her out on landlords, good or bad, and also mention the soup kitchen, if Bob hasn't already done so.'

'Don't forget she's a working woman, Moira. Check with Bob first and find out when she's likely to be in.'

'Yes, of course.' She paused. 'It's easy to slip into the mode of thinking that women have time on their hands, as I do, with a cook and staff to do the work that many other women do for themselves.' But I must live a useful life, she considered, otherwise what is the point of it all?

The door opened as they were both silently sitting in contemplation and Matthew came in, holding Floris's hand. 'Floris has been helping me with tomorrow's exam papers,' he said ironically, 'and we've stopped for a break.'

'I thought she was having a nap!' his mother said. 'I'm so sorry, Matthew. Have you been disturbed?'

Floris was holding up a sheet of paper and smiling. She came to Moira to show it to her and Moira murmured platitudes as she tried to keep up with what Matthew was saying.

'She came to find me. I've been learning another language, although I don't know what it is!' He shrugged his shoulders. 'What I've discovered is that a certain small person speaks a foreign language much better than she does English.'

His father looked up. 'So is that why this diminutive person doesn't talk much? Her English vocabulary isn't as good?'

Matthew looked from one to the other and nodded. 'I think so. I don't think she understands a lot of what we're saying. She came to look for me and we've had a long conversation, most of which *I* didn't understand, and I'm sure that's why she doesn't speak much.'

'Only words like cake or biscuits?'

Floris looked up. 'Mrs Evans bring cake?'

Moira gently tapped her cheek. 'Yes. Soon.' She looked down at the drawing. 'It's that man again! The man with the beard.' She smiled at Floris and said slowly, 'Who is this man?'

Floris put her head to one side and looked at it, then sighed. 'This man Baba.'

'Your papa?'

Floris nodded. 'Floris's baba.'

'What is his name?' James asked.

'Baba!'

'Of course it is,' James chuckled. 'Matthew, did you know my name when you were – well, roughly the same age as Floris?'

Matthew shook his head. 'I don't think so. I don't think I knew it until I could read. I remember bringing you the morning post and reading James Ripley on the envelope.'

'Let's try something,' Moira said quietly. 'Floris, what is Mama's name?'

Floris looked at her. 'Moira!'

Moira nodded. 'Your other mama?'

154

'Lay-lah!' Floris said triumphantly.

Yes!' They all clapped.

'And what is Floris's baba's name?'

Floris clapped her hands and jumped up and down on both feet. 'Ziki,' she said. 'Lay-lah say Ziki.'

Everyone clapped again and James murmured, 'Perhaps a nickname?'

They had no answer to that, but decided they might be a little further on in their knowledge of Floris and her parentage, although not much: James was inclined to think that his father could have been on the right track when he mentioned the Mackenzies, who had a daughter named Leila.

But how would they find out what had happened to her, and where was she now?

CHAPTER TWENTY-FIVE

Moira picked her way carefully to Mrs Walters' home. It was a small, narrow court of ten houses, five on each side; deep puddles of rainwater filled the uneven cobbles so that she had to edge round the sides, and then step over. Some of the houses had clean glass and curtains in the windows, whilst others had cardboard torn from boxes inserted in the frames to keep out draughts or rain.

She knocked on the door of number six, which was opened cautiously. Bob's aunt Lily stood inside and seemed startled on seeing her. 'Mrs Ripley? Ma'am. Is summat amiss?'

Why would she think that, Moira wondered. Does she never have visitors? Maybe none like me. She had deliberately worn a plain dress, bonnet and cloak, and carried an umbrella. Mrs Walters was neat and tidy and wearing an overall much too big for her.

'Nothing amiss, Mrs Walters, but I wanted to ask you something. May I come in?'

Mrs Walters opened the door wider, and with her back to a narrow staircase leading up from the tiny hall ushered her into what she thought was the parlour or a kitchen or possibly both. 'You mustn't mind the upset, ma'am. I'm in 'middle of a customer's ironing.'

There was a large basket on a chair filled with clean laundry: shirts, petticoats and snow-white pillow slips. A thick cloth was spread over the table and a flat iron heating on the bars of a glowing coal fire.

'I'm so sorry to disturb you. Bob said I might find you at home this morning.'

Mrs Walters nodded and then looked round the room as if wondering where she could seat her guest. Footsteps clattered down the uncarpeted stairs and the front door banged.

'I beg your pardon,' Moira said hastily. 'This clearly isn't a good time.'

'My neighbour.' She pointed a finger upwards. 'They don't know how to be quiet; up and down, in and out, all day long!'

Moira was startled. 'Oh, erm, someone else lives upstairs?'

'They do,' she answered prosaically. 'I used to rent 'whole of upstairs, but now just 'one room. My lads use that for their bedroom and I sleep downstairs. Won't you sit down, ma'am?'

There was just one empty cane chair by the fire and Moira carefully picked her way to it.

'I didn't feel 'need to have 'whole of upstairs once Bob came to live in at your place,' Mrs Walters went on, as if she should explain. 'So I saved a bit o' rent money and 'landlord was happy enough to have another lodger.'

'Of course,' Moira said quietly, feeling totally inadequate. 'It, erm, it was about landlords and property that I came to see you. I thought you might be able to help me – us – with some advice.'

Mrs Walters' eyebrows shot up and then she bent down, holding a thick cloth in her hand, and removed the flat iron from the fire bars, placing it carefully in the hearth.

She stood up straight. 'I don't know how 'likes o' me can help you, Mrs Ripley, but I'll do my best.' She crossed her arms in front of her, and then looked round. A pile of folded sheets had been placed on a low stool, and she picked them up and put them on the table, then sat down on the stool with a sigh.

'I'm so sorry,' Moira said with a catch in her voice. 'So sorry to disturb you when I can see you're so busy, and I promise not to take up too much of your time. I just wanted to ask you who would be a good landlord, if we were looking for one?'

Mrs Walters looked totally flummoxed, and Moira went on to explain what they had in mind. She added that she gathered Bob hadn't mentioned the project that he and their son, Matthew, had envisaged.

'Your son and Bob, ma'am? No, he hasn't, but then he wouldn't discuss owt – anything – that went on anywhere else. Bob's a good, honest lad.'

'He is,' Moira agreed. 'Absolutely.' She told Mrs Walters that the two boys would like to set up a soup kitchen during the winter, and went on to explain the project that she and Mr Ripley and possibly others would like to start if they could find a suitable property to convert into a house for the homeless. 'It's a question of finding a willing landlord who would allow us to do that,' she finished.

'You're not thinking of buying a property, then?' Mrs Walters asked bluntly. 'Then you could do as you liked.'

Moira shook her head. So many people would imagine that they had bottomless pockets; they were comfortably off, it was true, but not so rich that they could buy another property. James wouldn't take that risk, but if they could form a charitable company – well then, maybe.

'These are early days, Mrs Walters, and it's still a pipe dream. What we would like to do is to provide accommodation for those who can't afford to pay for rent themselves; to bring people in off the streets and give them food and somewhere to sleep safely.'

Mrs Walters looked at her sceptically. 'You have trust in these folk, do you, Mrs Ripley? You don't think they'll say thank you very much and bow and scrape, and then when you're not looking go off with what you've provided – your blankets, your chairs, your cutlery and what not – and sell 'em so they can buy another dose o' loddy to give them 'fix that they need?'

Moira swallowed. She recalled that young Tom had gone off with their blankets and they hadn't seen him or them since. She remembered how sad, worried and disappointed she'd been. Were they, after all, on a fool's errand with their altruistic ideas?

Mrs Walters shook her head. 'It's a grand thought, ma'am, but you've obviously got more trust in folks than I have.' She gave a deep sigh. 'You could try my landlord, Mr Thomas. I hardly ever see him, but he's allus been all right wi' me, but then I allus pay 'rent on time. He uses an agent to accept or turn out folk who live in his property. Or Leggott; he's all right, so I hear. He's been at rock bottom at some time in his life and then done all right for himself. Mebbe try him.'

Moira stood up to leave. Mrs Walters had given her some useful information, and it seemed she had nothing else to offer. 'Thank you,' she said. 'I'm very much obliged to you.'

Bob's aunt huffed as she got up from the low stool. 'Sorry if I seem cynical, Mrs Ripley,' she muttered. 'But it's 'way you become when life is hard and you get knocked back at what seems like every turn.' She paused and rubbed her chin. 'Well, mebbe not every turn; 'day that Bob found Mr Ripley was one of 'better days and I'm more than grateful for what he's done for him.'

'And do you not believe that there might be others just as deserving, Mrs Walters? Mr Ripley was thinking of Bob and other young people when he came up with this idea. And it was Bob's notion that they – he and Matthew – could run a winter soup kitchen on a fishing smack that's moored in the Old Harbour; if they're allowed, that is. They'll need support, of course,' she went on, 'and Mrs Evans said she was willing to help them with the making of soup and bread.'

'Well, I could help wi' that!' Mrs Walters burst out. 'If I could have flour and ingredients for soup it wouldn't be a difficulty at all.'

'That would be wonderful,' Moira enthused. 'I'll ask him to let you know when something is set up. Thank you so much, and I'm sorry to take up your precious time.'

With a nod and a smile, she said goodbye and walked from the house and down the entry, lifting the hem of her coat to skirt the puddles, and conscious of eyes watching her as she made her way home.

When she arrived back, James was in his study, which was also his office, and no one ever disturbed him in there; nor did Rosie do any dusting unless he asked her, but he allowed the brushing of the carpet and the laying and lighting of a fire in the small hearth each morning.

When he was working on the company accounts, or sketches for ships, he generally spent all day in there, only appearing for a brief lunch and ringing the handbell for coffee or tea throughout the day. Three days a week he left the house very early and went by either train or cabriolet to the shipyard, and the office which he and his brother shared in Daniel's home.

He opened the study door when he heard Moira come in through the front door. 'Rosie has brought coffee. There's enough for two.'

'Lovely. I'll just pop upstairs and change my shoes.'

She hung her coat on the clothes stand in the hall and ran lightly up the stairs. She reached the top and heard the chatter of Floris and Rosie, but trod quietly and went into her bedroom, where there would be soap and a towel and a jug of clean water to wash her hands.

I'll have coffee with James and then relieve Rosie of her charge, she thought. Not that the girl minded looking after Floris; she'd told Moira she was happy to any time.

James looked relaxed, and his slippered feet were up on a

chair when she went into the office, but he took them down straight away and turned to pour her coffee, for Rosie always brought in two cups.

'I've got some good news,' he said. 'The owner of the fishing smack has come to light. His name, appropriately, is Fisher. Ben Fisher. I don't know of him, but Howard did. They'd only just gone out of the estuary when he began to feel ill, so the mate immediately brought him back into the Old Harbour, which he thought would be quickest for sending for a doctor.'

'Goodness,' Moira said. 'And were they in time?'

'Yes. They took him off the ship and then to the infirmary, where it was confirmed he'd had a heart attack. He's going to be all right, his mate told Howard, but the man doubts that he'll risk fishing again.'

'So – would the ship be available for the boys?'

'In the short term, possibly.' James nodded. 'The mate, whose name is Wilson, is up for buying it for himself if Fisher decides to sell and if he can raise the asking price. He's said he'll ask Fisher if he'll agree to loan it out for a while in a good cause.'

'That's good news all round,' Moira said happily. 'They'll only want it when the snow falls, which it undoubtedly will; the weather's much colder today.' She changed the subject. 'I wonder how Matthew has done in his entrance exam. Do you think he'll be all right? He didn't seem nervous at all, did he?'

'No, he didn't. He seemed quite buoyed up when I walked to the school with him this morning; he's so pleased to be going there.'

'We don't know yet if he'll be accepted,' she said cautiously. 'Won't it depend on his results?'

'It will, but we know he's good at maths, and I saw his preliminary English paper and he'd written an essay on poverty and the poor. That's sure to do well.'

161

'Do you think that's because of their intention to provide a soup kitchen?'

James took a sip of coffee, and then said, 'Possibly, but also because of Bob himself. I think that Bob has told him about his aunt and his cousins, and how they can't always get work, and how he left school without being able to read. Matthew has discovered that there are divisions in society, which I don't think he quite took in when I first told him about the cellar and the people in it, or realized that that's where we found Floris. He's learning about real life, which is what we all do . . . or should.'

CHAPTER TWENTY-SIX

The next day James put on his raincoat to go out.

'Where are you off to this morning?' asked Moira, who was still sitting at the breakfast table, drinking coffee.

'A few ideas to explore,' he murmured. 'First to see Nicholas Howard and discuss raising a committee, and then to try to find this Leggott fellow that Mrs Walters mentioned. If he has had a rough life and managed to climb out of poverty, he might be willing to participate.'

He looked up as Rosie brought Floris into the room. As always, the little girl had a book under her arm. Matthew followed them in.

'Good morning, darling. Did you sleep well?' Moira asked Matthew. 'No worries as to how your results will be?'

He shook his head. 'I did the best I could,' he said. 'Maths were all right and I think they'll approve of my essay, just not sure about French, though I explained I'd only started a year ago.'

He looked at Floris, who was watching and listening intently. 'I should have told them I was learning another language,' he said, 'but not French.'

'*Je parle français,*' Floris piped up, and looked from one to another. 'Lay-lah say so.'

'Did she?' Moira leaned forward to take her hand and draw

163

her close. 'Where is Leila?' And wanted to ask, did Leila teach her French?

Floris pressed her lips together. 'Gone!' she whispered, and looked intently at James and Moira as if to say I've told you that. 'Gone to find Baba!'

'Of course,' Moira murmured. 'Where is Baba?'

Floris raised her arms wide. 'Not come on big ship.' She shook her head. 'Stay with—' She hesitated. 'With – man – soldiers! Lay-lah cry.'

Moira lifted her on to her knee and held her close, feeling the child tremble. She smiled down at her. 'It's all right. You're quite safe.'

'Floris not go in water! Papa Jamie say so.'

'Papa Jamie.' Moira looked across at James, who was tucking in a scarf and doing up his coat buttons. 'That's what Matthew sometimes called you when he was little.'

'Did I?' Matthew said. 'I don't remember.'

'Maff's papa,' Floris murmured, and Moira and James relaxed. There was so much more that they needed to know about this small child who had burrowed into their hearts.

After James had left, Rosie brought Floris a coddled egg and bread and butter for her breakfast. She had climbed into Moira's bed this morning and shared a cup of tea. She was eating better now and her appetite improving, yet sometimes she seemed pensive and Moira was sure that she was grieving over her missing parents. Sadly, they were no closer to knowing where they were.

The clouds that had prompted James to don his raincoat earlier had darkened, and Moira got up to light a lamp. 'It's raining again,' she said mildly. Matthew was sitting in his father's vacated chair, having already had his breakfast, and Floris was at the table eating hers.

Floris looked up. 'Floris not go in water,' she said again, staring intently at Moira.

Moira went across to her as the little girl slid down from the chair. 'That's right,' she said. 'Don't go in the water until we buy you some rubber boots. Then you can splash in the puddles!'

Floris shook her head. 'Not go in water,' she repeated. 'Papa Jamie carry me.'

She's thinking of the cellar, Moira thought. Why is she saying that now? It's rained almost every day since she was brought here. James was wearing the same coat he had worn that night, and although he had worn it several times since, perhaps Floris hadn't seen him in it; and then she herself had said that it was raining. Was that enough to bring back a memory of that dreadful night?

James had told her that women were screaming to get out of the cellar as water from the blocked drains flooded down the steps, crying out that they would drown. They wouldn't have drowned, she thought, but perhaps it had seemed that they might. It would have been dark in the cellar, especially at the back where James had said the women and children were.

Up to their ankles or knees in cold dirty water, they would have been terrified, and that fear would have been infectious as they all struggled out, especially to a young child who hadn't fully understood what was happening. We must do something to allay her fears and teach her not to be afraid of rain.

She looked at both children now. Floris had climbed up to share Matthew's seat and he lifted his eyebrows in a droll manner, rather as his father would do, as Floris sinuously squeezed herself in beside him. She trusts Matthew, Moira thought. Perhaps he is the answer.

James strode out. Rain! When was it going to stop? It was sleety cold, sharp as a razor that cut into his face, and he pulled his scarf up to his nose as he headed across town towards Nicholas Howard's house in Parliament Street.

Howard had lived in the same house all his life, just as James had. They had both attended the prestigious Grammar School, although Howard was older than James and had been in the senior class when James had first begun. They had known each other, but they hadn't been close friends.

The housekeeper opened the door to him and Howard came out of a side room to greet him. 'Good morning. Come through.'

'I won't keep you long,' James said. 'I've come to say I'm going to see Leggott if he's at home, and enquire if he has a property we could rent. He's been recommended.'

'Leggott! I've come across him,' Howard said. He led James into the room he had just vacated, and lowered his voice. 'Leggott's all right, I think; met him a couple of times. Not my sort really; had a tough upbringing, I'd say, and you wouldn't want to argue with him, but he's done well for himself. He has a house in Kingston Square, close to where he grew up.'

James nodded; he already knew this. 'I'm only going to ask him the ins and outs of renting property and if he has anything he would be willing to let to us; not every landlord would be if they knew it was meant for people without any means of support.'

'True,' Howard agreed. 'It's a fine concept, but it might not work. People can take advantage, especially if they have nothing and are mixing with people who are better off than they are.' He drew himself up, but didn't seem to gain any height. 'And don't think they'll be grateful, Ripley, because they won't be. Believe me, I have met all sorts of people in my life, and not everyone appreciates what others do for them.'

'But . . .' James was beginning to change his opinion of Howard, who had initially seemed so enthusiastic about providing shelter for the homeless. 'We're not asking anyone to be grateful; we're not asking for anything. We'll just be providing a service that's badly needed. We live in an unbalanced society.'

Howard looked at him and gave a little cynical smile. 'We'll give it a fair trial, see if we can get some initial sponsors—'

'Ripley and Sons have already agreed. We'll put our name and money into it. Perhaps your company would do the same?' James knew there was money in Howard's family. He had his nose to the ground as far as other businesses were concerned. 'Others will then follow suit; I'm quite sure of that. However,' – he had noticed the startled expression on Howard's face – 'I'd better be off and search out Leggott. I'll let you know how I get on.'

The housekeeper let him out and gave him a quick smile as she bobbed her knee. He turned left at the bottom of the steps and strode on, skirting the dock and cutting across George Street towards what was called the Georgian area.

There had been a massive clearance of narrow streets and houses in this part of Hull; he didn't remember it as it used to be, but his father did, and had come to watch as derelict houses were demolished. Others had come too, and some who had lived here, cheek by jowl with their neighbours, had cried.

He paused as he reached Albion Street, where the grand terraced houses were built, and stood to admire the dwellings opposite. A smart gig with a sleek young horse in the traces and a young boy holding the reins waited outside one of them. The shiny black front door opened and a man and a woman stepped out and came down the steps towards the gig.

His eyes ran along the row; all but one had pristine white lace curtains at the windows. The odd one out, he noticed, was in need of a touch of paint on the dark grey door, and the heavy window curtains top and bottom were tightly drawn as if to keep out any sunlight.

He continued on his way and came to St Charles Borromeo, where his thoughts turned to Tom, who had claimed to be Catholic and was unwilling to enter Holy Trinity. Poor lad,

167

he thought; has he survived? I must call in at the police station again and enquire.

Leggott lived in Kingston Square. James ran up the steps of the house he wanted and pulled the iron chain to clang the bell. Almost immediately a young girl of about fourteen answered the door and bobbed her knee as if she had been waiting for someone to call, and said, 'G' morning, sir, can I assist you?'

'I'm looking for Mr Leggott, please, if he's available.'

'I'll ask him if he's in,' she said, and James's face broke into a smile. She turned away, and taking a step further into the hall shouted up the stairs, 'Da! Are you in?'

James heard the answer floating back. 'Dunno! Who is it?'

The girl came back to the door and indicated over her shoulder with her thumb, raising her eyebrows.

'Ripley,' he said, trying to keep a straight face. 'James Ripley. I'd like to enquire about renting a house.'

She turned again and called upstairs, 'Mr Ripley. He wants to rent a property.'

'Hang on a minute,' James heard the voice say. 'I'm coming. Ask him in. Put him in 'parlour.' James warmed to this unseen man, and wondered how Howard would have reacted if he'd come with him.

He looked about him. The parlour had long green chenille curtains at the window, a comfortable brown sofa and two matching easy chairs. A round mahogany table bore a lacy tablecloth and a lamp with a domed glass cover in the middle of it. On the walls were oil paintings of whaling ships on rough seas, with blue-tinged icebergs in the background beneath an eerie stormy sky. Another was of a three-masted schooner with a slender hull: American built, he thought, as he stood beneath it, and another of a tall-masted clipper with square sails, built for speed like all trade ships and particularly for the transport of tea from Asia. Above the fireplace was a portrait of a fine-looking woman, plainly dressed, who had a passing resemblance to the young maid.

Heavy footsteps on the stairs indicated a big man, and when the door opened James saw that he wasn't mistaken. Leggott was enormous, and had to duck his head as he came through the door, a head of thick brown hair, a strong bristly jaw and keen blue eyes. Howard had been right: you wouldn't want to argue with him, but he took James's hand and shook it gently but firmly.

'You like my paintings, Mr Ripley? I commissioned them myself,' he said, and held out his large hand towards the chairs. 'Come, have a seat. Hubert Leggott. Everybody calls me Leggott.'

James sank into one of the chairs; perfect for an afternoon nap, he thought. 'I'm sorry if I'm intruding on your time, Leggott, but you were recommended to me as a decent landlord, and as I am hoping to begin a project before the full winter falls on us' – they both looked towards the window as a sudden gush of wind and rain rattled the glass – 'I thought I'd seek you out.'

Leggott shook his index finger towards him. 'Are you of 'shipbuilder Ripleys?'

'Yes, sir,' James replied. 'Ripley and Sons.' He grinned. 'I'm one of the sons.'

'Ah! I've met your father, then, a lot o' years ago when I was a young feller.' Leggott nodded sagely. 'Did me a good turn; put me back on 'right path when I slipped off it.'

James smiled. 'That sounds like my father.'

Leggott leaned back in his chair and stretched out his long legs. 'Then tell me what I can do for you, young Ripley. It's about time I paid back a favour.'

CHAPTER TWENTY-SEVEN

James outlined the rough plans he had in mind, explaining about the people living in the cellar and rescuing them from it. 'We took them into the church for shelter; we didn't know where else to take them. The old Charity Hall has closed, and the other charity homes were already full. It came to me that something has to be done. Another place must be found, and quickly.'

Leggott shook his head, rubbing his fingers through his stubby greying beard. 'It's wrong, totally wrong,' he rumbled. 'I spent a few months living rough when I was a lad, and I can tell you it's no joke. You feel as if you've fallen from a great height and'll never get back on your feet again.' He frowned. 'Is it just you, tekking this on?'

'No,' James said. 'I couldn't do it alone. Nicholas Howard has said he would be on a committee if we formed one, and one or two others I've mentioned it to have expressed an interest. My wife is with me on this, too,' he added. 'I, erm, brought a small child home with me from the cellar. The women in there had been looking after her; no one knows where her mother is.'

'A small child? What? You mean she . . .' Leggott seemed to have run out of words.

James nodded. 'She went in with her mother only a few days before, so they said.' He took a deep breath. 'It seems unbelievable, and it is. But then her mother went out for some reason and didn't come back. The women took care of the child even though they had little food themselves. Then came the flood. I had the option of taking her to the workhouse or an orphanage and decided on neither, so I took her home.'

'What did your wife think o' that?'

'Like me, she didn't think I had any choice. And now we all – everyone in our household – love her.'

We'll be devastated to give her up, he thought, and a lump rose in his throat at the idea of taking such a vulnerable child to a home for abandoned children; but we might have to.

Leggott sat silently pondering and then leaned forward. 'But for a child who mebbe doesn't understand what's happening . . .'

'She didn't – doesn't. We didn't even know her name to begin with. Her speaking ability wasn't good; it's much better than it was, but—'

'What do you mean?'

'Well, she speaks another language much more fluently than she speaks English, but she's getting better by the day at explaining to us what she wants.'

James pondered. If the blonde hair Lizzie mentioned means her mother was English, why isn't Floris's English better? Though if her father was foreign, as Lizzie suggested, perhaps he didn't speak it and they used his language at home, wherever that was.

They talked for an hour. Leggott's daughter Hannah brought them coffee and biscuits and then disappeared again.

Leggott was frowning. 'I know that cellar. It should be blocked up, but then where would folk go?'

James surmised that he wasn't asking for an answer. It was a comment. He finished explaining about the proposed project and finally said, 'Someone told us that you were a decent landlord, although you weren't theirs, which was why I came to you first.'

'Right!' Leggott breathed hard. 'Well, as I told you, I've been in such situations as them folk in 'cellar when I was young, and had a helping hand. I got a job on trawlers through your father's recommendation, and all he asked in return was that I'd respect his name and not sully it by misbehaving or getting into trouble. He'd bailed me out of jail. Did he ever mention it?'

'No,' James said. 'Your name came via a woman whose young nephew works for me as an odd job boy. She lives in a court off High Street and my wife asked her if she knew of a reputable landlord. She gave your name.'

Leggott crossed his arms across his chest. 'Mm, well, that's – rare. Landlords have a bad name on the whole, and I don't own any houses off High Street.'

'Well, word has got around,' James murmured. 'That you're fair and agreeable, and from what I've gathered there are some places owned by other landlords that you wouldn't keep a pig in.'

'Sometimes it works both ways.' Leggott gave a cynical twist of his mouth which wasn't quite a smile. 'I've had folk in my properties who've brought a pig and hens in wi' them!' He sat for a moment. 'It just so happens that I have a property that might be suitable. I bought it on a whim because it was cheap and a good sound building, but it's in a poor area.'

'That's what I was hoping for,' James said eagerly. 'I don't want a property close to where the neighbours might resent our residents. Are you thinking of selling, or renting?'

'Not sure.' Leggott sat forward and crossed his arms. 'I thought that mebbe I'd bought a pig in a poke, to be honest, and have been wondering what to do with it.'

'Can it be modified? Would you allow that, so that there

could be a dormitory and separate rooms and mebbe a couple of washrooms?'

'Yeh.' He nodded. 'It's not a house but a building that could be adapted into one. I can take you to have a look at it, but not today. Today's my daughter's bothday and I'm tekkin' her out.' He thought for a moment. 'I might make some conditions, though.'

'Ah! What would those be? No noise and so on?'

Leggott shook his head. 'No. This committee that you're setting up. I'd like to be on it.'

Most satisfactory, James considered as he left the house. Instead of making his way home, he continued up Mason Street to where he knew there was reputable stabling and hire of horses and vehicles.

A young lad was sweeping the yard, and when James came to the gate he asked if he could help him. James told him he wanted to hire a horse and trap for an hour. 'I'm only going up on to Anlaby Road, but it's rather a long walk and it's raining again, and I don't have a great deal of time.'

'Mr Snowden's out at 'minute, sir,' the boy told him, 'but I can arrange 'hire if you'll leave a deposit and your card.'

How very efficient, James thought as he fished in his pocket for a business card and handed it to the youth, who carefully looked it over.

'That's perfectly all right, Mr Ripley. Would you like to come into 'office to make payment? You can shelter whilst I get horse an' trap out. Would you like a canvas cover, seeing as it's raining?'

'I would, please.'

The boy led him to a wooden building where on the door was a notice that said, *There is no money kept here. Don't waste your time looking.*

Inside were two chairs, a very tidy desk and a cupboard.

The boy wrote out a receipt for the deposit, put the money in a strong box and locked it, then placed the box in the cupboard and locked it again, putting the key in his pocket and buttoning it up.

'If you'd tek a seat, sir, I'll onny be a minute.'

A short time later he came back with a young filly in the shafts of a neat covered trap and ready to pull away. 'This is a converted trap,' he said. 'Like 'American buggies, you know; me and Mr Snowden built this between us for days such as this. This is Nellie,' he added, stroking the animal's neck. 'She's nice and gentle.'

James thanked him and asked his name.

'Herbert, sir. I'm Mr Snowden's apprentice.' The boy touched his forehead. 'Tek it easy, sir.'

James nodded and flicked the reins. Much quicker than walking, he thought. Especially in this weather.

He was going to the workhouse. It had been his intention to visit Lizzie all along, though he hadn't mentioned it to Moira, thinking she might become anxious and unsettled and wonder if he planned to make enquiries about Leila, which was indeed his intention.

It didn't take long, and he enjoyed the drive in spite of the constant drizzle. He pulled through the gate and into the yard and two young lads came running; the first one to arrive tipped his cap and, breathing hard, gasped, 'Look after hoss an' trap, sir?'

James smiled, but saw the disappointment on the other youngster's face.

'Erm, hm! This is a *very* important horse and a *very* important vehicle which isn't mine, and both need special attention.' He looked from one boy to another and rubbed his chin. He gave a big sigh and tapped his top lip with his forefinger.

'Tell you what. I really need two lads for this important job, one for this young horse and one for this very unusual trap. Are either of you up to it?'

'Yes, sir,' they both shouted out.

'Very well,' he said solemnly. 'I'll take you both on, but first I want you to lead this young filly over to that corner.' He'd noticed that there was a rail there, presumably for the purpose of tying up horses.

The first boy took charge of the horse and the second, with a quick glance at James, jumped into the trap, took up the reins and shook them, giving a click of his tongue as he did so. Off they went to the exact spot that James had indicated.

'Sir,' the second boy said, when they joined him again, 'Would you mind tellin' Master or Matron that Ben and Harry are doing a job for you? Then they won't think that we're skiving off.'

James shook his thumb to say that he would and walked towards the door. I don't know their history, he mused, but I don't think those two will finish up in the gutter or a cellar.

He gave the message about the boys to Matron and asked if he might speak to Lizzie Chambers.

'She's in 'kitchen, sir. I'll fetch her for you. Is she a relation, sir?'

'No. No, she isn't, but I met her before she applied to come here and I was curious to know how she's settled; she was quite unwell at the time.'

Matron nodded. 'So she was, but she's much improved after a few days of regular mealtimes and a bed to sleep in. I think in time she'll become a valuable member of our community.'

He was astonished to hear that. 'That is good news,' he said, and meant it. He would have been sad to hear that the wily old woman had succumbed and died in what everyone thought of as the ultimate indignity of the workhouse.

'I'll fetch her for you,' Matron went on. 'She's been very useful in helping out in 'kitchen since she arrived.'

He smiled to himself; he'd bet any money that the Lizzie he'd met, who seemed to have prepared herself for what might be the final stages of her life, would be making herself indispensable.

He sat down to wait and gazed round the room. This, he thought, might be where the matron interviewed people wanting to stop their struggle with the life they were leading. The last stop, probably.

It had only the basic furniture: plain wooden chairs without cushions and a bare wooden scrubbed table standing on a wooden floor. Matron, it seemed, didn't allow herself any luxuries or fripperies, not even a vase of flowers. Perhaps that was deliberate, he pondered; not gloating over those who came in with nothing.

The door slowly opened and James got to his feet. It was Lizzie who carefully stepped inside, head down, shoulders hunched and walking unsteadily, but when she saw who it was who had asked to see her, her shoulders straightened, her head came up and she gave him a toothless grin.

'Well I nivver,' she cackled, closing the door firmly behind her. 'Nivver thought it would be you, Mr Ripley.' She lowered her voice. 'Thought it might be one o' them committee members, or a councillor come to see if I was fit for work. And course I'm not, as you'll see!' Her voice had turned into a whine. 'But I'm more'n glad to see you.'

Crafty old woman, he thought, and laughed. 'It's good to see you looking so much better, Mrs Chambers.'

'I'm not lookin' too much better though, am I?' she said in a conspiratorial whisper.

'Definitely not,' he grinned. 'Quite peaky, in fact. Would you like to sit down?'

'I would,' she said, and bent towards him; she smelt of carbolic soap as she whispered in his ear, 'I've been willing you to come.' She tapped the side of her nose. 'I've got some news for you.'

She looked towards the door and then shuffled towards

one of the chairs facing his, sat down and again bent towards him when he followed suit.

'We had a new intake yesterday,' she breathed in his ear. 'Late on, it was. Sometimes folk get brought in from Hull Infirmary; that was 'word I heard. Folks they can't help, you know, them that are on their last legs.'

She nodded and he nodded back. She lowered her voice again. 'A woman – she's been in Hull Infirmary. I heard 'nurse who came wi' her say to 'Matron that there was no hope for her. Foreign, she was.'

'Who was foreign?' he whispered back. 'The nurse or the patient?'

She looked at him as if he were an imbecile. 'Patient, o' course, and she's been sent to our 'ospital, the one here in 'workhouse I mean, cos they needed her bed at 'infirmary. I expect it'd be wanted by a paying patient,' she went on cynically. James was having difficulty in keeping up with her meanderings.

'And 'upshot is, Mr Ripley – cos I've helped out in 'ospital a couple of times, tekkin' dinner and supper 'n' that – I heard 'em say that they can't do owt more for her, so she'll have to stop here until . . . well, until she snuffs it, to put it crudely.' She gave a little shrug, as if it wasn't a phrase she would normally use. 'Onny I took a look at her, and I don't like to say it and I can't be truly sure, but I think she might be 'bairn's ma; I think it might be Lay-lah.'

CHAPTER TWENTY-EIGHT

Leila

Leila had shopped a little in the Nice boutiques but didn't overspend, as she intended to buy what she required once they arrived in Turkey. For now she bought soft cotton dresses that would keep her cool whilst travelling, and packed wool blankets in their trunks to keep them warm during the night.

'You do realize just how far it is, Leila?' her father asked as they began packing. 'We'll spend much of the year travelling, and there will be times when it will be difficult. We'll travel through Italy, Croatia, Bulgaria—'

'I know, I know!' she said. 'You and Mama have done it. But when we have finished this journey, Papa, we will know where we want to settle.'

She had been pacified by his promise that they would travel into the Ottoman Empire, which, from being the longest serving empire in the world, with Egypt, Syria, Greece and Jordan within its domain, was beginning its long decline. She wanted to see at least some of the countries as they were; Henry Mackenzie, looking back over the years, was curious to know how life was changing in this once important empire. He was quite looking forward to the expedition, but, he thought, I'm no longer young and this journey might possibly be my last. He gave an inner sigh. *My journeying hasn't been the same without my beloved Dorothy.*

Leila will soon be old enough to decide where she wants to make her home, he considered, for he wasn't the average father who would impose limitations on his daughter, any more than he had on her mother: if Leila should meet someone that she wanted to marry, she could continue her journeying if they wished, but for me, he reflected, no more. *I have done enough. I will go home to England and live a quiet life, catch up with people I used to know; maybe meet former school friends from the Grammar School, if there are any left.*

Before Leila was born, he and his wife had travelled extensively through the empire and through countries that had since broken free, becoming independent of the reigning sultan. Before the change began, they had trekked over mountain passes, kayaked in turbulent waters through the narrowest of gorges, stayed overnight with native country-dwellers in their rural homes, and been made welcome wherever they went.

They had dived into cool, clear, deep seawater beneath sheer mountains, visited ancient Roman ruins, castles and temples, and had never felt harassed, not even in bazaars where they'd haggled good-naturedly with local traders over the price of wool carpets and silken draperies which they bought and sent home to the house in Hull.

After Leila was born, they changed their routine to accommodate a small child and toured towns and cities, taking it in turn to carry her on their backs as they visited mosques and palaces, always obeying the rules of the Islamic state; and now he was rather looking forward to revisiting Constantinople, once the capital of the ancient Byzantine Empire, and showing his daughter its many treasures, for she of course remembered none of it.

Leila appeared to have been listening to his tales of the splendour they had seen, but actually she was not. She didn't have the curiosity or the same interest in ancient times as her parents had had: she was a modern young woman keen to make her own mark on the world; to form her own impressions. She longed for romance, and didn't seem to comprehend that in some countries she should walk one step behind her father, and yet she wanted to travel; it was as if she had an obsession, a need to constantly move on.

They left Nice at the end of March, once the cold weather had retreated. 'This is the easy part,' her father commented.

Leila nodded as she gazed out of the train window. 'I love France,' she murmured. 'Perhaps I might live here one day.'

Henry sighed. 'There's a house in England, don't forget; that's where I'll be heading when this journey is over.' She didn't answer. He didn't think that she had heard what he'd said, but he didn't repeat it.

Leila had a grasp of many languages but she didn't speak Turkish, and now they had begun this first leg of their expedition she bought books about Turkey, its history and religion, and began to teach herself some basic words that she considered would be useful.

She dressed simply in cool cotton, as did her father, he in wide trousers, silk shirts and a large hat, Leila in her flowing cotton skirts and loose tops and her head covered as always.

She loved Croatia, she said, and Serbia too; it was the mountains that attracted her, she told him. 'England doesn't have mountains, Papa,' she pronounced. 'It's such a flat little island.'

'It is not flat!' Henry said testily. 'It does have mountains and I have walked and climbed many of them in my youth. They are not as high as some that we will see as we travel, but they have their own special beauty and magnificence. Your mother and I travelled to Cumbria on one of our trips home, and saw high mountain peaks and the deepest of blue lakes that took our breath away. It is the home of poets!'

She had touched a nerve, she realized, and meekly said, 'Perhaps we might go there next time we visit.'

They arrived in Constantinople at the beginning of September and were driven in a bullock cart to a hotel, the name of which Henry had found in one of his old diaries. He was pleased to be told that it was still open.

'Take careful,' the driver said, in an attempt to assist in English, for which Henry was grateful. 'No religion,' he said, shaking his head and hands in a negative manner.

They were given two rooms with an adjoining door and Leila was impressed by her comfortable bed and the extravagant hangings surrounding it, the day bed with its silken cushions and footstool, and the piquant-smelling soaps and lotions in the washroom; but mostly she was struck by the view from the long windows, entranced by the domes and palaces below them, the scent of spices floating up from the stalls and bazaars, and the sound of flutes and drums and singing voices.

Her father went down to speak to the desk clerk to order dinner and ask about local customs. He came back ten minutes later to tell her that what the driver had said was perfectly true.

'We must be careful where we walk; you must always take my arm, Leila, and not make any comment on any religion, and we must only visit the tourist areas.'

'But we're not tourists,' she began.

'Then what are we?' he said.

'Travellers,' she said contentiously.

'It's the same thing.' He smiled. 'They only have to look at us to know that we're not local. We're visitors, come to look at their beautiful country, and in turn they will look at us.' He laughed. 'Well, not me, but my beautiful daughter.'

And so they did; children followed them everywhere and men turned their heads to gaze at Leila, even though she was covered from head to toe in drapery.

One young man, whom they often saw near the mosques and palaces, always clasped his hands to his chest and gave a short bow whenever he noticed them. There was always a group of people near him and Henry gathered he was probably a local guide; it seemed that he was right, for the young man came to the hotel and left a card which stated that he spoke English and could give private tours in the city or the mountains and had a dependable horse and carriage.

On the card was his name and address. He lived near the hotel in a respectable area. His name was Ziki Adem.

CHAPTER TWENTY-NINE

'It's wonderful news,' Moira said when James arrived home and told her that Leggott was not only keen to be on the committee once it was formed, but he also had a building that might be suitable for conversion into accommodation.

'But you haven't seen it?'

'No. He was taking his daughter out somewhere as it's her birthday today.'

'He sounds like a nice man,' she said. 'Does he have a wife?'

'I don't know; he didn't mention one.' James was reflecting on the best way of breaking the news of Floris's mother lying unconscious in the workhouse hospital.

'Did he say where it was and when we can see it?'

He was really grateful that Moira was caught up with this project; she had definitely come out of her shell and was wholeheartedly behind him. At last, she had cast off her mother's opinions and was forming her own. Had this happened since they'd had Floris to consider, or was it Tom, whom they had almost saved and who, distressingly, had escaped their good intentions? Perhaps this was why she was so committed: they couldn't save Tom, but there were others that perhaps they could rescue; so many more.

'Somewhere near to where he lives,' he answered. 'And he's free at the weekend,' he said. 'Tomorrow or Sunday.'

She gazed at him. 'May I come?'

'Of course you can come! Best to have more than one opinion. I was going to ask Nicholas Howard to come sometime too, and Harold Bell: you won't have met him, but he's another potential committee member. Leggott said he didn't mind when we came. Then, if the building seems suitable, I'll ask Daniel and my father to take a look too, as they've agreed that our company can be one of the sponsors, though we will need others as well.'

'But there's something else bothering you,' she said perceptively. 'Is there a snag? Some hurdle that we can't climb? Money, perhaps. Where will we get it from if there aren't enough supporters?'

'Most ordinary folk are usually generous; think of the women who are always ready with soup kitchens at every disaster. I think maybe we should ask their opinion once we've looked at the building. And we should let it be known what we intend to do; those who complain about people roaming the streets after dark might change their attitude if they knew they had nowhere else to shelter. I hope too that the Corporation might dip into the coffers and help with a grant. But more sponsors, definitely.' He paused. 'But yes, there is something else. I couldn't think how to tell you.'

He gazed down at the top of Floris's dark curls as she crayoned trees and stick people in an exercise book. Some of the stick people had what looked like oranges or balls on their heads; he guessed they might be turbans.

'I will have to be careful what I say,' he murmured, and Moira moistened her lips as her eyes widened.

'Does it concern someone we know?' she whispered.

'Someone's parent.' He glanced down pointedly at Floris. 'A woman I heard of this morning. She was unable to see me.'

'Why not?'

'She was semi-conscious following an accident.'

'Oh!' Moira covered her mouth with her hands. 'But where was she?'

'I went to visit Lizzie Chambers in the workhouse,' he murmured, 'and she told me she had seen her in the hospital ward, or at least she thought it was her.'

Moira opened her fingers and spoke through them. 'What can we do?'

'Nothing.' He shook his head. 'The authorities don't know who she is or where she came from. She was knocked unconscious by a wagon and taken to the infirmary; since then no one has reported a missing person and so she was sent to the workhouse hospital. They've strapped up the broken bones – arms, ankles and ribs – but it's the concussion which is the biggest worry.'

'Look!' Floris sat up and showed them her drawing. She pointed to a stick person with long yellow hair and another with a hairy chin and baggy trousers and a round hat or turban on his head. In the background was a building with long thin sticks at each side, another with a dome on top.

James bent down and put his chin on the top of her head. Pointing to the stick woman, he asked softly, 'Who's this?'

She opened her mouth and took a breath. 'Lay-lah!' Then she pointed to the stick man and said, 'This Baba Ziki.'

She lifted the drawing up to show Moira, who touched the stick woman. 'Mama?' she asked.

Floris shook her head. 'Lay-lah!' she said in a determined manner. 'An-neh!'

'I think I get it,' James murmured. 'An-neh must mean Mama. Perhaps Floris calls her Lay-lah because her father says it?'

'The name your father said was given to his friend's daughter,' Moira remarked, gazing down at Floris, who was looking first at her and then at James, as if she was trying to comprehend what they were saying. 'Are we getting a little nearer to discovering her family?'

'Perhaps we are,' James said thoughtfully. 'If it is her. Her head was covered, but I saw wisps of fair hair.'

'You saw her?' Moira clutched her throat.

He nodded. 'I spoke to Matron, but I didn't go in, simply opened the door and looked at her. Her face was bruised, and she had a cut on her forehead which had been stitched. The matron said that she had nothing with her, apart from a satchel containing paperwork they couldn't understand, and she's been drifting in and out of consciousness since she was sent there. Matron thought that she wasn't poor; when they put her into a nightgown they saw she had good quality clothing: silks and fine cottons and expensive shoes, the kind that someone from the upper classes might wear. The infirmary had packed them into a bag and sent it on with her. She was also wearing a wedding ring.'

'What can we do?' Moira whispered.

James swallowed and shook his head. 'Nothing.'

The next morning they all dressed warmly for going out to look at Leggott's building. Mathew had asked eagerly if he could come, and when James said yes he asked if Bob could come too. 'No. Maybe another time if we decide to take it. But this is not only our decision, Matthew,' his father carefully explained. 'Others too will have a hand in the project. Also,' he added, 'Bob is a working lad; he has a job to do – several jobs in fact – and Mrs Evans wouldn't be pleased if he wasn't there to do them.' He shook his head. 'Sorry.'

He felt he had to explain; he realized that Matthew and Bob were becoming mates, as Bob would have said, and although he believed in equality for all, some people were simply born further up the rung of the social ladder than others. It was the luck of the draw, but the whole point of the project was to help the lowest to reach a place from which they could better themselves. He sighed. Or not.

They took Floris with them, dressing her in a warm coat, hat and scarf, but as they crossed over High Street and came to the top of Church Lane she suddenly hung back, pulling at Moira's and James's hands as they walked on either side of her.

'Not go. Floris not go in cellar.' She began to cry, catching her breath in dry sobs.

'Oh, darling, we're not going to the cellar,' Moira reassured her.

Floris put her arms up to James; he picked her up and she buried her head in his coat as if trying to hide. Matthew patted her shoulder to console her, but she pushed his hand away.

'Go right,' James said to Moira and Matthew as they came out into Market Place and crossed the road. 'We can cut by the top of the dock; it's probably quicker that way in any case,' and when Floris peeped up over James's shoulder she relaxed when she saw they were going in a different direction.

From the long and wide George Street, they turned towards Mason Street. James pointed out the stables in Charlotte Street Mews where he had hired the filly and trap the day before, and then they turned left to Leggott's house. He was ready for them and James introduced him to Moira and Matthew. When he bent down to take Floris's hand she gave him a little curtsey, which he thought very sweet.

'Come and look here, Hannah,' he called to his daughter. 'See these perfect manners.'

His daughter appeared in the hall and dipped her knee to Moira and James before saying hello to Matthew and Floris. Floris obligingly gave her a curtsey too, and then another one to Leggott.

'Party piece!' James murmured, smiling.

'Are you coming with us, Hannah pops?' Leggott asked his

daughter as he buttoned up his coat. 'Mebbe you could keep an eye on 'little bairn while I show Mr and Mrs Ripley round 'property?'

'I'd be happy to do that, Mrs Ripley, if you'd like me to?' Hannah smiled down at the little girl. 'What's your name?'

'F-floris,' she said, and put her hand out to Hannah, so that was agreed. Hannah unhooked her coat from the stand and put it on, slipped on a beret, and said, 'Ready.'

They walked back to the top of the street and crossed over. 'You might not know this area, Mrs Ripley,' Leggott said. 'Mason Street. These are well-built houses along 'front, but some of 'courts behind are not desirable residences. Corporation should really tek charge of 'rubbish and get rid of it. Can't expect residents to shift it; not everybody's able to do that. Owd folk, for instance. I have some property at 'back of here,' he went on, 'and every month I have a gang of men come to clear it. Otherwise it encourages rats.'

He cut down another street to take them into an area of courts which led one into another; Moira thought it would be easy to get lost in them and run up against one of the brick walls which separated some of the courts from their neighbours.

Leggott led them across to another narrow street of workshops and foundries and some houses, and on the corner of a lane behind a tall fence stood a square brick building. Four windows downstairs and four above were boarded up, as was the glass at the top of the wooden door, which had planks nailed across it.

'This is it,' Leggott said. 'I had 'windows and door boarded up, same at 'front, so intruders couldn't get in. You'd be surprised what folks can do to a building in no time at all – light fires and *puff*, your property's gone. Back gate is padlocked for 'same reason.'

He fished in his deep coat pocket and brought out a claw hammer to draw out the nails that were holding the planks in place, and then searched in another pocket to find a door key, which he held up triumphantly.

Moira glanced at James, who seemed invigorated as he took a quick look around the area; was he seriously contemplating this? She felt uncomfortable, wondering how people would feel about coming into this gloomy area on dark nights; would they be as nervous as she was sure that she would be? She peered about her and then took in a deep calming breath. A gas lamp stood on the corner. No glimmering light now, but such a relief to know that as dusk gathered the lamplighters would be out to light the way through the darkness of night.

CHAPTER THIRTY

The door that Leggott had unlocked opened into a kitchen of sorts with a large white chipped sink, a tap, cupboards on two walls and a large cooking range. Through the inner door they could see a hallway which had two doors on the right and two on the left, and beyond the staircase ahead was the front door.

Moira and James caught each other's glance and both gave a slight nod and raised their eyebrows. This would be ideal, James thought, and it's situated in exactly the right place. He opened the nearer right-hand door to reveal a very large room which looked as if it had been a workshop of some kind but could be easily adapted as a living room. There was even space to fit in a billiards table, a very popular pastime in all spheres of society.

The opposite room was equally large, and the one next to it was slightly smaller. All three had fireplaces.

'This, in my opinion, would be perfect,' James told Leggott. 'It's not solely my decision, but I'll definitely recommend it.'

'There's a privy outside in 'yard, if you noticed.' Leggott pointed over his shoulder to the now unlocked and unboarded door. 'It would be easy enough to put another next to it. There's a shed, too, which is presently empty and a good size.'

They could hear the voices of Matthew and Hannah upstairs

and Floris jumping up and down in an empty room, probably enjoying the resounding echo.

'This is very promising, Mr Leggott,' Moira said. 'I think many women of the town would be glad to supply curtains, and we could ask for unwanted furniture; I'm sure we could find some from our own house too.'

She thought of a chair which her mother had foisted on her that she didn't want. It was a perfectly comfortable chair but it didn't match any of theirs. These walls could be painted in bright colours, she considered, to make the rooms welcoming, and maybe if the wood floors were scrubbed and polished it would look nice with a few cosy rugs. Oh, I'm getting carried away.

James had a grin on his face. 'What?' she said.

'I said shall we look upstairs? You were miles away; you're decorating and filling it with furniture, aren't you?'

She blushed. 'I suppose I am.'

'My wife was 'same,' Leggott said. 'A proper homemaker.'

Moira hesitated. 'Was?' she murmured. 'Is she . . .'

'Aye, died a few years back. If it hadn't been for my daughter, I might have gone to 'bad again.'

'I'm so sorry,' she apologized. 'Forgive me.'

'Nowt to forgive, Mrs Ripley.' He shook his head. 'It happens. Best woman in 'world, my wife was. Hauled me back onto my feet. Come on then, let me show you upstairs. You can look in 'loft if you wish. Sound as a bell up there and enough room for an army to bed down.'

When they'd finished looking over the property they went back to his house, and whilst Hannah made tea and brought out cake and biscuits, James asked Leggott about rent and what they'd be allowed to do and made notes of the answers to discuss with those who would eventually make up the proposed committee.

'I wondered if perhaps you might ask Mrs Evans and Mrs Walters if they'd like to be on the committee,' Moira suggested

191

as they walked back home. James carried Floris on his back, as she was flagging with tiredness. 'They'd see the practicalities that were required.'

'Mrs Walters?' James asked, puzzled.

'Yes, why not? She does other people's washing amongst other things. Even if she didn't want to do all the washing for the house herself, she'd know who to ask, and she's the one who suggested we approach Mr Leggott.'

'Of course,' he said. 'Sorry, yes, you're quite right; we must have women on the team. I would never have thought of the laundry!'

She smiled and gave him a little dig in the ribs. 'That's because you've never had to do it, let alone think of who does it for you!'

The clouds were darkening the sky and they felt the first few drops of rain as they hurried past St Mary's church into Bishop Lane towards home.

'It's sleeting,' James grumbled. 'Can you pull my collar up, Moira? I daren't let go of Floris. She's heavier now than— she was.' He had almost said *when I carried her from the cellar*, but remembered in time.

'Quickly quickly,' Floris mumbled into his ear, echoing James's thoughts as if she too remembered that dawn flight from the cellar.

'It feels like snow,' he muttered, 'and the temperature is dropping. We'll have to get a move on with forming the committee before winter comes in earnest, because we need to get started with any changes that have to be made to the building.'

'Winter is here,' Moira pointed out. 'But you can't do everything at once. Sponsor money will have to come first. How soon can you meet any of the men you're considering?'

'I'm going to try today,' he said, as they reached their front door.

'Shall I speak to Mrs Evans, or would you rather ask her

yourself? I'll ask Mrs Walters. Bob might be seeing her this weekend, so he could come with me, perhaps.'

James slid Floris off his back and felt in his pocket for his key. 'Yes, speak to them both, why not,' he began, just as Rosie opened the door to them.

'Heard you, sir,' she grinned, dipping her knee. 'Thought you'd be back soon. We've just put 'kettle on.'

'Not for me, Rosie,' James said. 'I just want another warmer scarf and gloves and I'm going out again.'

'Yes, please,' Moira said. 'We've had a cup already, but I'd love another, and if we're not in the way we'll have it in the kitchen. I want a word with Mrs Evans. Matthew, would you like cocoa to warm you up? Floris will too,' she told Rosie. 'It was very cold where we have been.'

Matthew helped Floris off with her coat, hat and shoes and she ran to get her slippers from the bottom step of the stairs where she had left them. 'Toes cold,' she said, as she put them on the wrong feet.

'She's learning more words, Mama,' Matthew laughed, and went to help her.

Moira agreed that she was. 'It's since you've been home, Matthew,' she said. 'You've been reading to her and it's made such a difference.'

'I think I'd like to be a teacher,' he said, sitting on the bottom step of the stairs next to Floris to change his own shoes. 'I think it might be more interesting than what Pa does, just working out numbers all day.'

'He does more than that,' Moira told him. 'He's a draughtsman as well as accountant and bookkeeper for the company.'

Matthew nodded, but she could see he wasn't convinced. He was sure to change his mind several times before he settled to a future career.

'Mrs Evans, are we being a nuisance by coming in the kitchen?' Moira asked as the three of them went in. Obviously the housekeeper couldn't say yes, but she felt she had to ask. 'Mr Ripley has had to go out again,' she went on, 'but I thought I'd put you in the picture.' She paused as the back door opened and Bob staggered in carrying a basket of logs. He put it down by the range and touched his forehead with his finger, mumbling, 'Sorry, ma'am. Excuse me, can I just ask—'

'No, you can't, whatever it is,' Mrs Evans butted in. 'You can tek some of them logs upstairs first.'

Bob touched his forehead again, this time to Mrs Evans, picking up another smaller basket to fill. Matthew went across to join him. 'I'll give you a hand,' he muttered, opening the door to go upstairs before picking up a large log and taking hold of one of the basket handles as Bob took hold of the other one.

Moira and Mrs Evans waited until the boys had closed the door behind them; both raised their eyebrows, Moira questioningly.

'I might seem heartless, ma'am,' the housekeeper said, 'but 'lad has to learn he can't interrupt.'

'I know,' Moira said, 'and you're teaching him well.'

'Aye, he's a grand lad,' Mrs Evans said. 'But I don't want him thinking he can do 'same as Master Matthew. He has to learn life's different for him.'

Moira pursed her lips; she wasn't sure that she agreed with her. Manners were important, it was true, but so was learning self-confidence. Also, she thought that Matthew should feel that he was lucky to have been born into a family such as theirs, and not take his privileges for granted.

'I wanted to tell you,' she said, 'that we might have found a property to convert into our house for the homeless. That's where we've been his morning. And if all goes to plan, we wondered if you might agree to go on the committee?'

'Me, ma'am?' Mrs Evans seemed startled. 'I know nothing about committees.'

'Neither do I, Mrs Evans, but I know that both of us can put across a point of view just as well as men can.'

Mrs Evans agreed. 'Well, that's certainly true, and we probably know more of what's needed for folk who have nothing. At least I do, ma'am, beggin' your pardon.'

'I understand, but I am quite practical too, Mrs Evans. I was the one who suggested that you should be asked to join the committee, you and Bob's aunt,' she added. 'I suggested her as well.'

'Aye,' Mrs Evans said on a sigh. 'Bob told me that one of his cousins, his aunt's eldest lad, is leaving home and going to sea. When Bob last visited her he found her crying cos she didn't know how she'd manage wi'out 'lad's wages. It won't be easy.' She shook her head. 'But they say when one door shuts another one opens.' She thought for a moment. 'They also say,' she added gloomily, 'that if it's a big enough draught they'll all blow shut at 'same time.'

Moira hid her smile. Mrs Evans can be such a sobersides sometimes, she thought, but said, 'This might be the right opportunity for her. However, I don't want to get ahead of myself, as we need to get others on our side and we need sponsors too; we don't aim to earn any money from this endeavour, and neither do we want to spend any if we can help it. We need charitable contributions.'

'Well, good luck wi' that, ma'am,' Mrs Evans said sceptically. 'But yeh, I'd be pleased to offer my services. A lot o' men wouldn't think about such things as washing and who's going to do 'cooking an' suchlike. I'm only going to offer advice as I'm busy here, but I'd be willing to interview cooks 'n' that.'

She considered. 'Mebbe think on having a live-in cook–housekeeper like me, except not me,' she added swiftly. 'And mebbe Mrs Walters might consider it, wi' board and lodgings thrown in.'

'Splendid, Mrs Evans,' Moira said triumphantly. 'I knew I was right to ask you.'

CHAPTER THIRTY-ONE

Leila

It was inevitable, Henry considered. Leila was at the age where she would attract the attention of young men; she was not averse to a little flirting of her own too, he noticed. I'm not sure if I know what to do about that.

Dorothy never flirted; at least not with him, and he could not imagine her flirting with anyone else. When they had met, at a summer house party in Hull, everyone had wandered outside into a lovely garden and they had accidentally bumped into each other. She had dropped her rather large bag on his foot and he had picked it up for her.

'So very sorry,' he'd apologized. 'Clumsy of me.'

'My fault entirely,' she'd said. 'I take this old thing everywhere with me. My mother insists that I don't need it and I maintain that I do.'

Henry had given her a small bow and said, 'Well, I would consider that you must know best if it's your bag and not your mother's,' and she'd replied that her mother thought she had an answer for everything.

She'd mentioned that he was awfully brown, adding, 'I say, you're not the explorer fellow, are you? Henry something?'

He'd introduced himself as Henry Mackenzie and not an explorer but a traveller, and told her he had been travelling for almost twenty years since he had come into his majority and could do whatever he liked.

'Oh, you lucky old stick!' she'd said enviously. 'I wish I'd been born a man and been able to do whatever I wanted. Even though I'm long past twenty-one, my parents say it's not the done thing for a woman to travel alone.'

'Rather risky, perhaps,' he'd said thoughtfully. 'But I often think that I would like someone to accompany me on my travels.'

And so it had begun. But Leila is different entirely from her mother, he considered, and women must naturally be careful of their reputations.

Ziki turned up at their hotel most mornings just as breakfast was finishing and, bowing deeply, would make suggestions as to where they might like to visit: the Blue Mosque one day, the Hagia Sophia Mosque on another; the open-air Hippodrome, used for chariot racing in Roman times; the Spice Bazaar with its enchanting aromas.

Henry couldn't fault him. He was polite but never obsequious; he told them that he wasn't a regular guide but a history student, and that he worked as a tourist guide during his vacations to earn money to help his widowed mother. He also supported three siblings, he said, his youngest sister who was seven years of age and two more of ten and fifteen, and that he himself was twenty-two.

'Very soon,' he explained, 'when I finish my exams, I will become a history teacher.'

'When did you lose your father?' Henry asked him one day.

'Good sir,' Ziki answered, 'I have not lost my father. He died four years ago and so I became the man of the family, but he remains in my heart.'

Leila looked from under her veil at her father, keeping her

head low. How odd we English people are; we don't like mentioning death in case the bereaved are still grieving, but we give it another name, like *lost* or *passed*, and mention it just the same.

'My sincere commiserations,' Henry murmured. 'We too have had sorrow in our lives when my wife, Leila's mother . . . died.'

Ziki bowed his head and put his fingers together, murmuring, 'My sympathies, sir, and young mistress.'

'Wasn't that very kind of Ziki?' Leila said later. 'So very understanding, and so helpful to his mother too! And to take on such responsibility when he is not so much older than I am.'

'Hm,' Henry mumbled. 'Indeed.'

Leila was very keen to stay longer and suggested they find an apartment for a few months. 'There is such a lot to see, Papa, don't you agree?'

'There is a lot to see, but I thought you wanted to see more of the empire, not only Constantinople? The hotel is very nice, and the food is good; if we rent an apartment we will have to go out for our meals three times a day. We can simply move on from the hotel when we have seen enough of the capital.

'The empire is constantly changing, Leila. We may never see its likeness again. The present sultan is not inclined to have Russian armies in Sebastopol, and there is a very real threat of conflict there at present. Another reason why we should move on.' He sighed. He was not on a winning streak. But there would be war, he was convinced of it. 'We'll ask Ziki to arrange a boat trip on the Bosporus Strait, shall we? He can tell you of its significance so much better than I. Of how it straddles Turkey and Asia.'

I give in, he thought; I'll take a sleep under an awning whilst we sail and let the young people chat about whatever they want. I'm tired. This will be my last long journey. Perhaps we will spend the winter in France and then travel back to England in the spring, when Leila must make up her mind what she wants to do with her life. I will support her in whatever she chooses.

They stayed in Constantinople for a further two months and Ziki took them exploring several times a week when he wasn't studying; driving them or booking excursions for them and always accompanying them. Henry suggested to Leila that perhaps she might like to ask Ziki's mother if she would allow his eldest sister, fifteen-year-old Banu, to accompany Leila on some of the excursions in his place.

Leila was thrilled, Henry could tell; she was probably tired of his habit of constantly adding more information to what Ziki was telling them. 'If she agrees, Leila, you must ask her if she will agree to meet me; I must ascertain that Ziki, charming as he is, is a trustworthy companion for you.'

'Oh, Papa, of course she will say he is. She thinks the sun shines out of Ziki.'

'How do you know that? Have you met her?'

'Yes.' Leila lowered her head. 'That day when we stopped for a rest, and you sat and had coffee at a little table and smoked a hookah pipe with a Turkish gentleman.'

'Ah, yes. I must admit I recall only some of that afternoon. The tobacco was far too strong, and I'm sure something had been added to it. You went into a bazaar, I remember, and Ziki said he would walk behind you and make sure that you were safe. There were mainly women shopping in there, you said.'

'Yes,' she agreed, 'mainly western Europeans. All buying silks and gold bangles and not knowing the price of anything. Ziki's mother was shopping with her youngest daughter, Derya. He introduced me to them.'

'I see,' he said, and didn't ask, as he wanted to, why their driver would introduce his mother to one of his clients. I'm being snobbish, he thought. I am, after all, asking if we might use her daughter as a chaperon. Is it the same thing, or not?

He decided that it probably was, and subsequently visited Ziki's mother.

Bayan Adem and Banu were delighted to be asked, and Mrs Adem assured Henry that Ziki would be very careful of their safety. However, as Mrs Adem didn't speak English, Ziki was translating his own reference, and since his sister didn't speak English either, Leila and Ziki would be able to have private conversations.

Henry gave Ziki money in advance to pay for lunch and other requirements, mainly to be sure that they only dined in hotels rather than in street restaurants, which he would have insisted on if he had been with them; he believed wholeheartedly in eating local food to help local traders, but he wasn't prepared to risk Leila's health if he wasn't going to be there to choose the restaurants and dishes for her. Ziki was always meticulous in showing him the receipts and would shake his head and say, 'Good sir, that is too much to pay for such extravagance; I know of better places for half the price,' but Henry stood firm.

One evening as Henry and Leila were dining in the hotel, Henry took a sip of wine and leaned back in his seat. 'Well, my dear, about time to move on, I feel,' he said. 'Winter will soon be here. I'd like to spend it in France and then in the spring go home to England – to my home town.'

'Oh, Papa! I really don't want to.' Leila's eyes filled with tears. 'I want to stay here. I've fallen in love . . .' She hesitated. 'With the country, the people – I . . .'

'And with Ziki?' he asked slowly.

She bent her head and gazed at him from under her lashes; for a poignant moment he remembered how she did the same when she was a child and couldn't have what she wanted.

'Yes,' she murmured. 'And he with me.'

'You know that he hasn't any money to keep you?' he asked gently. 'Not in the manner which you have always enjoyed.'

She nodded. 'But *we* have, Papa!'

Henry shook his head. 'If he's the man I think he is, he will want to work, and being a history teacher or a tourist guide will not be enough. You will have to make great changes in your life.'

'B-but Papa, will I not have a dowry?'

'When you marry, of course, but when that is spent . . .?' He shrugged. 'And what of his mother and his sisters? He provides for them too, doesn't he?'

Her eyes grew wide. 'Yes,' she breathed.

'And where will you live? In their family home?'

'I thought—'

'What did you think? That your papa would buy you a house? You are still so young, Leila, only twenty, and my only daughter. Of course I will help you,' he said gently, 'but you must be absolutely sure that Ziki is the man you want as your husband; someone who will be by your side for the rest of your life. Is he the one you really want?'

She gazed at her father, her lips parted, and he thought that although he was bound to be prejudiced, he had never seen anyone so beautiful.

'Yes,' she said softly. 'He is.'

CHAPTER THIRTY-TWO

Leila

They were wed the following spring in the Hagia Sophia, once a magnificent building but now in a state of disrepair.

Henry admitted that Ziki was very handsome, and that any young woman might fall in love with him. He was tall, much taller than Henry, with wide shoulders and a broad chest; a lithe and muscular figure with thick dark hair and eyebrows and deep brown eyes. Nevertheless, all eyes were on Leila's petite figure, her pale blonde hair half-hidden beneath the traditional cap embroidered with silver and gold thread and tassels that fell to just above her eyebrows; her fair skin barely visible beneath her veil when, on her father's arm, she walked down the long aisle: a special concession to an Englishman giving his daughter to a Turkish man.

Henry gave a deep sigh after the festivities were over and decided to head straight off to Nice. He had no role to play here, but in Nice he would meet friends he had previously made, French, English and others, enjoy good conversation and fine wine, and then decide whether or not to go to England to look at his house and the condition of it. As he considered, he recalled that he had stipulated in his Will that if Leila should marry the house should be put into the name of her firstborn child. His intention had been to prevent any money-grabbing husband from claiming it, according to English law. He hadn't in the least thought, when he signed the Will, that Leila would marry anyone other than an Englishman.

But there we have it, he considered, on the last leg of his journey through France. I could change the Will, and that would entail writing to my lawyer, or taking a trip to Hull.

Hull was where his lawyer's office was situated. But there was no hurry, he decided. Ziki did not seem the avaricious kind, and it was doubtful that they would have children within the year; and as for money, he had already settled Leila's dowry, which would last them for a considerable time, if indeed they needed it; they were going to live with Ziki's mother and his sisters and their needs would be very little more than they were at present. Ziki had finished his exams and would be looking for a post as a history teacher, for which he would be paid a salary.

Henry settled into his train seat and considered. I'll give it some more thought and perhaps I will visit Hull. But I'm weary of travelling. I need to rest for a month or two and reflect on my options. I feel a little lost now that Leila no longer needs me, and I'd like to spend the summer in Nice; but then I don't want to visit England in the winter, especially not if it's wet. It rains such a great deal in England.

A few months later, he received a letter from Leila to say she was expecting a child. 'We are all so thrilled, Papa,' she wrote, 'and I know that you will be too. I was going to come to visit you, but now it would perhaps be best to wait a little while; I am at present feeling rather unwell, but I'm assured that it will pass.'

So what shall I do now? He sighed. If I should die before changing the Will, the unborn child will have the house, but of course Leila will have a good settlement; plenty in the pot, he mused. Her mother and I were not spendthrifts by any means, in spite of our wanderings. But I'm not going to die yet. I'll go back to England in the spring.

But time moved on, and as Leila's child was expected in April he decided that he wouldn't travel in the spring, as he hoped she would visit him, or perhaps he should go to them. But Leila and Ziki were living with his mother and siblings in Mrs Adem's small house, and he considered that perhaps Leila might prefer to come to France with her baby and stay with him, enjoying some quiet time. He would like that. He'd forgotten what it was like to have a small child that needed care and attention, and how life changed; he remembered carrying Leila on his back as he and Dorothy kept on roaming.

No wonder, then, that travelling holds no fears for her. Distance doesn't faze her. Visiting another country doesn't intimidate her; it had become second nature for her to pack a bag and prepare for a journey, even into the unknown. Ziki had once affectionately said of her that she was a nomad, like the ancient Yoruk tribe.

'Hm,' Henry had said, and thought that Leila also enjoyed her comforts. He couldn't imagine her by any means living a full nomadic life, sleeping in a tent and travelling with goats.

And so once more he put off his journey to England and awaited news from Leila.

Which came in mid-April, when a telegram arrived from Ziki to tell him that Leila had been delivered of a girl child.

'She is as beautiful as a flower,' he wrote. 'Dark hair, the sweetest face, and we will call her Floris.'

She was as beautiful as Ziki had said when Leila brought her to France in September. Leila had travelled alone with her, and they stayed for almost a month so that her grandfather could get to know her. By then she was smiling and taking notice of things around her as he held her on his knees.

With her dark curls and olive skin Floris was totally unlike Leila, and she had eyes as dark as Ziki's.

'Papa, won't you come back to Constantinople? We would love you to; *I* would love you to. There is no reason for you to stay here, except, I realize, that you have made friends, but you will make friends in Constantinople too; in fact you already have friends there.' She smiled. 'The gentleman with the hookah was asking about you the last time I saw him in the market place.'

'Hah!' He gave a grunt. 'I won't be trying that again in a hurry. But no, dear girl, I won't. This suits me fine, and the weather is not as extreme as it is in Turkey. Besides,' he added, 'I still intend to go to England.' He perked up as he thought that he really must go before the winter. He would write to Thompson, his lawyer, just as soon as Leila left, outlining the changes he intended to make. 'I need to adjust my Will, now that I have a grandchild.'

'I thought all that was taken care of,' Leila said, puzzled.

'It was,' he said. 'It is. But that was before there was talk of marriage and children. It's nothing much, but it needs to be done.'

'You could make another Will here in France,' she told him. 'You don't need to travel to England to do it.'

'I know,' he nodded. 'But old Thompson would be upset if he hadn't crossed all the t's and checked the p's and q's.'

She sighed. 'Sometimes I don't know what you're talking about, Papa.'

Floris jiggled on his knee, and he reached across and patted Leila's hand. 'It doesn't matter,' he said. 'As long as I do.'

He had agreed to meet his friends on the same day that Leila, holding Floris in her arms, stepped into the carriage and waved goodbye. He felt unbelievably sad; he had been so pleased to see her and thought how well motherhood suited her, and that his baby granddaughter was even more delightful than he had expected.

Perhaps I should have gone back with them, for a short time at least, but there, the decision is made and I'm comfortable here.

He went slowly down the stairs to the very grand entrance hall and, turning right at the bottom, headed towards the garden door and the terrace, where there were several tables and chairs, and chaises longues with soft tasselled cushions for those who might like to stretch out for a nap. He had done that himself a time or two.

Might anyone want to know about my lovely granddaughter, he wondered as he walked towards the terrace, and concluded that perhaps they wouldn't. Some of the men were single or widowed; the older men probably had grandchildren of their own and wouldn't want to hear about his.

He didn't remember the step; was there a step? He put out his hand to steady the sway and swing of the room around him and the floor under his feet, and couldn't quite get into the rhythm of it. He heard the call of one of the younger men, who had stood up, but he couldn't understand what it was he was asking, or why he was running towards him in such a peculiar manner. Nor why, as he put out his hand towards him, he felt nothing but emptiness.

CHAPTER THIRTY-THREE

Plans moved on apace as some of the men whom James had approached on that wet day agreed to join him, as did some of their wives. James's solicitor, Ernest Hawkins, volunteered as well, and very quickly a meeting was convened in James and Moira's dining room to set up the committee.

As the first sponsor, James's brother Daniel stood in for his father and brought in a fellow shipbuilder who after listening to the proposals also agreed to be a sponsor.

'Mark Brewer,' he said, introducing himself. 'I was born in Hull into a poor family but made my way up. I'll be glad to help folk who have nothing and give them at least a place to lay their heads.'

His audience clapped their hands in a show of approval, for even those who had been born into wealth and considerable comfort could appreciate what it must have been like to climb out of poverty.

Leggott had slipped in late and sat quietly listening, and not everyone knew who he was. When James introduced him, some of the men looked at him cautiously; as Leggott himself had said, landlords generally did not have a good reputation.

But Leggott explained himself succinctly and told them that he was willing to let out the property for a peppercorn rent to make it legal and official, and to make a contribution to the repairs and renovations that were needed. Hawkins, the lawyer, nodded his approval and agreed to look after any legal dealings.

'Doing it this way,' Leggott explained, 'if it doesn't work out, though I feel sure it will, I'll still have a property in my name.'

'In better condition than previously,' Howard butted in.

Leggott eyed him curiously. 'Aye, indeed, sir. When you've hauled yourself up from 'bottom of 'heap, you need summat to hold on to in case you slide down again.'

His daughter Hannah, who was sitting next to him, smiled approvingly and raised her eyebrows at Moira, who was sitting opposite her. Mrs Evans and Mrs Walters stood near the door and Bob next to his aunt.

James stood up again. 'In view of Mr Leggott's generosity, I'd like a show of hands for approval of my next suggestion. Time is moving on and winter is just about here, and desperate people will be looking for shelter.'

He took a deep breath and thought, Now we'll find out how keen they all are. 'I suggest that we open up our pocket books and make a returnable donation so that we can start on the building work. Mr Leggott is willing to let us have access to the building, so we'll need tools, as well as bricks, wood, lath and plaster and numerous other materials. We must each keep a tally of our own contributions, and my wife has offered to keep the accounts in order, with the assistance of Miss Leggott. Once the sponsors come in, and we hope donations too, once we publicize, the original contributions can be returned.'

He paused as murmurings began. Most of the men and some of the women were nodding their heads in agreement, so he went on, 'If this is not convenient, I can assure you that physical help will be just as important. Each and every one of us will give only what we can afford, and only the account keeper will have knowledge of the amounts. Receipts of course will be given.

'Finally, I would like to introduce Mrs Evans and Mrs Walters, who will offer advice on domestic matters. They have already told us that we'll need sheets, pillows and blankets as well as beds; we hope we might get some furniture donated, but we'll need a budget for food and cooking. We should perhaps also be thinking of a live-in housekeeper or cook when we are further on with our plans, and for swift messaging we have a very willing young lad, Robert Wilton' – Bob stood up straighter when he heard his name and James indicated in his direction – 'who has agreed to give an hour of his time each working day for passing on messages or running errands. A small payment would be appreciated.'

Almost every hand went up to show approval, and several people clapped. Then, as groups split up for individual discussions, Mrs Evans and Mrs Walters slipped out to the kitchen to make tea and coffee and butter scones, and Rosie came downstairs with Floris, who had had her bath and was in her nightgown and dressing gown. When she saw so many people, she ran to Moira's side and clung to her skirt.

One of the women who had accompanied her husband came across to Moira. 'What a dear little girl,' she said, smiling sweetly at Floris. 'Is she your daughter?'

'No,' Moira said. 'This is Floris. She's staying with us for a while.'

'So pretty. She has a foreign look about her.'

Moira said nothing, but lifted her head to Rosie, who was waiting by the door, and signalled with raised eyebrows for her to come over.

'Time for cocoa, I think, Rosie. Will you take Floris into the kitchen and I'll be there shortly.' She bent down and kissed Floris on her warm cheek; she smelt of soap and talcum powder. 'I won't be long,' she murmured. 'And then shall we have a bedtime story?'

209

'Yes, please, Mama Moira,' Floris said, 'and can Matthew have one too?'

'Of course he can.' Moira smiled as Rosie took her off, and thought affectionately that Matthew never seemed to mind hearing his mother read stories that were far too young for him. He listened because Floris wanted him to sit by her and share the stories that he had heard so many times before.

She turned to the woman who was still standing nearby. 'We are looking for Floris's parents,' she told her. 'Floris was one of the children caught up in the flood, do you recall? People without a fixed abode who were sheltering in the cellar close by Holy Trinity church?'

The woman gazed at her with parted lips. 'I thought they were all men and women; I hadn't realized there were children in there too. But that's dreadful. It shouldn't be allowed. They should be in a children's home, not living rough out on the streets. They could get up to all kinds of mischief. I don't mean little tots like her, of course,' she added, 'but older ones left to their own devices.'

Moira hid an impatient sigh. Wasn't this why they were here? Wasn't this the whole point of having a meeting? Hadn't this woman even been listening?

She made her escape as soon as she could and slipped away, leaving Hannah Leggott, armed with notebook and pencil, already taking donations and meticulously writing down names and addresses and amounts, and giving receipts from a receipt book, which thoughtfully she had brought with her. She had already told Moira that her father had taught her how to keep his account books.

'I think that's gone well,' Moira said as she entered the kitchen, where Floris was sitting at the table with a rim of cocoa on her top lip. Mrs Walters was also at the table nursing a cup of tea, whilst Mrs Evans and Rosie were pouring tea and coffee, putting scones on to plates, and loading trays for Rosie to carry into the dining room.

Mrs Walters pushed her chair back when Moira came in: she clearly wasn't expecting to see her in the kitchen.

'Please don't get up, Mrs Walters,' Moira told her, sitting down next to her. 'Enjoy your cup of tea.' She handed her a knife and a plate, and then held out the plate of scones and the butter dish.

'I've – I've had one already, ma'am,' she stuttered.

'Can you not manage another? I can always eat two, though perhaps I shouldn't.'

'There's no wonder our Robert likes working here,' Mrs Walters muttered, taking another scone.

'Well, he's a good worker; he's very useful.' Moira smiled. 'Did you see how he straightened his shoulders and stood tall when his name was mentioned?'

'Aye, I did. It's not often he gets praise.' Mrs Walters pondered for a moment. 'He's a good lad, trustworthy. I did my best for him, but' – her voice thickened – 'but it mebbe wasn't allus as much as he deserved. I had less trouble wi' him than I did wi' my own lads.'

'I'm sure you did what you could, Mrs Walters,' Moira responded softly. 'It's different looking after someone else's child, as I've recently discovered. Not as instinctive, and even though you want to do your best, sometimes it feels as if it's not enough.'

She glanced at Floris, who was sleepily rubbing her eyes, and she felt as if she were bursting with love for her. I haven't put my thoughts into words before, she realized. Is it because Leila has now been found, if indeed it is her, and so we will probably lose her daughter?

James was alone at breakfast the next morning when Moira came down. He had an early meeting with his brother at the shipyard.

'James,' she said, 'would you mind if I go to the work-house to ask about Leila? I've been thinking about her all night.'

'You don't have to ask me. You can if you wish.' He shook his head at her. 'Don't get upset, will you?'

She gave a shrug, picked up the coffee jug and poured herself a cup. 'Ugh,' she said. 'That's very strong. I probably will, get upset I mean. It's just that I'll need to prepare myself over Floris.'

'Not yet you won't,' he told her. 'It will be a long time before she'll be discharged.'

'Do you think she's very ill?' she asked anxiously.

'Yes, I do.' He took a sip of his coffee. 'If you do go, ask to see Lizzie Chambers, will you? She has a good grasp of the situation. Will you ask Bob to run for a cab? He'd go with you if you don't want to go alone.'

She took a deep breath and shook her head. 'I'm perfectly capable of going alone.'

'Of course you are.' He smiled at her. 'But ask the cabbie to wait for you to bring you home again, won't you?'

'I'll do that,' she said. She didn't intend to linger, as she meant to spend most of the morning making notes of the kinds of things they would need for Friendship House. Also, she was going to write a short piece for the local newspaper outlining their plans; she would show it to James before sending it to the editor, but she thought there were several things she could suggest that would appeal to the better nature of the readers, especially as they were now creeping towards the coming season of Christmas and goodwill.

She caught Bob just as he was leaving on an errand for Mrs Evans and he said he would go straight away to order a cab. She changed her shoes, put on a warm coat and hat, and picked up her bag just as the cabriolet rolled up at the door and Bob, with a huge grin on his face, jumped off the step below the carriage door, tipped his forehead at the driver and dashed away on his next errand.

'I wish all lads were like that one,' the driver said, as he opened the door for her. 'Where to, ma'am?'

'Anlaby Road, the workhouse, please,' she said, 'and I'd like you to wait for me.'

CHAPTER THIRTY-FOUR

The driver pulled into the courtyard and jumped from his seat to open the carriage door and assist Moira down the high step.

'I should be no more than half an hour,' she told him, 'if that doesn't inconvenience you?'

'Not at all, ma'am,' he said. 'Are you Mrs Ripley?'

'I am,' she said, surprised.

He nodded. 'I met Mr Ripley that weekend when 'cellar flooded; I brought an elderly lady here at Mr Ripley's request.'

'Did you? That would be Mrs Chambers. I'm hoping to meet her if she's available.'

'She's not dead, then?' He grinned. 'She seemed to think she was at life's end!'

Moira smiled. 'Apparently not. According to my husband she's settled in very well and is helping out in the kitchen!'

The driver put his head back and laughed. 'Give her my best regards, ma'am. I knew she had plenty o' marra!'

Moira wasn't sure what he meant, but she nodded in agreement and walked across to the door, trepidation creeping into her as she pulled on the bell rope and heard it jangling down the hall.

She assumed it was Matron, dressed in black and wearing a

grey pleated bonnet, who opened the door and stood back, looking rather startled on seeing her. Moira introduced herself.

'Do come in, Mrs Ripley. I met your husband recently when he visited Mrs Chambers and enquired about the lady in our hospital ward.'

'Yes, indeed,' Moira said quietly. 'Is she any better?'

Matron shook her head. 'Please come in,' she said. 'Too cold to stand here. I have a fire in my room.'

Moira felt frozen through, but thought that it wasn't from the draught whistling under the door but her own fear of what she might find here.

Matron offered her a cup of tea, which she refused, saying she had just had one, but she accepted the offer of a chair by the fire. The matron sat opposite her.

'Most people who visit us are nervous of what they might find,' she began, 'but although it's not a place where anybody'd choose to live, well, beggars can't be choosers and we do our best.'

'I'm sure that you do,' Moira said quickly. 'I'm . . .' she swallowed, 'very nervous about seeing Leila, if that is who she is. Miss Mackenzie, as we believe she once was.'

When Matron expressed surprise, Moira replied that they had put two and two together when someone else had mentioned that name.

'It is an assumption only,' Moira told her, 'and if, as we think, she is married, she will now have a different surname.'

She hesitated, and then took her courage in both hands. 'Would it be possible for me to see her? You see, if she is who we think she might be, well, there was an abandoned child . . .' She went on to explain the flooded cellar. 'The people who were rescued said that the child's mother had been there with her but had gone out one day and didn't return.'

'Dear me!' Matron said. 'This gets worse and worse. The surgeons at 'infirmary said that in all probability she'd given birth, but not recently, and you think this is the child, do you, ma'am? But where is she? Has she gone to one of 'orphanages?'

'No, no!' Moira said. 'She's living with us.' Tears which had been hovering since she came into the building began to fall in earnest, and she reached into her handbag for a handkerchief.

'I understand,' Matron said sympathetically. 'A lovely gesture, but you have your own lives to live and probably children of your own to look after—'

'Oh, I didn't mean . . .' Moira was horrified that she thought they didn't want Floris. 'No, no, we're pleased to have her! She's adorable, no trouble at all; it's just that it's so sad, and I really wanted to tell her mother that she is safe with us.' She wiped away her tears and blew her nose. 'If she can hear me, I thought that I could reassure her. If she is who we think she might be.'

Matron folded her hands across her lap. 'I can certainly take you in to see her, but as for her hearing what you're saying, well, that's a different matter. Since she's been with us there's been no response except that she has taken sips of water.'

She sat gazing at Moira for a minute or two longer and then said, 'One of our other residents was also in that cellar and thought that this was the young woman who had been living there with a child. She pops in to see her now and again. But we couldn't assume that what she was saying was true.'

'Mrs Chambers?' Moira asked. 'My husband was instrumental in her coming here.'

Matron nodded. 'So I understand; she often sings his praises. She's an asset. Some of our residents do nothing at all, but Mrs Chambers does; she helps with 'laundry and in 'kitchen. Sometimes she has a bit of a turn of being unwell on cleaning day, but generally speaking she's very helpful. Come along then, Mrs Ripley.' She stood up. 'If you'd like to see the young woman, I'll tek you now.'

Obediently Moira rose from the chair and suddenly had the thought that a matron's role would have suited her own mother perfectly.

The hospital ward was dimly lit by one oil lamp and the curtains at the long window were tightly drawn. Only one bed was occupied, the others all stripped down to the thin mattresses.

Moira came up close to the bed. A wooden chair had been placed next to it and she sat down. The bedsheets covered the patient up to the top of her chest; her hands were clasped in front of her and her head was wrapped in a white bandage.

Matron leaned over Moira's shoulder and whispered, 'I'll slip out and try to find Mrs Chambers whilst you're having a chat. I'll come back to you.'

Moira looked around nervously when she'd gone. She felt most uncomfortable being so close to someone who was so ill that she couldn't say a word; Moira could not even detect the slightest breath.

She stood up again. It didn't seem right to be here, somehow, when she had never met the woman before. Had she been a friend it would have been different, but not knowing her in the slightest made being here seem like an intrusion, an imposition.

She leaned over the bed. She felt as if she wanted to apologize.

'Leila,' she whispered. 'Can you hear me?'

There was no response, and she gazed down at the motionless figure. That she was lovely, or had been, was obvious; the bruises were still visible, but her face with its high cheekbones, fine eyebrows and full mouth showed a natural beauty.

'I wanted to tell you that your daughter Floris is safe,' Moira murmured, 'and is waiting for you to recover. She wants to tell you all about what she's been doing. She's looking forward to seeing you soon.'

I'm telling her lies, she thought. Floris doesn't know where her mother is, and if she should see her now, in this sorry state, she would be afraid. Whatever can we do for her? We can't bring food. How are they feeding her?

Tentatively, Moira put her fingers to Leila's wrist and stroked it. Fragile bone that would snap so easily, even between Moira's own slim fingers. Her skin was so fine and pale, translucent almost; how was that? They'd assumed she had been in a warm climate from what people had said about the fine clothes she had been wearing when she was in the cellar; they were surely not the kind of clothes that she would have worn had she been a traveller, as James's father had said her parents were. We have been putting two and two together and making half a dozen.

The door slowly opened and an old woman came in, looking carefully about her before approaching Moira.

'I'm Lizzie Chambers, Mrs Ripley,' she wheezed. 'Good of you to come,' she went on, as if welcoming someone to her home.

Moira turned to her. 'I felt I had to. I was hoping to find out who this young woman is, and what happened to her.'

Lizzie carefully eased herself on to the end of the bed, avoiding sitting on the patient's feet. She sniffed. 'Aye, happens all 'time. You get these young fellers driving hoss an' cart and don't know how to handle 'em an' then don't stop when they knock some poor soul into 'gutter or kingdom come.'

'Is that what happened?' Moira was horrified.

'Dunno,' Lizzie admitted. 'But it seems obvious to me, lookin' at her bruises and the broken bones. And concussion,' she added. 'She's gone a right purler, I'd say, an' 'driver didn't stop to say sorry or owt. It might not even 'ave been his hoss!'

How does she know this, Moira wondered? She couldn't have been there, wherever it was.

'Somebody at 'infirmary said she was near Parliament Street or Quay Street when it happened.' Lizzie answered Moira's unspoken question. 'She could have been going anywhere.'

Of course she could, Moira considered. But it's just guessing.

'That's where lawyers an' them sort o' folk have their offices. I've seen 'em,' Lizzie went on. 'When I've been out and about. You'll know 'em if you've seen 'em, ma'am. Men wear black tailcoats an' top hats as if they're off to a funeral, but they're not. That's how they dress when they're off to work.'

She waved a finger as if something had just occurred to her. 'That'll be why she was tekken to 'infirmary, cos that's 'sort of street it is. Poor folk, say, knocked down in one of 'back streets, would've been tekken back home or to 'workhouse hospital. Not to 'infirmary where you've got to pay!'

Moira nodded, and gathered up her gloves and handbag. 'You're probably right, Mrs Chambers, but we're not any further on with our enquiries, so I'll bid you good day. I hope that someone will advise us if there's any change.'

'I'll remind 'em, Mrs Ripley.' Lizzie shuffled with her to the door and held it open.

'By the way.' Moira paused. 'The cab driver who brought me remembered you; he brought you here. He said to give you his best regards.' She didn't add what he'd said about her having marra, because she still didn't know what he'd meant.

'Oh, aye. I remember him. I told him to keep a lookout for my son.' Lizzie shook her head, and turned to leave. 'I don't suppose he'll ever see him. And I don't think I'd recognize him now, and he certainly won't recognize me.'

She shook her head. 'Good day to you, ma'am,' she said, and went back inside the ward and closed the door.

Moira walked to the front door. There was no sign of the

matron, so she opened the heavy door and returned to the waiting cabriolet, wishing she hadn't come.

Lizzie sat down on the chair and looked at the woman in the bed. Poor soul, she considered, she's hovering between this place and 'next. She sat quietly and then placed one hand over the young woman's.

'Come on, Lay-lah,' she murmured. 'I'm sure it's you. I've nivver seen anybody as lovely as you, even as you are now, all battered and bruised. Mek an effort!'

She thought she saw a quiver and a parting of the lips, and she bent towards the bed, putting her ear nearer. 'What did you say, Lay-lah?' she murmured. 'Did you speak?'

'Ziki,' Leila breathed. 'Ziki. Floris – where – are you?'

CHAPTER THIRTY-FIVE

Leila

There had been a letter postmarked Nice waiting for Leila when she returned to Constantinople, to tell her of her father's sudden death. She was glad that she had seen him that one last time, and that he had met her baby daughter. She didn't return to France for the funeral, as Henry had put everything in place. The only thing he hadn't done was return to England to see his lawyer, so Leila wrote to Thompson to tell him what had happened.

Ziki had finished his university education and began as a history teacher in a local school. His mother was very proud of him and said that his late father would have been thrilled. Ziki's sisters too made a tremendous fuss of him, bringing him his favourite confectioneries and baking him cakes. Leila stood back from these small celebrations, feeling rather excluded, and not fully realizing that, to the poor, the honour Ziki had brought to the family was truly glorious.

'Ziki,' she murmured one night as they made ready for bed, whispering so that they didn't wake Floris, who was sleeping in a cot next to the bed, and knowing that the walls were thin and his mother, in the next room with one of his sisters, might not yet be asleep. His other sisters slept in a curtained alcove in the main room.

'Mmm?' He pulled off his shirt and she ran her hand down his muscular back. He turned and gathered her into his arms, nuzzling into her neck.

'I wanted to ask you,' she whispered, 'when do you think you will be earning enough for us to have our own house?'

He drew back. 'What?' Then he smiled. 'This is our own house. I pay the rent for it. I have done so since my father's death.'

'But it would be nice to have our own, wouldn't it?' She pulled him down on to the bed. 'What if we have more children? We will need more space, and we can't be private here with your mother and sister sleeping next door.'

'Tsh! They will be asleep already. Besides, my anneh, my mama,' he teased, 'she already knows what happens between husband and wife. She has children and we have a child to show for it, eh?' He kissed her and nibbled her ear. 'There is no money for another house. My salary isn't enough for two rentals.'

'But I have money now,' she said. 'There will probably be enough to buy one.'

'To buy? You have?' He held her at arm's length. 'Where is it?' He lifted the sheets and then a pillow, and then stretched over to look under the bed. He grinned. 'Where do you keep this money, eh?' He made as if to lift her nightgown and she squealed.

'Not here,' she giggled. 'In England. My father has a house in Hull. It's where I was born.'

He gave a little shrug. 'I don't know where this place is. It is near London, England, yes?'

'No.' She pulled the sheets over her. 'The other end of the country. Well, not quite, but well up north. I've only been once, I think, and I don't really remember it. Papa had been thinking of going back to live there.'

He slid down beside her. 'Was he? Not staying in France? Perhaps he missed it. There is no place like your own country.'

'Perhaps he did,' she said on a sigh. 'He just left it too late.' She turned to him and ran a fingernail down his belly, and he gasped. 'That is why we should do something about it. The house is empty and probably neglected, and if we don't want to live there ourselves' – she saw the startled expression in his eyes and knew it wasn't anything to do with what she was doing to him – 'then we could sell it and buy a house here.'

'Will there be enough money? Perhaps to buy a house big enough for us and my mother and sisters, so when they get married there will be plenty of room left for the three of us? My anneh can help you look after more children.'

Mm, she thought. I hadn't actually counted on your mother and sisters living with us, and neither do I want a houseful of children. Just one more would be enough.

He constantly put her plans to one side. He couldn't travel to England: he had to make a good impression in school. 'I am on – what do you say – erm, probation, audition? I must prove my worth.'

'I'm sure you'll do that,' she assured him. 'You're so very clever, but maybe in another year? Floris is still very young to travel such a long way; another year will be all right.' Though my parents travelled with me, she thought. We were constantly on the move, or so they said. I don't remember, and neither will Floris.

'You want we take Floris with us?' He sat up and leaned on one elbow and looked at her. 'She can stay here with my mother and my sisters.'

'Of course she can't.' She flapped a hand at him. 'She won't be weaned.' And she thought that at least they couldn't offer to do that in her place.

'Is that not time enough? She can have bottle. We can travel much faster if we leave her—'

'No, no, no! Definitely not. She comes with us. So we'll wait another year. We'll buy her a baby carrier – a papoose,' she said. 'That's what the indigenous people of America call them, and we can take it in turns to carry her.'

There was nothing more to say on the subject; but later they agreed that they would wait until Floris was three years old before they went.

When Floris reached three, Ziki discussed their plans with his headmaster, telling him that he and his wife were thinking of travelling to England during the summer holiday and he would probably need an extension of his leave. His headmaster warned him that Europe was in turmoil, which Ziki already knew: the Poles were rising up against Russian rule; rumours were rife that Napoleon intended to attack Vienna; and then there was the whole question of the Crimea and the Russian attacks. Turkey, Great Britain and France were already involved. But the headmaster gazed at the strong, healthy young man and thought that if there should be conscription in Turkey, Ziki would be one of the first to be called upon. The headmaster would rather have him alive in England to come home when the war was over than dead on a battlefield.

'All right,' he agreed. 'Let's see what we can do.'

Together, he and Ziki trawled through maps to discover the best way to travel and how. Railways were almost non-existent in Turkey apart from one built by a British company, but it travelled in the wrong direction, so that was stalemate. The headmaster shrugged and raised his arms. '*Kim bilir?* Who knows? Are you used to travelling?'

Ziki nodded. 'My wife is; she is English, and travelled all her life until coming to Turkey. She wishes to visit her family home now that her father is dead. She has to sign papers.' He didn't mention the house; it meant nothing to him and he knew nothing about English law. He didn't think that Leila did either.

'My parents travelled the whole time,' Leila said to him later, for the thousandth time. 'There weren't any trains except in England. They journeyed on foot, by mule, by camel, by boat—'

'I know,' he said impatiently. 'But there was no hurry for them, no work waiting. I will lose my job if I take too much time, even though Emir says he will try to keep my position. But he won't wait for ever, nor will the schoolchildren; they have to be taught. You don't understand, Leila. This is a different life.'

'I do understand,' she said softly, 'and you will understand too when we arrive in England and see the house that I will inherit. My father was a rich man and my mother was rich too, and Papa told me she put money into my name before she died.'

She knew that she should be pleased that Ziki hadn't married her for money. He hadn't known that she had any, although he must have gathered that her father wasn't poor. Ziki had worked hard to keep his family in their home after his own father had died, but not once in her presence had he ever grumbled about money.

'Do this for me,' she murmured in his ear. 'Let us travel back the way my father and I came, when I found you waiting for me,' she whispered fervently. 'Or, we could go to France, as I did with Floris, and then travel across to England to the house in Hull.'

She didn't say home, because it wasn't and never had been, and this omission Ziki noticed. His wife, his beautiful Leila, still had this wanderlust in her; she had stayed here with him and his family and their child only to please him, but deep inside her she still had the nomadic desire to roam.

Henry had given Ziki's family a dowry before their marriage. This payment, *ceyiz*, was a traditional gesture and he knew the amount would please Ziki's mother. Leila had money in her own name which had come from her mother's Will and was hers alone, though she was quite willing to share it with Ziki if he would accept it. Proud man that he was, he refused, so she decided that she too would give a sum of money to Ziki's mother, and ask her to keep it for Ziki without telling him, or to use it for any emergency whilst they were away. Bayan Adem was more than happy to accept, and Leila knew that she had risen in her mother-in-law's estimation, even though Bayan was not pleased that they were taking Floris with them.

Leila looked into other forms of transport, as there were no trains, arranging to hire a wagon and driver for the first part of their journey. She had done this when she had visited her father with Floris but hadn't told Ziki how long it had taken, letting him assume that she had stayed with her father for several weeks, which she hadn't. She had searched out cheap hotels, or *pensions* as they would say in France, for their journey in Turkey and up through Bulgaria – the safest route – Romania and Hungary. No use planning yet for the whole journey, she thought, though we must know where we are going and not take the longest route, unless it is the safest.

Somehow she had absorbed a travel instinct from her parents and knew no fear of entering another country. She had all the necessary papers to show who she was, and she impressed on Ziki that he should take his too. One day, when he was in school, she looked in his satchel to be sure he had everything that was required. She had bought matching satchels which had buttoned-down pockets inside and out and could be carried across their chests, thus deterring any potential thieves.

Ziki's papers were in order. She sat down on their bed and sighed. 'That's it,' she said in a whisper. 'We're ready.' She felt excitement in her chest, in her throat and running through her body. 'At last, we are ready for our journey.'

CHAPTER THIRTY-SIX

Leila

Ziki's mother cried when they left. She hugged Ziki as if he was going away for ever, and clung to Floris until the child began to cry and Leila had to take her back.

Leila gave Bayan Adem a peck on her cheek and waved goodbye to her sisters-in-law. The youngest, Derya, muttered that she wished that she was going too. 'You should have said,' Leila murmured to her. 'Maybe next time?' And immediately she drew an ally to her side.

They climbed into the wagon. The wagoner had supplied cushions and blankets and a small mattress for Floris to lie on when she was tired, which wasn't often, as she was too busy looking over the side of the wagon and waving to people as they passed. She was now three and her Turkish vocabulary was very good, as that was the language she mostly heard.

'You must speak to her in English, Leila,' Ziki said as they travelled. 'It is the best time to learn, when she is young.'

'I do when we're alone,' Leila told him, 'but not when your mother or sisters are there, as they don't understand what we're saying. How did you learn to speak it so well?'

'We were taught English at school, but there were not many

girls there. In Turkey they mainly stay at home with their mothers and learn about home things.'

'I was lucky, then,' she mused. 'When my parents travelled in Italy or France we spoke in those languages. But I understand, because I believe that in England too the poor people don't always send their children to school. Even the little ones have to work to earn money.'

'So, much the same, eh?' He drew her close and kissed her cheek. He'd been rather short with her recently, as he hadn't wanted to make a journey which would take him away from his family of females. He thought he should be nearby to protect and provide for them. Leila's parents were so very different: they had brought Leila up to be independent, even sending her away to school.

'I won't let Floris go away to school,' he said, twining a dark strand of his daughter's hair around his forefinger, and Leila gave him a quick glance.

'It was good for me,' she said. 'I loved it, although of course I didn't go until I was older. I felt properly grown up having to make my own decisions when my father was not there. My parents were always very liberal, and I do miss them, particularly my father.' She gave a small sigh. 'My memory of my mother is fading, yet I still feel the essence of her. Her being,' she tried to explain, 'if not the physical image of her likeness.'

'So you see why I didn't want to come away?' Ziki clarified, for they were speaking in his language, not English, and Leila still sometimes had to struggle for words.

'It's different,' she murmured. 'Sometimes you have to leave people in order to appreciate them.'

Floris seemed happy as they travelled. Sometimes she leaned over the front of the wagon to talk to the drivers, who were entranced by this small girl who chatted to them and told them her name. She spoke in Turkish, but sometimes would use English words that amused them, and both Ziki and Leila smiled as they watched her, her elbows on the edge of the wagon and her chin cupped in her hand.

The drivers asked her where she was going, and she would clap her small hands and say 'To Enger land and Mama's house', and then she would say it again in her native language.

When they asked if she was coming back, she would sometimes purse her rosebud mouth and shake her head and say, 'No, I don't fink so.' At other times she would tell them, 'Yes, because my anneh would cry if I didn't.'

When they reached Bulgaria Leila suggested they should stay in a small hotel for a few days' rest, enjoying baths and good food, and then continue on their way towards Budapest with a different wagoner.

'Leila!' Ziki protested as they put their luggage in the hotel bedroom. 'How did I allow you to make this journey alone when Floris was only a baby?' He put his head in his hands. 'What was I thinking of? How was it that I didn't look at a map?'

'I think you did,' Leila murmured. 'Places look different on a map; nearer! And,' she added, 'I came by a different route from the one we are taking now; the Crimea wasn't a problem then. Besides, you're not a traveller as I am. Have always been.'

'I think we should go back. This is crazy.'

'I won't go back,' she said emphatically. 'I will go on and Floris will come with me as she did before, when I visited my father in France.'

'No,' he said.

'Yes,' she answered quietly. 'I have done this journey before,' she added. 'And once alone, as you just said. If I can do it on my own, then how much easier it will be with you by my side.'

She moved towards him and put her arms around his waist to lay her head on his chest. 'I want you with me, Ziki. I want you to share my travels and see sights you have never seen

229

before, and for us to share the experience of England, for I don't remember it.'

There was nothing more to be said. She knew he wouldn't leave her, and he certainly wouldn't leave their child. She was tender towards him as they lay in bed that night after supper. Floris was fast asleep in a cot that the hotel had provided for her.

'We will be all right,' she murmured reassuringly, not wanting him to feel demeaned that, rather than making the decisions as he normally would for his mother and sisters, he had allowed his wife's judgement to overrule him without even noticing.

They stayed two nights at the hotel. Refreshed, Ziki accepted that it was time to move on towards their final destination.

They used the same wagoner that Leila had hired on her last journey. Her father had hired him when they first travelled to Constantinople, and she felt safe with him. He was well travelled in his own country and in others too; he gave them names of reputable drivers that they could use on the next stages of their journey.

He talked at length about the political situation to Ziki but not to her, never suspecting that she listened and understood all he was saying and still kept her own opinion. 'Everywhere is war, war, war,' he muttered. 'The Ottomans are much to blame, they have had too much power for too long. We must settle with Hungary or we die,' he added gloomily. 'This is the peace we enjoy before war begins again.'

And so they took some of his advice and set off once more, some of their journeys not only on land but crossing rivers too as they headed steadily west. Leila thought that in Austria, Germany and France there would be trains to take them towards the Channel coast before they crossed that final stretch of water and arrived at the little island that was Great Britain – and England.

CHAPTER THIRTY-SEVEN

Moira didn't know how she would explain her feelings about seeing Leila when she returned home, and was relieved that she didn't have to say anything until James came back later in the day. To distract herself, she went upstairs and played with Floris until lunchtime.

She decided to drop a note to her long-time friend Emily, and took her writing paper and an envelope from a drawer. I'll ask her if she'd like to come for lunch and bring Susan. *We have a little girl staying with us,* she wrote. *So sweet. I'm sure she'd love a playmate.* She hadn't seen Susan, who was five, for several months, and thought that the little girls could play together while she talked to sensible Emily.

Earlier, Bob had raced into the kitchen to say he'd seen the trawler man Wilson who might be buying the ship, and he'd told him that Mr Fisher, who was still the owner, had agreed that Bob and Matthew could use it for a couple of Saturdays as a soup kitchen.

'Whoa, whoa!' Mrs Evans had said. 'We have to get supplies in first. What do you want to give these starvin' folk? Don't think of owt fancy, cos I won't have time to do owt more than 'basics.'

Bob swallowed. 'They won't want fancy, Mrs Evans,' he said

bravely. 'I like your ham and pea soup best of all, specially when I'm really hungry.' He rubbed his nose. 'It meks me nose run. And bread to dip in. Ooh, I could eat some right now.'

Mrs Evans glanced at the kitchen clock. It was just on twelve; lunch for upstairs was at half past. 'You'd better sit down then,' she said, ''cos that's what I've made for luncheon. You can have some now wi' a beef sandwich; that should last you till dinner.'

Bob dashed to wash his hands in the deep sink. 'Ooh,' he said again, 'I'm so lucky to have you, Mrs Evans. I love you better'n anybody else 'cept for my auntie Lily.'

Mrs Evans stopped with the soup cauldron in her hands. She felt quite moved, but gave herself a shake. 'Go on, you soft ha'peth,' she muttered. 'Sit down and eat.'

Bob looked up and grinned. He was no longer scared of her, just in awe of her, though he wouldn't have been able to describe the feeling. He felt secure in her presence, even more than he did with his auntie Lily, who used to make him a bit nervy.

'When is this chap turning up, then?' Mrs Evans asked. 'Is he coming here, or . . . ?' She left the question hanging.

Bob shook his head. He'd already taken a spoonful of soup and his nose was starting to run, and he pressed the back of his hand to it as he swallowed. 'Mr Wilson said Mr Fisher'd agreed to do the – erm, negotiating,' he said in a rush. 'And that he'd bring 'ship across to this side of 'Old Harbour where it'd be easier for folks to come to. I explained that it was a charity for poor folk.'

Mrs Evans was pondering how to serve the soup; mebbe large cups or mugs might be better than bowls and spoons, since she suspected the last items would disappear along with the soup. I'd better have a word with 'mistress, she thought. On the other hand, this was Bob and Master Matthew's project, not hers; mebbe just plant the idea and let them suggest it.

Rosie came into the kitchen and sat at her place at the table, and Mrs Evans served her and then herself.

'I was thinking,' Bob said. 'Can I talk this idea through with you, Mrs Evans?'

Mrs Evans paused in putting her spoon to her mouth; was this 'same lad who daren't say boo to a goose just a few short weeks ago? She turned to look at Rosie, who was staring wide-eyed and open-mouthed at Bob.

The housekeeper cleared her throat. 'Is this idea going to change 'world?' she managed.

'I don't think so,' Bob answered, carefully mopping up the remains of the soup in his bowl with a chunk of bread. 'But I reckoned – well, mebbe I'd better ask Matth – erm, Master Matthew first off and see what he thinks, but,' and he got carried away with enthusiasm, 'we need to plan out how we're going to serve up this soup, and—'

'You'd be better serving it in mugs,' Rosie chipped in. 'If you give 'em bowls and spoons the spoons'll disappear like a shot.'

Bob huffed. 'That's what I was going to say! This isn't your project! I was going to discuss it wi' Mrs Evans first.'

'Well, sorry I'm sure,' Rosie mumbled. 'Is there any soup left, Mrs Evans? That were lovely.'

'You soon finished that,' Mrs Evans said. 'There's only a drop, and I was going to give it to Bob. He's got to go out into 'cold again and needs building up more than you do. You'll manage till cuppa tea time, and there's cake' – thus softening the blow. 'I'll mek more next time.'

Bob went off on another errand to the butcher and then to the grocer for a bag of flour for Mrs Evans, and on his return, rather than going straight into the house by the back door, he placed his parcels on the doorstep and then turned round to continue down the staith and on to the waterway. He watched some of the men who were working along the wharfside, shifting wooden crates and unloading a tug boat, and across on the other side of the dock where the old ship was berthed he saw somebody moving stuff about on the deck.

Mebbe he's mekkin' room for when we have it, he thought. He was excited at the prospect of being on the vessel, even if he and Matthew would only be serving soup and maybe sausages, and not sailing on it. He thought of his father, who was a seaman, who as far as he knew could be sailing anywhere, and not only fishing. He'd once heard him saying to his sister, Bob's aunt Lily, that he'd do anything and sail on any old tub if it meant he could earn a crust.

She'd been sharp in her response. 'Well, don't forget to save me a few crumbs for lookin' after your bairn.'

It was years ago and Bob hadn't understood that they were talking about him; his father had been rather huffy, answering that it was either her or the seaman's orphanage. He still remembered his aunt Lily sitting in the battered old armchair crying into her apron after his father had left, and they didn't see him again for months.

He still handed his wages over to his aunt. He decided he didn't need money. He had decent clothes now that would last him for years if he didn't grow out of them, and he was well fed; giving his aunt his wages was the least he could do to help her. There was something else that he thought he might be able to do for her too, but he would have to get Mrs Evans on his side first. I wonder, he thought as he made his way back up the staith, if Mrs Evans would ask Mr Ripley if he would ask my auntie Lily to be the housekeeper at Friendship House.

He picked up the shopping from the doorstep to take into the house, looking quickly at the upper windows that overlooked the water as he did so. He'd forgotten that Mr Ripley's office was up there, but to his relief there was no one looking out. He was glad; he didn't want anybody thinking he was shirking.

He heard the bang of the front door. He wondered if it was Matthew home from school; his exam results had been good and the Grammar School had said he could start straight away and get settled in before they broke up for Christmas. But no, it was only just past dinnertime – lunch, I mean, he corrected himself; he still had trouble knowing which was which. His aunt Lily said dinner, but that could also mean teatime, as often there was just the one meal in the day.

He wanted to be the first to tell Matthew about the trawler, but he listened from the bottom of the kitchen stairs and it wasn't him. It was Mr Ripley back from wherever he had been; perhaps up to Hessle. He'd said that he'd take him and Mathew one Saturday to see the ships they were building. He'd have to remind him.

He wasn't afraid of asking anything now. Mr Ripley had said that if there was anything he didn't understand or wanted to ask, then he should do so, so now he decided that he would ask about going to Hessle just as soon as there was a right time. Not when Mr Ripley was about to go out, or if he was about to eat his breakfast or his dinner. Bob often saw him heading into the breakfast room when he was bringing logs or coal in, and taking log baskets and coal hods upstairs, but Mrs Evans said not to ask Mr Ripley questions in a morning, cos not everybody was cheerful first thing, or at least not as cheerful as Bob was with his whistling.

He nipped out of the back door again and up the staith to High Street and the front of the house. He wanted to meet Matthew as soon as he came home from school, and he didn't think he would be long. He listened; perhaps he would hear the chimes of Holy Trinity and would then know the time. Matthew finished at four o'clock. He wished he could tell the time; Matthew had said he would teach him, but Bob thought he might have forgotten as it hadn't been mentioned since.

I'm older than him, he ruminated. Why can't I tell 'time?

He kicked a stone out of the staith and watched it rattling into the road. Cos I'm a dunce and an idiot, that's why. He'd left school on the day that a teacher said that to him and he never went back. He hadn't told his aunt Lily, and she only found out when the school inspector came looking for him.

That was when they had the upstairs rooms as well as the downstairs ones and he'd climbed into a cupboard and hidden until the inspector had gone. He'd heard Aunt Lil's voice raised to the inspector and then the rattle of the bolt and chain as she'd slammed the door after him.

Then he'd heard Aunt Lil shouting to him. 'Come on down,' she'd yelled. 'I know you're up there.'

He'd come down slowly. She never hit him, though he'd seen both of his cousins get a clout from her. 'Sorry, Auntie Lil,' he'd snivelled. 'I didn't think he'd know where I lived.'

'Course he knows,' she bellowed at him. 'Doesn't he know where every little lad who skives off school lives? Course he does,' she answered her own question. 'Come on,' she said after a minute, in her normal voice. 'Let's have a cuppa tea nice an' quiet afore them hooligans o' mine get in.'

And so they'd sat in front of the low fire and drunk what was supposed to be tea, but as he later discovered tasted nothing like Mrs Evans's tea, and it was then that he had realized that she didn't really think that his cousins were hooligans, and she certainly wouldn't allow anybody else to say they were, any more than she would let a teacher say that he was a dunce and an idiot, and that was why the inspector had departed in such a hurry. Ever since then he'd known Aunt Lil was on his side, just like Mrs Evans.

I'm lucky, he thought as he stamped his feet on the ground to warm them as he waited, and was gratified to hear the bells chiming out the hour. He counted four bongs. Four o'clock. I *can* tell the time! I'd better go inside. I don't want Matt to think I'm hanging around waiting for him.

CHAPTER THIRTY-EIGHT

Leila

At last the ferry reached the port of Dover. They had travelled through Bohemia and on to Dunkirk before reaching Calais. Ziki had thought they were never going to get there. The journey had taken so long, even though they had travelled quite a distance by rail across Austria and Germany, that he knew they would never be able to complete the business with the solicitor and be home in time for the start of the new school term.

I'll have to send a telegram to Emir to say we've been held up. He won't be surprised. He did warn me, and he also said that life would change once the railways arrived in Turkey. I shall be an old man by the time that happens.

Floris was tired and whiny now, and even when he told her that they would be going on a big ship across the water she was not interested. He thought that, like him, she was exhausted by travelling and wanted her own bed.

'Calais to Dover is the best route, my father always said,' Leila had told Ziki as they queued to board the ferry. 'That's the way he always travelled. It might seem that we've come a long way round, but the roads are better in Germany and this way seemed safer. Now we just need to get to London and we can travel by train all the way to Hull.' She patted his arm. 'Have you got your papers to show who you are?'

He nodded. There was some money in both the satchels, but not much; they would be obvious target for thieves, but so far they had been lucky. Nothing had been stolen from them, and Leila had done the same as she always did and sewn money bags inside her clothing.

'If there is no one renting the house we can stay there whilst we sort out the business of selling it and so on, and we needn't stay too long. We might not want to. It depends on the weather: I believe it can be very wet and damp in the north of England.

'But,' she went on cheerfully, conscious that Ziki was feeling despondent, 'we can find a comfortable hotel in Dover and look around there if you'd rather, just for a day or two? Though Kingston upon Hull is a very fine town, my mother used to say. It has theatres and a fine shopping street, and as it sits so close to the estuary and the sea it has many docks and harbours. The first dock to be built there was the biggest in the country, and then even bigger ones were built. It became a very prosperous town.'

'Hm,' Ziki said morosely. He wasn't in the least interested in what she was telling him. 'I am impressed. You should be a history teacher, Leila.'

'In Turkey?' she joked. 'I don't think so. But if we ever run out of money I could teach English. That would be more useful, I think. Fortunately,' she lowered her voice, 'I think when we sell the house we will have enough to last us a lifetime.'

'And Floris?' he asked. Having money was a difficult concept for him to accept, as was the fact that his wife was making decisions when it was his role so to do. 'She won't remember anything about this journey. We should have waited until she was older.'

He'll be fine, Leila considered. Once we are back in Turkey

I will hand everything over to him to deal with; he can make the decisions . . . or most of them. I really don't want to live in a house with his mother and sisters, and I don't think they would like it either. We must buy two.

They were beginning to shuffle towards the gangplank. Women and children were being ushered off the vessel first; Leila listened and heard mostly French and English voices and looked round for the tall figure of Ziki. He spotted her first and held Floris high.

'Here you are,' he said to the child, holding her tight and reaching over the heads of other passengers. 'Off to Mama Leila.'

Leila reached up and took hold of her, and Ziki didn't leave go until he was sure that Leila had her safe. But Floris was having none of it and shrieked that she wanted Baba to carry her, not her anneh. Other passengers smiled and put their fingers up to touch her, speaking in various languages to mollify her, and eventually she was happy enough with so much attention to smile at everyone.

Meanwhile, Ziki moved further back as other women and children were sent in front of him, until he found himself right at the back of the crowd. Someone was calling out instructions, but he didn't understand what they were saying. He watched some of the other men being moved to another area of the ship; there seemed to be some sort of altercation, and men were shouting.

He looked to see where Leila was; he couldn't see her, but he thought he spotted the top of Floris's dark curly-haired head nearing the bottom of the gangplank and called to her in Turkish. His English was reasonably good; he was, after all, a travel guide and advertised himself as an English speaker, but most of the words he used described the magnificent buildings, mosques and other historic structures of Constantinople, and the history of the longest-enduring and largest empire in the world. At home all three of them spoke Turkish, for the benefit of his mother and sisters.

He saw Leila standing on the quayside and looking up at the ship, no doubt searching for him. He waved to her, but she didn't see him because of the overhang of the upper deck. He called again and she lifted her head, but then he saw a porter moving the women away from the ship and directing them towards a building outside which some passengers were already climbing aboard a long carriage hitched to two very large horses.

'Leila,' he shouted. 'Wait.'

Another man was putting a chain across the top of the gang-plank, and Ziki renewed his efforts to get through the crowd of shouting men. He picked up their bags. 'Excuse please,' he said, trying to force his way through, 'Excuse please.' He reached the side of the ship and saw Leila in a line of passengers moving towards the waiting carriage. She was talking to someone, probably another porter, and pointing to the ship.

The ship's klaxon sounded. 'No,' he shouted as the vehicle moved off with Leila and Floris aboard, and he gripped the rail in frustration. Despite the chain across the top, the gang-plank was still down and the ferry still tied to the bollards with thick rope. He was near enough to jump on to the quay, but he was hampered by the luggage he was carrying, his and Leila's, and Floris's blanket over his shoulder. He called to someone and tried to tell him he needed to get off. The man rattled something at him that he didn't understand, and then waved a finger at him as if telling him to wait and disappeared.

It seemed like an eternity before the man came back with another, who also asked Ziki questions he didn't understand. He patted his chest and then pointed to the quayside. 'My wife and child,' he said. The two men looked at him and then daylight seemed to flood their faces, and one of them unhooked the chain for him to get off. One of them patted his shoulder and said, 'Get on the next coach, mate,' which made no sense at all.

He ran towards the building at the far side of the quay where the coach had been standing, explained in English what had happened and asked when there would be another coach.

'Not yet,' a man sitting in a small cabin told him. 'Not until the next ferry comes in. Have you got any money?'

Ziki was suspicious. 'A little,' he said.

'Then I suggest that you go out of that gate and hire a cab – cabriolet – do you understand?'

'Yes, yes. I understand. But where did the other carriage go?'

'Goes into Dover, and then to London, if that's where you want to be, mate. Where are you going?'

'Erm, to Kingston up Hull, in the north of England.'

The clerk scratched his head. 'Blimey,' he said. 'That's a long way.' He blew out a breath and Ziki caught the smell of vinegar and something sour that he didn't recognize. 'Well, I reckon your best bet would be to head for King's Cross station and catch the first train. Might not be today, of course. Where do you think your wife will be?'

'I hope she will be at the railway station, but I don't know. I do not know why she got on the coach instead of waiting for me.'

'Women, eh!' The clerk gave a strange wink of his eye and screwed up the side of his mouth. Ziki had no idea what that meant, but he thanked the man and walked out of the gate as suggested. There were several cabriolets waiting and he approached one and asked the driver to take him to the railway station.

The cab driver nodded and asked him something that again he didn't understand, and after a few more attempts the driver shrugged, helped him to lift the bags inside, and set off.

'King's Cross,' Ziki called up to him, but the driver sitting above him couldn't hear him, so Ziki had to wait until eventually they pulled into a small station forecourt.

He asked again for King's Cross, and the driver pointed to a plaque on a wall which indicated that this was the South Eastern Terminus.

'You can travel to King's Cross from here,' the driver shouted as if Ziki was hard of hearing. Ziki nodded and stepped down from the cab. Right now he was so frustrated that he felt like turning round and getting back on the ferry.

He lifted down the luggage and opened the satchel to take out money to pay the driver. He fished about for his wallet and couldn't find it, only Leila's purse and comb, her handkerchief, and a small pot of face cream.

He frowned and opened the satchel wider; it wasn't his. He had been carrying both of them, his and Leila's, and had handed one of them to her as they joined the queue for the gangplank. Leila's had a deep pink ribbon fastened to one of the outside pockets. He gave a gasp of dismay as he saw it. A pink ribbon fluttering in the breeze.

CHAPTER THIRTY-NINE

Moira posted the letter to her friend Emily. She had asked her if she and her daughter would like to come to tea the next day, adding that they had a little girl staying with them of about Susan's age.

She was desperate to talk to someone, someone who might have a fresh opinion on their situation. She didn't want to worry James with her fears about what might happen to Floris, or Leila either, whether or not she recovered. James had been very quiet on the subject for the last few days. He was trying to continue with his normal working practice, but questions were constantly cropping up about Friendship House, and as he had been asked to take on the role of chairman he had to consider those too. It had been agreed at the last meeting that they would aim to have the building ready before Christmas, by which time the legalities of its charitable status had also to be completed.

'Oh!' he sighed one evening as he dropped into his chair. 'I'm beginning to wish we had left it until the New Year.'

'But we can't,' Moira implored. 'We're coming up to the time of year when the house is needed the most. Could we ask your father to help out with the legal requirements? He has more time on his hands than you do, and he knows his way round things, as well as knowing who to talk to.'

'He does.' He rubbed across his eyebrows with his finger-tips. 'I know, but he's supposed to be enjoying his retirement. I just wish there were two of me.'

In the next morning's post a letter arrived from Emily apologizing that they couldn't come to tea, as they were all about to catch a London train to see her husband's parents, since they were going to be away at Christmas staying with their other son and his family.

It's their turn, she wrote. *We'll have Christmas with just our own little family, but we will miss them!!!! Perhaps we will see you then? We're hoping to have Open House on Boxing Day.*

Oh dear. Moira let out a huff of breath. That's disappointing, but never mind. She tried again to think of someone who would listen to the details of their dilemma, and decided that if James wouldn't ask his father, then she would. She immediately sat down to write to her parents-in-law. They will love to be wanted, she reckoned. They are such good, kind-hearted people.

She wrote simply that James was drowning in a sea of bureaucracy regarding Friendship House and that they needed to start the building work if they were to have the house almost ready before the winter started in earnest. She posted the letter the same day, and received a reply on the next from James's mother. *Don't worry, my dear*, she wrote. *I'm packing a bag as I write. We'll be with you tomorrow. Have you still got the darling child with you? Don't worry about accommodation; we'll stay with my cousin Jane. She'll be delighted to see us.*

Oh, how lovely. Moira heaved a sigh of relief. James's mother was so practical, and she loved Floris almost as much as they did.

'They're coming here!' James said, when she told him his parents were coming to Hull for a few days. 'Oh, heavens. That's wonderful, but there'll be no time for entertaining! Not even Ma and Pa.'

'You won't have to,' she said. 'When have you ever had to entertain your parents? They're not like mine! Anyway, they're going to stay with your mother's cousin Jane for a few days; they're not staying with us.'

'They're going to Aunt Jane? That's all right then.' James gave a huge beam. 'And in that case I just might collar Father and ask his advice on one or two things.'

'I'm sure he'd want to know how everything is running along.' Moira smiled serenely and James gazed at her, suddenly mildly suspicious, but not knowing about what, or why. He dismissed the querulous thought. His dearest wife was not in the habit of subterfuge.

It turned out that his father did know a few people, and whom to approach in officialdom to get things moving, and he took himself off to talk to them, advising those in authority that he and his sons had already committed their company to sponsorship, and would be very grateful if the corporation would show their eagerness in supporting the venture so that they could announce the scheme to the general public.

He joined his wife and James and Moira at the house, vigorously shook hands with Leggott, whom he remembered well, and announced that short of James and Leggott signing some papers, everything was in place and they could begin immediately.

As it was still Leggott's house, he had already set in motion the ordering of materials: bags of cement, plaster and lime, and pots of plain white paint. A builder named Jack Keylock had already approached him, telling him that he had heard a rumour that there was to be a hotel or alehouse on the site, and he wanted to be in with a chance of work as there wasn't much about.

Appropriately, as the Ripleys arrived, Keylock had just called to see Leggott, who, to try him out, had asked him to build another privy next to the existing one. Keylock had said that he'd better check the drains first and make some adjustments to the pipework. 'I'm a time-served plumber,' he said, 'but then building work became more lucrative so I did that instead. Now I'll do either. Fencing as well, if you need any doing, although I reckon you'd be better replacing yon fence wi' a brick wall. We could use 'fencing to mek 'other privy.'

'You'll need more than two privies,' James's mother chipped in practically. 'Is there room for three, maybe one of them separate from the other two?'

The men looked at her, their faces inscrutable.

'Well?' she said. 'Aren't there going to be women here as well as the men? A cook and a housekeeper, for instance, and maybe a cleaner?' She gazed at them in turn. 'They're not likely to want to share with unknown men, are they?'

'Of course they're not,' Elliot Ripley said. 'And what about an outside tap?' he added. 'Or maybe a sink with a tap would be more useful?'

'Aye, it would, and you can have as many privies as you like, they'll be easy enough as long as 'drains are all right. I'll check them out now. Have you got a crowbar handy so I can move this paving slab over 'manhole?' They could hear the joy in Keylock's voice as he cottoned on to the fact that there'd be a lot of work ahead.

'Good thinking, Mrs Ripley,' Leggott said, with a nod to Moira as well as her mother-in-law. 'That's what we want. Ideas. Now then, Jack, afore you start that, I'll need a word, so come inside and I'll explain what this place will be, and it's neither an 'otel or a pub.'

Moira took Caroline Ripley to look inside and tell her what their plans were. Her mother-in-law was very enthusiastic and said that once there had been a few changes it would be perfect. She suggested that the room nearest the kitchen could be used for eating, set out with different-sized tables so that those who wanted to be sociable could use a larger one, whilst those who didn't want to talk could eat at the smaller ones.

'I'll ask around,' she said. 'We'll see if we can get some furniture for free. You'll need benches and chairs; church pews
maybe, a long table, that kind of thing.'

'I'm so glad you came,' Moira said enthusiastically as they
walked back to High Street. 'You have so many ideas.'

'Well, as you go through life, my dear, you have to manage
with what's in front of you. Not everyone can just dip down
into deep pockets, so you must use your initiative.'

'Yes, of course,' Moira murmured, and looked behind to
see Floris holding Elliot Ripley's hand as she skipped along
singing a song that no one would possibly understand. To
Moira's amusement, Elliot was singing too.

'So what do you think is to be done for a certain child whose
mother is alive but only just?' Moira asked, turning back to
Caroline. They had previously told James's parents that Leila
had been found, alive, but not well, and that her hold on life
was precarious.

'I think that you must wait and see what happens next, my
dear. Her mother might recover; I do believe in miracles,' Mrs
Ripley murmured. 'Perhaps she might not, but now you know
where she is you will eventually find out. Or Floris's father
might appear, if it's true that her mother was looking for him.
As to where they came from and why they were not together –
who knows? You can't possibly guess; there could be a hundred
reasons. Perhaps they became separated on the journey here.
We are assuming, are we not, that because the child has such
dark eyes and hair they probably came from another country,'
She lifted her shoulders. 'Refugees? There is conflict wherever we look. Did you say her mother spoke English?'

'Apparently she is English, or at least she looks it, according
to the women in the cellar that James spoke to. But they also
said that she wore foreign-style clothing.'

'So married to someone who is not English?' Caroline Ripley shrugged again. 'Maybe he is lost too!'

CHAPTER FORTY

Ziki

Ziki found loose cash, Ottoman lira, in his pocket to pay the driver, who looked at it and then at him, shrugged, and climbed back on to his seat. Ziki walked into the small train station and his spirits sank even further when he realized that he was the only would-be passenger.

He sat down on a bench and opened the satchel again and took out Leila's purse. He counted the money inside, all in Ottoman lira, and thought there might be enough for the train ride. He got up and walked across to the small office window. Through it he saw a man wearing a blue cap with some kind of insignia above the peak.

He asked, in as clear English as he could muster, 'King's Cross please.'

The clerk looked up at him. 'Not today, sir. Last train to King's Cross left about twenty minutes ago. Next one is tomorrow morning, eight o'clock.'

Ziki closed his eyes in exasperation. No! What shall I do? He opened his eyes to see the man staring at him.

'You got somewhere to stay, sir?'

He deciphered his meaning. 'No.' He shook his head. 'Is there somewhere near? Not expensive?'

'Just a minute.' The clerk closed the window and turned his back, and Ziki thought he was just going to leave him there, but he didn't. Instead he opened a side door, came out and locked the door behind him, and signalled to Ziki to follow him.

He took him out through the large wooden gates the cab had entered by and pointed to the backs of a row of tall, narrow houses. 'Last but one,' he said. 'Sea View. You can't actually see the sea unless you stand on the roof, but I don't suppose you're too bothered about that?'

'Not at all,' Ziki said wearily. 'Just a bed.'

'You'll get a bed and somefing to eat and drink. Clean and comfortable, I can vouch for it; belongs to my sister. She'll look after you.'

'Thank you so much. Will she take Turkish lira? My wife has the English money.' He lifted the satchel to show him. 'We have mix up!'

'Come here.' The man indicated with his hand. 'I can change it.' He went back into his office and opened the window again and Ziki took the money out of Leila's bag. The clerk opened a drawer and brought out a notebook. 'We often get foreign money from folk coming off the ferry so I keep a note of the rates; don't think I've had Turkish before. We have to charge a bit extra for doing it, you know, so's we're not out of pocket. How much do you want to change?'

Ziki shrugged. 'All of it, please.'

'What? All of it? Staying for a bit, are you?'

Ziki nodded. 'Please. I am going to Hull in the north of England.' On impulse, he asked, 'Have you seen my wife and' – he searched for the right word – 'child?'

The clerk looked up. 'Little girl? Does she look like you?'

'Yes, yes! Dark hair' – he tousled his own, then put his hand down to measure just below his hip – 'so big. My wife is

English, erm, blonde,' and he lifted both hands and narrowed them to indicate someone slim.

The man twirled his hands above his head as if describing a scarf. 'Yes, yes,' Ziki said eagerly. 'You have seen her?'

'Yes. She got on the London train. The one that's just left. Will she be waiting for you?'

Ziki put his fingertips together almost in a prayer and swayed back and forth, his eyes closed, and when he opened them the clerk was holding up one thumb.

He changed Ziki's money and wrote something down in his notebook, and then said, 'I'll have your ticket ready and waiting for you in the morning. I've taken enough money out for your ticket right through to Hull so you don't need to bother at King's Cross. It's always busy there.'

Ziki thanked him profusely. Thank heaven above – at last, perhaps everything will turn out all right after all.

The following morning he woke in a strange bed, and it took him a few minutes to recall where he was and how he had got here. Someone was knocking on the door.

He called out, 'One moment,' forgetting that he was in England and using his own language.

'Hot water, sir.' A voice he recognized from last night; the railway clerk's sister, who had kindly taken him in, showed him a room with a bed and a chair with a towel neatly folded over it, and then another small room with a water closet and washbasin. She had given him a supper of soup and bread, which was as much as he needed as he was quite exhausted with worry; he had tossed about in bed for a long time, unable to sleep, but must have succumbed and woke to her knocking.

'Breakfast is ready, sir,' she said from outside the door. 'Don't forget the train goes at eight o'clock.'

He jumped out of bed, dressed quickly and went to the

door. The woman had left a bowl of hot water, and he carried it into the washroom.

At the station, he heard the clerk call, 'Ziki Adem! Your ticket, sir,' and bypassed the queue to collect it. Thanking the man again, he hurried to the waiting train; a guard was standing by an open carriage door. 'Ziki Adem, sir? Here's your seat. Good luck – hope you find your wife.'

He could hardly believe his good fortune, or the courtesy that had been shown to him. The booking clerk had obviously told the guard to look out for him. He thanked the man, who tipped his hat. 'Have a good journey,' he said as he moved away. 'Ask for the Hull train at King's Cross.'

In the privacy of the bedroom last night, Ziki had opened Leila's satchel again to check that he had not overlooked any remaining money it might hold and had discovered a couple of gold coins tucked into folds of material in the corners. Then he saw that there was another buttoned pocket in a separate section of her bag. His heart hammered; he had never looked in her personal things before, but now, he told himself, it was an absolute emergency.

There was English money inside. There was also Leila's legal documention.

The booking clerk had told him that it would be a long journey from King's Cross to Doncaster, where he would have to change trains, then not so long. He had eaten a substantial breakfast of something the landlady had called porridge, which he didn't like much but was quite palatable after he had added a spoonful of honey at her suggestion. She had then given him a plate of eggs and sausages and thin strips of bacon, and another plate of bread. She had also handed him a small parcel of food which she'd told him was lunch, and he'd put it in the satchel.

This was only a short train, but already full of travellers, and he was pleased to see that the guard had placed a reserved ticket on his seat. People continued to board at various small

251

stations nearby; at one, called Folkestone, he caught a glimpse of the sea. The train picked up speed as they headed towards London, and he noticed that the passengers were mostly men, who he thought might be going to their offices. He tried to guess from their clothing what kind of work they did. A few were dressed in tailcoats and top hats, and he guessed they were probably businessmen. They all moved towards the front of the train, which might have been a higher-class way to travel, he thought. In his carriage the men were dressed more casually, some in tweed jackets and flat caps, which they took off as they sat down.

In about an hour passengers began shuffling about, patting pockets, putting on caps and hats, some standing up and moving towards the door. Ziki leaned towards a man sitting opposite. 'Excuse me, please. Are we arriving at King's Cross?'

'Yep,' the man said. 'This is it. Prepare for a rush.' He pointed to Ziki's satchel and indicated that he should put the strap over his head and place the opening of the bag across his chest, not his back. This he did, and thanked him, and the passenger asked where he was going.

'To Hull,' he answered, and added 'In the north of England,' when the other man frowned and pursed his lips.

'Don't know it,' he said. 'You'll have to ask one of the porters; they'll know.'

He was told there wouldn't be a train to Hull for an hour. By the time he arrived he reckoned that this journey would have taken two days and he still didn't know where Leila and Floris were, or why Leila hadn't waited for him to disembark from the ferry. He decided to try to find someone he could ask whether they had seen a woman and a little girl getting off the last train the day before, but the porters he spoke to just looked at him pityingly. 'Loads, mate,' one said, and the other joked that he wished he could lose his. Then he shook his head. 'Too many passengers for us to remember,' he said. 'Ask the driver of the Hull train.' He looked up at the station clock. 'Fifteen minutes and it'll be in.'

'Thank you,' he said wearily. Leila and Floris will be waiting at the station for me, he thought. I would be, if I were waiting for them.

Fifteen minutes later, hoisting their luggage in front of him, he climbed aboard. He showed his ticket when the ticket collector came, then put it back into his pocket and closed his eyes, and slept and slept, and slept.

CHAPTER FORTY-ONE

'James!' Moira was sitting in an easy chair next to a small side table on which there were several notebooks and pencils. Floris was sitting on the floor with Matthew, who was showing her how to draw a house, and James was reading the newspaper.

James looked up. 'Hmm?'

'Do you think it would be an act of kindness to ask Mrs Walters now if she would be interested in taking on the role of housekeeper-cum-cook at Friendship House, rather than waiting for the builders to start the work? She could start planning the move, and what would be needed in the kitchen, for instance, if she agrees. I do hope that she will, for at least we know her.' She saw Matthew look up, and said immediately, 'We won't mention it to anyone else just yet, Matthew.'

The two boys, Matthew and Bob, were as thick as thieves and had been planning their course of action as soon as they were given permission to set up the soup kitchen.

'Yes, I do,' James said. 'She maybe won't want to move in just yet, though. There'll be a lot of brick dust and rubble when the builder starts. When were you thinking of asking her?'

'I was thinking of *you* asking her, as a matter of fact. Today would maybe be a good day to catch her, being Sunday; the reason being,' she went on, 'that Rosie is off today and I can't expect Mrs Evans to look after Floris, so I'd have to take Floris with me. Besides, your parents are coming for lunch at one o'clock and I said I'd do the table as Rosie isn't here.'

He huffed. 'I can look after Floris.'

'You might forget that you're in charge of her. You're a touch absent-minded when you have a lot going on in your head.'

'Am I?' He seemed astonished.

'Yes.' She smiled. 'And I'm not blaming you. You do have a lot to deal with just now. But also it's your project, and I think that Mrs Walters will be impressed and more inclined to agree if you ask her.'

He got to his feet. 'All right, I'll go now. I could do with a short walk – and I was going to say some fresh air, but there won't be any where Mrs Walters lives. Poor woman.'

It was a damp day, though only raining intermittently. The cold dank air held tangs of fish and oil seed from the factories and mills that were further downriver; James pulled his woollen scarf over his mouth and nose to obscure it. He sighed; he often thought of moving from High Street, but it seemed traitorous somehow. This had been a street for shipping and fishing merchants since time immemorial, and he felt a fond attachment to it, even though he and his family had been and still were shipbuilders, not merchants. His brother Daniel, though, had moved out as soon as he married to live in the village of Hessle, sitting close to the Humber estuary; he said he didn't want to bring his bride to such a confined area as High Street.

But James loved the house and was happy to move in when he and Moira married and his parents left for the sweeter yet bracing air of Scarborough. When his mother, a country girl, had been a young bride, she had made a garden in the yard at the back of the house and employed someone to take up the

255

paving and fill the space with compost of horse manure and pig muck, as she called it in her forthright manner, and soil which she'd begged from the town corporation when they were creating public gardens. She planted roses and lilies, spring flowers like narcissi and tulips, shrubs and apple trees and, in tubs, climbing honeysuckle. Moira, who had never gardened in her life as her parents had employed a gardener, really loved it, taking it over enthusiastically once it was hers, growing climbing shrubs up the walls and tender plants in a cold frame and a small glasshouse. It was her own special place, she said.

But the small court where Mrs Walters lived was a different scenario altogether. Like Moira when she visited, James stepped carefully to avoid the pools of muddy water that had gathered on the uneven ground, and knocked on her door.

He heard someone cursing as a chain rattled and a key was turned; the door was wrenched open. 'For God's sake, what now?' Mrs Walters was in full flow, with an arm raised as if ready for battle, but she dropped it in horror when she saw who it was and drew in a gasp. 'Sorry. Sorry, Mr Ripley.' She wiped the back of her hand to her red face. Her eyes too were red – red, James thought, from weeping.

'I gather this is not a good time, Mrs Walters. Can I assist in any way, or would you prefer me to come back later? I hope you haven't received bad news?'

He didn't think anyone had died. She would have had sadness written on her face, not the fury he saw.

She sniffed and shook her head. 'No. Nobody's died, though I could wish somebody had. But I won't; it's not my nature to curse anybody, however often I've wished to from time to time.'

'In that case, may I come in? I might be able to brighten your day.'

She opened the door wider. 'I doubt it, sir,' she answered miserably, 'but you're welcome.' She let him in, drew a large handkerchief from her pocket and blew her nose, loudly. 'Will you tek a seat, Mr Ripley? I apologize for my bad manners.'

'Thank you.' He sat down and unbuttoned his coat. 'What I wish to speak to you about won't take long, but may I ask what has put you in such a . . . tizzy?' It was an expression his mother used to use if she'd been out of sorts in any way. 'Can I help?'

Mrs Walters gave a sardonic grunt. 'It's more'n a tizzy, Mr Ripley, I can tell you. It was 'last straw – last chance of any improvement in my life. Landlord has put 'rent up so high that I can't possibly stay in this palace, which, as you will have noticed, is so desirable.' Tears were running down her cheeks in spite of her attempts to make a joke of it.

'I pay weekly, so he's given me a week's notice. In a week's time I'll be out on 'street.'

'You mean he came on a Sunday to tell you this?' James was astounded.

'Oh, he doesn't come hisself, Mr Ripley. No, he asks his agent, who generally comes on a Monday to collect. That one has a little bit of humanity left in him despite 'job that he does, and he called this morning to give me an extra day to find 'money. He forgot, though, that 'bank isn't open on a Sunday.' She choked on her sarcasm as tears streamed faster.

'I think – erm, I think I'm going to have to ask you to come back tomorrow, sir; as you'll see, I'm not quite myself today.'

'Indeed you're not, Mrs Walters.' James put his hand inside his raincoat and brought out his pocketbook, and she frowned. 'The Mrs Walters whom I met last time was a much more resilient woman than you are today, although I do realize that you've had rather a shock, but . . .' He opened his pocketbook and she stood up.

'Don't even think, Mr Ripley, that I would accept charity from you or anybody. I know how well you've looked after my nephew, but I'm—'

'I wasn't going to offer any, Mrs Walters,' he interrupted, 'and if you'd like to sit down again, I'll explain.'

She did as he bade, sitting on the edge of a rickety cane chair and holding on to the edge of the table as if she might unbalance.

'Do you recall that at the meeting regarding Friendship House,' James began, 'we mentioned that we would need to employ a live-in housekeeper-cum-cook for the people who'll require our services? My wife has suggested that we should ask if you would be willing.'

He fingered the pocketbook again, and the notes inside it. 'The money I have brought with me today was not to give you something towards your rent, as you might have assumed. It is not my money in any case' – this last statement wasn't actually true, but he continued anyway – 'it is money we have collected from sponsors to start off the Friendship House funds. I thought that if you agreed to take the position, we should show our good faith by paying you part of the first month's salary.'

'Oh,' she breathed; it was almost a sob. 'And you mean I'd have to live in?'

'Well, it would be more convenient all round if you did, but if you'd prefer to ...' He paused, and looked round the cramped damp room. 'We have yet to start knocking down walls and rebuilding, but the man we're employing is gathering his tools together. You'll have to speak to Mrs Ripley about the things you'd need, should you decide to take up the offer. You may take your own furniture if you wish, but there will no doubt be furniture donated and you could have the first pick.' He gave a conspiratorial grin. 'So if you'd like to think about it and let us know in a day or two ... ?' He left the question hanging in the air.

She stood up again. 'I've thought about it, Mr Ripley,' she said, her voice cracking and fresh tears running down her face. 'And yes please, I'd like to tek 'job!'

'Excellent!' he said. 'I'm so pleased. You've met our housekeeper, Mrs Evans? She's been with our family since she was just a girl. I'm quite sure she'd be willing to give you a few hints if you need them, not that I think you will, but perhaps the two of you could organize the kitchen together? It will be a fresh start; it's an empty building, so it will be quite a challenge.'

'I'm up to it, Mr Ripley,' she said hoarsely.

'I'm sure you are, Mrs Walters. Now, are you the original Mrs Walters I met a while ago? You've got rid of the one who opened the door to me?'

'Oh, aye, she's gone, sir.' She gathered her handkerchief up again and blew her nose, and gave a watery smile when she saw his broad grin. 'I've got rid of that scaredy cat! Don't want 'likes of her hanging about when there's work to be done!'

CHAPTER FORTY-TWO

Leila

Leila and Floris had arrived at King's Cross. Leila was still feeling confused; there had been so much hustle and bustle when they had arrived at the Dover railway station and been shepherded towards the London train.

She'd approached a guard who was standing by an open carriage door, urging passengers to hurry along. 'My husband is still on the ferry,' she told him as she put her foot on the step.

He'd pulled his pocket watch from his top pocket and said, 'Well, if he don't come in the next three minutes, lady, he's going to miss the train and will have to wait for the next one, which will be tomorrow morning. Best get on, ma'am. There's a seat on the left.'

He turned to walk away, but then turned back and said, 'It's possible he boarded further down the platform; there's been a right crowd rushing from the ferry.'

I don't know what to do, she thought. Shall I stay on? Perhaps he is on the train, and we'll meet in King's Cross. She commandeered a double seat; if Ziki appeared Floris would have to sit between them.

Too late. A whistle blew, smoke and steam obscured the

windows, and as the wheels began to turn she realized what the guard had said: the next train to London was tomorrow morning.

I have seriously mismanaged this, she thought. I should have waited. Why did I allow myself to be marshalled along with everyone else? I'm used to making my own decisions, but it is so long since I travelled that I'd forgotten how it can be.

It will be all right, she decided. I'll just find lodgings in London and meet him in the morning.

It was then that she opened the satchel to check her papers and realized that she was not carrying her own bag, but Ziki's.

When the train reached King's Cross Leila stood back on the platform checking the other passengers as they got off, but Ziki wasn't there. She spotted a Hull train waiting at one of the other platforms, and made an instant resolution. It was almost midday and the journey to Hull would take several hours; she had enough money in Ziki's purse for the fare but not for a night's lodging, and although she had money sewn under the clothes she was wearing she couldn't get to it without undressing. Carrying a weepy Floris and what little luggage she had, she boarded the Hull train, and was told by the guard that she would have to change at a place called Doncaster.

When the train reached Doncaster there was an hour to wait for the connection. The station was cold, with a bitter wind rushing through it. It was also dark and raining and she was tired; I'll find a small hotel where we can eat and sleep, she thought, retrieve some of the money from beneath my garments, enough to last until Ziki comes, and catch a train to Hull in the morning. Tomorrow I shall meet Papa's lawyer and take possession of the house, and by then Ziki will have arrived.

It was whilst she was lying in a strange bed with a sleeping Floris beside her that she realized that the paperwork for the lawyer, including the proof of her identity, and most of her money was hidden inside the satchel that Ziki was carrying.

Leila had been born in Hull, in the very house that she was hoping to sell and thereby release some money, but she had no memory of either. Her parents had continued on their travels as soon as she was old enough to sit up in a papoose on her father's or her mother's back, and when she and Floris arrived at Hull station the next day and stepped out of the concourse, she was looking out at a completely unknown and very damp town.

'Well, Floris.' She looked down at her small daughter. 'We're on an adventure.'

Floris was in no mood for coaxing. 'Want Baba Ziki,' she said plaintively.

'So do I, darling, but he's not here.' I really hoped he would be, she mused. He surely isn't far behind us, but then I don't know how often the trains run into Hull. She sighed. And it's a long way from London.

We must find lodgings as soon as he arrives, but I do not know how long the money will last. I should try to find the lawyers' office and get another set of keys for the house, and then we can stay there.

She went back inside and enquired about the arrival time of the next train from Doncaster; it wasn't for another two hours. She wrote a hasty message on a scrap of notepaper, in Turkish, telling Ziki to wait there for them, and asked the booking clerk if he would give it to her husband, who would be arriving on the next train. He looked at it, and then looked at her.

'Will he understand it?' he asked.

'Yes, of course. He's Turkish,' she explained. 'But he speaks English too.'

He nodded, and put the note to one side. 'Right-oh,

missus. I'm going off in an hour, but I'll leave it for 'next bookin' clerk.'

Outside again, she saw that there was a hotel next door to the station, so she took Floris by the hand and walked to the entrance. She knew as soon as she went through the double glass doors that it would be too expensive to stay there even for one night.

'When Baba comes, then we can stay here,' she murmured to Floris, who wasn't in the least interested and dragged her feet. Leila turned round again and went back out through the doors, wrapping her shayla round her head; she was feeling cold. Although the rain had almost stopped, the dampness wasn't conducive to lingering.

A small inn is what I must look for, where we can get food and a bed for the night. She crossed over the road and cut down a side street to look for a welcoming hostelry, one that would be safe for a woman and her child, thinking that even though she had travelled many hundreds of miles on her journey she must still look respectable in her silk gown and flowing long coat and shayla. Floris, in her pretty cotton dress and warm jacket, with her dark eyes and tangle of curls, could never have looked anything but lovely.

'Here we are, Floris,' she murmured as they approached an inn where a single-horse carriage was waiting outside. 'We'll ask if they can accommodate us.'

The woman at the reception desk looked at her so quizzically when she asked for a room for one night that Leila felt compelled to explain that her husband had been held up in London and they were waiting for him to arrive. The room she was offered was small but adequate, and they provided a cot for Floris. Leila asked if she might have use of a bathroom and hot water, as they had been travelling for a long time. At the lodging house in Doncaster there had been no bathroom, only a jug of hot water, a bowl for washing and a bar of soap.

They still had an hour and a half to wait for the next train, so Leila went downstairs again to ask for a bath to be filled in the meantime. She bathed Floris first, then popped her into the cot and covered her with a blanket, and within minutes she was asleep. Leila then locked the bedroom door and went to have a luxurious bath herself, imagining a blissful reunion with Ziki.

Floris was still fast asleep when Leila dressed to go out to the station again, and she pondered whether to leave her in the cot rather than wake her and carry her across to the station. She decided to leave her; she would probably sleep all night, except that Ziki would wake her to give her a hug.

I'll tell them to listen for her at the desk, she thought, and glanced at the clock on the bedroom mantelpiece. She had fifteen minutes before the train was due. I'll go, she decided. Floris was a good sleeper.

It was the same young woman at the desk when she went down, and she told her where she was going and that she'd left her daughter sleeping. 'I'll be straight back,' she said and told her the time of the train, and the woman just nodded.

She walked as quickly as she could, and noticed that a few of the people she passed looked at her rather strangely. Remembering where she was, she thought that perhaps people in Hull rarely saw a woman wearing a shayla; she removed it from her head and wrapped it around her neck. She would wear it on her head when she returned with Ziki.

Except that she didn't. She watched the train steam in and the passengers disembark, but Ziki wasn't one of them. She walked slowly back to the inn and wondered what to do next.

There was only one thing to do next, and that was try to find the lawyer who had looked after her father's affairs for as long as she could remember. But what was his name? Something beginning with T, she thought, but no, maybe not, was that a first name? An aitch, perhaps. Hawkins? Yes, I think that might have been it. Or was it Henderson? I'm no longer used to English names, or Scots ones for that matter. I used to be a Mackenzie and now I'm an Adem. I just hope I remember his name when I begin my search.

They had had a good breakfast at the inn, and Floris was in a happier mood after a good and long night's sleep. Leila collected their few belongings, paid the bill and ruefully realized how much it had depleted the small amount of money at her disposal. She asked the man at the reception desk if he had a directory of Hull lawyers or attorneys, and he took from under the desk a booklet that listed various professional people, businessmen, lawyers, bankers, shipbrokers and other merchants who worked or lived in the town.

None of the lawyers' names jogged her memory, so she asked the obliging young man where legal offices might be. 'In the older part of town, ma'am,' he told her. 'Parliament Street, High Street, Market Place, any of those.'

He gave her directions, but first, she decided, she must go back to the railway station to enquire about Ziki and the London trains. It was a different booking clerk, and he shook his head when she asked if anyone had been looking for her. She glanced in the booking office window and saw that the note she had left for Ziki was sitting on a shelf, probably where no one would see it, and if they did they wouldn't understand it.

Is there any point in trying again, she wondered, and decided there wasn't, so instead she asked when the next train would be in. The clerk looked up at the clock on the wall. 'Eleven fifteen, ma'am. Do you want a ticket?'

'No.' She shook her head wearily. 'Thank you. I'm waiting for my husband to arrive.'

'Is he handsome?' the man joked, and she answered seriously that yes, he was.

'I'll tell him there's a lovely lady looking for him.'

'Please, if you will,' she said, not realizing that he was joking. 'I wrote a note for him yesterday,' and she pointed to the shelf. 'There, the white piece of paper. Would you give it to him, please, and tell him I will come back.'

He shook a finger at her and winked; she didn't understand what that meant, and walked away. The clerk watched her cross the road, then he picked up the note and looked at it. 'What sort of language is this?' he asked a porter who was passing by.

'Where did it come from?' the porter said as he looked at it.

'No idea.' The clerk grinned. 'The lady said she'd left it for her husband yesterday. Can't read a word of it. Double Dutch to me.'

'It's not Dutch.' The porter handed it back. 'It might be Turkish. If it is then she's missed him. A foreign fellow came in first thing this morning; he'd fallen asleep on 'train from London yesterday and missed 'stop at Doncaster. Didn't wake up 'till he reached York, and caught 'first train back to Hull this morning.'

'Where did he go then?'

'No idea.' The porter shrugged. 'He asked where he could find lodgings. We sent him next door to 'Station Hotel.'

'I hope he had enough money to pay.' The clerk chuckled.

'I told him it'd cost him,' the porter said, 'and he said he didn't care, he just wanted a bed and a pillow to lay his head!'

CHAPTER FORTY-THREE

Lily Walters was so elated that as soon as James Ripley had gone she put on her bonnet – the pleated one that she'd stitched herself, her one and only coat, her best shawl, which she wrapped around her head and shoulders, and her only pair of boots, packed with newspaper in a vain attempt to keep the rain out; she locked the door and laughed as she did so, for there was nothing in the house that was worth stealing, and set off to the top of High Street and across Lowgate, past the top of what was now called the Old Dock, and headed towards Mason Street and the building that Mr Ripley had described as Friendship House.

She thought that was the quickest way, not that it would matter once she was in the new place, somewhere near St Paul's Street, he'd said, for she would have no reason to go back to the hovel she was living in at present. There were no neighbours that she would miss, for everyone kept to themselves, and from Mason Street it would be easy enough to get to the market or Whitefriargate, where, if she was careful with the new money that she'd be earning, she might have enough to buy a little something for herself, or even young Robert, who really, she considered, had brought all of this about, simply by plucking up the courage to knock on Ripley's back door to ask if there were any jobs available.

The house was on a corner of a narrow lane with a gas lamp above it. The gate to it was latched but not locked and she heard men talking inside the yard, so tentatively she opened it and stepped inside.

There were two men there, both kneeling and looking down a hole where a paving slab had been removed and pushed to one side.

'Hello,' one of them said, looking up.

'Hello.' Looks like 'gaffer, she thought. She wasn't shy of talking to men like these, they were of her ilk, whereas Mr Ripley, nice as he was, wasn't – he and Mrs Ripley were of a different class. 'I'm – I'm Lily Walters,' she said. 'Mr Ripley has asked me if I'd like to tek on 'job of housekeeper when 'house opens up.'

The taller of the two men got up and stepped forward, putting out his hand to shake hers. 'Oh, well done! Can I call you Lily, or do you prefer Mrs Walters? I'm Leggott; 'house was mine but transfer is just about done.'

'Lily's fine, Mr Leggott,' she said, putting out her hand to his. She couldn't recall ever shaking anyone's hand before.

'Just Leggott,' he said. 'Do you want to have a look round and see what you think afore you sign up? My daughter's inside tidying up a bit.'

'Yes, please,' she said. 'If that's all right?'

'Course it is; you need to know where you're coming to and what's in front of you. It's a bit of a mess at 'minute; it's been empty for a couple of years.'

She was astonished that a house could have been empty for so long and nobody had vandalized it. She stepped inside the door into what she thought must be the kitchen and saw a young woman cleaning out the sink. The girl looked up. 'Hello!'

Lily nodded. 'I'm Lily Walters.' She took a deep breath; she was going to say it. 'I'm going to be 'housekeeper here. I've just met your da. He had his head down a drain hole.'

'That sounds about right.' The girl laughed. 'I'm Hannah.

Would you like a cup o' tea? I've just got 'range to fire up, but it might tek a while for 'kettle to heat.'

'No, you're all right, thanks, but I'd like to have a look round.'

'Help yourself.' Hannah picked up a sweeping brush. 'I'll leave 'kettle on just in case you change your mind when you come down. It might have boiled by then.'

Lily nodded her thanks and went out of the kitchen and into the hall. She'd never been in such a big building before, except for a church. The hall had rooms on either side and she took a look in all of them, saw the tall windows and wondered if she'd be able to reach the top to clean them. I'll need a tall stepladder. Must make a list. Stepladder, bucket – two buckets. Could bring mine.

She went upstairs, noticed the dust on the steps and thought, it's a big house for me to clean on me own, mebbe I could have a girl in to help, like that one that Mrs Evans has got; but then, she pondered, Rosie was there for 'family. I'll have to recruit some of 'folks that come to stay; aye, that's it. They can't be sitting around doing nowt while I'm cleaning up after 'em. I'll set up a roster – think that's what it's called – aye, and mebbe speak to Mrs Evans and ask what she thinks. I'll mek a list when I get home and think on what to take. Not that I have much, but I'll manage.

She went upstairs and explored all the rooms, wondering which one she could have. She wouldn't want to share with anybody; she'd want her own room with a key. I quite fancy that one overlooking 'gate and on to 'street, so's I can see who's coming and going. I've been stuck without a view all these years, never knowing what's happening outside my own four walls. Oh, she thought, I'm going to love it, and to think that there'll be folk coming here who are worse off than I've ever been. I've never thought that there could be anybody, but now I'd guess that there are plenty.

Ziki

Ziki had indeed been lost. So worn out was he that he hadn't woken when the train stopped in Doncaster, and they were stationery for the shortest time only, as it was already running late. He'd opened his eyes as they were steaming out of a station and picking up speed. He closed his eyes, and when he opened them again he heard a guard shouting out a place name. Was this Doncaster? People were getting off. It was dark. He'd had the satchel over his neck for the whole of the journey for fear of its being stolen, and his neck and shoulders ached.

He decided to get off the train; a guard was standing by the door. 'Have you got a ticket, sir?' the man asked. 'I didn't like to wake you.'

'Yes, yes.' Ziki put the luggage down on the platform and patted his jacket pocket, then fumbled in the satchel.

'Don't bother now,' the guard said. 'Is this your stop?'

Ziki looked about him. It was pitch dark outside of the station, which was lit by tall gas lamps. 'Is this Doncaster? I need the Hull train.'

The guard gave a muffled grunt. 'We went through Doncaster well over an hour since, and you won't get a train to Hull till morning. You've slept through. You're in York!'

Ziki put his head to his forehead and groaned. What an idiot. Leila will wonder where I am. Will she be all right? Sense told him that she would be, she was used to travelling, but she had Floris with her and she would be tired.

'Is there somewhere I can stay until the morning?' he asked the guard, who was unfurling his flag and putting a whistle to his lips.

The guard looked along the length of the train and slammed the door behind Ziki, then waved his flag and blew a shrill, ear-piercing whistle. Only then did he turn to him and say, 'Aye, you can sit in the waiting room; there's a fire burning. Hull train is due in at seven thirty in the morning. Don't miss it. You can pay 'conductor for a single ticket. Fancy a cup o' tea or coffee?'

'Oh, yes, indeed I would,' Ziki said. 'I have been travelling all day.'

The guard nodded. 'I'll see what I can find. Wait in yon waiting room and I'll bring you summat.'

Ziki opened the door cautiously and saw a small fire burning in a grate; there was no one in the room, so he pulled one of the wooden chairs nearer the fire. There were long bench seats set against the walls, but he thought the wooden seats looked to be slightly more comfortable, and although he wasn't cold the fire looked comforting. He sighed. How in heavens did I miss the Doncaster stop? Of course I didn't know how long it would take the train to get to Doncaster, but still . . .

He was unused to train travel. His first was in Germany, then Dunkirk to Calais and then from Dover to London. Now I am well travelled, he mused, and to prove it I have 'missed my connection'.

The guard brought him a cup of black coffee and a strange-looking item of food which he called a sausage roll. Ziki thanked him and reached inside his pocket for change, but the guard brushed the payment away.

'You are very kind,' Ziki told him. 'When I arrive in Hull, I must look for my wife; we became separated in Dover and she got on the train without me.'

'She got on the train to London?' the guard asked, astonished. 'Will she be able to manage? Does she speak English?'

'Oh, yes!' he explained. 'She is English, but mostly she speaks Turkish because we live with my family. Sometimes, though, she teaches our daughter English words also.'

'But why are you in England, sir, if you don't mind me asking? Especially in this weather.'

271

Ziki leaned forward and gazed into the fire. It is a good question, he thought; Leila could perhaps have signed the necessary documents in Constantinople. It might have taken a long time to send details to England, but a lawyer could have done it for her by telegraph, perhaps. It is a new way of doing business, though I have heard it doesn't always work. He realized the guard was still waiting.

'Her father, sir. He died in France and my wife wishes to come to England to claim the house where she was born.'

'Ah!' the man nodded. 'And so you'll be coming to England to live, will you?'

Ziki was startled. Surely not. That wasn't Leila's intent, was it?

'Weather will be better where you come from, I expect?' the guard went on. 'We get some cold weather in winter.'

'We get cold weather in Turkey too,' Ziki said, 'but warmer summers. But no, we will go home when the house business is finished.' He sighed. 'England is a long way from my homeland. I could not live anywhere else.' He shook his head. 'My wife, Leila, she is a traveller always. She has, what is it they say? The wanderlust.'

He didn't sleep well. The chair was uncomfortable after all, so he tried one of the benches, but it was narrow and he thought that if he slept and then turned over he would fall off. He decided therefore that he would walk up and down until he was tired enough, and then he would lie on the floor with his head on the satchel.

The next morning the guard was there to make sure that Ziki caught the right train. 'Straight through to Hull terminus, sir. Good luck.'

'Thank you, thank you, you are good kind gentleman,' Ziki said sincerely as he climbed on board, on what he hoped was his last journey until they started for home.

CHAPTER FORTY-FOUR

Leila

Leila had shivered in her light clothing, and whilst at the inn had taken some clothes out of the small bag that she had been carrying since Dover. There was a wool tunic for her, and some leggings and another jumper for Floris, and she dressed her in these on top of what she was already wearing; she hadn't yet worked out where they would stay that night. She was depending on finding the lawyer whose name she still couldn't recall. Was it Thompson, or Hawkins? The name seemed familiar, but she had no address for him.

Her remaining money she would have to use for food for Floris and rent at a cheap lodging house, and it was with a mixture of hope and anxiety that she took Floris's hand and set off, this time to search for the elusive lawyer. She called in several offices in the area of town that the desk clerk had mentioned, but heads were shaken when she mentioned her father's name and she left feeling more and more uneasy.

Then at the end of a long shopping street she came to a row of tall houses, some private dwellings without a nameplate and others with plates that denoted companies. One was a registry of births and deaths . . . and then another highly polished brass plate that announced the office of Hawkins, Thompson and Hawkins, Solicitors.

She felt her heart flip. This was it, she felt sure; didn't her father call him old Thompson when he was talking about him? They were educated at the same school, she was certain.

She climbed the steps to the front door and pulled the bell chain, hearing its peal echoing through the hall beyond. Floris tweaked her skirt. 'Can I do that please, Anneh?' The little girl spoke in Turkish, and Leila smiled down at her.

'Say in English, Floris,' she coaxed her. 'We are in England now.'

Floris stumbled over the translation, 'Mama', and Leila nodded. 'Good girl. Listen – someone is coming now.'

A young man opened the door and invited them in. 'Good day, ma'am. May I be of assistance?'

Leila let out a huge sigh. 'I really do hope so. I am looking for Mr Thompson, who I believe looked after my late father's legal matters. His name was Henry Mackenzie.'

The young man's mouth shaped into an O. 'Ah, won't you come in? I'm afraid Mr Thompson isn't here today. You might not be aware that he has taken semi-retirement and is only here for two days a week.' He must have seen the dismay on Leila's face as he hastily added, 'Perhaps Mr Hawkins junior can assist you? He is attending to some of Mr Thompson's clients.'

Leila felt dizzy; this was yet another blow. Why had she not thought of contacting Mr Thompson to tell him they were travelling to England; and did she ever write to tell him of her father's death? She thought that she had, but couldn't be totally sure. There were not many people that she knew her father had kept in touch with, and she had received only one or two replies when she had notified them of his death. He and her mother had virtually cut themselves off from former English friends, as they rarely came back to England and Hull.

'May I sit down?' she asked. 'I have travelled such a long way to see Mr Thompson. I – I don't know of any other person who might have advised my father.'

'Of course, of course, I beg your pardon.' He led her to a padded velvet chair against the wall. 'You said your late father, Miss—' he glanced at Floris, 'erm, Mrs—'

'He was Henry Mackenzie. My name was Leila Mackenzie, it is now Leila Adem. I am married and it is a Turkish name. We live in Constantinople.'

'How wonderful,' he enthused. 'How very interesting and exotic!'

'What am I going to do? Will Mr Hawkins allow me to have the keys to the house? I have no proof of who I am.' She put her fingers to her forehead and rocked, not really aware of what she was doing.

'Mrs Adem?' The clerk bent towards her. 'Are you all right? Would you like a glass of water?'

'Yes, please,' she whispered and put her arm round Floris, who seemed to realize that all was not well and clung to her mother. 'I'm so sorry,' she began, but the young man had scurried along the hall and through another door to fetch a glass of water.

'Thank you,' she said softly, her fingers trembling as she took it from him. 'You're very kind.'

'Would you perhaps like to speak with Mr Hawkins junior?' he asked her. 'I can make an appointment for you. I'll explain to him about your father and we can search out his documents.'

'Make an appointment?' she gasped. 'No, I need to speak to him today. I'm – I'm . . .' How to explain in a few words the predicament she was in? 'Please. I won't keep him long but I must speak to someone.'

'He, erm, he's with a client at the moment. I will have a word with him when he's finished. The thing is, Mrs Adem,' – he

pulled up another chair close to her and sat down on it, lean-
ing towards her – 'the thing is that we have hundreds, probably
thousands, of documents down in the cellar and in the loft
relating to our clients, and it will take some time to find your
father's. How long is it since he last saw Mr Thompson?'

Leila stared at him, and then shook her head. 'I don't know.
Some years, I should think. He rarely came back to England.
He was living in France for quite some time.'

Had he maybe come after her marriage? He was always talking about it, but did he actually make the journey? He would
have told her, and yet she couldn't recall him doing so, and then
she remembered that of course he hadn't; when she had visited
him with Floris, the first time he had seen his granddaughter, he
had said that he must come to England to see 'old Thompson'
to sort out his Will. But he didn't, because he died so soon after
she left; the letter had been waiting for her when she got home
after the long journey back to Constantinople, vowing that
never again would she travel so far alone with a small child.

She told the young man, who said his name was Alfred
Wright, about their journey here, and the mishaps that had
followed, and how her husband had her satchel with the legal
papers, and that she really desperately and urgently needed
the keys to the Albion Street house so that she and Floris
could stay there until Ziki arrived.

She saw a shadow of doubt cloud the clerk's eyes and she
understood; it could be considered a make-believe story, an
invented tale with intent to deceive.

One of the inner doors opened and an elderly man came
out; Leila glimpsed a younger man saying goodbye behind
him. Alfred Wright stood up and escorted the client to the
front door and opened it for him, wishing him a good day.
Then he turned back to Leila and murmured, 'I'll have a
word with Mr Hawkins now to explain your circumstances. I'll
be back in a moment.'

Floris climbed on to her knee and she held her close. The little girl whispered in her ear, 'Where is Baba Ziki? I want him to carry me.'

'Speak in English, Floris,' Leila whispered back. 'You know the words.'

Floris shook her head, her curls dancing over her forehead. 'Want Ziki,' she repeated.

'Soon,' she said softly. 'On the next train.'

The inner door opened again and Alfred Wright came out at the same time as the doorbell chimed. 'Excuse me,' he said to Leila as he passed her, and greeted a man at the door who entered and followed him through to the inner office.

'I'm so sorry,' the clerk said as he came back. 'It's a very busy morning; Mr Hawkins said he will see you tomorrow at noon. Today is frantic, I'm afraid, as he's covering for Mr Hawkins senior who is at York Assizes all day.'

'And – and the keys to the house, could I have those?'

He shook his head. 'I'm afraid not. Not without the paperwork, which I will look for later this afternoon. I'm so very sorry that I can't do more.'

She lifted Floris down to the floor and rose wearily from the seat. Her head felt empty. What could she do? Did she still have enough money for lodgings? She should go back to the railway station and try to find out if Ziki had arrived.

'Thank you,' she said mechanically. 'Tomorrow.' She turned to the door and then turned back. 'May we use your toilet facilities?'

The clerk hesitated for a second. 'Oh, yes, of course. Erm, upstairs, the second door on the left.'

She followed his directions and found a small room with a flush water closet and sat Floris on it, and when she finished she lifted her own skirts and took out the last of the packages that had been sewn into her underwear.

Fingering it, she had no idea how much the Ottoman lira

277

was worth in England. Currency in the empire had been changing over the years, especially when other countries had established themselves independently and created their own.

She had one gold coin and a few paper notes left. 'I must find a bank,' she muttered. 'I can't offer gold for one night's lodging.'

They both washed their hands and headed back downstairs. Mr Wright was waiting for them with his hand on the door.

'I'm sorry to have kept you,' Leila murmured. 'Is there a bank near here?'

'Yes, ma'am.' He pointed back up the street they had come along. 'Just on the corner.' He gave a bow. 'I hope you have a pleasant day. A pity about the rain. It will perhaps clear later?'

She nodded. 'I sincerely hope so. Goodbye, see you tomorrow.'

They walked back the few yards to the imposing building Alfred Wright had indicated and up the steps. A doorman gave a courtly bow and opened the doors for them. 'Good morning, madam. I hope you are well today. Pity about the rain.'

Father said that the English always talked about the weather, but I don't know why when it's always raining, she considered, taking her place in a small queue. I never thought of the weather when I was planning this journey. I should have known better. Ziki will be quite dispirited. He doesn't like the cold or the wet, and here we have both on the same day.

We won't stay, she thought. I'll sell the house; Father always said it would be worth a considerable amount of money. Perhaps I should take a look at it, although I don't remember him mentioning the name or number of it, he only ever said the house in Albion Street.

It was her turn at the desk and she opened up her palm and dropped the gold coin on the shiny counter, then took from her tunic pocket two crumpled lira notes.

'Will you exchange these for English money, please?' She pushed the little pile towards the bank teller.

He peered at the gold, turning the coin over in his hand. 'Is this old currency, ma'am?'

'Old? I don't think so.'

He looked at her and then leaned towards the clerk next to him and showed him the coin. The clerk shrugged, and shook his head.

The teller looked back at Leila. 'Begging your pardon, ma'am,' he said, 'but I'll have to take advice; I'm not familiar with the coinage. It's Ottoman, I think?'

'You're quite right,' she said. 'Turkish.' Before she married, her father always dealt with monetary matters. She'd used Turkish lira and French francs the last time she travelled to see him, and Ziki had paid for their needs as they travelled towards Europe on their way here. She was so tired, her brain seemed dead, and she felt she couldn't think straight. The teller was speaking to her. 'Sorry,' she said. 'What did you say?'

'I asked if you'd care to take a seat whilst I enquire?'

'Oh, yes, I would. Thank you.' She looked about her and spotted a seat against the wall, next to an iron radiator. Perhaps it will be warm, she thought, and holding Floris's hand she hurried towards it.

The radiator was barely warm, but she put her hands on it and suggested that Floris should do the same. 'Want Baba Ziki,' Floris said plaintively, and climbed on to her knee. Leila put her arms around her to warm her, as she felt cold.

'He won't be long,' she murmured, holding her close. 'We'll go to the train station next and perhaps Baba will be there waiting for us.' But by now she was feeling extremely anxious.

She saw the bank teller come out from another door and look round. He saw her and signalled for her to come across.

'I'm so sorry to keep you,' he said, settling in behind the glass. 'I'm sorry to say that the coin is old Ottoman lira and as

279

such we can't change it as it is no longer legal tender. We can, however, change the paper money.'

'But surely the coin is gold?' she stammered.

'It is gold,' he agreed. He bent closer to the glass. 'There is a shop in Silver Street,' he said quietly. 'Only a few yards from here. They deal in old coinage and rare stamps; you could try there. I believe he is an honest trader.'

She looked at him, not knowing what to say, and put her hand out for the coin's return.

'The paper money isn't worth much, I'm afraid; might buy you a cup of coffee and a bun.' He smiled, shrugging his shoulders as if that would be a treat.

She said nothing; there wasn't anything to say. He counted out a few pennies, a sixpence and a farthing. It might buy a hot dinner, she thought, but not a bed for the night.

She left the bank, holding Floris's hand. A woman was sitting on the steps under the portico which kept off some of the now steady rain. Leila and Floris sat on the step behind her. The woman turned round and gave them a nod. 'Blooming miserable weather, en't it?' she said.

'Yes,' Leila said, and put her hands over her eyes and began to cry.

The woman turned round. 'Now then, now then, hit a dark spot, 'ave you?' She reached out a hand to her and patted her arm. 'D'you want to tell Peggy about it? I've heard enough dark tales to fill a book, and not all me own. Sometimes it helps to talk.'

Leila didn't answer, but she nodded and moved down a step to sit beside her, and Floris wriggled to sit between them.

CHAPTER FORTY-FIVE

'James,' Moira said after supper, 'I think the boys could be ready to open the soup kitchen by the coming weekend.'

'Really? That's good. I'm sorry, I haven't been very helpful over this, have I?'

'You've been busy. Have you a lot on at the yard?'

He nodded. 'Yes, really busy. We've one ship almost ready to launch and have taken on another order.' He smiled. 'Not grumbling; we need the work. Coming in like this, with one almost finished, another halfway, we're happy to take an order for the next. We don't want to expand further just yet, as long as we keep our clients happy. So tell me about the boys?'

She laughed. 'I haven't told them yet, but I've made these for them.' She reached behind the cushion on her chair and brought out a bag, opened it, and pulled out two white aprons and two chef's hats. She had starched the cloth on the toques to make them stand up. On the front of the aprons she had stitched in red thread the words *Friendship House.*

'I thought that if they'll wear these, people queueing for soup will ask what Friendship House is.' She looked up at him. 'What do you think?'

'Yes! A great idea. It will help spread the word. Mrs Evans

told me that Mrs Walters has been to see her to ask her advice on something, and she's also started cleaning up at the house.'

'Mrs Walters has?'

'Yes.' He raised his eyebrows. 'Can't wait to move in, according to Mrs Evans. She's chosen a room for herself, and I think that's the one she's been cleaning!'

'But surely there'll be more mess when the inside walls come down to make dormitories?'

'Leggott suggests that just one room could be made into a dormitory of six to eight beds, for those who come for say one or two nights and then move on. The other rooms could have perhaps four beds each, which is probably as many people as can be accommodated at any one time. Mrs Walters couldn't possibly be expected to cater for more than that number if all the beds are filled.'

Moira nodded. 'We should perhaps find someone else to help her; someone like Bob, do you think?'

'Yes, but not Bob, we need him. Perhaps those who intend to stay and look for work could work out a rota to help with the cleaning?'

They went on suggesting various ideas, and then Matthew came in, having finished his homework, and Rosie brought Floris in after her bath. The little girl scrambled on to Moira's knee, laying her head on her chest and putting her thumb in her mouth.

Moira twisted one of Floris's curls round her finger as the dark eyes closed. 'We're having a melancholy moment,' she murmured. ''They seem to be coming more frequently, but what can we do? We can't let her see her mother whilst she's in the state she's in.' She kissed Floris's forehead. 'I have told her that Mama Leila will be coming soon, but am I giving her false hope?'

James watched as Floris's long eyelashes flickered sleepily. 'It isn't false hope. We can only keep faith that her mother will recover, at least to some extent, if not completely.'

'And her father,' Moira said. 'Just where is he?'

Matthew was watching them both. 'What will happen to her if her father doesn't turn up and her mother doesn't . . .' He hesitated, not knowing whether he ought to suggest that she might not recover. 'You know,' he said awkwardly.

'We do know, Matthew, and if you're worried that we might send Floris to an orphanage, then don't be,' his father told him. 'You can be sure of that; we will keep her safe here with us until . . . circumstances change. Which they are bound to do eventually. We can't change anything just now; we simply have to be patient and hope that things turn out for the best.'

'Look what we've got here for you and Bob.' Carefully, so as not to disturb the sleeping Floris, his mother brought out the aprons and chefs' hats she'd made for him and Bob.

'Oh, that's great,' Matthew enthused, putting on one of the hats. 'Is it all right to go down and show Bob?'

'Of course. The other one is for him.'

'We're going to open next weekend, aren't we? Mrs Evans has told Bob that we're ready. We've just got to be careful not to splash anybody with hot soup or drop the bread overboard and suchlike. Bob says he's clumsy, so he wants to ladle the soup into the mugs and I'll hand them over the side with the bread.'

Moira smiled. 'It's so exciting, isn't it? What about putting the bread in a basket and then people can help themselves?'

They tossed a few ideas about. When Matthew suggested supplying napkins, Moira said that perhaps they wouldn't be needed in this instance, but there could be a bowl of water and soap and towels that people could use if they wanted to wash their hands. Matthew went downstairs then to take Bob his apron and toque; Moira and James smiled at each other.

'How wonderful it is,' Moira spoke with a catch in her voice, 'to think that two young boys could have come up with such a brilliant idea.'

Downstairs, Rosie said, 'Let's see you wearing them,' and dutifully they fastened the straps of the aprons round their waists and put the hats on their heads. They fitted perfectly.

'Do you know what the hats are called?' Mrs Evans asked, and both boys shook their heads.

'Cook's hat?' Bob offered.

'Toque blanche,' the housekeeper said. 'White hat. But not spelt the same as when you talk about something. It's a different spelling because it's French. You can check that out, Master Matthew, with your French master when you're at school.'

'I've got a French dictionary upstairs which I can use,' Matthew said gleefully, 'cos I'm not very good at French yet.'

'Well, don't let 'em drop in 'soup, will you?' Rosie told them. 'Or you'll ruin 'em. I wondered what 'mistress was mekkin' when she kept hiding away her sewing every time I knocked.'

'Now then,' Mrs Evans interrupted. 'This is what you're going to be doing. Chicken soup; I've got four chickens simmering in 'large pot right now, and I thought we'd do a Scotch broth, something hearty to warm folks up. Lots of vegetables: potatoes, turnip, carrots and suchlike, mebbe pearl barley and lentils.'

'What! All of that? Crikey, I didn't think there was so much in Scotch broth,' Bob exclaimed. 'Auntie Lily used to mek it when I lived with her. It allus made me nose run just like ham and pea.'

'That's cos it's hot and peppery,' she told them, 'and best of all, if you haven't got much money you can put in as little or as much of anything you've got to mek a good meal, so don't forget that if ever you fall on hard times.'

That was their first lesson. The next one was how to peel and chop a mountain of vegetables so that they didn't think they could just heat and pour out mugs of soup. They had to learn how to prepare it and cook it.

Mrs Evans didn't trust them to make and bake the bread, but Mrs Walters had come in to help and she showed them how, after scrubbing their hands, to mix the flour, add the frothing yeast and lard and finally a sprinkling of salt, and then knead the dough, a process which they both enjoyed. The loaves were left to prove in the larder until Saturday, when they were baked and proudly presented on what the boys had named Soup Day.

CHAPTER FORTY-SIX

The rain had eased during the night and a biting northerly wind had risen, dropping the temperature and making everyone – or at least everyone who could afford to do so – reach for warmer clothes and bring in extra coal and logs to build up the fires. Those who could not afford it huddled further into the corner of a favourite shop doorway until such time as the owner came to open up and moved them on.

Realizing that she was superfluous to the making of soup in the kitchen, Moira decided that she would take a cabriolet to the workhouse and ask if she might see Leila. James was at home and said he would look after Floris and put his hand on his heart, promising that he wouldn't take her out and risk losing her, as Moira seemed to think he would.

He offered to walk to the cabriolet rank by St Mary's and order her a vehicle but she said no thank you, she was perfectly capable of walking there herself, and he grinned and put his arms around her waist and warned her that he would tell her mother that she had been out alone.

She gave him a light slap with her gloves, and then kissed his cheek and Floris's too and said she wouldn't be long. She felt icy tingles cutting into her face as she crossed Lowgate, and pulled her wool shawl closer around her neck. There were two vehicles waiting at the rank and she recognized the driver who had taken her to the workhouse the last time.

He greeted her, and lifted his hat. 'Good morning, Mrs Ripley. You've chosen a cold morning to be out.'

'Yes, indeed. Pity the poor souls who are living outside. There's snow to come, I think. Can you take me to Anlaby Road, please?'

'I can, ma'am. The same destination as before?'

'Yes, please.' She stepped inside the carriage just as a gust of cold wind caught the door he was holding for her, threatening to snatch it from his grip. Pity the poor indeed, she thought as she sat down. There will be a queue of people wanting soup on this cold day. The boys had decided that it would be best to serve it up after the regular market shoppers had left. They didn't want those who could afford to buy soup queueing up for it; this was free and intended for those who had no money for food. 'PIP folk,' as Bob said to Matthew.

There was little traffic out that morning and they arrived at the workhouse within fifteen minutes; the driver asked if she would like him to wait.

'I would, please. I shouldn't be very long.'

'No hurry, ma'am,' he said, tipping his hat as once again he held the carriage door.

'Thank you,' she said, and he nodded.

She pulled the bell rope and waited until one of the residents came to open the door, a woman of perhaps Lizzie's age.

'Good morning,' Moira said. 'May I see Matron, please?'

'Come in, missus,' the woman said. 'I'll go an' fetch her.' She shuffled down the long hall, past the room where Moira had previously been seen by Matron, and disappeared.

Moira waited while five minutes went by, and then took matters into her own hands and knocked sharply on Matron's door. No reply. She could be anywhere; it was a huge building with many rooms and corridors off the main hall. She thought she could remember where the hospital ward was so started walking that way, and went round a corner to find Matron coming towards her.

'Mrs Ripley!' she said in astonishment. 'How did you get in? I didn't hear the bell.'

Moira smiled. 'The door was opened for me by one of the residents; she's gone looking for you.'

Matron gave an impatient huff. 'Gertrude!' she said. 'She loves to open the door when she hears the bell; she'll be looking for me all morning but won't remember why.'

'It will keep her occupied,' Moira said warmly. 'No harm done. I wondered if I might see Mrs Adem again; is there any change in her condition?'

Matron pointed down in the direction of the hospital ward and turned about to walk beside her. 'There might be. Mrs Chambers said she had heard her speak after you were here last time, and her heart beat is stronger. We're giving her sips of boiled water. I haven't heard her speak myself.'

She opened the door to the ward. Leila was still the only patient in there. 'I'm considering asking the surgeon to come again,' Matron said. Drawing herself up, she folded her hands in front of her. 'We are not nurses here, though I know the rudiments of nursing.' She appeared to consider. 'In my opinion, Leila needs more than we can give her, and we have our hands full dealing with the elderly residents like Gertrude and Mrs Chambers.'

'But is Mrs Chambers not able to do most things for herself?' Moira asked uneasily. 'She seems very capable.'

'She thinks she is more capable than she actually is. She comes and sits with Mrs Adem most days and then gives me her opinion, but I'm never sure if she's spinning a tale. You can judge for yourself. If you'd care to take a seat with the patient, I'll be back shortly. I have pressing things to attend to.'

'Don't worry about me,' Moira assured her, as she opened the ward door. 'I'll stay for only a short time and let myself out. But if you should see Mrs Chambers, perhaps you would tell her I am here?'

Matron nodded and left her there, and Moira drew up a wooden chair and sat beside Leila. She was breathing more easily today; Moira could see the slight rise and fall of her chest, but her hands, which were folded in front of her, and her face were still very pale.

Moira took off her gloves and put them on her lap, then placed her warm hands over Leila's cold ones. Instantly, Leila opened her eyes, making Moira jump. She didn't speak, and it was as if she was staring at Moira and yet not seeing her.

'Leila,' Moira whispered. 'Are you awake? Your daughter, Floris, is asking about you.'

Leila didn't answer, but closed her eyelids for a second before opening them again and staring at Moira as if surprised to still see her there.

'You don't need to speak just yet,' Moira continued quietly, 'but if you can hear me, my name is Moira.'

She paused for a moment, not wanting to bombard Leila with too much to think about. Matron was quite right, she thought. She needs more than just a bed to sleep in, and she wondered what medicine Leila was taking. Had she been given something to help her sleep, or take any pain away? Had she any injuries?

Leila continued to look at her, and then she licked her lips. 'Would you like something to drink?' Moira asked. A full glass of water was on a small bedside table, with a teaspoon beside it.

Moira got up and went to the other side of the bed. She knelt down by the table and picked up the glass to sniff at the water. It seemed fresh, and dipping the teaspoon into the glass she drew up half a spoonful of water. Awkwardly, she put one hand round the back of Leila's neck and head and with

289

the other held the spoon to her mouth. Leila parted her lips and Moira carefully tipped in the water, trying not to spill any.

Leila briefly closed her eyes, then opened them and licked her lips again. 'More?' Moira asked, and Leila blinked. Moira gave her a little more water and was convinced that it was what Leila wanted. She was dehydrated; no wonder she wasn't speaking.

She gave her another spoonful of water and then put down the glass and spoon and waited a few more minutes before asking quietly, 'Do you understand what I'm saying?'

Leila gave a slow nod of her head and Moira wanted to weep tears of joy. She took hold of her hands and ran her fingers over them, gently smoothing them; warming them. Leila's skin was thin and papery and felt cold, despite the blanket on top of the cotton sheet.

Moira looked round the ward. One wall had tall cupboards from end to end and she got up from where she was kneeling and opened one of the doors; inside were shelves of nightgowns and underwear, long johns and vests. She opened another and found sheets and pillow cases, and on a higher shelf were piles of folded blankets.

She fetched the wooden chair she had been sitting on and carried it across to the wardrobe, then unfastened the laces on her boots, took them off, and climbed up on to the chair to reach the blankets. She pulled two out and let them drop to the floor.

She was just getting down when the door opened and Lizzie Chambers peered round it. 'Ah!' she said. 'Can I have one o' them? I'm freezin' cold.'

Moira climbed up again and dropped another into Lizzie's arms.

'Leila has taken some water,' Moira told her. 'But her hands feel very cold, so I'm going to wrap her in a blanket and put another on her bed. Will you help me with that, Mrs Chambers?'

Lizzie took the thin coverlet off the bed and together they placed a blanket over Leila, then Moira doubled the other blanket and wrapped it round her neck and shoulders; although the blankets were thin, she thought they would surely make a difference.

'You know nothing about this, Mrs Chambers,' Moira murmured. 'I did this before you came in.'

'Aye, so you did, ma'am. Who knows what you toffs will get up to when nobody's watching?'

Moira laughed, and then remembered that the cab driver was waiting for her and she had said that she wouldn't be long. Leila was lying with her eyes closed and her hands inside the blanket. She seemed to have dropped off to sleep.

'I can't stay,' she said quietly, as she put on her boots and fastened the laces. 'But I came to find out if there was any improvement. Will you sit with her for a while?'

'Aye, I will. I like to be useful, and I'll tell Matron that you suggested that some warm soup wouldn't go amiss, shall I?'

'Why not?' Moira thought of the gallons of soup that Matthew and Bob were making under instruction, and quickly told Lizzie about it.

'Good lads,' Lizzie said. 'They'll mek you proud.'

As soon as Moira arrived home she looked for James and found him with Floris down in the kitchen. The boys were about to pour the soup into metal containers with lids, load them into a wooden trailer, and pull it down the staith towards the ship that was now berthed on this side of the Old Harbour.

With the help of some warehouse men who had heard about what they were doing and offered to help, they were going to hoist the containers aboard and reheat the soup on paraffin stoves. Bread was already packed into baskets, which Rosie had offered to carry to the ship.

'My word, it smells good,' Moira said. 'Well done, boys.'

'Can we put our aprons and toques on now?' Bob asked. 'We've sent some of my mates out to round up 'PIP folk to tell them there'll be soup later, but we've warned them only to tell those who've got no money.'

'You might want to wait until you get on board,' Moira told them. 'It's started raining again, and you'll need your coats on. Mr Ripley and I will come over and see you later.'

'Me go as well?' Floris said, and then gave a squeal as Moira swept her up and gave her a great hug. James raised his eyebrows and wore a questioning look.

'Tell you in a minute,' she said. 'But better news!'

The three of them went upstairs, leaving Matthew and Bob tucking into bread and beef standing up, as they were too excited to have a proper sit-down lunch.

'I do hope this goes well for them,' Moira said. 'It has to prove popular so that they know they're making a difference.'

'I think they do know,' James said. 'Bob says that some of his mates are jealous of what they're doing, so let's hope that the enthusiasm rubs off.'

In the sitting room Floris headed towards the box containing her books and toys and sat down on the floor near the guarded fire. James dropped his voice. 'So what's happened? Is there news?'

'Yes,' she said, subduing her delight. 'She was awake for part of the time, and I gave her sips of water which I'm sure she was gasping for; then I took blankets down from a cupboard and wrapped one of them round her and put another on top. It's not the warmest of places; there was a small coal fire but it didn't give out nearly enough heat for such a long room.' She released a sigh. 'I think there's real hope now, but I'm trying to imagine what might have happened to put her in a hospital bed in the workhouse, or Floris in the cellar.' She glanced towards where Floris was chattering quietly to herself. 'And how and why did she leave her child behind in the first place?'

He shook his head. 'And what happened to her husband?'

'If, or I hope *when*, she improves,' Moira said quietly, 'what should happen next? Do we take' – she nodded significantly towards Floris – 'to see her, or . . .' She hesitated.

James gazed at her for a long moment. 'Bring her here?' He shook his head, not negatively, but as if he didn't have an answer to her question, which he hadn't. 'We can't take in everyone who is in difficulties, Moira,' he said softly. 'That is why we are creating Friendship House. But, yes, there is something special about these circumstances.'

'I know.' A tear ran down her face and she wiped it away with her fingertips. 'And they seem to have come to our attention for some reason.'

She released a deep sigh and shook her head. 'Something happened to her; and no matter what, as soon as she improves enough to be moved we have to bring her home, to her daughter.'

CHAPTER FORTY-SEVEN

Leila

Leila had wiped her tears away and silently mulled over her options, which seemed to be few or none, and then began to talk to the woman sitting alongside her. Judging by the old clothes she was wearing, and the boots, from which bare toes were protruding, this Peggy, as she named herself, was hardly in a position to help anyone, but just talking seemed to reduce the misery and pain and the sheer terror of wondering what she could do.

Tomorrow might be better if I'm able speak to the lawyer, she thought. Was there really a chance that he would agree to see her? Did he have the authority, when it was Mr Thompson whom her father had known?

'So what d'ya think, m' dear?' The woman was clearly waiting for an answer.

'Erm, I'm sorry, I was miles away.'

'Somewhere exotic, I bet.' Peggy gave a cackling laugh which became a croaky cough. 'I said, do you want to come wi' me?'

Leila wondered how she could be so cheerful when clearly her life couldn't have been good. 'Wh-where did you say again? I didn't quite catch . . .'

'We – that is, 'folks who live there – call it *the Cellar*, cos that's
what it is. Used to be a wine merchants until it was burnt down,
ooh, I don't know, years ago, afore I was born, but 'cellar is still
there, and very useful it is too for them as have nowt else – nothing else, I mean.' She looked at Leila as if reconsidering whether
or not she understood English. 'And it'll cost you nothing.'

'A cellar?' Leila repeated. 'And, erm, is it dry?' She really
did long to be somewhere dry. She didn't want Floris to catch
a chill.

'Aye, it's dry!' Peggy grinned sardonically. 'Can't say much
else for it, but it's dry; unless 'drains block,' she mumbled as
an afterthought, 'and 'water comes under 'door. An' there's
allus somebody wi' a candle or a spare blanket,' she went on.
'We share, you see; folks do when they have nowt. You could
mebbe just come an' stop for tonight and your fortune'll
change tomorrow.'

She scrambled to her feet. 'Well, I'm off,' she said. 'I've had
a rest so I've 'strength to walk back.'

Leila had seen how her face creased as if in pain as she got
up from the cold stone step. 'Well, if you think it's all right for
us to come; if no one else will think we're intruding . . . erm,
yes, please.' She took hold of Floris's hand. 'We'd like to come
with you.'

She didn't know what she had come to or even where she was.
She had lost her bearings as Peggy had led her only a short
distance from the bank towards a square. Neither had she
noticed that there was a door set into the wall immediately
opposite the north side of a magnificent medieval church.

'Oh, aye,' Peggy had muttered when Leila had remarked
on it. 'We're under 'shelter of one of God's houses. We're safe
enough here.' She'd rattled the planks that served as a door.
'It's Peg,' she called through the gaps. 'Let me in. I've brought
a friend and her bairn.'

One of the planks was pushed to one side. 'There's no room for anybody else, Peg,' a male voice said. 'We're full up as it is.'

'Open 'door!' Peg demanded. 'They can sit wi' me. They're in dire need and besides, women and bairns have priority over men, so hurry up.'

The makeshift door swung open and Peggy with a toss of her head invited Leila and Floris inside.

Leila couldn't see anything immediately, but as her eyes became accustomed to the darkness she saw flickering lights from short stumps of candles set in cracks in the side walls, in alcoves, and on top of the maze of low walls that divided the cellar into small spaces where people, women and children mostly, were sitting.

Her first thought was that she must get out, that she couldn't possibly bring Floris into such a place. She was halted almost immediately by the realization that there was no other option; where else could she get free shelter and be out of the rain?

'This is my place.' Peggy led her into a corner at the back of the cellar. 'I've got it quite cosy. I found a cushion a fortnight back that somebody'd discarded.' She picked it up from the low wall and stroked the worn velvet. 'Just look at that,' she said to Leila. 'Proper velvet, that is. Little bairn can sleep on that. I keep it on 'wall so's it doesn't get damp on 'floor.'

From an alcove she drew out a wad of cardboard and placed it on the floor with the cushion on top, and pulled down a blanket that had been hanging on a nail hammered into the wall. 'Here you are, m' darling,' she said to Floris. 'There's your bed for tonight.'

Floris looked up at her and then at her mother, and obediently sat down on the cushion and curled up, tucking herself into her own arms and drawing up her knees. Peggy placed the blanket round her.

'There you are,' she said softly. 'She'll sleep safe tonight.

Now then,' she added to no one in particular. 'Where's my little lad?'

'He's over here wi' me, Peg,' came a disembodied voice from another part of the cellar. 'He's asleep, so best not to disturb him.'

'Oh, thanks, Lizzie, you're a pal. I've got a newcomer here; she's got a little bairn with her. Sort of lost her way, haven't you, honey?' The question was directed towards Leila. 'She won't be stopping long, but she's in dire straits just now so I brought her home.'

'Good lass,' said the other voice. 'Well, we'll talk in 'morning cos I'm going to sleep now. I'm dead beat.'

'Night, then,' Peggy said. 'May 'good Lord watch over you.'

Is it night already? Leila wondered. I was sure it was still afternoon, though it is very dark. She shuffled about, trying to find some small comfort on the cold stone floor and then decided to sit on the satchel. I won't sleep, she thought. I have too many things on my mind. But she closed her eyes, and slept.

The following morning, one of the men who had their places at the front of the cellar by the door was going into Trinity Square with one of the young boys to buy or be given yesterday's bread at the baker's. He collected coins from those who had any and stopped in front of Leila.

'I can only give you foreign money,' she said croakily. 'I'm hoping I might get some English later.'

The man looked down at her. 'We don't tek ill-gotten money,' he said roughly. 'Keep it for yoursen and your bairn.'

'What? No, I don't mean—'

'Leave her alone, Isaac.' Peggy sat up. 'She's not on 'game. She's just had bad luck. She might or might not have a better day today.'

The fellow glanced at Leila again, but only grunted and

went out, but when he came back he gave her a bread roll. 'Sorry,' he said. 'I just thought . . .' and turned away.

'He don't mean any harm,' Peggy said. 'He's a God-fearing man; fat lot o' good it's done him.'

Leila gave the bread to Floris, who tore into it with her sharp little teeth. 'I don't suppose there's, erm, anywhere to wash?' Leila asked Peggy hesitantly.

Peggy looked about her. 'I go to 'church.' She'd lowered her voice. 'There's a privy and a washbasin. I'll tek you and show you. Verger turns a blind eye, and if 'door is locked there's allus 'back of a gravestone.'

She saw Leila's recoil. 'Folks resting there've been gone a lot of years,' she murmured. 'None of 'em would object.'

I have dropped as low as I can possibly get, Leila thought, as, holding hands with Floris, she followed Peggy outside into the cold damp air. *Ziki!* She wanted to shout out his name to bring him to her, but dawn was only just breaking and people would still be sleeping. It's another day; perhaps it will be a better one.

She asked Peggy if she would watch over Floris when she went to see Mr Hawkins. 'I don't think it will take very long,' she told her. 'If they have located my father's paperwork I hope to see the lawyer who always looked after his affairs, but that depends on how busy he is.'

She gave a deep sighing breath. I am praying that he will allow me in the house, unless of course there is someone living in it. That would be a worry, as I don't think I could turn them out; it would be very unfair. I wonder if they'd let us have a bed for the night. The possibilities reeled through her head, but she couldn't be sure of any of them. All she knew was that she must stay positive.

When it came to almost midday, the time she had arranged to meet the lawyer, Peggy agreed that she would watch over Floris until Leila came back. 'Don't get lost, will you?' she warned her.

'Cos it's easy to walk past 'door. Trinity Square is what you want. Just look out for 'church. Good luck.' She put her hand to her chest and took a short, shallow breath. 'See you in a bit.'

Leila stepped outside the planked door and looked up. She shivered; her silk gown and cloak were not suitable for wear on an English winter day, and the cold cut through her, in spite of the wool tunic she also wore.

The church was magnificent; medieval, she thought, and even to one who had visited mosques and churches of all denominations, this ancient church built of mellow brick had a special glow in spite of the dull sky.

Gazing at it as she walked, she gave a silent prayer that her fortunes would change today: that she would see the lawyer and that Ziki would find them. She came to the end of the narrow street and looked about her. This didn't look right. Had she come the wrong way?

To her right the long road stretched out, with carts and delivery wagons trundling towards what looked like warehousing and maybe butcheries. She narrowed her eyes, and saw what looked like a statue glinting like gold through the mist. In the other direction, on the opposite side, was another church, smaller than Holy Trinity and not so grand, but it was old and stately and again built of brick and stone; an archway protruded over the footpath, and as she walked towards it she saw people sheltering beneath it, keeping out of the drizzle that had begun again.

If I turn left at the top of this road I should find Parliament Street from this end. It was a through street, a short cut to the dock, she supposed. Just as quick as going the other way.

This road was very busy. It led in and out of town; she saw a bridge over a river and small ships with their masts lowered going through. On the road there were many wagons pulled by heavy horses as well as carts, barouches, broughams and commercial vehicles, many of them being driven faster than necessary, she thought.

She came to the top end of Parliament Street. It was a fine street, very elegant, and judging by the lace curtains many of the houses were homes, whilst lawyers, accountants and other professional people perhaps used some as offices. She thought she was a little early, and hesitated on the footpath, looking about her before turning.

On the other side of the road she saw the dock, and the tall masts of some very large ships moored there; there was also a great deal of commotion: crates being unloaded, she surmised, and the shouts of men's voices that seemed very close; and then the clatter of wooden wheels and metal hooves striking the road.

She turned slightly, looking up and behind her, and saw men racing behind a driverless wagon pulled by a pair of galloping horses, their trailing reins advancing on another, smaller wagon. A youth was struggling with the reins of his horse as it shied and skidded as the loose wagon came abreast. It crashed into the smaller one, unseated the driver almost under her feet, and Leila knew no more.

CHAPTER FORTY-EIGHT

Ziki

Ziki had moved from the Station Hotel. He'd asked the desk clerk how much his stay there would cost and was astonished and horrified to be paying so much. When the clerk told him that Her Royal Majesty had once stayed there, he realized why.

'Thank you,' he said politely. 'That is a most wondrous thing, but now I must be leaving you. Be assured I will tell everyone that I have slept in the same hotel as Her Royal English Majesty.'

He quickly repacked Leila's satchel, and checked the papers within it. He saw the card of Hawkins, Thompson and Hawkins, lawyers, and the address on Parliament Street.

'Excuse me,' he said to the clerk when he paid his bill. 'Can you advise me where is Parliament Street?'

The clerk drew a sketch to show him, and told him to look for a long shopping street. Parliament Street was three quarters of the way down it.

'Three quarters,' he murmured. 'More than half, but not quite one whole.' But first he must find another place to stay. It wasn't his money he was spending, after all, but Leila's, and now most of it had gone on the most royal hotel. He still had a few Turkish lira and some French currency, and of course there were Leila's gold coins.

He found an inn not far from the railway station which was half the price he had been paying, and after taking the bags upstairs to his room he set out again to change the money. A young woman at the reception desk told him where to find a bank. 'You'll need one of the bigger ones, sir, to change for-eign money to English.'

Following her instructions, he found the place immediately and ran up the stone steps. It was quiet, with few people inside, and he was soon attended to.

'I wish to change my foreign money into English, please. M-mixed denomin-nations,' he said carefully, spilling the coins on the counter.

'Denominations.' The clerk smiled. 'Certainly, sir. I will check the rates for you.'

He came back almost immediately with a list in his hand, and picked up one of the gold coins.

'Oh, but this is old Ottoman currency, sir, which we can't exchange, I'm afraid.' He looked curiously at Ziki. 'A lady came in with the exact same coin; I suggested that a coin dealer in Silver Street might buy it from her.'

Ziki stared at the clerk. 'Sorry, what did you say, please? A lady? Did she have a child with her?'

'Yes, sir, she did. The lady was very fair; the little girl had dark curly hair.' Obliquely, so as not to stare, he glanced at Ziki's dark curly hair, which reached his collar.

'Where did she go?' Ziki said urgently. 'Which way, please? Did you see?'

'I'm sorry, sir, I didn't. We were quite busy.'

Ziki put his hand to his head. 'Please, if she comes in again, ask her to leave the name of the place where she is staying. She is my wife.' A sob gathered in his throat. 'And my daugh-ter. I am looking for them, but cannot find them. Please

302

change the rest of the money. I must go again and look for them.'

He collected his English money and hurried down the steps, asking the first person he saw where he could find Parliament Street. He was given instructions and began to run. Perhaps the lawyers know where she is staying. Perhaps she has gone to the house. I will go and look for it. Albion Street, he recalled. That is what it is called, and I have the number in the satchel. But first I must ask to see the lawyer.

He rang the bell and waited, and as soon as the door was opened he stepped inside, saying who he was and showing the young clerk who had opened the door to him the papers that he had kept in his hand.

'I am looking for my wife,' he said urgently. 'She is lost, and my daughter too.' His words seemed to be jumbled up. 'Has she been here?'

The clerk looked astonished. 'Yes, sir, she came yesterday. One moment, please.' He hurried down the hall, knocked, opened the door at the end of it, and leaned inwards so that Ziki couldn't hear what he was saying. He opened the door wider and another man came out. 'What is your name, sir?' he asked.

'Ziki Adem,' Ziki told him. 'I am looking for my wife. Leila. She was Leila Mackenzie before we married. Her parents once lived in Hull and had a house in . . .' He paused to consult the sheet of paper in his hand. 'Albion Street.' He put his hand to his face in despair. 'I can't find her, or my child. We were separated on the ship.' Tears streamed down his face. 'The bank people said she had been there yesterday, but . . .' He shook his head. 'I don't know what to do to find her.'

The man's face softened and he invited Ziki into his office, calling to the clerk to bring coffee.

'Forgive me,' Ziki said, taking a handkerchief from his pocket and wiping his face. 'I was sure that she would come to see Mr Thompson. Are you Mr Thompson?'

'No. I am not. Mr Thompson is our senior partner. My name is Hawkins and my son is our junior partner.' He shuffled papers about his desk. 'Your wife came here yesterday, but as she didn't have any proof of her identity and as Mr Thompson wasn't here, there was little we could do until we had spoken to Mr Thompson, whose client Henry Mackenzie was. We immediately sent a telegram to him to ask for his advice, and we made an appointment for your wife to come back at noon today.'

He looked up at the clock on the wall. 'It is now two thirty, Mr Adem, and we have had no word from her.'

The door opened and the clerk came in carrying a tray bearing a jug of coffee and two cups and saucers. Ziki breathed in the aroma of strong Turkish coffee and hoped that one of the cups was for him. It was, and as he slowly sipped he told Mr Hawkins exactly what had happened on the ship when the women were allowed to disembark at Dover while the men were held back because someone had said there had been a knife attack.

'When we were finally allowed to leave, the coach with the women on it had already gone to the station, and there wasn't another train to London until the next morning. It took me days to get here, for I mixed connections, and I have been to' – he lifted his hands – 'I don't know where. I got off the train in York.' He sighed heavily. 'And I can't find Leila or my daughter and I think they won't have much money for accommodation.'

'I can't discuss the detail of Mr Mackenzie's Will, Mr Adem,' Mr Hawkins said. 'Not without your wife here, but I can tell you that Mr Thompson sent a telegram to confirm that he did know your wife's father had died, but had received no official confirmation of his death. So until Mrs Adem is found and can show us such confirmation, there is little else we can do.'

Ziki didn't draw any comfort from what he had learned. He

finished the coffee and left the lawyer's office to wander around the small town, hoping to catch sight of Leila and Floris. He turned into a market square where a great church stood and stallholders were packing vegetables and bakery items into wooden crates and handcarts as if they had finished for the day.

He walked alongside the church and crossed over a wide busy road to an older area, where he cut down a very narrow street with just enough space for a small horse and cart to drive through. He came out on to an ancient street, with inns and elegant houses, and commercial shipping offices, and soon saw that the alleyways alongside some of the buildings led on to a harbour where coal barges and cutters, keels and sloops were berthed. He was interested, and thought he might return to explore further when he had found Leila and Floris.

Now, however, he was hungry, and he went back to the inn and asked if he might have something to eat. The young man at the reception desk asked if he would like a sandwich. He said yes he would, wondering what that would entail, until a plate of beef and chicken, thick slices of bread and a small dish of mustard was brought up to his room on a tray, with a pot of coffee. He was cautious at first, but it was very good, and when he had finished he stretched out on his bed and fell asleep.

When he woke it was pitch black in his room and the fire was almost out. Through the window he saw how dark it was, with gas lamps flickering in the street below.

He heard the shout of men's voices calling to one another from the inns and hostelries, and caught the echoes as the yells rebounded off the walls of narrow streets, passages and alleyways. They could have been coming from anywhere in the vicinity.

Almost immediately, he got up from the bed, put pieces of

305

coal on the almost dead fire, and then poured water from the jug into the bowl, and washed his hands and face and dried them on a towel.

He dressed in a warm wool jumper that Leila had bought him especially for this journey, put on his jacket, and wrapped a scarf around his neck. Then he locked his door and went downstairs.

It was quiet in the inn; there were only a few customers in the bar and the barman, who also served on reception, came over to him. 'Can I help you with anything, sir?'

Ziki shook his head. 'I think not, thank you. There is something I must do. Do you lock the doors at night?'

'Not until midnight, sir. If you are later than that, just pull 'bell rope and I'll hear it.'

Ziki stepped out into the night. The sky was dark and clear with myriad stars, and it was cold, a biting frost in the air which made his nostril hair crackle when he breathed in. It reminded him of Constantinople, where the winters were often sharp and harsh; he wondered if his mother and sisters were managing without him.

I hope that they are, for I cannot go home again until I know where Leila and Floris are, and I swear in every God's name and by every religion in heaven or on earth that I will search every corner, every alleyway and every street, until I find them.

CHAPTER FORTY-NINE

Ziki

For the next few weeks Ziki stayed at the inn, losing track of time as he spent his days wandering the streets of Hull, hoping to find his wife and child. One evening his search took him back to the waterway, and he stood looking down at the dock below. Fishing boats were berthed along the quayside, some with lanterns casting an amber glow from their bows, and in the dim light he saw neat piles of nets and blankets in the sterns; he guessed the crews were preparing for an early start the next day.

There was a trawler also, with a crowd around it and two boys on deck handing out cups of soup. A woman helping them glanced up and stood for a moment, catching his gaze and then looked away.

Sitting on a bench a little way along the quay, he put his head in his hands, his thoughts in turmoil. He must have sat there for longer than he knew, or perhaps he had dozed off, for when he came to he realized that night had fallen.

Behind him stood a tall monument with a statue at the very top. He read the inscription on the base stone. William Wilberforce. Ah, of course, he thought, a well-known man the world over. Abolitionist of slavery, and born in Hull. How proud the people here must be.

Walking on, he approached the long shopping street, White-friargate; the gate of the White Friars, in fact; he had heard of the order of friars who wore white robes, and realized that this place must once have housed a religious community. On the left of the street there were narrow alleys with buildings behind them, but he thought the buildings must have a wider entrance elsewhere, perhaps behind Parliament Street.

He was a big man, broad-shouldered, but not obese, and with narrow hips, and in spite of the narrowness he was able to squeeze through one of the alleys. He peered about him and shook his head. This was not the kind of place where Leila would be, and he turned back.

On the other side of Whitefriargate was a fine building with a locked gate and a brass plate denoting Trinity House. This, he thought with his history guide's hat on, might once have been part of the friary. He wouldn't find Leila and Floris there.

He walked on, passing by Parliament Street to where the road divided. Going by instinct only, he turned right, and was led into the square with the great church that he had seen earlier. It was quiet here; there was no one about as far as he could tell, though there were shadows in deep dark shop doorways. If Leila were seeking sanctuary, she would perhaps be here. On impulse he stood tall, took a deep breath and shouted, 'Leila! Leila! Where are you?'

An answer came from a doorway. 'Jigger off! Get lost, will you? Some folk are trying to sleep.'

'Sorry.' Ziki backed away. The last thing he wanted was to become embroiled in trouble. He was sure to be blamed for breaking the peace, being a foreigner.

Once again he cut through the narrow street that ran along-side the north side of the church; there was no gas lamp here to show his way, but a light was dimly flickering at the top of the street, which he now knew led to a wide road. He turned briefly, looking over his shoulder as he saw, or thought he did, a flickering light behind a boarded-up door, but then dismissed it as a reflection of . . . what? The only dim light was from an oil lamp swinging on the corner of the church wall.

He crossed the road, and before cutting through another narrow street named Church Lane he lifted his voice again and called. 'Leila! Leila!'

He stepped cautiously down a cobbled staith leading to the waterside and saw the shapes of barrels and boxes and neat piles of ropes and nets, and wooden sack barrows for transporting heavy objects. The dark water gleamed and he heaved a sigh. He felt emotion creeping up into his very pores, running through his veins and into his heart. 'Leila!' he cried out in desperation. 'Leila! Leila!'

Moira stirred in her bed. In her dreams she heard Floris crying for her mother, and saw how Leila in her hospital bed moved sharply as if she had heard her. Moira stirred again and woke. Had she heard Floris cry? Usually the little girl slept well. But there was something; something or someone had called.

Someone who had dined and drunk too well, perhaps? She sat up. No. Not a drunk. Her window looked out on the Old Harbour, as did James's on the opposite side of the landing. She slipped out of bed and drew back the curtain.

James, too, woke with a start. Matthew? Was his son calling? They had all been triumphant over the success of the soup kitchen, and Leggott had come to tell them that he and Keylock had knocked down the wall between two of the upstairs rooms in Friendship House, had moved all the mess that came with it and swept up, and, whilst the builder took down the fence and began to build an outside wall, he had begun painting what was to become the dormitory.

He sat up, but who was calling out? A man, no doubt of

that, but a man in distress? He got out of bed and went to the window, lifting the curtain aside. A man stood by the ship, his head and shoulders bent, his hands clasped to his head.

'Ah!' James let out a heavy breath and turned to take his dressing robe from the hook behind the door just as it slowly opened.

'Moira?'

'James, there's someone out there.' She held a flickering candle in her hand.

Upstairs in one of the top rooms, Mrs Evans sat up in bed. What was that? she wondered. What did I hear? There definitely was someone or something.

In the other bedrooms, Rosie stirred and turned over in her sleep, whilst Bob next door didn't stir but gave a little snore and smiled in his sleep. Matthew, on the floor below, turned over and didn't hear the slither of the book he'd been reading as it fell softly on to the rug.

James took the candle and reached for Moira's hand as they slipped quietly down the staircase and crossed the hall to the kitchen stairs. On the ground floor the kitchen was still warm from the cooking range, and they passed through into the back lobby. James eased back the bolt, turned the key, unhooked the chain and opened the door that led to the staith.

All was silent outside, and James raised his voice, not enough to waken the sleepers in the house but enough for someone outside to hear. When there was no response, he nipped out the candle flame, which was flickering in the cold air, and locked the door again from the inside. 'I'm going out of the garden door,' he said.

'No! There's no light,' Moira protested. They rarely used the garden door that led on to the waterway. In the summer roses grew around it.

'There's enough,' he answered. Whoever was calling was out by the edge of the Old Harbour, not on the staith side.

He opened the door and stepped into the garden. The air was bitterly cold, and a breeze blew in off the water. 'Hello,' he called. 'Who's there?'

'Leila! Leila!'

The voice had moved further down the waterway towards the warehouses and Rotting Herring staith, which led to the old South End, the Custom House watch house, and eventually the estuary itself. Not areas for strangers to enter, particularly at night.

'James, be careful,' Moira pleaded; he was wearing only slippers on his feet, and though the collar on his dressing robe was turned up he was hardly dressed for a walk outside on a winter's night.

'Go inside, Moira. I'm not going far.' James moved on, but she could still see him.

They heard the call again, and this time James answered. 'Leila! Here! Come here!'

Ziki stopped. What was that? Someone mocking me? Or an echo? 'Leila!' he called again.

He listened and there was nothing, and then: 'Baba Ziki! Baba Ziki! Come here!'

'Who knows me?' His voice cracked. 'Who are you?'

'James Ripley. Come here, please. This is no trick. We have news of Leila. Come!'

And then James found Moira by his side and she took his hand.

'Ziki!' she called. 'Ziki, we have your daughter Floris sleeping in our house. Please come. You are safe.'

'I'm coming! I'm coming!'

They heard his voice coming nearer and then saw the tall figure looming in front of them. Moira moved from James's side and walked slowly towards the stranger, stretching out her hand. James held his breath. And then the stranger took the hand and Moira held him fast.

They brought him into the kitchen. Moira lifted the kettle on to the range and James pulled out a chair for Ziki to sit on. He sat with his hands clutched to his head, shaking it.

Then he looked up. 'I am dreaming, I think? Is my wife here? My daughter?'

James drew up another chair and sat opposite him. 'Your daughter Floris is asleep upstairs. Leila is not here, but we know where she is. Tomorrow we will take you to her and perhaps bring her back here. She is in hospital.'

He had no idea how much English Ziki understood, but it was quite obvious that he was Floris's father: those deep brown eyes, the dark curly hair; do all Turkish people have dark hair? Probably not, James thought, but this was not a coincidence.

Moira handed Ziki a mug of coffee, which he drank gratefully, and there was a silence that no one quite knew how to fill, until the staircase door slowly opened and Mrs Evans came in holding a stout stick with both hands.

Moira and James both hid a smile as she looked about her suspiciously. Her eyes fell on Ziki and she took in a short breath. 'I saw you yesterday,' she croaked. 'You were near 'soup kitchen in 'Old Harbour.'

Ziki nodded. 'I was,' he said, his words choked with tears. 'I was looking for my wife and daughter.'

'Well, my word,' she said, and picked up the kettle to refill it. 'You certainly took your time!'

Mrs Evans made more hot drinks and took hers to bed.

'Thank you, Mrs Evans,' Moira said gratefully. 'Don't rush to be up early in the morning.'

The housekeeper looked askance at her. 'I'll be up as usual, ma'am,' she said. 'I'm not one for sleeping in.'

Moira told Ziki he could stay the night if he didn't mind sleeping in James's bed, and James took him up to see Floris, who was sleeping soundly in the nursery. Tears ran down Ziki's face when he saw his child safe and well.

'We'll take you to see Leila tomorrow,' James promised. 'We understand that she has probably been in an accident, but as she hasn't been fully conscious we haven't been able to ask her. Moira has visited her.'

'You have been more than kind,' Ziki murmured, almost overcome. 'I can never thank you enough.'

James showed him where he could sleep and where the bathroom was, said goodnight, crossed the landing and knocked softly on Moira's door.

'You don't need to knock, James,' she said. She was sitting up in bed waiting for him with a warm shawl around her shoulders. 'Do you think all will be well now?'

He sat on the side of the bed where she had drawn back the sheets for him. 'It has been a wonderful day, hasn't it?' she said.

He heaved out a breath. 'I feel both elated and exhausted, and' – he leaned towards her and kissed her – 'as for you, my darling brave wife, I love you more than I can say.'

'I'm not brave,' she whispered. 'You're the brave one going outside to meet a stranger and inviting him into our home.'

He drew her close and shook his head, murmuring, 'You're the one who held your hand out in friendship to someone we didn't know, unafraid to take that step.'

She put her head on his shoulder. 'Shall we say we make a good team?'

CHAPTER FIFTY

The work was moving on at a fast rate. Jack Keylock had easily run pipework through for two more privies, and was waiting for supplies of sanitary ware, so in the meantime, after he and Leggott had brought out the bricks of the inside wall they'd demolished, he took down the fence and leaned it against the original privy, prepared the base foundations and began mixing the mortar, and by the end of the day the wall was halfway up.

Lily Walters called to him to say she'd made a pot of tea if he'd like one. She'd also been to a local bakery and bought two potted meat sandwiches and a Yorkshire curd cheesecake.

'This is, in a way, a backhander,' she admitted. She looked at the half-eaten slice of cheesecake in her hand, adding, 'This isn't as good as mine,' and Jack looked impressed. 'But I want to ask a favour. If I hire a cart, will you help me unload my few bits of furniture and carry them upstairs? Cos I've decided to move in.'

'No need to spend your brass on hiring a cart,' he told her. 'I've got a small wagon and I can borrow a hoss from a mate o' mine, and we can do it in one go.'

He asked her where she lived, and when she told him he said she'd be glad to get out of there and he'd do it just as soon as he'd finished tidying up and before it got too dark; he could finish the wall the next morning. He grinned and she smiled back. She was going to like it here.

Moira brought Floris downstairs in her nightgown and dressing gown the next morning, whispering to her that there was a big surprise waiting for her in the dining room. Floris put her hands to her eyes, and Moira smiled when she saw how she'd spread her fingers so that she could peek through. James was waiting to open the door and Ziki stood up, anxiety creasing his face as he wondered how his daughter would react.

She began to cry when she saw him and clung to Moira's hand, but he crouched down and held out his arms and after a mere second she rushed into them, wailing with joy as he wrapped his arms around her and stood up, holding her tight and showering her with kisses.

Moira wept and held out her hand to Matthew, who was crying too.

'I wanted to keep her, Mama,' he sobbed. 'I don't want her to go.'

'Nor do I,' she said, choked with tears, not of sadness, for she was overjoyed for them, but with emotion at the thought of losing this little girl whom she had loved so much.

Bob was sent to order a cabriolet after breakfast and Moira dressed Floris in a pretty fine wool dress and warm coat and bonnet. She went with Ziki and Floris in the carriage and James said he would call at Hawkins, Thompson and Hawkins to apprise them of the latest information on Mrs Adem, formerly Mackenzie, now reunited with her husband. Coincidentally, he already knew the younger Hawkins, as they had been at school together and both were now on the committee of Friendship House.

Floris sat on her father's knee as they drove the short distance

315

to the workhouse. Moira saw the flickering frown on Ziki's fore-head as they drove through the gate and on to the forecourt, as if he was working out what kind of hospital this was.

Ziki lifted Floris up to pull the bell chain, and she moved her head to one side to listen to the peal.

Matron opened the door, and she greeted them cautiously. 'Please come in,' she said politely, and glanced at Ziki's impos-ing presence. Moira made the introductions and asked how Mrs Adem was today.

'Improved, I would say,' she answered. 'But perhaps it would be better not to have too much excitement.'

'May I go in first?' Moira asked, glancing at Ziki. 'To pre-pare her?'

He nodded, and Moira walked down the hall to the hospi-tal ward. There was someone else in a bed opposite who appeared to be asleep; Leila was propped up on pillows with her eyes closed and only stirred when Moira sat down beside her, opening her eyes and gazing at her visitor.

'I'm Moira. Do you remember me?'

'Yes,' Leila said huskily. 'You came to see me. Gave me water.'

'Leila,' Moira said softly, 'do you remember what happened to you?'

Leila shook her head slowly. 'No. I don't know how I came to be here in a strange bed, or where Ziki and Floris are. I think I have lost them.'

At least she remembers their names; Moira reached out to hold her hand. 'They are here,' she said quietly. 'Ziki and Flo-ris. Would you like to see them?'

Leila's eyes swam with tears and she nodded. 'Yes, please,' she said quietly, and Moira rose from the chair. She went out of the room and into the corridor where Ziki was sitting with Floris on his knee. Moira put her arms out to her and lifted her gently down to the floor.

'Go in, Ziki. I have told her that you are here. I'll bring Floris in in a moment.'

She sat down in his vacated seat and Floris climbed on to the one next to her. 'Where is my anneh . . . Leila?' she asked.

How confusing for her, Moira considered; she's juggling two languages. 'You will see her in a moment,' she told her. 'Leila has not been very well. She has a headache.' She hoped the child would understand that, and she did, for Floris stroked her own forehead and made a little *aww*-ing sound.

A few minutes went by, and then the ward door opened and Ziki was beckoning to Floris to come and greet her mother.

Whilst she was waiting, Moira sought out the matron and asked if she thought Mrs Adem was fit to leave and stay with them; she had been working out that Leila and Ziki could sleep in James's room if she organized it for them. 'We can also ask our doctor to call on her and assess her injuries,' she added, and so it was agreed. Whilst Ziki and Floris stayed with Leila, Moira went home alone in the cabriolet. The driver waited as she went into the house and gathered together one of her own warm hooded dressing gowns, a pillow, blankets and slippers, and then he drove her back to the workhouse where Ziki tenderly carried his wife to the carriage and made sure she was warm and comfortable for the journey home.

The doctor visited her every day, and day by day she improved. She had one broken shoulder and one broken leg, both of which were healing, bruising all over her body, and concussion. The doctor had made it his business to ask the hospital what had happened to her, and it was revealed that they had been told she had been trampled by a runaway horse and hit by the wagon it was pulling.

'She is lucky to be alive,' he said, 'but if she has a strong constitution she will pull through.'

And so she did, safe in the arms of her husband and

knowing that Floris was safe. Bit by bit, the story of what had happened came back to her, including living in the cellar, which shocked and horrified Ziki.

'If I hadn't been called out on that dreadful night of the flood,' James murmured to Moira as they sat side by side in her bed, propped up by pillows, 'we would never have found Floris and their story would have had a different ending, but it would always have begun with Ziki delayed on the ship and Leila going ahead on the train without him.'

'Fate,' Moira said softly. 'And we wouldn't have had the joy of a daughter coming into our home that winter night. In the short time she has been with us she's brought us such delight with her sweet ways, her laughter and her love.'

He turned her face towards him and saw tears in her eyes. He kissed her and whispered something; she smiled and gently traced his lips with her fingers and returned his kiss.

ENDING

Floris sat on the edge of the bed. She wasn't happy about being ordered to have a rest in the afternoon; she was perfectly well and healthy, she'd argued: expecting a baby was quite normal. But the doctor insisted, as did Tom.

If I have to rest, I'll write my diary, she decided. The diary she had begun ten years before, when she was ten years old, drawing on precious childhood memories before she forgot them.

She got up from the bed and picked up her writing materials, a very large notebook and a sharpened pencil, from the table by the window, and then looked down to the street below.

It was an interesting view. There were museums in this English street, doctors' surgeries, commercial houses and residents' houses just like this one; this was a fashionable area in the heart of the town, and she loved to see elegant ladies strolling by, some with parasols, who were so different from women in the country of her birth.

She got back into bed, adjusted her pillows and began.

'I had been told many years ago that my English grandfather, Henry, whom I don't remember in the slightest, as he died

319

whilst I was still a babe in arms, had left this elegant English house to me in his Will. He had lived here as a boy in this fashionable part of Hull in the north of England, with *his* parents, and my mother, Leila, was born here. Although my mother and I can live in it, it won't be completely mine until I am twenty-one, which I will be in April of this year, by which time I will be a mother too.

'I have often wondered why my grandfather hadn't left it to my mother, but she said that she didn't mind in the least, and he had left her a substantial amount of money, as had her mother. She said she wouldn't ever have lived in the house, and would have sold it had it come to her. Except, she told me rather vaguely, there was a clause in English law about women and property and that was why it was left to any child that she might bear if she should marry. Tom laughed when she told us that and kissed my cheek and said, lovingly, that it wouldn't apply to us.

'Interestingly, the house has an aura of other countries and is not purely English as one might expect in a Georgian house. There is pottery from Portugal and the Netherlands, like the Delftware for instance, and ceramic tiles, and the most beautiful carpets and silken hangings that can only have come from Turkey. My grandparents, it seems, were collectors as well as travellers and they obviously had excellent taste.

'I like to come back to this fishing and shipping town, even if it is so far from my homeland of Turkey. It has a friendly feel to it; there is no conflict, as sometimes there is in the great landmass of the Ottoman Empire; and besides, there are people here that I love. So Tom and I decided that we would come to Hull for the birth of our first child in our English family home; I am half English after all, and Tom's parents are so thrilled, especially after the difficult time that they and Tom went through when he was a boy, until he settled down to home life and schooling again.

'Tom is extremely clever and after university he trained to

be a teacher and then followed me out to Constantinople, which is my home city in a country that has many languages and religions, and now he teaches English in the same school as my baba, Ziki.

'I forgot to write this down before, but of course I must document everything, and especially about meeting Tom for the first time on one of our journeys back to Hull. Baba and I come back every three years or so to see Moira and James, and Matthew of course, whom I love as if he were my real blood brother, which is how I always think of him; he is married to a lovely golden-haired, sweet girl called Iris, and they too are expecting their first child this year.

'I have a sister too; I will write about her later. Strictly speaking she isn't my sister, but I feel as if she is, as she is the daughter of Moira and James, whom I will always think of as my foster parents.

'Leila doesn't always travel to her home country with Baba and me. She has many anxieties about coming to England and sometimes her bones ache; she is much better in the sunshine of Turkey, and whilst we're away my grandmother Adem takes care of her very well.

'About three years ago, when Baba Ziki and I were here on one of our visits, we went to Friendship House to see the further changes that had been made, and it was there that Tom and I met. He helped out at the house whenever he could, he told me, to give something back for the friendship and understanding he had received from Moira and James when he was a troubled, mixed-up boy.

'I didn't remember him from when I was a child, of course, but he remembered me. We struck up an immediate friendship when we met, and agreed to correspond with one another, as we had much in common.

'I don't recall much of the time I spent in the cellar; my mother says that perhaps I have blocked it from my memory.

Sometimes when we're in England and it rains, I remember being carried through the dark old streets, clinging on to someone's coat. Tom told me that it was Papa James's, and that he was carrying me to the safety of the church.

'Papa James never mentioned the flooded cellar to me. It was only Tom who did. He's older than me and remembers that night very well, so he's filled in the gaps in my memory.

'He's told me about his own life, too, starting with the time when he was just a schoolboy and ran away from home in an act of bravado. But he was afraid out in the streets; he had thought it would be an adventure and it wasn't, it was very frightening for a young boy. But his friend Bob worked for Papa James, and together with dear Matthew they found him and took him home with them. Unfortunately, someone had given him laudanum and told him that it would make him feel better, but instead it made it worse and he ran away while everyone was asleep.

'Tom said that when he heard about Friendship House he went and found James and Moira again, and told them that he was ready to meet his parents if they were willing to take him back. He was still only a boy, and had been so afraid when the cellar flooded, and then after spending time on the streets he had finally realized that he wanted to go home as he missed his parents after all, but he was anxious that they might not want him after the heartache he had caused them.

'Papa James had gone with him, to break the ice, which is such a strange comment to make, and yet is so exactly right, as relationships can be frosty sometimes. But not on that occasion, as his father and mother, who had searched the streets of Hull for him, were really relieved and happy to see him safe and sound.

'Friendship House is still in great demand. Papa James says that the poor are always with us, and I think that perhaps he is right. Bob, who used to be in charge of logs and coal and ran errands for everyone in the Ripley household, is the manager there now; he says he knows what it's like to be poor, but that he was given a chance and he wants the same for people who come to Friendship House. His aunt is the housekeeper there and between them there is a great welcoming spirit.

'I love it here in this old town, and we'll stay after the birth until early summer before returning to Turkey. Baba Ziki came with us, and we brought his sister, my aunt Derya. She had always wanted to travel and my mother suggested that we ask her to come. She said she would be a great help with the child when he or she arrives.

'I know that this is why Baba Ziki has come too. He can't wait to see the baby, although he jokes that he is far too young to be a grandfather. He will return home after the birth; he doesn't like to stay away too long from Leila, and he gets anxious about her. He knows that she is uneasy when he is away from her. They are such lovebirds. Only happy when they are together.

'Will Tom and I be like that when we are old? We are both very independent and yet he is so protective of me; he remembers how I used to cry out for *Lay-lah* when we were in the cellar, and the women used to try and console me, but I remember very little of that.

'I haven't yet written about the most important thing of all. The first time I returned to England after being at home in Constantinople, I was nearly ten years of age. Ziki had said that we should all go, including my mother if she felt strong enough, and see James and Moira again, and I very much wanted to see Matthew, who used to read to me and showed me how to draw; I also wanted to see Mrs Evans, and Rosie too, who will eventually take on the role of housekeeper, but what I wanted most of all was to meet my little sister.

'Not a sister through blood, but Matthew's sister, born at the end of the year after we came home to Constantinople. I longed to see her and will always think of her as my baby sister.

'She is as fair as I am dark, and so beautiful. She was not a baby any longer when we first met, but nearly five by then, roughly the age I had been when I was rescued. James, Moira and Matthew, Ziki and Leila and I, we stretched out to clasp hands and form a circle and bring us together.

' "Rosanna," Mama Moira said softly to this shy little girl, and I could see her eyes glisten, and heard the happiness in her voice as she said, "Rosanna, meet your sister Floris." '

ACKNOWLEDGEMENTS

At the beginning of this, my twenty-eighth book, I found myself once again turning to my old and precious history books. The oldest, Sheehan's *History of the Town and Port of Kingston upon Hull*, with the preface written in 1866 and so small and faded that I must now read it with the aid of a magnifying glass.

My search was for the section on the cellar below the burnt-out warehouse, which I first used in my third book, *Children of the Tide*, and wished to resurrect for this new one.

Throughout, James Joseph Sheehan tells of numerous fires that had broken out in the old town. These fires, described variously on the pages, were defined as violent, alarming, destructive, shocking and a terrifying conflagration; well, yes indeed. Fortunately, it also rained in torrents, a deluge, a surge, and with high winds the Humber frequently broke through the town walls and flooded the streets so one would hope that some fires would be extinguished also.

Another book, *Living and Dying: A Picture of Hull in the Nineteenth Century*, was written, I believe, during the twentieth century, but unfortunately not dated; nevertheless, it is a treasure chest of information regarding every possible aspect of life and death, as described in the title, written and privately published by Bernard Foster.

So, my aim here is to give my thanks to these long-gone history writers who have left such a wonderful catalogue of information for fiction writers such as me, and, in particular, to Mr Sheehan, who was in some instances writing of events happening in his lifetime.

I would also like to thank the Transworld team once again – editors Alice Rodgers and Francesca Best, long-standing copy-editor Nancy Webber and production editor Vivien Thompson; Sally Williamson, Lara Stevenson and the whole Transworld Penguin Random House team – for bringing the book together, not forgetting Richard Ogle and the design team who create the lovely covers; nor my faithful local Divine Clark PR team who guide me through the terrors of social media and publicity.

To Catherine Wood, who steered me through the intricacies of nineteenth-century travel in the Ottoman Empire to make sure I was going in the right direction and didn't get lost – yes, I know that I did!

For the encouragement and support of friends and family, I thank you all.

ABOUT THE AUTHOR

Since winning the Catherine Cookson Prize for Fiction for her first novel, *The Hungry Tide*, **Val Wood** has become one of the most popular authors in the UK.

Born in the mining town of Castleford, Val came to East Yorkshire as a child and has lived in Hull and rural Holderness where many of her novels are set. She now lives in the market town of Beverley.

When she is not writing, Val is busy promoting libraries and supporting many charities. In 2017 she was awarded an honorary doctorate by the University of Hull for service and dedication to literature.

Find out more about Val Wood's novels by visiting her website: www.valwood.co.uk